PURGATORY

SWALLOWS AND PSYCHOS

K.L. TAYLOR-LANE

SYNOPSIS

Some say I'm a psychopath, others say sociopath.

Deranged, demonic, unhinged.

And I am, unashamedly, all of those things and so, so many more.

I'm the lone daughter of The Swallow Family crime syndicate.

A bloodied, violent queen reigning from a throne of bone and ash, hands and soul bathed in crimson.

The one thing I'm not, though?

Crazy.
Or so I thought...

But when I start receiving threats, start 'seeing' people that only I see and get forced to take time out, I start to wonder if they might be right about me after all.

Just a crazy girl made up of twisted, shattered pieces, a half dead organ decaying inside her wounded chest and a tendency for violence.

I’m Kyla-Rose Swallow and this is the beginning of my downfall.

So, welcome to Southbrook, the city where Swallows rule and psychos raise hell.

To my baby sister,
Thank you for always fighting for me,
I love you more than you'll ever know.

NOTE FROM THE AUTHOR

This is a reverse harem, meaning the female main character will have three or more love interests and will not have to choose. The harem grows throughout the series, meaning there is not an established harem in book 1. It is a medium/fast burn romance.

Please be aware this book contains **many dark**/taboo themes and subjects that may be uncomfortable/unsuitable for sensitive readers. This book contains **very** heavy themes throughout so please heed the warning and go into this with your eyes wide open.

For more detailed information, please contact the Author.

The characters in this story all deal with trauma and problems differently, the resolutions and methods they use are not always traditional and therefore may not be for everyone.

This is book 1 of a planned trilogy and DOES end on a cliffhanger.

TWO YEARS AGO

Blue and red strobe lights slice through the thick haze -a mixture of smog, some from the smoke machines, the rest from cigarettes and blunts- as I weave my way through the heaving mass of bodies. Beads of sweat drip from the dark curls at the nape of my neck and race down my spine.

The deeper into 'The Pit' I get, the hotter the temperature climbs and the thicker the humidity gets, making each breath I draw in more laboured than the last.

I'm definitely overdressed and I feel like I'm hardly wearing anything. Ripped, skinny jeans, unlaced biker boots, a sleeveless hoodie thrown on my back, the zip all the way open. Baring my inked chest and tattooed arms, my hood flipped up and a bandana covering the lower half of my face.

I don't need everyone seeing my face here tonight. Anyone

who's not currently drugged up or hopped up on booze by this point in the night is a possible witness to my presence here and the last thing I need as a twenty-five year old, single, son of a top politician, is my name plastered all over the local papers in the morning. I can just see the tabloids now; *'Elizabeth Harrington-Griffin's only son, spotted leaving illegal rave at 4am'*.

Yeah, I'd rather keep this little visit to myself, thank you very much; I'd never hear the end of that one.

Down here, underground in the concrete maze, nothing but sin survives. All of the crime factions that run in these parts and are any part of the criminal underbelly of Southbrook, more than likely will have a presence here. But I'm not here for that, not tonight, I'm not here scoping out a target, I'm just here to let loose.

The raised DJ booth is the focal point in the huge space; sitting centrally on a raised platform, towering over everyone in the room. That's the only way you could get eyes on someone in a place like this and I'd really rather not take on the job if it involved coming down here.

I dive deeper into the crowd, weaving my way through the grinding bodies. With my military background, shit like this should bother me, the cramped space, no clear visual on the exits, being here alone, without backup, without my *brothers*. But not tonight, tonight I need to forget what my life is and just do *something,* something that's not the norm.

Hundreds of people are crammed in here. Half-naked bodies' slick with sweat, grinding their heated, writhing cores up against strangers and I'm suddenly wondering why the fuck I came here.

Oh yeah, motherfucking childish rebellion, that's why.

A strobe of blue casts a sweep of bright light across the top of the crowd and as it cuts through the fog and darkness, a white haired beauty catches my eye.

Dancing in the mass of bodies, her long, tattooed arms thrown up in the air, her head thrown back in ecstasy and heavily made-up eyes closed as she moves to the beat in the centre of the sea of people. I find my feet subconsciously moving closer, intrigue carries me until I'm standing in a tiny circle of space before her.

Up close -even in the darkened space- this woman is even more captivating, my heart starts to beat a little harder in my chest as I look at her. Hundreds upon hundreds of lines of black ink cover every visible inch of her almost translucent skin, I can't make any of them out in detail but she's covered.

In contrast to my darker complexion, she's visually the light to my dark in every way. Her waist-length hair is the palest shade of white-blonde I've ever seen and compared to my thick dark curls we're stark opposites.

"Are you going to dance with me or just stand there?" her husky voice asks, goosebumps prickle my skin as her plump lips tilt up slightly at the corners.

Her head still thrown back and kohl covered eyes shut tight. How she's even aware of my presence is unknown to me, her eyes haven't even opened to slits. Before I can answer, her eyes still hidden from me, she drops her arms.

Her long, thin fingers encircle my wrists, dragging and dropping my heavy hands to her hips. She steps into me, eradicating any and all distance between us and the little space she vacated is quickly filled by others. Her lean arms drop onto my shoulders, her soft body pressing into my firm chest, my body reacts to hers and quickly we start to move as one.

Without taking my eyes from her, I strain them hard to take in her features every time a light cuts through the darkness, but not once does she open her eyes. The black thin-strap vest she's wearing is wet with sweat, clinging to the curves of her heavy breasts, as tight as a second skin, revealing the outline of her hard, pierced nipples. The feel of them rubbing against my bare chest has my dick stirring.

Fuck me, this girl.

She spins in my hold, pressing her back to my front, forcing me to suck in a sharp breath as she grinds the round globes of her arse against my hardening dick. My fingers flex on her waist, my grip tightening as her arms wind up behind her. She shoves my hood down, latching onto the back of my neck, her fingers running through the thick curls at my nape.

Her head drops back against my shoulder, her silken hair sticking to the sweat of my bare chest. She tilts her face back and presses her plump lips against the scruff on my jaw, the little sliver of skin not covered by my bandana, a rush of electricity pulses through me.

She grips my hand suddenly and spins out of my hold, her chest heaving with untamed breaths as she finally pops open her eyes.

Stark grey orbs capture me, twisting something low down in my stomach as she looks at me, like, *really* looks at me, *sees me*. Then her other hand is coming up and shoving me sharply in the chest, the heat of her skin against mine gets me all sorts of excited as she steps back into me and shoves me again, *hard.* Gesturing with her head to one of the dimly lit alcoves on the far side of the room, I spin on my heel, shoving people out of my way as I barge through the crowd.

Her fingers cling onto mine in a vice-like grip, her lithe body staying plastered to my back like a human cloak, a finger through the belt loop of my jeans, she follows me through the masses.

Just as we hit the break of people, she stops, tugging a phone from her denim cut-off shorts, she scowls down at whatever she sees. The bright white light from the screen finally illuminating her face but just as I start to get a look at her, the screen goes black again engulfing us both in the smoggy darkness.

"I have to go," she yells huskily, a shiver rakes up my spine as her lips brush the shell of my ear, separating our linked fingers she rushes to leave.

I immediately start to follow, calling out to her, but by the time I make it outside, the cold air hitting my sweat covered skin, she's already long gone and I didn't even get her goddamn name.

Well, fuck.

CHAPTER 1

KYLA-ROSE

Carefully making my way down the winding steel staircase, descending into the darkness of the industrial sized basement, I walk a few blind steps before long strip bulbs begin to light my way. My thin stiletto heels click against the metal steps, the sound-proofing of the basement forcing the sound to echo around the long hall below me. I make my way down the stairs and follow the corridor to one of the rooms at the very end.

As I reach the end of the hall, I stop myself in front of two large men, their backs against a big steel door, both wearing hard, unrelenting scowls.

“Boss,” they nod, greeting me in unison as they un-bar the door they’re guarding and swing it open.

As the door closes behind me I’m instantly assaulted by

the tangy scent of blood and piss in the air, it's enough to turn anyone's stomach, but all my body feels is excitement.

"What made you think you were going to get away with selling knock-off drugs in my territory? Do I not provide you with sufficient, *safe* product and a more than generous cut?" Dee calmly asks, but I can sense the hint of irritation in his otherwise relaxed tone.

My Uncle Dee taught me everything I know. How to slice and dice a man whilst still keeping enough blood in his system to keep him alive, if not only so I can exact more pain and gain more information. I know just how to make a grown man squeal like a little piggy. He taught me how to disarm someone quicker than I can blink and how to school my features in times of stress or rage. He's a man of many, many talents, each of them usually bloodier than the last.

Dee sits on a folding metal chair. His legs casually crossed one over the other with his large hands –fingers laced together- atop his knee. His short greying hair styled to one side and a ridiculously expensive grey, pin-striped suit covers his lean body. He's the epitome of class. Anyone could be fooled into thinking he's a fucking aristocrat or some shit, well, that is, if it weren't for the blood splatter across his face.

The man he addresses is quivering. Naked, bleeding and sweaty, bound to a matching metal chair across from Uncle Dee, his bloodied back to me.

Just how I like them.

"I, I…-" the greasy man tries to choke out when my cousin –Charlie- cuts him off, smashing his large tattooed fist into the side of the man's head, he knocks him out cold as his knuckles penetrate his temple.

Charlie is one of the four cousins I grew up with, Dee's second son. Charlie -by clinical definition- is a psychopath, who fortunately or unfortunately -depending on how you look at it and what position you happen to find yourself in- is also built like a brick shithouse.

He's tall, standing at six-foot-four, painted head to toe in tattoos -much like my own- having the typical Swallow family traits; white blonde hair and glaring emerald green eyes -although you can definitely see the crazy reflecting in his.

He offers me a sardonic smile and I reciprocate the action *–okay*, so maybe it's not *only* Charlie that has a little bit of crazy in him.

Silently stepping around the bloody puddle pooling at the base of the restrained man's feet, folding my arms across my chest, I take in the scene.

The greasy fucker tied down is completely naked, already marred with fresh cuts and bruises. Spit and snot, in equal parts, drip down his mouth and chin with his scraggily hair sticking to the sides of his sweaty face. I wrinkle my nose, screwing up my face before turning my attention to my Uncle.

Clucking my tongue and tapping the pointed toe of my stiletto against the concrete, I ask, "so?"

"Nothing yet," my Uncle sighs, like he's already so over today. Wiping the blood on his face with a silk handkerchief *–yes, really-* he pockets it and uncrosses his legs, leaning his forearms on his knees, he looks up at me. "Says he doesn't know where the shit came from, according to him, he doesn't usually deal in anything but weed." My cousin, Eli, scoffs as my uncle continues, "but apparently this bag of blow came unexpectedly in his delivery. Thought it was added by mistake and he'd hit the profit jackpot so to speak," Dee smirks, it's sinister and cold but there's a glint of excitement in his deep green eyes, he likes the violence just as much as the rest of us.

"So, he says we *accidently* gave it to him?" I scoff, trying to clarify the ridiculous tale, our guys never make mistakes, especially not like *that*.

"In a word? Yeah, that's exactly what he's insinuating," my uncle confirms, "sticking with his story too," he harrumphs, as I nod. "Eli, spoke to Stumpy, he said it is absolutely not ours," Uncle Dee finishes, a deep set scowl creasing his lightly aging face.

Stumpy oversees the drug sector of our business. He checks the product, dishes it out, takes in the money. He's probably the only guy outside of my own family that I trust with such an important role, that and he's been doing it for my uncle for the last fifteen years. If he was a dodgy guy, Dee would have sniffed it out like a bloodhound.

"This scumbag mention anything about the other thing?" I ask, nudging the foot of the unconscious man with the point of my shoe, Uncle Dee shakes his head.

I widen my eyes, shaking my head at that utter bullshit. Letting out a small scoff I tilt my head, tucking a long strand of silver hair behind my ear, I slowly circle my prey. This fucking sleazebag is a paedophile, after his little indiscretion –selling someone else's product on our turf- we looked into him a little more and found out he recently abused his niece, his own fucking *blood* and I am not having anyone that works for us do shit like that.

In this line of work -running the underbelly of a city- people usually let any illegal shit fly.

Not us.

Not that.

And not in our fucking city.

We will not have children stripped of their innocence. That is something I absolutely will not condone. I would have killed this scum for that alone, however he's also fucking with our business; a business Charlie and I are set to take over one day. And this guy's out there selling drugs for someone else on my fucking turf to my fucking customers and I point-blank refuse to be insulted like that.

No fucking way.

So today I shall set an example.

"Wake him up," I instruct.

My cousin Eli emerges from the shadows. He's six-foot-six and huge -the youngest of my uncle's four boys- and at twenty-seven he still seems to just keep on growing, if that's even possible. I mean, I'm not exactly short; I stand at a solid six-foot myself, which for your average woman is tall but having someone Eli's size towering over you, is intimidating to say the least.

His large emerald eyes pierce through the darkness as he steps forward, his pale blonde hair illuminated under the light of a single bulb, swinging to and fro from the ceiling. Unceremoniously, Eli wastes no time, ramming a smelling salt stick into the guy's nose, gives his face a harsh slap with the back of his hand, knuckles splitting the skin of his cheek, the guy's head whipping to the side. The slime ball starts to regain consciousness with a low groan.

Moving myself down to his eye level as if I were disciplining a child, bent at the waist, fingers splayed wide on my thighs, I cock my head to look at him. His dark eyes fluttering back to life, his chin lifting at the same time his eyes finally land on mine.

"Oh, *shit*," he exhales, hissing in pain as his face drops in realisation.

"Hello, Pat," I greet him, a feral grin splitting my face.

"Look, *please*. I already told them everything!" he stutters, his voice wheezing with his breaths. *I wonder who broke his ribs.* "I really, honestly, don't know whe-" I stop his blithering with a single raised finger.

I straighten up, clasping my hands behind my back and tut. Without taking my eyes from him, I circle his restrained body, like a starving vulture waiting for the animal below to die, so I can pick apart his carcass and have my fill. Once I've gone a full three-sixty, I stop in front of him again, his eyes so wide they might pop out of their sockets.

Now, wouldn't that be a pretty sight!

Eyeballs -once removed from the socket- are seriously weird fucking things. Their shape is *strange*, there's all these sinewy bits attached to it, it's totally gross but I love the process of removal, especially the brutal way in which Charlie does it. There's something so satisfying about it, especially when the fucker's still awake. I internally sigh to myself.

Great, now I'm gunna be thinking about eyeballs all day.

"I'll give you two minutes to tell me *exactly* what I want to know and then I'm going to get a little bit testy," I tell him calmly, his bottom lip trembling. "If you can convince me you're telling me the truth, the *entire* truth. I'll let you go," I offer with a raised brow, "If I think you're lying, I will take that rather personally, I *really* don't like liars," I smile, "do you understand?" I ask gently, only my voice and Pat's ragged, unsteady breathing can be heard in the open space.

He frantically nods his head as I take a single menacing step towards him. I have to make sure all my moves are calculated perfectly to ensure the intimidation is more than horrifying, women are seriously underestimated. You have to be a seriously deranged bitch to do well in this line of work, luckily for me, I'm exactly that.

"Where did the cocaine come from?" I ask very carefully, calmly, letting my voice elongate the words.

He starts mumbling, incoherent words fall from his split lips, heavy tears dropping down his cheeks and snot bubbling from his nose.

Okay. Eww.

I try to hold back the look of disgust on my face but honestly, snot, not something I handle very well. Give me blood and entrails any day, snot? No fucking way, that shit makes me heave.

"Well?" I ask, "only ninety-seconds left to answer me, times a-ticking," I cackle sinisterly, tapping my bare wrist like I'm wearing a watch.

"He'll, he'll-" he stutters through a choking sound, the back of his throat gurgling, "he'll kill me," he hushes out, drool hanging from his bottom lip.

"Uh-huh, I see," I say, "it's okay," I assure him, trailing my pointed black fingernail down the side of his bleeding face. "I understand," I say sarcastically, jutting out my bottom lip in a pout.

"Yo-, you do?" Pat stammers, swallowing as he calms a little.

"Sure," I shrug, bending down so my face is close, my eyes staring directly into his. "I understand perfectly," I whisper, "you lied to my men, forcing me to come all the way down here, just so you could tell me that you're more afraid of someone else, over *me*. Did I miss anything out?"

"No, no!" he panics. "That's not what I meant! Please! You have to understand!" he blubbers and I take in a deep steadying breath as I straighten up, trying to keep myself from lashing out and tearing his fucking head off.

"You think you should fear this other person because he'll kill you?" I ask for confirmation, cocking a brow at him, he nods manically. "Sooo…what the fuck do you think *I'm* going to do to you?" I ask almost silently. "Oh and Pat," I say, tapping my index finger against my chin, "other than the fact we don't take kindly to traitors," I spit, sneering at him in disgust, my lip curling over my teeth, disloyalty is not something I take very well. "I also know what you did to your niece," I hiss in his ear and I kid you not, he pisses himself, forcing me to take a step back to keep my expensive shoes from being soiled.

"NOT IN FRONT OF THE LADY!" Charlie roars, landing another earth shattering blow to Pat's beaten face, blood spurting from his droopy mouth.

"Lady?" I snort at Charlie, who shrugs his shoulders and

cocks his head.

I am most definitely *not* a lady, that shit right there is fucking laughable; a lady is the last thing I'd ever wanna be. Pat mumbles incoherently under his breath as blood and drool slithers from his swollen face.

Is he fucking praying?

I curl my top lip up over my teeth and wrinkle my nose.

Oh, fucking hell.

I raise an eyebrow and step over to Uncle Dee, who hasn't moved a muscle from his comfortable sitting position; I stand beside him, laying my hand on his shoulder, tilting my head to the side at the mess of a man before me.

Honestly, why do they always have to piss?

I sneak a glance at Charlie. His green eyes glaze over as he mimics my head tilt, clearly mirroring my thoughts, his eyes snap their attention to me and he shrugs, silently asking me what I want to do and I heave a deep sigh.

"Charlie," I say loudly, Pat's attention finally resettling on me. "Be a doll and remove one of his eyes, I'm feeling… thirsty," I shrug, "and it's five o'clock somewhere," I smile, a maniacal slightly deranged grin.

Pat starts to struggle in his binds, which is pointless. Then comes the begging, again, *pointless*. I could have ended it all nicely if he just gave me the information I wanted, I mean I was never gunna let him go, he deserves to be killed for what he did to his niece but still, I probably would have let him keep both his eyes.

Oh well.

Instead, he chose the hard way; which I've gotta give him

props for, not many stand up to me, not many stand up to any member of my family to be honest, which is why I'm not usually needed. But something like this, for someone as unhinged as me? A morning like this is like taking me to the fucking carnival.

Strangled screams of pain and a couple of long minutes later, Eli holds out a perfectly prepared martini –minus the olive- to Charlie who proceeds to drop one of Pat's beady little eyeballs into it, the clear liquid sloshing over the rim of the glass. Eli screws his face up in disgust holding the glass out as far as his arm will stretch, before handing it over to me. I hold the glass up into the air, peering into it from the bottom of the glass, coming *eye to eye* with Pat's. I chuckle to myself.

Well I thought it was funny.

"Nicely done, Charlie-boy," I praise, winking at my cousin and partner in crime with a maniacal smirk.

He flashes me a feral grin before re-awakening a –once again- passed out Pat, throwing a bucket of ice water over him.

"I really wish you had just told me what I wanted to know," I sigh heavily, pouting as he comes to, "well, here's to me, Pat," I toast, raising the glass above my head, "because why the fuck not!"

I laugh as I knock back my martini, the overwhelming metallic tang of blood assaulting my taste buds, the eyeball bumping up against my lips as I drain the glass dry. All to the perfect background symphony of screams and moans of pain, I drop the glass –still containing Pat's eyeball- to the polished concrete letting it shatter across the floor. The glass crunching beneath my feet as I once again make my way to Pat, bending at the waist to look at him.

"Mmm," I moan, "*delicious*," I exhale the taunt, licking my lips and smacking them together loudly, "your beautiful niece is safe from you now, you sick fucking pervert," I hiss.

Making sure he knows this isn't just about lying to me over a bag of coke. No, I know what he did and although I can't fix what happened, I can make sure she grows up never having to worry about her paedophile uncle ever again.

I stand, tucking my long silver hair behind my ears and straightening my silk camisole.

"Goodbye Pat," I toss over my shoulder.

My fist pounding against the large steel door, it opens from the outside, swinging wide and allowing me to step out. I whistle a chirpy tune as I walk down the hallway, hearing just a small roar of pain as the steel door closes behind me, a smile lifting my lips, I swipe at the corners checking I didn't smudge my lipstick and then head for the metal stairs.

CHAPTER 2

KYLA-ROSE

The autumn nights are turning bitter as winter fast approaches and it's fucking freezing tonight. The wild wind howling, thrashing what's left of the golden, rust coloured leaves free from the safety of their battered branches. It's getting dark already, considering it's only late afternoon, the sky threatening a downpour at any moment. That earthy, damp smell filling my nostrils as storm clouds roll in for the night ahead.

I lean further out over the railing of my balcony, closing my eyes and breathing deeply. I find something so calming about storms, which is sort of ironic considering I was petrified of thunder as a child, now I seem to revel in it; I guess the darkness it brings with it speaks to my now tarnished soul.

A small clicking sound behind me catches my attention,

just as I expected and I lazily turn to look through my half open, sliding glass doors. Turning around fully, I rest my back against the glass panel railings, my elbows on the bar behind me; I arch a brow at my cousin Cam aiming a gun straight at my head through the open door.

"Too slow, you're dead," he taunts with a wide grin, his deep green eyes glistening with excitement.

"I heard you the second you came in the front door, dipshit," I laugh, rolling my grey-green eyes as he huffs out a disappointed breath.

Charlie and I play games with each other that some might say are *dangerous*, I laugh at that, they don't know what danger really means. But Cam, on the other hand, is always trying to be the silent assassin, trying to sneak up and get one over on us. Even though he's stealthy for a guy his size, he's still too obvious. I've got ears like a motherfucking bat, nothing is getting past me.

"If that's so, why didn't you call me out?!" he huffs, running a frustrated hand through his messy blonde hair.

Cam is a fucking beast. Standing at six-foot-seven, he is almost as wide as he is tall, he could take you down with one hit and that's with little to no effort considering his fists are the size of sledge hammers. Underneath all that height and muscle, he's cute as a button, pale, ink-free skin, which is more than can be said for the rest of the Swallow family, even my oldest cousin Jacob *–the Doctor-* is covered in ink, but not Cam, he's terrified of needles, which only ever sets me off into fits of giggles every time I think about it.

His dark blonde hair is shaved on both sides, long in the

middle, just enough length that he can tie it up in a little bun at the back of his head. His emerald green eyes are buried beneath thick black lashes that brush over his high cheekbones and dimpled cheeks, just like mine, little crescents either side when he smiles –rarely but it happens. He's a gentle giant with a heart of pure gold but he'll be damned if anyone knows it.

"Because it's funny when you think you've finally got me, I'm impressed it only took you seventy-eight seconds this time too, so at least you're improving," I chuckle, tapping my imaginary watch as he mumbles under his breath about '*know it all women*', tucking his gun back into his underarm holster.

"You get the kid out?" he asks seriously, joining me to look out over the city.

I nod, "yeah, Eli finalised everything and they're long gone, safe and sound."

"Good," he nods, the scowl on his face lessening some. "Coming to Fight Night on Friday? I've got a few newbies on the cards," he says, rapidly changing the subject, teasingly nudging my elbow with his and waggling his eyebrows so they dance across his forehead making me scoff.

When I got out of juvie, one of my first jobs found us shutting down an underground dog fighting ring and taking control of the premises. It was my idea, as punishment –and entertainment- to make the men -who thought it was appropriate to let dog's rip each other to pieces- fight to the death, just like they did to innocent animals. Let's just say that helped solidify my idea of turning the shithole into an underground fight club but for people this time instead of dogs. *Willing* people, that is.

Cam controls it now, deciding who fights and when. It's

totally illegal like pretty much everything else we do but if *we* didn't do it some other fucker would and I highly doubt this city would be run the way we do it. Even the police keep off our backs, they know full well what we're up to but if we keep trouble from them, they let our other shit slide under the radar. We have a good relationship with the law and as long as we keep our boys in check, everything's peachy.

There's absolutely zero tolerance for bad drugs, the skin trade and harm to children -hence the situation with Pat- and Dee rules with an iron fist. You break his rules, I break your face and everyone fucking knows it.

My Uncle Dee is the big boss, top dog, the man in charge. I'm shadowing him currently, learning everything I can, so that when he decides he's had enough, he can pass the baton onto Charlie and I. None of his other sons wanted to take over completely, they'll still run their businesses but we both needed to find more purpose and this is our way of finding it.

Currently though I'm still just the psycho niece of the King with a taste for chaos and violence, which is exactly how I like it. I can still live my life, party, go out and not have to worry about anyone wanting something from me, no favours. And as far as most know, I'm just a soldier working for my uncle, on the *little* jobs.

"Was that sound you made supposed to mean yes, Cuzz?" Cam laughs, pulling the joint from behind my studded ear and lighting it for himself.

"Suppose," I shrug, "haven't got anything else to do, unless Charlie finds us another toy to play with over the weekend," I smile lightly at that idea and accept the joint back from Cam.

"Did you really drink a mojito with a fucking eyeball in it, Ky?" Cam asks with a look of disdain, making me laugh and choke on the heavy smoke in my lungs.

"No," I answer and he raises a brow. "It was a martini," I correct and he throws his head back with a roar of laughter, his shoulders jiggling with the rest of his huge body.

"Honestly, Dad has raised a fucking monster," he laughs, "you were supposed to be the princess of the family," he says, making me flinch at the nickname, not that he notices as he takes the joint back from my fingers.

I never want to be treated like a prissy princess.

"Takes one to know one," I wink and he smiles, exhaling his smoke in little 'O's' before the wind whips them away into the darkness.

"Wanna talk about whatever it is that's bothering you, Kyla?" he suddenly asks without looking at me, *smart boy*, avoiding eye contact with a question like that.

"Nope." I answer, popping the 'P' and twisting my head to look up at him.

Cam stares down at me with a slight pinch to his eyebrows, pursing his lips around the last of the blunt as he narrows his eyes. Realising I'm not going to talk about it, he flicks the butt of the joint over the balcony and runs his hand over my hair, cupping the back of my head firmly in his large hand.

"Love you, Lala," he says seriously, using my childhood nickname.

"Love you too, Cam," I say with a small smile, letting him know I'm okay.

He releases the back of my head and drops his hand lazily

to rest back over the balcony railing.

"Wanna stay for food?" I ask, "we can order pizza?" I offer and he gives me a half smile.

"Sure, but no pineapple," he says with a wink, knowing full well it's my favourite.

"I can have fucking pineapple on my pizza if I fucking want it!" I shout and he belly laughs his way back inside the penthouse.

Friday Fight Nights are always a highly anticipated event. The first few fights of the night are always new or newish fighters who've recently come onto the scene, or rather, are new to *our* scene and that gets the crowd thrumming with excitement, ready for blood to splay, fists to crash, adrenaline pumping through their veins for the unexpected.

I don't attend every week, it's held on Friday's but if Cam has enough new players wanting in –or old rivals wanting to fight it out sooner rather than later- he adds in a few more dates during the week.

It's a semi-controlled environment, controlled in the sense that we don't allow fights to the death, but there are very few other rules. It's just the first one to knockout wins, or someone taps out, however you get to that point though is more or less up to the fighters.

Cam makes sure everyone behaves; no fights that he hasn't sanctioned and no under the table bets so to speak. It has to go through our organisation or it doesn't happen. It's always a good time though. I crave the blood, there's something so therapeutic about fighters beating the shit out of each other, I'm not gunna lie about it, the sound of flesh being pummelled gets me kinda hot, especially if the fighters are something to look at.

I push into my master bedroom, decorated similarly to the rest of my penthouse; all dark colours and low lighting with gold accents. The walls in here are painted a deep maroon red, the floor covered in a thick black carpet –the heavy, plush kind your feet sink into when you walk- and a large four poster bed; all carved black wood with maroon drapes hung around its posts.

The bedding is black silk, right down to the throw pillows and there're gold fixtures and fittings for the lights, door handles and wall sockets. The walk in closet is to the far left of the room and the en-suite bathroom sits to the right. The entire back wall of the room is made up of floor to ceiling windows with a glass door leading out onto the wrap-around balcony. I'm not one for bright colours, I like the darkness, it's safer to hide in the dark, shadows and hidden corners.

Checking my reflection in the floor length mirror, I tuck my waist-length, silver hair behind my heavily pierced ears. I've gone with a thick black smoky eye and a blood red lip. Over my tattooed skin I've pulled on an old black t-shirt which I cut into a crop top, it's one of Jacob's old shirts so its baggy causing it to slip off of one shoulder.

A red lace bra beneath it; which just peeks out if I lift my arms but not quite enough to flash my nipple piercings. Black fishnets, black leather, mini-skirt, all finished off with my trusty black combat boots. My outfit is probably not weather appropriate, given that we're in England and it's fucking freezing out, but the warehouse gets so hot your skin would melt off like it were dunked in acid if you wore much more.

I walk down the long dark corridor when I'm ready, stopping at my babies' room -my two rescued pit-bull babies that is- on my way to the elevator. Brute is my big boy, he's raven black nose to tail, with piercing grey eyes, he's soppy as fuck. He looks scary but really he's petrified of his own shadow, apart from the odd occasion he goes into protective mode. He definitely lacks a bit of intelligence too, let's just say he's not the brightest bulb in the box.

Then there's Angel; she's definitely the boss of the two. White fur with striking pale blue eyes, her looks may make her the definition of an angel but that's where the angelic qualities end. She has a *slight* temper problem, she's a little aggressive and isn't a big fan of strangers but the two of them together are the perfect fit for me. Brute is the light to Angel's dark, just like both sides of my personality.

I'm cool, calm, collected, super laid-back, but in the right moments I get a little… *excited*? Okay, deranged is also probably a good description but in what world would I wanna be normal?

Boringgg.

Crazy should be the way of the world, I *thrive* on my psychotic tendencies rather than hide them away. I always get my most *creative* ideas when I let my demon loose.

My babies are wrapped up together on their couch when I head into their room. One end of the couch has been chewed open, the stuffing falling out of the split fabric but after replacing it three times already, it can stay as it is. Whatever makes them happy.

I scrub my hands over Brute's exposed belly at the same time Angel leaps up to nuzzle my face, I kiss their heads goodbye, then carry on down the hall to the elevator. I press the call button, waiting for that familiar *ding*, before taking the elevator down to the underground parking level. I climb into the back of the waiting, blacked out SUV.

"Evening, boss," the driver greets me as I slide across the leather and buckle my seatbelt.

"Frank," I nod, "how's your day been?" I ask pulling my spare Glock-26 from the seat pocket in front of me and checking it's loaded.

It's the perfect size gun to carry in this tiny skirt.

"Nothing to report, boss, all's been quiet," he replies as he starts to pull out of the car park.

"That's good to hear, how's the wife?"

"Carol's well, thanks," he swallows, his eyes flicking to meet mine in the rear-view mirror, "speaking of, if there's any extra shifts this weekend I'd be grateful."

"Oh, yeah? Saving up to buy that holiday home she wants after all?" I wink and he laughs.

The last time I saw Carol she was showing me photos of a big ski lodge up in Switzerland.

"Nah, her parents are coming this weekend and I'd be real happy to be away from them for as long as possible," he grimaces, making me laugh.

Frank's been my driver and a member of my security team for the last couple of years. He's one of the good guys and I like him a lot.

He's in his early forty's, his dark hair shaved short with

beautiful bright blue eyes that remind me of the Mediterranean, he's tall and lean and loyal to the bone, a very trustworthy guy with a mean face and a friendly smile. He's managed to get me out of more than a few sticky situations with his mad driving skills too.

"Sure, you can work the weekend, I'm sure I can find a safe spot to hide you until they leave," I chuckle knowing I'd be the exact same way if I had in-laws too, I'm not a meet the parents kinda girl.

Scooting forward to the edge of the seat I tuck the gun into the back of my skirt.

"Thanks, boss, appreciate that," he smiles warmly.

"Just make sure Carol doesn't come breaking down my door because she's pissed I made you work," I warn, pointing a finger at him as he watches me in the mirror.

"Cross my heart," he chuckles, mimicking a cross over his heart with his finger.

We pull up in the abandoned warehouse district -which we now own- it's full of dilapidated buildings including the one I burnt down when I was sixteen, the events of which ended with me being sent to juvie for nearly two years but that's a story for another day.

We renovated the very central warehouse, which is the largest, just enough that it's safe for people to be packed in like sardines and feel at ease knowing the roof isn't about to cave in on them.

Frank jumps out, rounding the car he opens my door, holding out his hand for me to take, I latch my fingers around his and hop down onto the wet tarmac, my heavy boots sending little splatters of dirty rain water up into the air.

"Want to watch a few?" I offer over my shoulder before turning towards the building.

"Wouldn't say no," Frank shrugs.

"Come on then," I nod, gesturing my head in the direction of the warehouse, Frank checks his gun is loaded and flicks on the safety before locking up the car and leading the way.

I check my phone messages as I absently traipse behind his large frame –knowing he's got eyes everywhere- and delete most of them without reading them first. There's one with a picture of a blood-soaked Charlie, which makes me laugh but a little jealous, what fun is he having without me? And one from Jacob, warning me to behave myself and telling me he misses me which makes me smile.

Jacob is the oldest of Uncle Dee's four sons, he's a Doctor. Well, a surgeon now, he worked his fucking arse off in med school for nine fucking years and then last year he finally got promoted to specialist surgeon. Specialist in what exactly, I don't know, all I know is he's a handy guy to have around; especially with the lives we lead. He's pulled more than a couple bullets from me and his brothers and reset more bones at our kitchen table than I could even count over the years.

We're really fucking lucky to have him.

Jacob's been working away the last six months in Ghana on some charity project and I don't know when he's gunna be back but I wish it'd be soon. It's weird having one of the boys I grew up with not around all the time when the rest of them are.

Frank pounds his curled fist against the door, a small slider opens revealing a pair of dark eyes peering out before it slams shut and the door swings open. Frank stands to one side with his arm out gesturing for me to go in first.

As soon as I step inside everything overwhelms my senses at once. Heavy bass music pounds assaulting my ears as I work my way down the dimly lit corridors, nodding to various staff and security members as I pass. They all nod back with respect or greet me with a bow of the head, they know I can be violent and unpredictable and most have heard what I'm capable of. Not that I'd ever attack a member of my staff. *Well*, unless they deserved it…

The smell of beer, sweat and blood fills my nose and my eyes slowly adjust to the brighter lit areas as we approach the main room. I push my way through a *staff only* door and enter out into the packed room, closely followed by Frank.

Scaffolding fixed at various levels around the room gives a heightened view of the action for spectators to sit or stand, keeping the warehouse with that raw, industrial feel. There are three bars located in different areas around the room, all serving the same beverages but spread out to avoid a large crowd gathering in one particular spot at a time. The ring is a raised platform with a thick mat, boxed in with wide blue ropes.

I spot Cam right away, standing off to one side of the ring with Eli, their heads drawn together in private conversation. Cam is tapping ferociously at the scheduled fight card and Eli is throwing his arms wide in what looks like frustration.

What the fuck is going on?

"Frank, get yourself a drink, I'm popping over to see the boys," I tell him, he looks over, following my eye line then nods.

Not that I expect he'll get a drink, he'll probably watch me like he normally does until I'm safely beside one of my cousins, even though I'm probably the scariest fucker in the entire room.

I weave my way through the sweaty crowd, working my slim body between people, popping up on the other side of the crowd. I step between the ropes, hop up into the ring and cross the mat.

"What's happened?" I half-shout, rocking my weight forward on the ropes, rolling back and forth on my tiptoes, I look between Eli and Cam with a raised brow.

"*Jesus!* Kyla-Rose!" Eli jumps, "you scared the shit out of me, fuck's sake," he says dramatically, slapping his hand over his heart and shaking his head.

"Always be prepared for the unexpected, *Swallow,*" I scold with a grin and he rolls his eyes at me.

"Hey, Ky," Cam greets with a half-smile, if you can actually call it that.

Grumpy fucker.

"Hey, sooo…" I start, raising my eyebrows expectantly, waiting for them to fill me in, my eyes flicking between the two of them.

Eying each other before looking back to me with hesitation and that's all the confirmation I need to know somethings going down.

"Well?" I ask impatiently.

"There was a bit of a brawl earlier, the *off-the-card* type and Cam was dealing with it, along with some of the team but Charlie got involved and you know how he is," Eli, grimaces.

"Yeah… and?"

"And one of them mentioned you and him being a little, ya

know, that word that triggers him," Cam heaves a sigh and runs a large hand over his tired face.

"They called us crazy?" I ask and they both nod.

It's okay for us to call ourselves crazy, hell, even call each other crazy but no other fuck has that sort of permission, Charlie's very sensitive to the word.

"So… what are you trying to tell me right now?" I ask, my eyes darting between the two of them.

"He's still *playing*, he says he's not done yet and he won't come down," Cam tells me and I narrow my eyes.

"Okay, where is he?" knowing it's only me that has any real chance at getting some sort of control over my psycho partner in crime, I'll find him, reattach his leash and retake control of the hell beast.

Simple.

"In the back, top floor, old office," Eli sighs, scrubbing his hand over his face, his fingers stopping at his chin to massage his jaw.

"Okay, I'll be back," I chirp before ducking under the ropes, "don't put on anyone good before I get back!" I call over my shoulder, heading to a door on the opposite side of the warehouse.

As my boots hit the steel stairs I instantly hear muffled cries. Charlie must really be on one tonight, I wonder how long he's been at this. He can get a little carried away when it comes to violence. Not that I blame him, it's thrilling, the feel of blood seeping between your fingers and toes, the warm splatters that spray across your skin when you really get into it, there's honestly nothing better.

Control.

I tried to get Charlie to wear a muzzle once –which I thought would be fucking hilarious- he was open to the idea, well, he didn't openly verbalise his objection… but when I started to put it on him, he bit into my hand so hard that by the time he released me I needed eleven stiches. Still think it was one of my best ideas, it could have been his whole thing, like all the murderers in horror films, they all have their signature masks and shit, that could have been his, but oh well, you win some, you lose some.

As I hit the top floor I follow the low groans down to a dingy room at the end. I swing the door open, wedge my body to lean in the jamb, crossing my ankles over each other and fold my arms across my chest. A very bloodied man is tied to an old office chair in the middle of the room, Charlie hunched over him, blood dripping from Charlie's large tattooed body, as he works away at whatever it is he's doing.

"Hey, Charl," I call softly as to not startle him but his body snaps to attention anyway as he slowly sweeps his gaze in my direction.

"This man called you *crazy*," he hisses gruffly, baring his bloody teeth -blood that I don't suspect is his.

"I heard," I say casually, as though it doesn't bother me one way or the other, it does though, I don't like being called crazy.

You must never enter a room unannounced when Charlie's *working*, he gets a bit carried away, zoning out if you like and if you surprise him, well, he's not always aware of who's around him immediately and that's when accidents happen.

"You almost done?" I ask gently, tilting my head to one

side taking in his bloodied appearance.

Charlie's coated in blood, he looks like he bathed himself in it for some demonic ritual or something, blood is dripping from his shaggy blonde hair and running down his face, he blinks some from his eyelashes as he looks at me, his hands and clothes saturated and the butterfly knife –I know to be purple- he's holding is a deep crimson red.

"I want you to come watch the fights with me," I state melodically and he cocks his head at me in response.

"You don't want him punished?" he grumbles through gritted teeth, the huskiness of his damaged vocal cords straining to get sound out.

"He looks pretty well punished to me, Charl," I chuckle, glancing back over at the whimpering creature behind him.

"You sure that's enough? He insulted you! *Us!*" He hisses, his muscular arms spread out wide in outrage, blood running down his corded forearms.

"I know," I placate, "but I want us to go downstairs, be with your brothers, how about we go to the locker room and get you showered real quick?" I reach my hand out to take the knife, giving him a small smile as he thinks over my offer. "I've got a new toy to play with lined up for Wednesday," I throw in for leverage and he grins wide.

"Okay," his grin turns menacing, releasing the sticky knife into my custody, he drops it into my open palm. "I'm done with you now," he smiles slapping the guy hard on the cheek. "Don't ever insult my family again," he warns with a growl, "GOT IT?!" he shouts, clacking his teeth together like a hungry alligator as the trembling man cries out a babbled reply of agreement.

"Good," Charlie plasters on a simple smile before turning to face me, slinging a bare, bloodied arm over my shoulders and steering me from the room.

The locker rooms are small and basic but functional all the same. There are two, one for women, one for men, although we rarely get any women fighters -much to my disappointment- both rooms are laid out identically. Each holds three rows of red lockers, a large square, wooden slatted bench in the very centre and showers to the left which veer round the corner with a couple of toilet cubicles and a long worktop holding two sinks and a large mirror hanging above them.

Lying on my back on the bench in the middle of the room, all of the fighters abandoned the space and hurried off into the other locker room as soon as we walked in. Both of us entered caked in blood -we must have looked a right pair, the infamous Chaos Twins at their finest- we made quite the entrance, emptying out the room in about a fifth of a second. I chuckle to myself at the image of those guys' faces, all those large, scary men waiting for a bare-knuckle fist fight paled at the sight of us.

I managed to clean up my bare shoulder and the side of my neck from where Charlie had slung his bloody arm around me, leaving me crimson too and now I'm just waiting while he showers off, we like to always have one of us with him at all times. I might be just as crazed as he is but I generally have better self-control.

Sometimes…

Charlie?

Charlie has *none*.

He often sneaks off, hiding torture victims and bodies here, there and everywhere. He often thinks we don't know, but *I do*.

"I can hear you laughing to yourself, you fucking weirdo!" he calls out, his deep, growling voice echoing from the showers only serves to make me laugh harder.

"Hey! I'm not weird!" I shout back with a grin, I most definitely, *definitely* am.

"Whatever you say!" he bellows back gruffly, making me laugh more.

I close my eyes and drop an arm over my face, my silver hair fanning out around my head and trailing onto the floor, swinging my legs off the end of the bench, I flick Charlies little, purple butterfly knife around in my other hand. I smile.

I count my blessings every goddamn day for this family.

I may not have had the best start to life, what with my daddy being in prison since before I can remember and my mum a careless addict, but my Uncle Dee always made sure I was alright.

Mum died when I was sixteen, the same night I got arrested. I cringe at the memory, it was a stupid fucking thing to do but I wasn't exactly in the right head space I guess, after everything that happened that night, I shudder just thinking about it.

At the time I thought burning that shitty warehouse to the ground would give me some sort of peace after what happened there but all it did was get me banged up in juvie for nearly two fucking years –two really *long* fucking years.

A cold shiver rushes through me at the onslaught of

hideous memories. I'd burn that fucking juvie to the ground too if I could, with all of those fucking men inside it. I snort at the thought, knowing I've already spent enough of my life locked up in one way or another. Trapped by my mother and her addiction then thrown from that cage into another, only this one had shiny metal bars and abusive prison guards to keep me locked inside.

The door opens into the room and a single pair of footsteps enters making me sigh. What fucker would even dare walk in here once they see who's occupying it? I'm sure they were warned before even stepping over the threshold, so they must either be really brave or really fucking stupid. I can't wait to find out which.

"This room's occupied, the fighters go next door," I sigh without moving from my spot.

"Oh, I don't know, I kind of like the view in here," a deep voice rumbles with humour from somewhere beside me, somewhere way too *close* beside me.

I bolt up into a sitting position, throwing my legs around to the side of the bench with a scowl on my face.

"Oi! Arsehole, I-" I stop myself abruptly with my mouth slightly agape when I look up into a pair of mischievous gold eyes.

God, he's fucking beautiful.

"This is the *men's* locker room, right?" he asks with a smirk and just like that…

BOOM!

I think my ovaries just exploded.

"So you *can* read, Big Man, good to know," I deadpan and

his smile widens.

Jesus Christ, have mercy.

I stand up, flicking the little purple blade I was playing with away before tucking it into the waistband of my leather skirt. He doesn't even flinch at the knife I carelessly tossed around, though his eyes track its movement as it disappears from his sight. I tuck my long hair back behind one ear, leaving the other side to curtain across my face as I stare up at the god-like creature before me. We're standing so close together, we're practically touching tits to chest, barely a hair's breadth apart causing me to involuntarily suck in a sharp breath.

Looking up at him he's easily six and a half feet tall, if not taller, the guy's a fucking giant. His pale blonde hair is shaved bald on one side revealing the lines of a thick black tattoo curling around the side of his skull. The rest is a shaggy mess on top, flopped forward onto his forehead almost completely covering one of his unusual amber-yellow eyes.

His jaw is square, chiselled so sharp it could cut glass, with a light dusting of day-old gold stubble covering it. His throat is tattooed with black ink which runs down disappearing beneath his baggy vest, a distinctive thick scar running right across the centre of his throat, which only serves to make him even sexier.

His entire look screams 'bad boy' and I want to scold myself for practically panting at him like a cat in heat.

God, I hope I'm not dribbling.

He is literally intoxicating; I'm dizzy just looking at the fucking guy.

Jesus, god, down girl.

"When you're quite finished eye-fucking me," he purrs

knowingly, seductively, "I'd like to get changed if you don't mind," he smirks, slowly reaching out his large tattooed hand, his thick fingers tuck the long curtain of silver hair behind my other ear, taking away my hiding spot and revealing my face.

His knuckle brushes my neck, a shockwave rolling through me at the contact, making me clench my traitorous thighs together. I narrow my eyes at him, placing one hand on his *way* too muscular chest, pushing against him lightly, *god he's firm, holy Christ.* He moves with my hand, creating much needed distance between the two of us, voluntarily that is, there's no way I could have gotten him to move if he didn't want to, the man's a body-building beast.

I smile sweetly at him as I raise my gun in the air and point it at his big head –metaphorically big that is, *his normal size head is really quite beautiful-* I jerk my own to the right as my smile widens.

"Fuck off next door, Big Man. I don't need to look at any more of you, that ridiculously sized ego of yours certainly doesn't need any more attention," I tell him but much to my surprise, he doesn't back off like any other sane person with a gun to their head would.

Well that's a fucking first.

In fact, he shocks me even more by taking a step towards me, quickly closing the newly built distance I created. As he gets in my face, the small gun pressing into his forehead, he doesn't flinch, he simply presses himself against it harder making my grip stiffen at the pressure, the metal biting into his skin.

"You gunna shoot me, cherub?" he teases, running his tongue over his front teeth, a maniacal grin engulfing his square face, his lips upturned and perfect pearly whites gleaming.

Fuck me. That's hot.

"Yes." I answer definitively without fault, my face blank and emotionless even as I work hard to hide my body's overt reaction to him.

I've been doing this shit for years and my pussy isn't about to betray me now, no matter how hot the piece of meat standing in front of me is because at the end of the day that's all he is, all he could ever be.

Thinking about what's beneath his loose white vest –not that it covers much anyway, I could easily tear it off- I almost bite my lip but internally slap myself at the very idea. Chiselled abs covered by tight tattooed skin, I imagine his huge arms, which are finely on display in his baggy drop arm vest, wrapping around my slim frame and lifting me with ease, my legs winding around his tight waist.

Fuck me.

If he thinks he somehow knows me already from a thirty second conversation and feels confident enough to think that I *wouldn't* shoot him right between his *–gorgeous as fuck-* gold eyes then he is deadly mistaken.

"I like you," he breathes with a cocky grin, close enough to my face that I can feel his hot breath on my skin, halting any and all words I'd prepared myself to spit at him.

Likes me… who *likes* a manic woman holding a gun to their head?!

Well… I mean other than me?

Clean soap and mint fills my nostrils, there's something earthy there too, but the clean, fresh scent sends a shiver ricocheting down my spine, hitting me like a bolt of lightning, before he takes a large step back. Scooping up his duffle bag from the floor, tossing it over his broad shoulder, he turns his solid back to me, more tendrils of ink swirling out beneath the racerback cut of his vest, he silently exits the room, leaving me to gape at the door sweeping shut behind him.

"Jesus, *fuck*!" I hiss under my breath, squeezing my eyes shut and tapping the side of the gun against my own head as I pace an anxious circle.

No one's ever stepped up to me like that before.

Staring me down without an ounce of fear in his eyes, not even the prospect of a fully loaded weapon –one that was literally pressing into his forehead- being emptied inside his skull was putting him off.

Something about that got me so hot it's fucking disorientating.

"What're you doing?" Charlie asks, his gruff rumble pulling me from my thoughts.

Wandering out from the showers in a pair of low slung, black joggers, his tattooed top half still bare and running with water, he cocks his head at me.

"Cursing myself for not shooting someone," I grumble, roughly shoving the gun back into my skirt.

Charlie's rough chuckle echoes around the empty room as he rubs a white towel over his wet hair, dropping it into the laundry bin beside the lockers. He tugs his leather jacket from the hook on the wall, throwing it over his right shoulder, forgoing a shirt as per usual.

"Come on, cuzz, let's go watch the bloodbath then maybe

I'll help you hit your target," he winks throwing his arm over my shoulders, dragging me through the door and leading me back out into the main room.

I sit myself up onto one of the higher scaffolding levels which gives me a view of the entire floor, resting my sticky forehead against the cool metal pole railing gives me a moment of reprieve from the heat. I swing my legs back and forth over the edge, it's so hot in here my blood feels like it's close to boiling.

I wonder if we could get air-con?

Looking down into the heaving crowd, money's exchanging between gambling hands, grubby fingers betting on which newbie they think is worth a shot, as well as which regulars they anticipate will be their winners.

I spot Cam talking to someone at the side of the ring, heads pulled together, Cam shakes his and eventually dismisses the kid by turning his back on him.

Charlie plonks down beside me, passing me a beer in a clear plastic cup.

"Thanks," I say, chugging down a few gulps of the – thankfully cold, although cheap- beer.

That was one of the best decisions we made for this place, setting up generators to run the refrigeration was a top priority, no one wants to drink warm beer. *Gag*.

We sit together quietly, waiting for the first fight and my tense body starts to relax into the familiar bustling atmosphere.

Rain pelts down onto the tin roof; vibrations of sound rolling through the warehouse give it an even darker vibe, the lack of windows makes it dark and intimidating, uninviting even on the best of days. We have tall free-standing lights set up around the place, mainly at the bar and directed on the ring, the rest of the place is fairly shadowed with just enough light to stop you tripping over your own feet. The clash of thunder and occasional flashes of lightning only heighten the deviant atmosphere of the place.

The first few fights were bloody. One kid lost a few teeth before tapping out and Cam had to haul another guy off of his knocked out opponent. They get carried away, what can I say.

During a break, Eli drops into the space beside me, there's always space around wherever Charlie and I are. Everyone always giving us a wide berth, no one brave enough to sit close to the '*Swallow family psychos*', no matter how packed out the place is.

"Hey, kid," Eli greets me, nudging my arm with his elbow as he passes me another beer.

"Hey," I smile up at him as he reaches across me, passing another drink to Charlie.

Accepting it, he swallows down the whole pint in one and tosses the empty cup over the railing into the crowd below. The empty cup catches a guy's shoulder on its decent and he looks up with a scowl to see where it came from, when his eyes lock onto us, quickly realising who we are he bows his head in our direction before he turns back to face the ring.

Sometimes I hate that. The way people fear us so much, no one daring to challenge our authority, it's as much a blessing as it is a curse. We need to rule with an iron fist and be respected because ruling the underworld is a tough as fuck job; you're dealing with criminals day in, day out. But at the same time I just want someone to challenge me. I want the fight, the back and forth. I want the danger, the excitement of not knowing if I'm going to win. Even an argument would help sate some of my desire.

Sure, I like torture as much as the next whack-job –when the person deserves it- but it's predictable. I want the chase, the thrum of excitement at the unexpected, someone who is equally as fucked up as I am, giving me a run for my money, I guess. I'm a predator but I want, on occasion, to feel like the prey, not be fully in control all the time and let the excitement of the chase rush through me.

As long as I win in the end, that is.

Taking another sip of my beer, my grey-green eyes wander around the room, stopping when they land on a hulking, tattooed figure. It looks like Gold eyes is up next. Adrenaline coursing through my veins, my leg begins bouncing of its own accord in anticipation. I don't know if I've ever been this excited to watch a fight before. Without changing the direction of his head, Charlie raises an eyebrow at me and peers out the corner of his emerald green eye.

"Kyla-Rose," he whispers my name, "that the guy you wanted to shoot?" his question laced with suspicion, his eyes roving back over to the bulldozer sized man with the intricate head tattoo.

"Yes," I answer quickly, too quickly apparently, if Charlie's reaction is anything to go by.

He smirks and turns to face me fully, "what exactly happened in that locker room?" his eyes narrowing in on me, assessing my face for the tiniest of reactions.

"I threatened to shoot him, he stared down the barrel of my gun without flinching and practically dared me to do it, smiled like a loon, told me-" I excitedly rush out all too fast, stopping before I say to much but the thought of someone standing up to me, makes heat pool rapidly in my lower belly.

"Told you what, Lala?" Charlie smirks, his tongue flicking out and running over his unnaturally sharp fang tooth.

My cheeks heat, my chest blushing a violent red, I lick my dry lips and turn my gaze to Charlie.

"He told me he-" I swallow past the dry lump in my throat, my eyes flicking to Gold eyes and back, "he said he likes me."

"Was this before or after the gun to the head?" Charlie questions, that smirk growing more feral with every passing second.

"After, well, *during.*"

"Wow," Charlie whistles lowly, his eyes wide as he looks between me and the golden eyed fighter that's just stepped up into the ring.

"What's going on?" Eli leans forward studying both Charlie and I.

"Nothing," I try to say, but of course Charlie talks over me.

"That guy," he says, boldly pointing Gold eyes out for Eli, Eli's line of sight travelling in the fighters direction, "stood up to Kyla in the locker room and now she's totally hot for him," Charlie answers for me, making me scowl.

"Charlie!" I growl.

"*Fuck!*" Eli hisses, "Kyla-Rose! You gunna kill him?" he asks, genuine curiosity in his dark green eyes.

"No," I snap back defensively, "I'm not going to kill him, he didn't *do* anything," I hiss making him chuckle along with Charlie.

Eli throws his hands up in surrender, still with a stupid smile slapped on his face.

"Maybe you should marry him, I can't remember any guy stupid enough to stand up to you and live to tell the tale!" he howls, slapping his thigh and making me frown harder.

I'm not *that* bad.

The more Elijah laughs, the more I think about tearing one of my boot laces free and wrapping around his thick neck. I wonder how long it would take him to free himself whilst I plant my feet on his back and pull the string tighter.

"Careful, Eli, or it might be *you* that I shoot tonight," I say quietly with a -fake as fuck- sickly sweet smile.

"You'd never kill me, kid. I'm your favourite cousin," he chuckles slinging his arm around my shoulders, dragging me into his side and squeezing me tight, I tuck myself under his thick arm and lean into his chest, absorbing his comfort.

"Mmm, sure, whatever you say," I mumble, continuing to stare down at the golden eyed guy, who I hate to admit is already holding a little more than my attention.

"You've got that look, Kyla-Rose," Charlie mumbles his accusation at me.

"What look?" I frown, knowing exactly what he's referring to, *the obsession.*

"The look that tells me, that guy's got your attention," he

observes, speaking almost silently and he's not wrong is he? "The look that says you either wanna spend a weekend torturing him or fucking him but you still can't make up your mind on which," Charlie finishes.

That's because I'd like to do both.

I wrinkle my nose in denial at his comment and stare up into my older cousin's green eyes that are so similar, yet so much more intense than my own.

"I'm not going there, Charl, don't worry about me," I whisper back.

"You're exactly who I worry about, Kyla-Rose," he says, returning his attention back to the ring and instantly stiffening in his seat.

I slowly follow Charlie's line of sight and find myself stiffening too, my back snapping ramrod straight. Gold eyes is glaring up at me from his corner of the ring, his unique coloured eyes locking onto my own, smirking when he knows he's got my attention, throwing me a devilish wink just as Cam calls the start of the fight.

The guy he's fighting is huge, easily rivalling Gold eyes' height and build, they're more than equally matched in this fight but neither party looks deterred. The other fighter has beautiful dark skin, a shaved head and lots of colourful ink down both arms, covering his back and chest. He lightly bounces on his toes and has his arms up protecting his head.

Within seconds he throws a hard punch directly at Gold eyes, who doesn't even try to block the punch that hits him square in the temple. His arms hang loosely at his sides, he bounces on his toes, shaking his head, grinning as if taking that hit was enjoyable. The crowd erupts into cheers, the noise almost deafening as Gold eyes smiles wider, a big grin that splits his face, like the demon inside him is coming out to play, his perfect white teeth shining brightly in the dim light.

This guy is a fucking psychopath and I mean, I should know; I'm one too.

The dark skinned fighter, still guarding his face, jabs out a few times, landing his blows, making him get a little too cocky and just as he throws out his fist to land another solid punch, Gold eyes dodges to the left landing an uppercut to the chin that's so hard it has the guy sprawling out on the mat, knocked out cold with one hit.

The crowd erupts. Cam's team step in to attend the knock out as Cam grabs Gold eyes wrist, thrusting his arm high into the air, announcing him as the winner. Gold eyes looks up directly at me and smiles, not a smirk, a real fucking smile, wide and toothy and perfect and completely crazed. My pussy clenches, heat pools low down in my belly and my thighs squeeze together painfully.

I watch Cam take notice of where his fighter's attention is drawn, raising his eyebrows in surprise but I can't stare him down like I usually would, all I can do is stare back and be all consumed by the golden eyed boy who has undoubtedly, now, got my full fucking attention.

CHAPTER 3

KYLA-ROSE

The mattress dips heavily beside me and I groan. My head's fuzzy, my eyes are aching already and I haven't even forced them open yet. Hot breath on the side of my neck has me twisting so I'm lying flat on my back, a slobbery wet slap to my warm cheek has me launching myself upright.

"Eurgh!" I moan, wiping my palm down the trail of slobber on my face.

I open my eyes slowly, two sets staring back at me, one pair grey and one pair blue.

"You two will be the death of me," I grumble at Angel and Brute who have parked their huge bodies on either side of mine.

Brute's huge black body lunges forward, knocking me down onto my back and pinning my shoulders with his huge paws, his tongue darting out, licking me all over the face and neck making me squeal. Angel just changes her lazy position from sitting to lying so she's closer to my face.

"Okay! Okay! Breakfast, I get it!" I laugh pushing Brute's heavy paws from my shoulders removing his weight with a grunt.

He really is fucking heavy, weighing in at just over sixty-pounds, it's a lot. He backs off, jumping to the floor and racing down the hallway towards the kitchen. Angel just gives me a lazy yawn laying her big paw over my forearm; I lean over and kiss the crazy bitch on the forehead before pushing myself up and following the sound of Brute's skittering feet.

I find Hazel in the kitchen, already filling two silver bowls with dog food. Hazel has been my housekeeper for the last few years, her shiny brown hair is always neatly pulled back into a low bun at the nape of her neck and her large brown eyes bring her smile to life, making her white teeth look even brighter against her olive skin.

She's one of the only women on my staff, but I have to admit it is nice having a woman around for a change –not many women fancy getting into my line of work- although I rarely bump into her. She's silent as she works around the house and keeps all of the other staff on a tight schedule, so I never really run into any of them –I think that's probably more for their benefit than mine.

I smile at her gratefully, placing the filled bowls down onto their mat. Brute's head immediately disappears into his, swallowing every last scrap of food before Angel has even bothered to saunter down the hallway from my bedroom. Brute looks up at Hazel with wide eyes, she laughs patting the greedy dog on the head, shaking hers at him. A silent message being passed to him *–no you greedy shit, you're not getting anymore.*

"Good morning, Hazel," I yawn, finally being awake enough to speak, I take a seat at the breakfast bar, propping my elbows on the counter and resting my chin in my hands.

"Good morning, Miss Swallow," she greets me and I cringe, I know she's being polite and professional but I hate being called something so *official*.

I give her another smile as she turns her back to me, carrying a basket of laundry out with her. My phone rings from somewhere nearby and I wrinkle my nose trying to remember where I dumped it last night.

Ah, last night.

After watching Gold eyes in the ring, I thankfully didn't see him again after that, so I got myself well and truly wasted, I haven't consumed that much alcohol in a *long* while and I can already tell I'm gunna pay for it today.

I slide off of the bar stool and begrudgingly follow the incessant ringing. I wind my way towards the elevator and screw my face up when I can't see it on the centre table. Wandering over to where the sound is coming from and low and behold, there it is, tossed in the plant pot that sits next to the elevator. I wipe the dirt from it down my sleep shorts before pressing it to my ear.

"Yeah?" I answer, easily sliding into boss mode.

"Morning, boss," Frank says down the line and I scrub a hand over my tired face.

"Morning, Frank, what ya got for me?" I ask, making my way through to the main bathroom.

"Few things happening down at the warehouse, boss, think you should get down here," he says in a disgruntled tone.

"Talk to me, what's happening?" I demand, switching on the shower, letting the water run as I shove a toothbrush in my mouth, scrubbing my teeth while I listen.

"Couple of your boys down here saying some shit about being approached last night, they came to talk to Dee but no one can get hold of him. So thought I should at least see if I could get you and see what you wanted me to do," he tells me respectfully.

I spit out my toothpaste into the black marble sink and shimmy my shorts down my legs, moving the phone away from my ear, I pull my loose t-shirt over my head and then place the phone back to my ear.

"Keep them there, I'll be twenty," I tell him, hanging up and tossing the phone into the sink.

I step under the hot spray, tipping my head back, letting the water run over my face and soak my hair. I lather citrus scented soap all over my body, shampooing my hair and following with coconut scented conditioner. I rinse off and climb out, wrapping myself in a fluffy white towel. I pad my wet feet down the hall into my bedroom, wet hair slapping against my back, crossing the thick black carpet, I push open my closet.

Stepping inside I drop my towel and select a bright red, two piece pant suit, red wide leg trousers and a matching red fitted blazer. I step into a black lace thong, forgoing a bra; I pull on a black lace body suit, followed by the red pant suit. I slip my feet into red soled, black pointed stilettoes, applying a thick layer of mascara and a bold red lip, I ring my soaking hair out with the towel and pull it up into a high ponytail.

Grabbing the Audi R8 keys –knowing that baby will get me there in next to no time- I make my way down to the underground garage. I slip into the driver's seat, adjusting it to fit me and not Franks hulking frame, throw it into first gear and gun it up and out of the garage.

Hitting the main road, I fly through the gears until I hit seventh and then thrash it towards the warehouses. I jump two red lights and pass three police cars on my way –all of them recognising my bright orange sports car and ignoring it- I hit hands-free and dial, Uncle Dee.

"Kyla-Rose," he greets almost immediately and I can tell it's with a smile.

"Uncle Dee," I reply warmly.

"It's a Saturday, why you up this early?" he asks with a light chuckle.

I imagine him now, out on the stone balcony off of his bedroom in a button down shirt and slacks. Designer, tortoiseshell sunglasses perched on his nose and a newspaper in his lap, an ankle resting on his knee as he sips espresso.

"Business as always, Sir," I sigh and I can practically hear his smile being replaced with a frown.

"Talk to me," he demands and so I tell him what Frank called me with and that I'm heading there now.

"You want me to come down?" he asks.

"Nah, I'm good, just informing you," I shrug.

"Okay, catch me up later."

"Love you."

"Love you too, Lala," he replies as the line goes dead.

Switching contacts, I call my partner in crime who answers on the second ring.

"Kyla-Rose,"

"Charl,"

"What's up?" Charlie asks.

"May need you, meet me at the warehouse."

"Already in the area, see you in a few," he growls without hesitation before ending the call.

I can always count on Charlie to be available for me. No matter where he is or what he's doing, he always makes time.

Pulling into the warehouse grounds, I skid to a complete stop, kicking up gravel; Frank is there immediately, pulling open my door, holding his hand out to help me from the car. I follow him into one of the warehouses we don't use for more than storage, my heels tapping across the cracked concrete.

"Who is it?" I ask Frank just as Spider and Hatchet come into view.

Spider is pacing back and forth in a slow but anxious manner; his tall skinny body draped in clothes two sizes too big. His shaved head and large ginger beard a stark contrast to one another as his dark gaze snaps in my direction at hearing my approach.

Hatchet, however, is leaning his short muscular frame casually up against some stacked wooden pallets, arms folded across his firm chest and one leg bent at the knee, his foot kicked up against the pallets behind him. His pale grey eyes follow me as I enter into the open space and he pushes his flop of dark hair from his eyes.

A couple of my other security guys are in the space but have backed off to give us space to talk.

"Boys," I greet, receiving a head nod from Hatchet in response.

Charlie's familiar presence crowds my back before standing at my side and that's all it takes for Spider to practically self-combust.

"Boss. Bosses… Boss-lady, Boss-man," he stumbles over his greeting, confused as to who to address and I roll my eyes impatiently, widening them at him in an urge to get on with it. "I didn't do anything," he sputters. "That's why I'm here, to tell you what happened," he babbles and I roll my eyes, he's anxious this one, that's how I know he'd never fuck us over, he's too easy to read.

"Spider," I say his name firmly, forcing him to stop pacing, "I just want to know what happened, you came to me remember?" I ask with a raised eyebrow.

"Don't mind him, boss," Hatchet's deep voice rumbles as he moves towards us from his leaning position, "we just wanted to let you know as soon as possible," he says respectfully and I nod.

"Right, well, why don't you start talking then," I instruct and they both share a look.

"Well, I was on my usual corner and a guy with his hood pulled up came over, I thought he was looking to score," Hatchet shrugs, "he slapped a piece of paper in my hand and I was confused because you know, it wasn't cash," he scowls. "Anyway, I said to him, 'what the fuck man?' and he said, his boss sends mine a message," he says jerking his head in my direction. "The guy said, *'he's coming for you, Kyla-Rose Swallow, to take what he's owed'*, I grabbed at the guy but he ran and was disappearing in an unmarked car before I could even blink, I didn't even get a good look at it," Hatchet finishes and I crease my forehead.

"Okay…" I say slowly, still taking in his words –which mean absolutely nothing to me- "and you, Spider?" I ask, drawing my attention to the guy who's now pacing once more.

"Similar thing, boss, I was all out of product, waiting for a drop off, some random dude, in a literal *suit*," he spits as though seeing someone in a suit is the worst thing he's ever seen in his life, "approached me, I gave him a wary once over, cause I thought he was a cop," Spider shrugs, "but then I thought that'd be weird seeing as, you know, I work for you and all and then he said some guy paid him to give me a message," he swallows. Stopping his pacing to look between me and Charlie, "he told me to give my boss a message, tell *her*, *he's* coming and she better be ready," Spider says and I frown.

"What was on the piece of paper, Hatchet?" Charlie asks, his gruff voice soothing the anxiety bubbling in my chest, always the epitome of calm.

Hatchet pulls it from his pocket and approaches us confidently; I stretch out my arm, my hand open as he places the small crinkled paper into my palm. I eye Charlie for a moment before opening it, trying to soak in some of his calm. I place it over my thigh, trying to smooth it out somewhat before bringing it back up to read, holding it in such a way, that Charlie can see it too.

I won't be kind or gentle when I come for you.
You can't hide from me and mine.
We are everywhere you think we're not.
Everywhere you go, we already are.
Everyone you trust, we've already won.
There's nothing left for you.
The only thing you can do now is run.
You already know how much I love the chase, little bird.

I read the twisted words over and the only thing that sinks my stomach is the *little bird* reference, but even that could just be a coincidence, Swallow, bird. Like seriously what the fuck is this supposed to mean? But the 'I already know' part… that implies I already know who this is from? Is this some sort of joke? If it is… why do I feel so fucking weird right now?

I look up into Charlie's concerned emerald eyes, his eyebrows knitted together and an unusual expression pursing his lips. He looks down at me, giving me what he thinks is a reassuring smile but all it really does is make my stomach churn and my weak knees feel like they'll buckle at any moment.

This is a threat, threats I can deal with, *we* have been dealing with them since day one, it's not easy running an operation like the one we do, there's always someone wanting to take what's yours. So I'm not going to let something as minor as a fucked up note –that doesn't even rhyme, like, Christ, put some creativity into it, *just saying*- put fear into me. Even if this *does* feel different to other times.

"Thank you, boys. I appreciate you coming straight to me," I nod, straightening my spine and slapping my game face back on, trying to keep my voice strong. "I trust if you hear anything else, you'll do the same," I say without it being a question.

"Yes, boss," they both utter in unison.

Spider looks slightly more relaxed, now that he knows neither Charlie nor I, are going to be cutting him up into little pieces today. Frank silently steps in front of us, opening up the door, we walk out across the crunchy gravel in the direction of our cars.

"It'll all be fine, cuzz," Charlie stops me with a hand on my shoulder; I turn, looking up at him, my knight in shining armour. "I'm not gunna let anything knock you from your throne," he winks, his rough voice gravelly with a genuine smile and I feel my lips turn up to return it.

"I'm not worried," I say truthfully, even with the small niggle of doubt nipping at me, "I'm good," I lie. "Want to come to the gym with me?" I ask as I continue my way over to the bright orange Audi.

"Not that shitty gym on the other side of town?" he asks with a grimace, knowing that's exactly where I mean.

"That's the one," I grin broadly, loving that familiar little hole in the wall.

"Think I'll pass, we've got a perfectly good gym in the basement of our building, I can't understand why you like venturing all the way over to that shithole," he scoffs and I laugh.

"It's authentic, no one takes any notice of me when I'm working out there and I like Fat Tony, he's a riot," I laugh and Charlie shakes his head.

"Whatever floats your boat, I'll call you later," he calls over his shoulder, climbing into his sleek black Ferrari.

The ride over to Fat Tony's is quiet; I don't need to stop on the way because I always have a duffle bag of work out gear in the trunk of all my cars, just in case the need ever arises.

It's Saturday morning, so I know it's gunna be dead, especially before nine-am.

Fat Tony is a burly ex-boxer in his late fifty's with a thick Italian accent and more muscles than most men his age.

When I was thirteen I accidently broke one of his windows. Obviously, Mum and I had no money to replace it, so I worked off my debt by helping around the gym. It was nothing much, just sweeping and wiping down surfaces, but during that time we got on well and he took me under his wing.

I liked him straight away, that day a brick went sailing through his window –I didn't actually intend on smashing a window, I just threw a brick in temper- was a good day in the end, I got a lifelong friend out of it.

It was three days after my thirteenth birthday and I was in a strop, like a typical teenager, because as usual, my mum had forgotten all about my birthday in her drug haze and we ended up in an almighty row. I think that was one of the only times I was ever truly angry with Mum.

Anyway, working there every day after school and on the weekends to work off my debt, Fat Tony and I had more than a few cross words. I remember him practically pulling his hair out at my antics; he said I was the most Italian woman he'd ever met for someone who wasn't even remotely Italian at all. He said my fire rivalled even that of his own mother –who sounded like a very scary woman, I bet I would have *loved* her- he told me he liked my fire and he could teach me how to channel my rage into something productive, so I took him up on his offer and that's how I learnt to fight.

I don't get to come here very often now, since I'm always so busy with work –that's why we put the gym in at our place- but when I do, I feel like I'm coming home. Plus, Fat Tony's always so pleased to see me, it makes me feel all the warm and fuzzies that I don't get anywhere else.

I pull into one of the many empty spaces outside the large glass windows, grabbing my duffle bag from the trunk, I click the button on my keys, locking up the car and push open the glass door.

The musty smell of sweat greets me as I enter and as weird as it sounds it's comforting. The gym in our building is ultra-modern and new and smells like fresh paint, there's nothing quite like an old, well-used gym.

As predicted, the gym is more or less empty. There are a couple of older guys sparring in the ring but other than that it's deserted. I head toward the door in the back, knowing that's where I'll find Tony and knock once.

"What?" he growls from the other side of the wood and I laugh as I push open the door.

"That any way to greet your favourite girl?" I chuckle with confidence and his eyes widen in shock at seeing me.

"Kid!" he exclaims, a grin splitting his face that could rival even one of Jacob's.

"Hey, Tony," I smile, crossing towards his desk as he stands from his chair, meeting me on the other side of the wood.

He folds me into a bear hug, lifting my feet clean from the floor, pressing a hard kiss to the top of my head.

"I'm so happy to see you, *bella*!" he beams, placing me back down.

"Me too, it's been too long," I agree as he swipes one of his bear-sized hands through his grey hair.

"Although, you only seem to visit me when shit's going down… you okay, kid?" he asks me in a serious tone, a frown now covering his once smiling face, he narrows his suspicious gaze on me.

"I'm okay, just need to train a little," I shrug and although he knows something's not quite right, he doesn't press me for anything.

"Get out there then, kid. I'll catch you in a bit," he smiles, returning to the large leather chair behind his desk.

I smile, making my way back out of his office, heading into the changing rooms. There's only one but I'm sure if I asked, Tony would tell me the same thing he always tells me; '*women don't want to train in my gym, why would I put in a women's locker room just for you, when I know you don't give a shit.'*

I chuckle to myself at the memory of a particular conversation we had when I was fourteen. I told him it was sexist to only have one locker room labelled *men's* and he essentially told me to suck it up or go home. So I did –suck it up that is- but I also laugh in triumph at the sign now marking the locker room door as *unisex*. So, I think perhaps I won that round.

I dump my duffle bag down in the middle of the room, kick my shoes off and shred my red suit to the floor. Once I'm only in my tiny thong I pull on my black sports bra and shimmy into my tight black leggings before kicking on my white trainers, stuffing everything else back into my bag -which I shove into one of the old lockers.

I make my way out onto the floor and the two guys who were sparring when I first arrived, have gone, leaving me by myself.

Perfect.

I head over to the old stereo, which is at least thirty years older than me but still punches out sound like most of the new high tech ones and play on some metal. Anything loud and brash to help drown out all other thoughts from my mind.

I jump rope until I can barely see, my eyeballs rattling about inside their sockets from the vibrations of my feet hitting the punishing concrete. Sweat trails down my spine, wisps of hair sticking to my sweaty face, I drop the rope, swiping my arm across my forehead. I scoop down and grab my water, cracking open the top, I inhale half of the bottle in one gulp, just as Tony emerges from his office.

"Want to spar, kid?" he offers, stepping into the ring without waiting for an answer. "Noticed you haven't been fighting lately, want to tell me what that's about?" he asks, no accusation in his voice just fatherly-type concern.

"Sure," I shrug stepping up into the ring, "and how'd you know I haven't been taking any fights?" I raise my eyebrows in question, "you been watching me, Tony?" I smirk and he lets out a loud chuckle.

"You know I do, kid, now, we bitching or we fighting?" he deadpans and I grin wide from ear to ear.

"Come on, old-man, show me what you got."

After taping up my hands and slipping on my gloves, Tony bounces gracefully in front of me. That's one of the things I love about Fat Tony, he doesn't look at me as anything less than who I am. He looks at me and just sees Kyla. Equal to anyone else he spars with. That's a special skill that not many people have these days. Everyone's always trying to label everything and everyone but not Tony, he just see's what's in front of him, takes everyone as they come.

"Kyla-Rose, come on. Head in the game," he barks, jabbing out and tapping my chin.

We go hard for an hour, beating the fuck out of each other, my arms feel like jelly, my entire body soaked with sweat but I don't want to stop or even slow down, all it does is make me want to push harder, fight harder.

I throw my fists at him, wild left and right hooks, jabs and uppercuts. I push forward, he pushes back, giving everything that I've got, I go on the offense, fuck self-defence, I just need to hit something.

Summoning up every shit thing in my life, dragging the memories up through the darkness, slamming them into the forefront of my mind, I channel my rage. I think of where I grew up, my mother, my daddy, high school, the heartbreak of the boy I loved -who took my virginity then fucked me over all on the same night- the abusive juvie guards and the sick things they did to me, all the things I've never told anyone about. Every little thing that gives me an edge, I throw it all into the weight behind my fists, my ribs ache, my heart pounding so hard, I'm sure it'll explode from the confines of my chest.

"KYLA-ROSE!" Tony bellows and I blink, suddenly back in the room.

I drop my hands, my arms feeling like lead, my legs weak,

I fall to my knees, resting my weight forward onto my gloved fists. Sweat runs in rivulets down into my eyelashes and I blink it away, swiping at my forehead with my forearm, I rock back sitting on my feet.

“Sorry,” I hush out, my eyes closed as I try and fail to catch my breath, “I guess, I needed that more than I thought,” I splutter between ragged breaths.

After a moments pause, “Kyla, you gunna tell me where the fuck your heads at, kid?” Fat Tony asks, leaning back on the ropes.

My head too heavy to even look up at him, all I can see are his feet, I shake my head once in response, because honestly there’s nothing to say. I am not weak.

“We’ve been doing this dance the last few years and your control seems to slip more and more every time, I get you might not wanna talk to me about it, but talk to someone, kid,” he’s almost as out of breath as I am.

I tear my gloves from my fists, struggling to rip off the tape, tearing into it with my teeth, I nip my skin, a trickle of hot blood running down my knuckles.

“Whoa, whoa, whoa! Kid, cool it, let me get it,” he rushes out, dropping to his knees before me.

I stop struggling and after he quickly removes his own gloves, he takes each of my hands in his and gently removes the tape from my knuckles.

“Thank you,” I whisper, my eyes still closed as my chest continues to heave.

“I’m worried about you,” he says earnestly and honestly, I think I’m a bit worried about me too.

"I-" I start as I'm interrupted by a loud, deep voice, speaking words I can't hear over the buzzing inside my head.

Multiple pairs of feet enter the room but I can't bear to move, I can hardly keep myself upright.

"Boys, give me a minute," Tony calls over my head, his rough, thick Italian bellow vibrates his order through the thick mat, the laughter instantly subsides, the footsteps retreat.

"Kid, get yourself showered, you're done for today," he tells me as he stands and as much as I respect him and would never talk back, today I can't seem to help myself, I *need* this.

"Tony," I call breathlessly as he crosses to the ropes, he stops looking back at me. "I *need* this, just a couple more hours," I almost plead and he frowns, a deep line appearing between his eyes, darkening his deep olive skin, shadowing his face.

"Kyla-" he all but growls in warning, I interrupt him.

"Please, no more fighting, I'll just hit the bag, I'll run out my aggression on the treadmill, *fuck*, let me just jump rope, anything, Tony," I beg from my sitting position on the floor, "*please*."

I guess that little note I received this morning threw me more off balance than I thought. It's like the shadows in the room are moving in too quickly and I'm scrambling backwards to stay in the light, a constant battle of hiding my fear.

"I know you're some big hot shot in the underworld now, Kyla-Rose, but not here you're not, this is still my gym, my domain, my rules and if I say you're done, then you're done," he warns me in a low growl and I know I should just shut up before I piss him off but it's just not in my nature.

"Tony," I push to my feet, my legs wobbling with

exhaustion, "please, I can't look weak in my position and I fucking *need* to keep my shit together. I promise, I won't cause you any problems if you let me stay."

With a deep sigh, he massages his closed eyes with his thumb and forefinger, grinding his teeth.

"*One* fucking hour, Kyla, and then I'm throwing you out my goddamn myself," he snarls, threatening in a low rumble, huffing heavily and turning towards the front door.

"Thank you," I breathe, barely above a whisper but I know he heard me; his shoulders visibly relax as he punches the door open and yells out to whoever he made wait outside.

I restart the stereo that Tony silenced while we were sparring and hit the treadmill. I crank it up as fast as my aching legs will carry me and tune out everything else. Letting the heavy bass reverberate through my body and clear my mind. My feet hit the belt heavily as I pump my arms as hard as I can. I hear the hustle and bustle as Tony re-enters the gym with his other customers and I block out their conversation.

A few moments later I feel a presence, a large body steps onto the treadmill beside me, the machine beeping as they set their pace. Squeezing my eyes shut hard, I force myself to ignore them. Suddenly my pace comes to an abrupt halt as someone pulls the emergency stop cord.

"What the *fuck*?!" I roar as I grab onto the handrail in an attempt to stop myself careening off the end.

"You following me?" a deep voice chuckles.

I jerk my head left, my trigger finger twitching, if only I had my gun, I really should stop letting my guard down when I come here. I turn my head, immediately met with a piercing pair of amber-yellow eyes, an all too *familiar,* pair of amber-yellow eyes.

"No, I'm not fucking following you, *Big Man*, I was here first," I growl defensively, making him laugh.

"Good point, still, I'm happy to see you again," Gold eyes shrugs, pressing pause on his warm-up, turning to give me his full attention.

His huge arms, muscles stacked on muscles bunch beneath his tattooed skin, his loose black vest hanging off his broad shoulders, the drop arms gaping and the neckline non-existent, leaving absolutely nothing to the imagination. My eyes roam over him appreciatively without my consent, my demon practically purring inside.

The way his gold eyes, the colour of sunflowers wrinkle at the corners, his thick lashes fanning over his cheekbones, his strong nose just a little crooked, probably from being broken a few too many times. Intricate swirls of black ink cover one side of his skull, leading down his neck and blending with the ink at his shoulder, a flop of thick blonde hair, the straight length covering one eye before he pushes it back.

But the smile, the smile he gives me knocks the wind straight out of me.

Defensively I scowl at him, hating the way my body reacts to him, climbing off the treadmill to escape, he follows me.

"Leave me alone," I grit out, making him chuckle again, a deep, smooth rumble that works its way up from his chest, only enraging me further.

"But I like you, I already told you that," he shrugs, as if following me is how you get a strangers attention, like a stray alley mutt, hoping I'll take pity on him.

"We're not five! You can't follow me around, pull on my pig-tails and hope that lets me know you like me!"

"Well, if we're talking about tugging on pig-tails-"

"I threatened to shoot you!" I more or less shout, cutting him off before he can finish his sentence.

Spinning on my heel, I throw my arms out wide, coming face to face with the hulk-sized god, his looks momentarily halting my tirade.

Fuck. Me.

He really is pretty, but pretty people tend to tell pretty lies.

"I know," he shrugs again, like it's the most normal thing in the world, pushing a tattooed hand through his flop of blonde hair.

"What the fuck is wrong with you?" I screw my face up at him and he smiles.

He fucking *smiles*!

"Argh! You are *so* annoying, just fuck off, Big Man!" I yell, turning my back on him again.

"Kacey," he calls behind me, forcing my feet to stop, I slowly turn, looking at him over my shoulder with narrowed eyes. "My name," he clarifies with a small throat clearing cough, "is, Kacey."

And fuck me sideways, the way his own name falls from his lips, has my belly doing somersaults.

"Great, well then, I'll repeat my earlier instruction, fuck off, *Kacey*," I say with a grunt.

"And yours?" he calls after me.

"My name?" turning back to face him, he nods with a smile.

"Your worst fucking nightmare, sunshine, so leave me the fuck alone," I grouch, spinning on my heel and heading straight for the locker room.

I grab my duffle bag, swing it over my shoulder, deciding I'll shower at home, I pull the door open just as someone pushes it from the other side and the fucking thing hits me straight in the forehead. My bag drops to the floor, the force of the hit sending me staggering back a few paces.

"*Ow*! Fuck!" I hiss on a groan, pressing the heel of my hand to my pulsing eyebrow.

"Shit! Sorry!" the person rumbles and of *course* it's Kacey, "are you okay? Let me see," he instructs gripping my wrist.

His thick fingers curl around my thin arm, the pain suddenly dissipating at his touch as I focus on his hot skin scorching mine; he tugs my hand away from my face, scowling at my head assessing the damage.

"Fuck! That's gunna bruise, let me get you some ice," he offers, but I am so fucking done with today, I just want to leave.

"No!" I snap, "I think you've done enough, don't you, Big Man?" I seethe, trying to get my shit together, I tear my wrist from his grip, instantly missing his touch.

He's too goddamn pretty and I really don't need any fucking distractions, especially not after this morning. I take in a deep breath, my eyes clamped tightly shut, I exhale a slow shaky breath. What is it about this guy that turns me into a massive bitch? I'll tell you what it is, he's a fucking distraction and he's not afraid of me, which just messes with my fucking head.

Fuck my complicated life.

Why couldn't I be one of those normal twenty-five year old

women, someone who meets a hot guy and oh, I don't know, *doesn't* tell him to go fuck himself?

Oh yeah, because I'm not fucking normal. I am so far from fucking normal, it's comical.

"I *am* sorry," Kacey says, this time his jaw is clenched tight and he looks irritated, *huh*, guess my attitude *is* having an effect on him after all.

"It's fine," I mumble, feeling a little bad, my thumb wanting to rub over a weird aching spot in my sternum.

Ignoring the feeling I break eye contact, stooping to grab my bag. Beating me to it his big hand clutches the handles before I can, making me exhale in irritation.

"Don't leave on my account, I won't bother you. I really am sorry, I'm not trying to be a creepy arsehole and I really didn't mean to fuck up your eye," he gestures with his head in the direction of my face. "I was just," he sighs heavily shaking his head to himself. "I guess I was just excited to see you," he mumbles under his breath, so quietly I almost don't catch his words. "I'll go. Honestly, I can train later," he offers gently with another shake of his head and guilt floods me, needles pinging in my chest.

Fuck's sake.

"No," I sigh, "don't go, its fine, I've been here for too long anyway and I've got work to do and don't worry about my face, seriously, I've had much worse," I say honestly, looking up into those beautiful fucking eyes, that I hate to admit haunted my dreams last night.

"Well, maybe I'll see you here again some time," he tilts his head, his blonde hair flopping forward onto his handsome face as he gives me a soppy grin.

"Yeah, maybe," I reply coolly, taking my bag from his ridiculously sized hand, our fingers brush against one another, a jolt of electricity pulses through me, surging all the way down to my toes.

Instead of letting go of my bag, he tugs it sharply, my body slamming into his solid one.

"What are yo-" I start to say, a frown creasing my brow as I try to push away.

"Let me make it up to you," he breathes, interrupting my question, looking down into my eyes, his hot breath fanning over my lips. He's so tall that even being six-foot myself, I have to crane my head back to look up at him, "come to a party with me tonight," he says seriously, "as my date," he clarifies, his lips barely a hair's breadth from mine, my breath catches, his cocky smile nowhere to be seen.

What the fuck is happening right now, did he just ask me to be his date?

I don't think any guy has ever asked me out on a date, like literally never. Every guy I was ever interested in was either not in it for the right reasons, knowing who I am and the power I wield or my cousins scared them off. Which if I'm being honest, did me a favour in the long run because if they're scared of my family, I'm not interested. I lick my lips anxiously, my mouth suddenly as dry as the Sahara.

I look back up into his gold eyes, my own confused and flicking between his.

"I don't know…" It's not that I don't want to say yes, but the *why,* is what I can't figure out.

"Please?" he asks again, almost pleading in a whisper.

I'm suddenly desperate to close the distance between us, the tiny sliver of space between our lips is too much yet too little all at the same time, it's dizzying.

"Why do you even want to take me out? I've been a bitch to you, I threatened to shoot you. I would have done it you know," I tell him seriously, my eyebrow raised, words coming out sharp, like the crack of a whip but a little more breathy than I would like, *fuck*, this guy sure has some weird voodoo effect on my greedy cunt.

"I know you would have, but I like that about you, I guess. The gun pointed at my head kind of just sealed the deal," he shrugs casually and I pinch my eyebrows together.

What in the world is wrong with this man?

Is he as fucked up as I am?

Surely not…

"You like me because I gave you shit?" I make a confused face, tilting my head to one side to assess the truth of his words.

"Yes," he answers definitively.

"And held you at gunpoint?" I clarify, my eyebrow cocked.

"Yes-"

"Kyla-Rose," I cut him off before he can say anymore, my name sounding like a confession, my heart thrashes wildly.

"Kyla-Rose?"

"My name."

"Kyla-Rose," he repeats, like he's testing out how it tastes on his tongue and *fuck me,* if hearing him say my name doesn't get me wet, "I like it," he smiles.

And Jesus Christ, there go my knickers.

"Okay," I say, making his head snap down to meet my grey-green gaze.

"Okay?" he asks with a small frown, searching my face for clarification and I laugh.

"I mean, okay, I'll go to the party with you. How bad could it be? You already know I'm a raging murderous bitch, so at least I can completely relax and be myself," I laugh mirthlessly and he beams down at me, his gold eyes glowing with delight.

"I'll pick you up from yours," he offers, releasing a breath, of what? I'm not quite sure, relief at me saying yes?

"No!" I suddenly snap, thinking over his offer, his eyes widen. "Sorry, I mean, I can meet you some place and we can go together? Just, my place, is a little, erm, busy," that's a complete fucking lie but this guy clearly has no fucking idea who I am or what I do, so giving him my address at Southbrook tower would more than give it away and that's the last thing I want right now.

"Okay," he laughs, "I get it," he says with a shake of his head, "how about I meet you at the old movie theatre? You know where it is? The one next to the Thames," he clarifies and I nod.

"I know the one."

"Ten then?"

"Ten." I agree, I can't help but return his beaming smile with a small one of my own.

"It's a date," he sings after me as I head toward the exit, luckily he can't see my face and I don't turn back, because I'm one hundred percent sure that I blush.

CHAPTER 4

KYLA-ROSE

Once I get home, shower and ice my throbbing eyebrow, I pull on some fresh clothes; high-waisted black leggings and a loose, black cropped t-shirt that slips off of one shoulder. I brush through my wet hair, parting it down the middle, giving it a rough towel dry.

Walking barefoot through the empty halls of my penthouse, my footsteps echoing through the silent space, I let out a heavy sigh. I love my space, it smells good, it's clean and tidy, it's dark and full of all the things I like, yet, it's still not what I *need*.

I step into the back living room; it's the largest and my most favourite room in the penthouse. Running the entire length of the building, it's a huge open space with large white couches, a ridiculously sized TV -that is never used-, an ostentatious grand piano and a floor to ceiling glass wall that runs the entire length of the room, giving the best bird's-eye view of Southbrook in the entire city, you can see everything from up here. I step up to the glass, looking down over the city I help lord over and can't help but feel really small.

I'm up here in my fancy tower whilst there're little girls and boys going hungry below me, all because mummy or daddy just gave their food money to Hatchett or Spider on the street corner, buying up a supply of heroin.

That was me once, not buying heroin but being little, my tummy cramping with pain after not eating for three days, watching while my mum shot up in the kitchen. I always said I was going to do better, *be* better. I may not be anything like her but I'm not any better either. I sigh heavily, my breath fogging the cold glass as I rest my forehead against it. My mind's already hazing with exhaustion and the day's barely begun. I mean, after the morning I've had, what with bumping into Kacey, resulting in a literal *bump* to the head and that note.

A fucking *note.*

Like, the complete opposite of a love letter. I got a literal death letter. I almost want to snort.

Who even sends notes anymore anyway, what are we ten? It's nothing, it's less than nothing, just some kind of sick joke, it's not really a threat, well, it *is* but it's not a serious one anyway, it can't be. My chest cramps at my own lies and I squeeze my eyes shut tightly, rubbing the heel of my hand between my breasts, a lame attempt at giving myself a sense of comfort.

I've had threats before, *fuck,* people have actively been trying to take me out for what feels like ever, but this one, it just, it hits different.

Someone's playing with me. Fucking playing with me and I won't lie, I'm… *anxious*. Usually, the 'big bad' that's trying to off me is a little more fucking obvious about it, none of the past threats have tried to hide their identity, in fact I think they quite liked being bold as brass about it.

I'm not that much of a big player in the game, not in the grand scheme of things, anyway. I mean, yes, I am learning what's expected of me for if and when, Charlie and I eventually take over from Uncle Dee but I'm just a lackey currently, a henchman, an enforcer of sorts.

Honestly, I just beat the shit out of people and torture them until they talk. Don't get me wrong, I fucking *love* what I do. Playing with their eyeballs, using amputated legs as golf clubs, playing games of tug of war with various bones, seeing how much force it takes for them to splinter and snap. That sort of thing. Okay, yeah, perhaps that's not *entirely* normal, okay, I won't lie, I *know* that shit's not normal but I live for it and that's why I'm so damn good at my fucking job.

Hell, they even preached to us in primary school about deciding what we want to be when we grow up. My teacher's advice to me –when I told her I didn't know what I wanted to be- was to get a job doing something I was good at or enjoyed in my free time. I release a dark chuckle, the tension in my chest easing a little. If only Mrs Fisher could see me now, learn what my career of choice was, oh, hell, who am I kidding? She's probably turning in her grave right now. If she's even dead, *that could be arranged*, no.

No.

Bad demon.

She was an okay teacher.

Blowing out a breath and deciding I can't stay in this empty room any longer, I make my way back down the darkened hall, stopping at the circular table in the foyer where I threw a pair of chucks earlier. I kick them on my feet, leaving the laces undone and press the call button for the elevator.

The doors slide open one level below my own and I step out into a dark hallway. The walls and floors are all painted jet black, the only light illuminating the space is from an emergency exit sign glowing at the opposite end of the hall.

Scuffing my feet along the wood until I get to a set of large double doors, I enter the security code and scan my fingerprint. The bolts start to glide open, one by one clicking open until all seven are disengaged. Placing my palms flat against the smooth mahogany I gently push them inwards, where I'm met with yet more darkness. Only unlike the hall, there's no light coming from anywhere at all.

My eyes struggle to adjust and when they finally do I spot a pair of emerald ones staring back at me from the far corner of the room. I turn, pushing the doors closed behind me, the locks effortlessly sliding back into place. Knowing the room like the back of my hand –even in pitch darkness- I take a few steps further inside and pull the fridge open, which unsurprisingly, also does not have a light in.

"Got any of that tropical juice I like?" I ask the figure lurking in the shadows, when I get no answer; I peer over my shoulder finding the green orbs closer. I attempt to hide the smirk that's trying to break free.

"No?" I sigh.

Turning back to the fridge I feel around the shelves once more before deciding there's no juice and close it. Who in their right mind would remove the bulb in the fridge? How does he get midnight snacks?

"What are you doing, Lala?" the low, menacing growl carries across the room like a gentle whisper.

"I'm bored."

"No. You're thinking too much."

I nod in answer, knowing all too well that -even if I can't- he'll be able to see my movement in the darkness.

"Come," he orders.

I turn, finding Charlie right before me, his large tattooed hand outstretched for me to take. Slipping my delicate hand inside his, he tugs me through the dark, twisting through hallways until we stop. A glow of red light emits from under the door in front of us, Charlie's shadowed features twist into a feral grin as I look up at him, his hand squeezing mine with excitement. My knuckle bones grinding together from the force, I squeeze him back just as hard as he pushes the door wide open, ushering me in ahead of him.

The black painted room is lit by a strip light, the red bulb within it cloaking the room in an eerie shade of crimson. Charlie steps ahead of me; his shirtless body gliding across the room toward a small electrical box, flicking a switch, the dark room is instantly bathed in clinical bright white light. I flutter my eyes heavily as they adjust to the drastic change in brightness and look back to Charlie, he remains unfazed, the change in light seemingly not affecting him in the slightest.

Moving focus, my gaze eventually rolls over the

unconscious body in the corner of the room. Strung up high with thick black rope like he's ensnared in a spider's web, his naked body already slashed, torn and burned, I tilt my head to one side, assessing. Charlie really is an artist when it comes to torture.

"What did this one do?" I murmur the question, taking in every inch of his damaged flesh.

"He deserves it," is all Charlie growls and my eyebrows jump to attention, my gaze snapping to his.

"That bad, huh?" he never has a reaction like that unless it's something seriously *bad.*

"Yes," he grunts.

I whistle lowly, "wow."

"I thought we could take a blood bath, it's supposed to help stop your skin aging," he shrugs casually as he too assesses the man with a head tilt like my own.

"Ooo!" I clap my hands together excitedly, "I love trying new things! We've not done this before!"

"Hold on," he grumbles, the huskiness of his tone sending vibrations of adrenaline through me.

Charlie disappears back out of the door and not a second later, I giggle at the sight of the thirty-one year old, six-foot-four, murderous beast, dragging in a bright pink paddling pool.

"This should work," he grins, placing it perfectly beneath the bound man.

Our heads tilting to the right in unison, we trail our gaze up his unconscious body, our eyes finally meeting each other's, our faces dressed in matching grins, our silent agreement clear. Charlie, grabs two matching blades, handing me one as we both step into the empty pool.

Then we get to work.

A piercing howl echoes around the four walls, the sound bouncing around as Charlie and I hack and slash with all the gracefulness of blind butchers. Before long, the screaming stops and our paddling pool begins to fill. Although, looking at it now, I can't see it filling with much, most of the guy's insides are already sprayed across the two of us. But I suppose I do feel a bit better, maybe I just needed the distraction of inflicting pain on someone deserving to distract me.

"I don't think this pool is going to fill with blood like I expected it to," Charlie grunts, flicking a rogue piece of flesh off of his bare shoulder.

"You don't say," I chuckle, patting his chest as I step out of the measly puddle beneath our feet. "We'll have to try again but with more bodies," I suggest with a shrug, it would be interesting to take a literal blood bath.

Charlie grunts in response, turning to face me, he too, steps out of our paddling pool. Little spatters of blood across his pale face, he blinks some from his lashes and throws an arm over my shoulders, peering down at me with those deep, dark green eyes full of shadows and rage.

"Lala."

"Charl?" I answer, gazing up at him.

"Cry."

"What?" I blanch with a shake of my head.

"Cry." He shrugs, "that's what people are supposed to do when they're sad," he states clinically.

I blink at him.

"I'm not sad."

"Liar."

"I am not," I counter like a petulant child, a pout to my bottom lip.

"I know I don't really understand that stuff," his rough voice forces out, "but I *know* you're sad and I don't like it. I don't like it one bit, Lala, and it makes me *murderous*," he growls aggressively, my chest constricting at his affection for me.

Charlie doesn't understand or relate to emotions and feelings, sure, he feels them and can sometimes read them on others but he processes things *differently*. We both struggle with trauma and emotion has always been something we don't discuss much, we will kill and die for one another but we don't really *talk* about feelings and stuff, we read each other so well we don't really ever need to use words to understand how the other one is feeling, we can just sense it.

"You came to me because you're struggling. What do you need me to do to make it better? Is this about this morning? Or something else?" his scratchy voice continues, even though it's so hoarse now that his words are barely making it out, I can hear the concern in his voice.

"I'm n-"

"Stop lying to me."

"I- you-" I swallow as realisation hits me, "you knew we couldn't fill that fucking pool, Charlie," I state quietly, a small frown growing in the space between my eyes. "You're a motherfucking genius! You calculated all that shit in less than point-four seconds; you knew we'd need more bodies, what the fuck was this?" I smack his arm off of my shoulders, turning to face him fully, his expression marred with irritation as he looks down at me.

"I'm helping y-"

"I've got shit to do," I snap, turning away, tears burning the back of my eyes, I race through the apartment and make it back to my own where I take a deep breath and pull myself together.

The rest of the day passes by in a blur. I spend the time looking over planned shipments and deal with a few phone calls from some of my guys. Then before I know it, Eli's walking into my office and switching on the light. Expelling the darkness that's fallen, I squint through the sudden invasion of light, rubbing at my tired eyes.

"You been in here all day?" he asks, casually leaning in the door jamb.

"Yeah, guess I have," I answer without looking up, I'm not good at lying, so best to avoid eye contact.

I don't want to mention the fact Charlie and I spent time in his playroom this morning because Eli won't like that, none of them will, they don't like it when we lose control, but Charlie and I are good at keeping our secrets.

"Kyla-Rose, its six o'clock, have you even eaten today?" as if right on cue, my stomach grumbles with hunger, "guess that answers my question," he laughs, I drop my pen, reclining back in my seat.

"I haven't felt very hungry today, that's all," I spin left to right in my chair, folding my hands across my stomach.

"Charlie filled us in. Dad's looking into it, we'll figure it all out," he says confidently and I nod, knowing Charlie hasn't filled him in on *everything*.

"Sure," I reply, closing my laptop.

"Charlie said you went to Fat Tony's today, you been feeling that bad, huh?"

"I'm good," I tell him and I know he won't push me further, like I said; I'm not much of a talker when it comes to feelings.

"Cam and Charl are coming by, Cam's bringing dinner, thought we could all eat together for a change," Eli watches my face for reaction, I narrow my eyes on him.

"Why are we having family dinner? Without me even knowing about it? Is this an ambush?" I question sternly, raising an eyebrow at him, slouching down in my seat.

"No, we just wanna spend time with you, and Charlie said you seemed a little freaked out this morning," he shrugs again casually but I can tell he's nervous telling me all this.

"Charlie's going to be eating his own fucking dick for dinner if he doesn't mind his own goddamn business," I warn, venom dripping from my tongue with every word, stress from this conversation infecting me like poison.

Charlie never tells his brothers my shit, what the fuck has gotten into him today, first telling me to cry, now *this*.

"No, no, no. Ky, we're all in this life together and we all support each other no matter what, so when one of us is noticeably down, we fix that shit, you know that," Eli pushes off the door frame moving into the room, he reaches across the desk, gripping my hand. "We love you. Can't we just enjoy dinner together and forget the world for one night?" he implores, my resolve shattering at the sincerity in his tone.

"It better be Mexican, Elijah, or I swear," I trail off, wagging a finger at him with raised brows, causing a laugh to spill from his throat.

"This is Cam we're talking about, of course it'll be Mexican," he grips my hand tighter, dragging me out from behind my desk.

I follow him out into the living room, both planting ourselves onto the large white couch, I snuggle down in the corner with Eli dropping himself down in the middle, legs spread wide, taking up enough space for three as he flicks through the channels for something to watch.

A little while later, noise from the entrance hall grabs my attention. Brute barks an almighty chorus and Angel starts to snarl, I rush to my feet at the sound. Angel's not the friendliest dog, probably because she suffered so much abuse before I rescued her but she loves the boys as much as I do, so to snarl at them is totally out of character for her.

Brute's barking intensifies and Angel growls low and loud.

Shit.

"Angel!" I shout, gaining her attention as I thunder down the hall towards her.

Her large white body is tucked beneath the round table in the hall, her hackles up. Brute's huge body guarding her protectively, his hackles raised in similar aggression, which is more than unusual for him since he's the softie.

"What the hell has gotten into you? It's just the boys, calm down, girl," I frown, never taking my eyes from her, I slip my hand gently into her collar to keep her at my side, I don't like seeing her get herself so worked up.

"Sorry, cuzz, that's my fault. I probably smell different after being away so long," a familiar rumbling voice says, my eyes snap up.

"You!" I squeal with excitement.

"Me!" he grins.

I release my hold on Angel, Eli comes up behind me to take over and I run full pelt at him. Knocking into Jacob like a battering ram, I throw myself at him, his arse slamming onto the floor with me wrapped around him like a spider monkey.

"Fuck, Kyla-Rose," Jacob chokes out from beneath me with a grunt-laugh combo.

"Sorry, I'm just so happy to see you! Why didn't you tell me you were coming back?!" I cry, smacking his chest, scampering off of him.

Charlie reaches out an arm, pulling us both up.

"Wanted to surprise you, you happy to see me?" he beams and I beam right back, it's impossible not to smile at Jacob when he looks at you like that, he makes all my fears dissolve with just one look.

"Of course I am! Holy fuck, what the hell is even happening right now?" I exhale in disbelief, tucking my hair behind my ears.

"Good, cause I'm starving," he chuckles, throwing an arm over my shoulders and leading me back into the living room, his three brothers trailing behind.

The rest of the evening, we laugh, eat tacos and catch up on all the things Jacob's been doing in Africa and the shit going down here. It feels so much like home now, it's perfect how quickly we all fall back into our normal ways, it's like he's never been away at all.

I get snuggled up with him, tucked protectively under his thick arm, gazing up at him like he hung the moon, while he tells us all of his stories about saving people. Jacob's honestly amazing and I find myself even more in awe of him as his stories continue.

"Kyla-Rose has an admirer that she didn't attempt to kill yet," Eli mocks, making my spine stiffen.

"Oh, yeah?" Jacob asks teasingly, a raised eyebrow and smirk on his peach coloured lips.

Twisting his body to look at me, where I'm still hooked under his arm, he taps me on the nose and winks. I feel my cheeks flame at the thought of my big, blonde fighter, how *his* thick arms would feel banded around my body when suddenly I shoot upright on the couch, knocking Jacobs arm from my shoulders as I jolt.

"Fuck! What's the time?" I suddenly shout, realising that I totally fucking forgot about my *date,* I cringe at that, pushing to my feet, letting the blanket pool at my ankles.

"Nine-fifteen," Cam states, eyeing me suspiciously.

"Fuck, fuck, *fuck!*" I panic, moving my arse towards the living room door.

"Whoa! Ky, where you going?" Jacob calls, twisting his upper half to hang over the back of the sofa, grabbing hold of my jogging bottoms, stopping me in my tracks.

"Oh, um," I stutter, looking down at my feet, "I sort of," I huff out a breath.

My eyebrows pull together, why the fuck am I so nervous to tell them I have a date? Oh yeah, because *I'm* nervous that I have a date.

"You sort of, *what*?" Jacob echoes.

"I have a date, well, sort of," I announce loudly on an exhale, "it's not really a date," I wince. Watching as four pairs of protective eyes hone in on me, "but I'm late already," I sigh, scrubbing a hand down my face.

"Who are you going out with this late? Sorry to sound like an old man but that's the definition of a booty call, Ky," Eli warns me and I scowl over at him.

"I'm going to a party and it's not a booty call, you fuck-head," I growl, making them all laugh.

"Okay, okay! I'm just fucking with you," Eli laughs, raising his hands in surrender.

"Who you going out with?" Jacob asks, looking less than impressed, ever the over-protective alpha.

"Not the fighter from last night!" Cam accuses, making my body tense and I feel myself getting a little defensive over the golden eyed boy, who seems to have apparently gotten under my skin.

"Yes, actually, it is him," I shrug nonchalantly, making more than one pair of eyebrows in the room rise at my confession.

"You like this kid?" Jacob asks me and I sigh.

"I don't *know,* this *kid,"* I tell him, rolling my eyes dramatically, "that's why we're going out, to see if I like him," I plant my hands on my hips, *god*, it's like my high school days all over again.

"What's his name?" Charlie asks with genuine interest,

Cam answering before I can.

"Kacey."

"Last name?" Jacob demands and I look to Cam, who shrugs at the same time I do.

"I dunno," we answer in unison, making Jacob flick his gaze between the two of us.

"I'll find out for you if I ever get out of here! Can I *please* get dressed now?!" I plead with a whine.

Jacob narrowing his eyes once more he waves a dismissing hand at me. I hurry down the hall to my bedroom and rush into my closet.

Okay.

Party.

I'm assuming it's a house party because what other kind even is there? It's not a kid's birthday party with a clown and balloon animals, although that would be kind of funny wouldn't it? Taking me on a date to a kid's function, or better yet, an adult party but dressed up as a kid's party, everyone likes piñatas and cake, right? I chuckle to myself.

Focus, Kyla-Rose.

Goddamn.

I don't have a lot of time, so I grab a tight black mini dress with spaghetti straps, a small slit up one thigh. I rush through my make-up, coating my eyes in thick heavy liner on the top lids, pairing it with a classic red lip, the shade's called *American Dream* and it's my trusty go to. You can't go wrong with a red lip, it's classic.

Taking a brush through my already straight hair, I decide to leave it hanging down my back; I pull some grapeseed oil through the ends, smoothing out the little fly-away strands, tucking it back behind my ears. I hook chunky gold hoops through my lobes, leaving the rest of my ear piercings as they are –each one filled with little black, ball studs- and stack gold rings onto my fingers, my nails pointed and already painted black.

I strip off my baggy clothes, put on a matching set of black lace underwear before shimmying into my tight dress. I pluck out my favourite pair of Valentino's; open toe, strappy, black stilettoes studded with gold pointed studs and buckle them up around the ankle.

Taking one last look at myself in the mirror, *something's missing.* I turn back into my room, rifling through my top drawer I pull out two small switchblades. Grabbing a garter I hike it up my thigh so it's sitting high under my dress and lace the two blades through it. Sure, you can see their outline through the tight fabric but I don't give a fuck, I'm not going anywhere without easy access to a weapon and I think an underarm holster might be a little too obvious.

"I called down to Frank. He's waiting for you," Jacob says, emerging from the kitchen as I make my way down the hall.

"Thank you," I smile and he returns it with a blinding one of his own.

That's Jacob's superpower, blinding smiles, just one look at it and he could get you to do anything he wanted.

"You'll call me, if you need to," he tells me, less of a question, more of an instruction.

"Jacob, I'm twenty-five years old and running part of the biggest crime syndicate that England's ever seen... I think I can handle a little house party," I laugh, but his features don't soften and I find myself rolling my eyes, "of course I will." I promise, pressing a kiss to his cheek.

Cam appears, handing me my black leather jacket, I take it from his fingers, giving him a small smile.

"You look killer," he winks, making me throw my head back as laughter flies from my throat.

"Thanks, dude," I laugh, shoulder checking him as I pass, pressing the button for the elevator I shrug into my jacket.

Frank drives like a rally driver to the old cinema, racing down the quiet roads, other headlights flashing by, we end up making every green light, luck must be on our side because I end up making it just two minutes after ten, when I expected to be super late.

Maybe it's a good thing I forgot and had to rush about, that way I didn't have time to obsess over my looks too much because if I did, I might not have even bothered coming, I'd be too nervous. In fact, I wonder if it's not too late to turn back. What the fuck am I doing? Why on earth did I think a *date* would be a good idea? Oh my god, what the hell am I doing?

Jesus, I hope I look okay.

The sky is dark, ominous thick rain clouds looming over the old abandoned cinema. I peer out of the window, instantly spotting Kacey leaning against a street lamp, the soft orange glow illuminating half his features, shadows hiding the rest. Frank clears his throat drawing my attention, I look towards him, his gaze holding mine in the rear-view mirror.

"Boss, you want me to pick you up, you just call, I'll be available," Frank tells me.

"I'll be fine, thank you, Frank. You get home and tell Carol I say hi," I smile fondly, reaching across the seat, I give him a reassuring squeeze on the shoulder.

That's the thing about being a woman, whether I'm a ruthless killer or not, I have all of these people worrying about me, concerned about my safety and as much as it's touching and I genuinely am grateful that I'm so lucky to have such a great family and team, it's just sometimes so stifling I want to scream.

I make grown men piss themselves on the regular for fuck's sake but I want to go on a date? That's a different story. Suddenly, I'm thrown back in time to being fourteen years old. Danny Evans held my hand and Charlie more or less tried to kick the shit out of him, he nearly tore his arm off. Luckily, Jacob was there, handling it all but that fucking kid never looked at me again. Too frightened of my family of delinquent monsters to even talk to me in class and that was the end of that.

Not that I resent them for that, or anything for that matter. I love my family and I wouldn't trade them for anything, but still, the alpha-male, over-protective bullshit they radiate is a little bit like suffocation, phantom hands closing around my throat. Still, could be worse I spose, they could have sent a chaperone. I snort at that, not putting it past them and roll my eyes, sliding from the car, I slam the door shut behind me.

And deep breath.

Kacey's golden eyes rake over my body –in what I hope is appreciation- as I step towards him. He pushes his large frame from its leaning position, stalking towards me. His bulging thighs are wrapped in black skinny jeans, leaving very little to the imagination and a crisp white t-shirt that shows off the impressive ink covering his muscular arms. Kacey's light blonde hair is perfectly tousled in that *freshly fucked* sort of way, the shaved side completely bare, allowing the black ink of his head tattoo to stand out sharply.

His buttery-gold eyes glint with mischief as a smile tilts up one corner of his lips.

"Fuck, your eye!" Kacey almost yells as soon as his eyes land on mine, his smile disappearing as though it were never there to begin with.

"It's honestly fine, I forgot all about it," I grimace, remembering our earlier collision with the door in the gym.

"Kyla-Rose, seriously, I am so sorry about that," he breathes, gently running the pad of his thumb over the bruise, my skin heating at his touch.

"Please, seriously, forget it, it was an accident, shit happens," I shrug, desperately wanting him to move on from it.

The last thing I want to do tonight is go over and over his apology, I'd honestly forgotten about it already, it's a tiny faint line in my eyebrow, sure it's bright blue and a little puffy where the edge of the door caught me but it's not a black eye, you'd think he'd scarred me for life the way he's panicking over it.

"Thought for a minute there you might stand me up," he smirks, changing the subject, retracting his hand, his chest deliciously stretching the cotton of his shirt with each movement.

"Nearly did," I smile innocently and his eyes widen at my confession. "Accidently, of course," I laugh lightly nudging him with my elbow as we turn side to side and I start walking in the direction he leads.

"No way! You were actually considering it? I am crushed!"

he exclaims with mock horror, slapping his hand over his heart.

"No, I was just kind of distracted and didn't realise the time, sorry I'm a bit late," I tell him honestly, looking up into those glittering pools of golden sunshine.

Honestly, you could so easily lose all sense of time looking into those eyes, they're mesmerising.

He looks down at me, a genuine smile on his lips, he grips my small hand inside his, his thick fingers lacing through mine like it's the most natural thing in the world. It's such a small action that feels strangely intimate, I'm not sure anyone has ever held my hand like this before, not except for Charlie anyway, but my cousin hardly counts.

Someone holding my hand, like they want to keep me near, they want to hold onto me, make sure I'm still there, close by. It feels comforting. *Safe*. Seeing my long slim fingers, threaded through his, makes butterflies soar in my belly and heat creep up my neck. It feels…*nice*. I like it.

Kacey must look down and see me eyeing our joint hands because he pulls his away gently, making me look up at him, my eyebrows drawing together.

"Sorry, I didn't mean to force that on you," he tucks his hands deep into his pockets.

I frown to myself at the loss of contact, my skin still tingling from his touch. However, the fact that he just admitted he doesn't want to force -even that small level of touch on me- makes my tummy do summersaults.

We walk along the quiet path a little while longer and I find myself missing the feel of his hand in mine. I keep glancing up at him as we walk, trying to take in his features a little more as if I'm subconsciously committing them to memory. I shake my head, attempting to keep my focus forward, concentrating on putting my feet one in front of the other.

"Sooo… where we going?" I ask, breaking the silence.

"Just to my place," his grin wide at my look of confusion.

"Err, I thought we were going to a party?" I question suspiciously, not that I'm particularly fussed about a party but still.

He releases a mischievous chuckle, "we are, it's at my place," he smirks.

"So, let me get this straight, you came to meet me, to take me to your own party?" I ask, my eyebrows knitting together, my face scrunching up a little. "I don't understand… why not just give me your address so I could turn up?" I ask in confusion, he looks at me with an expression that is just as bewildered as I feel.

"Isn't it obvious?" he furrows his brow and I feel my own brow crease deepen.

"Um, not really," I shake my head, looking up to meet his gaze.

"If I just invited you, you could have just, not turned up, or worse," he shudders.

"What could be worse?" I giggle, his eyes lighting up at the sound.

"You could have brought another guy with you and I don't think I could've controlled my jealousy if you did," he shrugs, watching my face for reaction; I look away quickly, feeling heat creep up my cheeks.

Wow.

I don't really know what to say to that. What does that even mean? Honestly, you threaten to shoot a guy one time and look what happens when you don't follow through! Not sure I'll be making that mistake again any time soon.

Although, looking up at Kacey -who is by far one of the most beautiful men I've ever laid eyes on- I'm kinda glad I *didn't* shoot him, not that I'll ever admit that to anybody, but let's face it, it would be a tragedy to waste such a fine specimen.

We hook a left at the corner and I can already see which house is his. The dead-end street is lined on both sides of the road with identical two story houses. The road is packed with cars, all parked haphazardly along the paths and in neighbouring driveways, most of the houses look dark and empty, bar the one at the very end of the cul-de-sac.

It's painted pale blue with a small ivory porch, a large wooden front door has been painted to match and a large bay window sits on the left, giving a direct view into the living room, two large windows line the second floor and a separate garage sits to the right of the property, a concrete driveway leading up to it.

A half wall encases the property and we come to a stop simultaneously at the top of a path; lined on either side with pretty bluebells. The path leads up to a couple of steps that take us to the front door.

Kacey glances down at me with a smile, offering his hand to me once more. I look down at it, only a moment's hesitation, I slowly slip my hand inside his, giving it a gentle squeeze. He tugs me closer into his side, leading me to the house.

CHAPTER 5

KACEY

Kyla-Rose's hand is so fucking soft, I can't stop imagining her delicate fingers wrapped around my cock, which is *such* a typical fucking guy thing to say, I'm actually kind of pissed at myself for my serious lack of self-control but there's just something about her. I don't know what it is but that first moment I laid eyes on her I knew I'd never get enough. I saw her demon come to life in those enchanting green-grey eyes as she pressed a gun into my forehead and I wondered if maybe she could handle mine. My demon, I mean. Could Kyla-Rose handle my brand of crazy?

I walked into that locker room last night –which already feels like a lifetime ago- my mind whirring from all the shit I'd been dealing with during the day, I was trying to get my shit together ready for my fight and bam. I step not a foot into the locker room and this beauty was spread out on the bench looking like a goddamn fallen angel.

Her long silver hair fanned out around her, trailing down to the floor like a smoky halo. Her long lean legs casually swinging off of the other end, her tattooed arm resting over her eyes, the other playing with a little purple knife and *fuck me* that little leather skirt. I bite my lower lip just thinking about it.

And as if her mere presence alone wasn't enough to captivate me, her threatening to shoot me, sent every fucking drop of blood in my veins straight to my already hard cock. I had a semi all through my fucking fight which was thankfully over as quickly as it started –I like to put on a show usually, especially when it's somewhere I've never fought before- but I couldn't stop thinking about those big eyes. This strange green-grey colour and what was hiding behind them caught my attention and that was that. It may as well have been over then and there because when she sat up from that bench and locked those eyes with mine, that scornful look on her perfect face, I practically came in my pants.

I looked for her after the fights were over but I couldn't find her anywhere and not knowing her name I couldn't exactly ask around. After wandering around for a while, Huxley said to leave it and just go home, so after one last circuit of the warehouse I decided he was right, so I called it a night.

That didn't stop my mind from conjuring her though, I thought about her all night. Lying restlessly in my bed, my mind replaying our meeting over and over. That maniacal grin she gave me when she held that tiny gun to my head, excitement all but soared through me and only served to make me more curious. Who is this beautifully wild girl with balls of steel, a menacing grin that could literally make children cry and the devil himself shudder?

I tossed and turned all night thinking I probably wouldn't ever see her again, I'm not ashamed to admit that I jerked off to the thought of her and then I worried about not seeing her again, *again*, repeating the cycle until I just couldn't lie there any longer. That's how I wound up in the same gym as her. I got up and hit the gym in an attempt to work out my frustrations.

And my infatuation.

I never normally hit the gym that early on a Saturday morning but not being able to sleep must have been fate calling because as I stepped through that door and spotted a tall lean girl up in the ring, hunched over on her knees, without even needing to see her face I knew it was her.

I could *feel* her, like I was already tethered to her in some way.

My heart thumped a million miles a minute. It beat so fucking hard in that second that I thought it was going to rip free from my chest, fluttering manically like a bird trying to break free of its cage. I physically rubbed my chest with the heel of my hand as Tony kicked us out, I don't know what was going on in there but I ached to get to her, my demon roared and snarled, snapping its teeth, demanding to get closer to her.

Pulling the emergency stop cord on her treadmill –yeah, I know, not my finest hour, fucking dangerous- to get her attention threw me through a fucking loop. Her eyes pierced mine and the murderous look on her face got me all kinds of hot and bothered. Something about this girl just, *eurgh*, I don't even know how I feel but she does something to me.

So the fact that she agreed to come here tonight?

With me?

Fucking spectacular.

I tug Kyla-Rose into my side as she takes my hand and lead her into the house. It's already full of people, even more so now than when I left to meet her.

The front door opens up into the open plan first floor, the stairs are immediately opposite the front door, to the right is the dining room and downstairs bathroom and to the left is the living room leading to the kitchen, separated by the kitchen island. We pushed all the furniture out of the way so the floor space is clear for dancing.

People greet me as we walk in, fist-bumping and slapping me on the shoulder, but the noise seems to settle somewhat as we walk in, people are noticeably dropping their volume and whispering amongst themselves, usually you can hardly hear the music over the noise of people talking but not tonight, tonight the music is very much noticeable and so is the whispering.

"Kyla-Rose," Tommy greets, giving her a firm and respectful nod of his head, "bro," he greets me second, offering me his knuckles which I tap with my own; all the while his blue eyes fly between Kyla and I.

I scrunch my face up at that.

What is that all about?

We make our way to the kitchen, Kyla-Rose quiet and taking everything in. I wonder how she knows Tommy. *Did they hook up?* Nope, I'm not going there, not thinking about it.

I release Kyla's hand –albeit reluctantly- and step around to the opposite side of the island. I place my palms flat against the countertop; my fingers splayed wide and give her a grin. I don't know what it is about this girl but without even trying she gets more smiles out of me than any other fucker I've ever known. I normally only smile like this when I'm cutting someone up.

"What would you like to drink?" I ask her, a normal mundane question. "We have pretty much *anything* you could want," I waggle my eyebrows at my double meaning and she giggles.

Fuck. Me.

That fucking sound is like music to my ears.

She shrugs her slim shoulders beneath her jacket and I'm just itching to see her in that tiny dress without it.

"Can I take your coat?" I blurt out and she raises an eyebrow at me.

"Err," she smiles shaking her head, "I guess so," she laughs as I walk back around to her side of the island, pinching the leather at the shoulders as she shakes it free from her tattooed arms, "thanks," she murmurs with clear confusion in her voice at the formality but still with a soft smile on her gorgeous face.

Her grey-green eyes shine with amusement as I take her face in properly for the first time. Her eyes appear almost a little too big for her slim face but at the same time seem to fit perfectly above her high cheekbones. Doe-eyed and inquisitive, slightly more green than grey, a small narrow nose sits above plump red lips, the cupid's bow of her top lip perfectly symmetrical and her bottom lip -slightly larger than the top- is practically begging for me to sink my teeth into it.

By god, I swear this woman is going to fucking kill me.

Taking in her body I have to hold myself up to stop my weak knees from fucking buckling. Her creamy white skin is tattooed almost as much as my own –and that's saying something- I mean I noticed a fair bit of ink on her last night but I didn't get to look at her for nearly long enough.

Kyla-Rose's completely inked from the collarbones down, the long column of her ivory neck completely free of anything and then boom; an explosion of black ink, swirls, lines and shading coating her chest and shoulders continuing down both arms, hands and fingers included, even her back and both legs. Every inch of her I can see is touched by black ink, no colour but I can already tell that's just not her style.

Her chest piece sprawls wide, spanning across both shoulders, trailing down the tops of her arms, a shaded array of swallow birds, thorny branches and climbing plants but no flowers, not until the design hits her elbows, that's when the roses begin to appear between the thorns. Tight buds open into full blooms as they weave down to her hands and fingers, all intricately woven together with smaller swallow birds inked between. It's hours upon hours of work and absolutely stunning.

"No problem," I shrug, tossing her jacket over the back of a bar stool before turning back to her, "so, Sweetheart, drink?" I ask again and she raises a dark blonde brow at me.

"Didn't you hear me?" she laughs and my eyes go wide.

"No, sorry, I must have spaced out for a sec," shaking my head to clear my thoughts, I push a large hand through my mess of blonde hair.

"Am I boring you already?" she chuckles with a small shake of her head.

"No!" I almost shout at her, surprising the shit out of her, her eyes widen and she stops laughing, looking up at me through her thick black lashes.

Fuck me.

Doesn't she realise what she's doing to me?

"Why're you shouting at me now?" she laughs harder, recovering from her shock, my own head shaking without instruction.

"Honestly, because he's a fucking idiot. I'll get you that vodka-cranberry now, Darlin'," Huxley says, crossing the small space of the kitchen, his eyes raking over her appreciatively, forcing me to glare daggers at the back of his head.

I look across to Kyla-Rose but just as I should have expected, her attention has shifted to my very attractive best friend –not that *I* find him attractive but I do have eyes, all the girls want him. Huxley's an attractive guy, dark caramel skin and a lean build, not as broad as me but cut with defined muscle nonetheless. He stands a couple inches shorter than me, which still puts him at a decent six-four and his dark brown curls are shaved close to the scalp, his eyes, a deep brown, so dark, they're almost black in colour.

His silver eyebrow piercing glints in the spotlights of the kitchen as he bends down into the fridge and retrieves the cranberry juice. I watch him grab a crystal cut tumbler from the cabinet and drop some ice into it before pouring a generous splash of vodka and topping it off with the juice. He places it down on the counter in front of Kyla and she gives him a small smile which he responds to with a flirtatious wink.

God fucking damn.

And then it hits me. I've lost her already. I feel myself deflate and kick the toe of my shoe into the black tile floor.

What the fuck is wrong with me?

Fuck's sake.

I finally thought I'd found the girl. I know that sounds premature but I can just feel something between us, I hoped she might too.

Unless she's game for sharing?

I'll have her in any way I can. That thought starts to take over everything else, having her between us, my brother and I with a girl we both like…

"Kace," Kyla-Rose sings my name, my eyes snapping up to once again give her my attention, "got any lime?" she asks with a soft tilt of her lips.

I notice Huxley's abandoned us in the kitchen again, moving across the room to where he has the attention of two girls, maybe he isn't interested, only time will tell. I nod, returning Kyla-Rose's smile with one of my own.

I cut a lime into four pieces passing her a wedge; she runs it around the rim of the glass applying a small amount of pressure before dropping it into her drink. Still looking into her glass, she brings her finger and thumb to her lips, popping them into her mouth, she sucks on them gently.

Jesus, fuck.

Cracking open a beer I watch as she places her glass against her red painted lips, sipping it slowly she watches me from beneath her thick lashes. She swallows gently, the ivory column of her throat working it down as I imagine my thick fingers curling around it, restricting her air and filling her lungs with my own. Her pink tongue darts out, licking the remainder of lime from her lips. I'm fucking entranced, I couldn't look away from her if someone plucked out my eyeballs, I'd still be staring at her.

I stop mid-air with the spout of my bottle a couple of centimetres from my parted lips. I watch her and *try* –discretely- to adjust my now *very* hard cock beneath the restraints of my tight jeans. She takes another sip, larger this time but still watches me over the rim of her glass and I swallow, *hard.* Her eyes catch my movement and a small smile tilts one corner of her red lips, she averts her gaze, swallowing down her drink in its entirety, dropping the glass to the counter she looks back up at me, something unknown dancing in her eyes.

"Another?" I ask her almost breathlessly as I finally manage to take a swig of my beer.

"Little stronger this time, please," she smiles, that perfect action lighting up her whole face, perfectly matching dimples carved in either cheek.

I repeat what Huxley did but double the vodka and half the juice, copying Kyla's earlier step I run a lime wedge around the rim of her glass before dropping it in. I pass it over, her long delicate fingers brushing mine as she takes it. A cold shiver works its way up my spine and I swear it does weird fucking things to my brain. I can't think, can hardly fucking see anything around me but this beautiful woman, I'm blinkered like a horse at the races, my eyes only seeing what's directly in front of me.

How the fuck did I manage to get her to come here with me?

"Better?" I ask her as she takes a sip.

"Yes, thank you."

"Come on, let's sit," I jerk my head in the direction of the empty couch.

Rounding the island once more, I drape my arm possessively over her slim shoulders, drawing her into my side I turn her towards the room, dropping us onto the navy couch. My dick's got a complete mind of its own and as I watch her scope out the room, it's begging to find that warm wet place between her thighs, searching it out like a fucking heat-seeking missile and I find myself adjusting my cock for what feels like the hundredth time. I lay my arm across the back of the sofa and she turns to face me, her knees twisting into my body.

"You have a lot of friends," she comments, glancing at the people around us.

"Yeah, I guess, me and Hux know most of these guys from college and the gym," I shrug.

"Huh," she nods looking around, "is Hux the guy who made my drink?" she asks.

"Yeah, Huxley, sorry about that, him not introducing himself I mean," I laugh nervously but she just smiles at me. "I bet you have tonnes of friends, you should bring some with you next time, the more the merrier and all that," I tell her, nudging her shoulder with my hand, my fingers lingering a little on her bare shoulder, she shivers under my touch making me smile.

"Sure," she says but I get the feeling that's not something that will be happening in the near future, "you both live here?" she asks and I nod.

"Yeah, the two of us and our other friend, Nox, but he's still deployed at the moment," I tell her as she nods along.

"You were in the army?"

"I was, *we* were. Huxley, Nox and I were deployed together, Nox was our Lieutenant, we all just clicked and the rest is history so they say," I chuckle.

She smiles brightly at me, her eyes soft, "people bond going into battle, you need good people in your corner, especially for something like that."

"You do," I agree, "you got experience of that?"

"Sorta," she shrugs gently, "you fighting for Cam again?" she queries taking me by surprise with the sudden change in subject, but I brush it off, I don't want her to feel forced to talk about things that make her uncomfortable.

"Yeah, I think so, he offered me a fight next Friday, told me to let him know by Monday, I'll probably say yeah, the money's pretty good," I shrug, "why, you wanna come watch me?" I ask mischievously, looking back down at her with a teasing wiggle of my eyebrows, but her focus has shifted from me to some dark haired guy, I don't recognise, across the room.

Kyla-Rose watches him with undeterred focus, her shoulder tensing under my hand, her free hand clenching and unclenching into a fist in her lap, she inhales a sharp breath through her nose.

"I'd love to," she murmurs distractedly, "may I use your bathroom?" she asks, suddenly standing without looking at me.

"Err, yeah, to the left of the front door or you can use mine upstairs if you want, second door on the left," I tell her, her eyes not wavering from the dark haired guy.

"Thanks," she mumbles.

I watch as she crosses the room towards the guy, moving through the crowd until she reaches him, latching onto his elbow she tugs sharply gaining his attention, he snaps his head around to face her, his dark eyes widening as she drags him toward the stairs and he follows her up.

What the fuck was that?

I can't help but see red. Jealousy soars through me, filling my veins with a rush of anger, I have no fucking claim to her but I can't stop myself moving. My demon growls possessively as I slam my beer down onto the side table, froth and bubbles overflowing from the neck of it, soaking my fist. A squeal of surprise escapes the woman sitting the other side of it, I murmur my apology before taking the stairs two at a time. If I brought Kyla-Rose here for her to take another guy upstairs, I'm gunna lose my goddamn mind.

I know inviting her here doesn't give me some sort of special permission to fuck her or even get her undivided attention but I didn't tell her where my bedroom was so she could pull some other dude up there. I march down the hallway towards my room, stomping heavy footsteps as I go, my door's open ajar and rather than burst in there –ignoring my raging primal instincts- I shove my demon down and instead lean against the wall to listen.

"You shouldn't fucking be here, Polecat," Kyla hisses, "I fucking warned you to get your shit together or get the fuck out of my city, what you're pushing down there isn't my shit, don't think I didn't see you trying to slip shitty cut drugs to that woman, do you think I'm fucking stupid?" she seethes in a whisper.

What the fuck is going on?

"Boss, I'm sorry, I real-"

"Shut the fuck up or I swear to *fuck* I will rip your tongue out of your head with my bare hands and shove it so far up your arsehole, it'll appear back in your fucking mouth. Now, get the fuck out of here or your tongue won't be the only appendage you need to worry about losing tonight," she snarls.

"Yes, boss," the man –Polecat- replies as hurried footsteps pound in my direction.

I rush to push open Huxley's bedroom door, stepping inside I hide myself behind the door just as the guy pulls open the door to my room and bolts down the stairs. I listen for more movement but all I hear is the string light in my bathroom being pulled and the door clicking shut. I walk back out into the hallway closing Huxley's door behind me, then I dither. Do I go back downstairs and pretend I was nowhere to be seen? Or do I wait right here and ask her what the hell that was all about? Is that a bit of an ambush?

Deciding it's really none of my business, I play it safe and head back downstairs to retake my seat. I know nothing about this woman and although I *want* to get to know her, eavesdropping on a conversation, that is very clearly none of my business, is probably not a great start to what I hope is some sort of relationship. It'd make me close up, zip my mouth and throw away the key if someone I just met was listening in on my private conversations.

A few minutes later Kyla's sexy body sways back into the room, all male eyes are drawn to her and I even spot a few of the women glancing in her direction, some look on with jealous disgust, others in awe, appreciating what they see. Then as if searching me out, her eyes find mine across the crowded room, the biggest smile forms on her face, flashing me her pearly whites as matching dimples indent her cheeks. Her green-grey gaze never shifting from mine, she wears a smile that says she's genuinely happy to see me and I get a little pang in my chest at that, only now realising her eyes *are* just for me tonight.

"Everything okay?" I ask her.

"Yeah, I used your bathroom upstairs, thank you," she says casually, dropping her slim frame back down into the space beside me.

Her hand finds my thigh automatically as if it's the most natural thing in the world, she squeezes gently and rests it there.

"Oh!" I say a little loudly startling her, she plucks her hand from my thigh like it burnt her. I almost grab it and shove it back but manage to resist the urge, "don't drink that," I say as she lifts her drink, "let me make you a new one, I left them unattended and well, you know, you can never be too careful," I say with a shrug, there's always some fucking arsehole looking for an opportunity to spike someone.

"Oh, Kacey, seriously, no one would *dare* spike me," she chuckles like she really truly believes it and I raise an eyebrow at her. She looks at me quickly swallowing her laughter, "sorry, yeah, you're probably right," she agrees, passing me her glass, I look down at the glass and then back up at her with what I know is a confused as fuck expression on my face.

"Why would no one *dare* spike you?" I ask with a raised eyebrow, still clutching her half full glass in my hand.

Kyla-Rose swallows, glancing down at her hands, she twists them in her lap, knotting her fingers together she looks up at me through her lashes.

"No reason, I'm just being silly, I'd love a fresh drink, thank you," she says quietly and I can tell it's utter bullshit but I don't push it.

Leaving her on the couch I start mixing her a fresh drink, glancing over at her every now and again, I tilt my head. No one steps over to speak with her, no one sits next to her, in fact, everyone seems to be giving my girl a wide berth. The women seem to be point blank ignoring her or glancing at her before turning back to their friends whispering, something just doesn't feel right. I don't like that one bit, everyone we invite here is usually super welcoming and friendly, so what the fuck is wrong with them all tonight?

I pass Kyla her fresh drink and she thanks me as I glance back around the room. I feel my muscles tense up and my jaw clench, I grind my teeth together so hard I swear I could crack a molar.

"Kacey?" Kyla-Rose whispers, my head snapping down to meet her gaze.

Her eyebrows pinched together, lips slightly parted, she looks up at me.

"Is everything okay?" she asks, sensing I'm different to how I was not five minutes ago.

"Yeah, yeah, everything's fine. Here," I say, offering her my hand, "let me introduce you to some of my friends," I offer.

A flash of hesitation crosses her before she composes her features, taking my hand, I pull her up from the sofa. Her delicate fingers encased in mine, her silky smooth, tattooed skin warm against my palm makes a low growl rip free from my chest as I think about handcuffing her to me for the rest of her life.

I wonder if she'd let me?

"Ladies," I smile at the small group of women as we approach.

We went to college with these four and they're usually super sweet and polite, always welcoming any newbies into their little group and taking other girls under their wing at parties when it's obvious they don't know anyone but not tonight. I expected them to jump on Kyla as soon as we stepped foot in the door but instead every time I've looked over at them they've been having hushed conversation and I don't like it one bit.

"Hey, Kacey," Alice says and I offer her a forced smile.

"This is Kyla-Rose," I introduce, tugging her forward a little harder than necessary and pulling her to stand in front of me.

I wrap my arm around her waist pulling her back flush to my front and I swear to fuck she must be able to feel my dick pressing into her lower back, she makes me hard as fucking rock but she doesn't comment or try to move away.

"Hey," Kyla says confidently, head held high, "nice to meet you," she says and the four women all glare at her like she's some sort of fucking alien and I feel my temper growing.

"Hi," Maddie chokes out, glancing between the other three girls who each look uncomfortable.

"So, Kacey, I hear you went to the fights in the warehouse district last night," Tina says, glancing at Kyla-Rose and I raise a brow at her.

"Yeah," I confirm gruffly and she looks down at her feet.

Okay, this is fucking weird.

"So are any of you gunna speak to Kyla-Rose or just stare

at the fucking floor, if you've got a fucking problem, now's the time, I wanna hear it," I almost snarl.

Feeling Kyla-Rose stiffen in my embrace, she presses her hot body back into mine but I can't appreciate holding her like this when I'm so worked up. The four women all look between themselves and then back to Kyla, then to me and then back to each other.

"Well?" I demand a little too loudly, sure I'm drawing the attention of others but I really don't give a fuck about causing a scene.

Out the corner of my eye I see Huxley shift, staring at me from across the room as Kyla-Rose presses herself even further back into me, obviously sensing I need something to help ground me.

"It's fine," Kyla suddenly speaks up, "I get it girls. I'm just spending some time with Kacey, I'm sure you understand," she says diplomatically, demanding the attention of all four pairs of eyes.

"Yeah, of course!" Alice almost squeals, the sound instantly making me wince, "we totally get it, *don't* we ladies?" she rushes out, elbowing Maddie in the ribs as she does so.

"Of course, there's no problem," Stacey chimes in and I narrow my eyes on them.

"Well, you girls have a good night," Kyla-Rose smiles at them.

Wrapping her delicate hand around my vibrating forearm, that's somehow found its way across her chest. Her gentle touch slightly diffuses the tension in my stiff posture, giving me a small tug towards the front door, she slips her hand through mine and leads me away.

I follow her willingly, my hand latched onto hers, very aware that all eyes are on us after my little outburst. My feet carry me of their own accord until we push through the front door, venturing out into the frosty night air. Kyla-Rose leads me down the garden path only stopping at the very end, she carefully steps over the row of bluebells that Huxley's mum *insisted* we plant. Pulling me with her across the small patch of grass, she tugs me down to sit beside her on the brick wall.

"Thanks," I breathe, closing my eyes and taking in a deep breath, the winter air crisp in my lungs.

Still holding my hand Kyla gives it a reassuring squeeze, I feel her shuffle slightly beside me and when I open my eyes and look down at her she's turned herself into me, her bare knee brushing my own.

"It's okay, Big Man, I lose my shit sometimes too," she says softly, earnestly, "it takes a lot to get me to drop back down to earth, if you know what I mean," she offers with a small smile and I can see just how honest her words are, she's not just trying to make me feel better, she's giving me a small glimpse into who she is.

"Yeah, I know what you mean," I agree with a short nod of my head, still feeling the tension in my shoulders, "I don't like the way people were looking at you in there," I admit with a growl, looking at her from the corner of my eye with a frown.

"I'm used to it," she shrugs nonchalantly, "girls don't really like me, I don't have friends," Kyla-Rose shrugs again trying to appear unaffected, looking out across the lawn back to the house, where the party still rages on whether we're inside or not and wrinkles her nose. "I don't need friends Kacey, that's just the way it is."

I inspect her face, searching for anything that might tell me that's untrue but I find nothing but truth in her eyes. Something inside me settles uncomfortably. I don't want Kyla to feel like that, like she doesn't have friends and shouldn't, that's not *just the way it is*. I want her to know there's at least one person in her corner, whether she wants me there or not, I already find myself wanting to bat for the wild girl with the pretty green-grey eyes.

"Well, you have at least one friend," I tell her quietly, her eyes find mine in the dark, flicking between them before she exhales a deep breath.

"You want to be my friend, Kacey?" she asks quietly looking away again, her silver curtain of hair hiding her expression but I can practically feel the vulnerability seeping from her pores.

"If you'll have me."

"Just friends?" she clarifies, her tongue darting out to wet her red lips.

I'm enthralled by her, the moonlight falls across her ivory skin, revealing all the little bumps and scars her dark tattoos try to hide, it only makes her that much more beautiful to me. If I was never able to look upon another person again, I'd be happy knowing she was the last I saw, the best. I'd happily replay her over and over again in my mind's eye, brand her image to the inside of my skull, carve her into my skin.

"If that's what you want," I tell her, trying not to sound too desperate because in reality I want to scream just how much I already want to be around her, bind her wrists and shackle her to me.

Little does she know I've never chased after a woman in my life. Then I met Kyla-Rose and fate decided to drop her back in front of me twice in the space of just two days and I swear I will follow her to the ends of the earth if she doesn't shoot me like a stray dog. I'm possessive by nature, among *other* things but I've never felt *this* before.

"That's not what I want," she exhales so quietly I almost miss her words completely.

"No?" I tilt my head, "what is it that you want, Kyla-Rose?"

She stares up at me, her green-grey eyes flashing a deep emerald, I reach over tucking a long strand of silver hair behind her pierced ear, my thick fingertips brushing over her cool skin. I run my index finger down her round jaw, stopping to pinch her chin between my thumb and forefinger, I tilt her face up to meet my gaze.

Her eyes darken as she drags her plump bottom lip between her teeth, nibbling on it thoughtfully, she glances back down at her tattooed hands, one of which is still encased in my own. I splay my fingers wide across her cheek, cupping her face I drag the pad of my thumb across the apple of her cheekbone, forcing her to draw her eyes back up to meet mine. I dip my head down, tilting Kyla's back as I go, I lean into her slowly, inhaling deeply, I can't help but smile at the excitement of my demon.

"You smell so fucking good," I breathe forcing her to tilt her head back further to look at me.

"Yeah?" she grins, "I guess that's as good a compliment as any," she snickers.

Moving my hand to the back of her neck, I tangle my

fingers into her silken hair and tug as I lean in. Roughly nuzzling my face into the crook of her neck, my light stubble scraping across the ivory column of her throat, marking her like a male lion bunting his mate. Breathing in her sweet coconut and citrus scent I note there's something else there too, something that is just *Kyla-Rose*, its heady and intoxicating and it makes me wanna throw myself down at her feet.

I know what lust feels like, it's usually the only thing I feel when I'm with a woman but the way I feel when I'm around Kyla-Rose is so astronomically different I can't even put it into words. The effect she's had on me in such a short amount of time is insane. I can already feel myself being drawn in with the tide and dragged under and I really hope she decides I'm worthy enough to be drowned by her.

I've never been so captivated by a woman before. I'm no saint, I've had my fair share of women and I won't lie, I love women, everything about them, the hard parts, the soft parts, the calm and the fire. But none of the women I've ever had the pleasure of meeting before have had *all* of that.

And no one has ever had something inside of them like Kyla-Rose has. A shadow, a darkness, a hell dimension that burns inside her, thrives even but she isn't consumed by it. She *rules* it. A demon akin to my own, a sickness, a plague of darkness with devilish intentions; she's the queen of her darkness and I can only hope I get to be the slave that surrenders to her every wicked whim.

Her free hand traces up my back, making my muscles ripple under her delicate touch, a scorching trail left in its wake, she brings her fingers up to the nape of my neck curling them around the taut muscle, massaging the spot like she's trying to soothe the beast in me, my shoulders relaxing at her touch.

She sighs heavily as my lips ghost over her cool skin, I press a tender kiss to the point her neck meets her shoulder, her skin smattering with goosebumps under my warm breath. I kiss along to the bony point of her shoulder before doubling back and working my way back up her neck. Kissing, nipping and sucking a trail, her hand slips from my neck, gripping onto my shoulder; her long black nails dig in, holding me in place like a cat with a prey it wants to devour.

Releasing her fingers from my own, I place her hand on my thigh. I grip her waist with both hands and in a single move I spin her body to face me completely, making her gasp. She leans into me, her breasts pressing up against my solid chest, the hard peaks of her nipples brushing against me. I nibble the soft skin behind her ear, making my way along her jaw until I find her lips. I rub the tip of my nose against hers, her eyes fluttering shut, her thick lashes dusting over the tops of her cheekbones. She sucks in a sharp breath as my lips hover over hers, brushing against them as I say my next words.

"I want to kiss you, Kyla-Rose," I breathe into her lips; which part like I ordered it.

Her big eyes slowly peel open, flickering between my own.

"So, what you waiting for, Big Man?" she whispers, challenging me, daring me, a wicked smile tilts the corner of her lips, her mischievous eyes dropping to my mouth.

My lips find hers, instantly sending a jolt of electricity hammering through me, my inner animal taking over, my large hands grab at her hips, digging in the skin, pulling her flush against me. Lips, teeth and tongues battling it out for dominance, she locks her fingers into my shaggy blonde hair, her nails scraping over my tattooed scalp and fingers tugging at the root. She sucks my bottom lip into her mouth, her other hand closing gently around my throat, her thumb stoking across the thick scar there. I never let anyone touch that jagged line of tissue, but strangely, the way she strokes her delicate fingers over it and then down to the base of my throat, I find it soothing, giving permission for the low rumble of a growl I've been trying to contain to rip free.

She gasps at the feral sound, opening her lips more, I find myself trying to taste every inch of her, my tongue delves deep, my lips massaging hers. Her teeth nip at my tongue forcing it to retreat. Her weight pressing against my chest making me straighten for her, allowing her to take control. I finally break the kiss on a groan, a little whimper escaping her parted lips, I straddle the wall, one leg dropping either side of it before pulling her back into me, her swollen lips automatically finding mine once more, the curve of her arse resting between my open knees as she twists her lithe body into me.

My hard cock nudges against my tight jeans, pulsing painfully beneath my zipper, the tip weeping for contact. Her hands slide up my rough, jean clad thighs, fingertips brushing painfully close to where I need them most. She groans into my mouth as I pull her closer, every part of our bodies touching, her bare thighs trapped between my own. My hands roam over the exposed skin of her shoulders, gripping them tightly, drawing her flush to the hard planes of my chest.

Kyla's delicate hands ghost over the waistband of my

jeans, forcing me to hold my breath as her cool fingers find their way beneath my shirt. Her hands roam over my hard ripple of abs before reaching my muscular chest. My arm bands around her tiny waist as I stand, bringing her with me, her feet lifting clean from the floor, without breaking our kiss she draws her legs up wrapping them around my waist as I carry her towards the house.

Kyla-Rose tears her lips from mine, "not in the house," she orders in a hoarse, breathy whisper before re-attaching her luscious lips to mine, I groan at her tongue sliding effortlessly back into my mouth.

Switching direction, I stumble over the bluebells, her thighs tightening around my waist, she laughs into our kiss, I smile against her, pillaging her mouth with my tongue. My tongue darts in and out, dancing with her own as I carry her down the side of the house.

Flipping us around, I slam her back into the exposed brick at the side of the house. She groans into me, biting down on my bottom lip so hard she draws blood, pulling her lips from mine, her eyes flicking between my own. Never taking her eyes from me, her tongue darts out, painfully slowly lapping up the trickle of blood from my chin to my lips before sucking it back into her mouth soothing the sting. Her nails claw aggressively at my back, gripping my t-shirt in her small hands she tugs at it, leaning back, still holding onto her with one hand, I use the other to rip my white shirt over my head and drop it to the grass.

Kyla wastes no time tearing her swollen lips from mine, her teeth burying themselves into the trapezius muscle of my shoulder, my head drops to hers as she bites and sucks, running her tongue up my neck to my ear, pulling my pierced lobe into her mouth, biting and sucking as I rock my hips into hers, my hard cock pulsing against the heat of her core.

One of her hands drops between us, her fingers effortlessly flicking open the button of my jeans, hastily peeling my zipper all the way down she slides her soft hand to the waistband of my boxers. The heel of her hand resting against my abs, her eyes on mine, I can't look away with her looking at me like that, her eyes boring their way into my soul.

Seeing nothing but desire in my eyes, Kyla-Rose wriggles her small hand under the waistband of my boxers, slipping her smooth hand completely inside, her cool, silky fingers wrapping around the steel shaft of my cock, her thumb tugging on my piercing.

"*Fuckkkk,*" I exhale the growl as she pumps me with her small hand, my head dropping forward once more against her shoulder as my breathing quickens.

She works my shaft slow but firm, her fingers circled around me tightly, her thumb swiping across the pierced tip dragging the bead of pre-cum all the way down to the base, repeating the action over and over.

"Fuck, Kyla-Rose," I say between ragged breaths, "I need to feel you."

"I want you, Kacey," she breathes into my ear and everything else falls away.

I grip her wrist, removing her hand from my pants. I push her firmly into the wall, holding her there with one hand, my other working its way up her creamy thigh, under the last bit of her dress that hasn't already bunched up over her hips, when my fingers run over something cold and smooth.

Metal.

My hand stills, she sucks in a sharp breath as my fingers run over two knives attached to a garter.

"What's this?" I murmur almost excitedly, peeking down between our bodies to take a look before flicking my gaze back up to hers.

"We don't have to play with those today, Big Man," she answers in a whisper with a teasing smile.

"That's so fucking hot," I pant with a chuckle and she throws her head back with a loud laugh.

"You and I are gunna get on great," she laughs breathlessly, "but now's not the time to discuss knife play, Big Man," she winks and my cock stiffens even more at the thought, the *promise*.

Sliding back over the switchblades, my rough fingers resume their mission in finding the lace of her knickers, sliding beneath and seeking out her warmth.

"*Fuck*, you're soaked," I hiss as my fingers run over her wet folds.

Kyla-Rose whimpers into my neck, her tongue tracing across my scar, her hands pushing at the waistband of my jeans as she wiggles in my arms, I pin her in place.

"Patience, Sweetheart," I chuckle darkly, earning me a huff of frustration, "don't pout, I've got you." I promise.

Hooking a single finger through the black lace I yank her knickers to the side, making her hiss through her teeth at the exposure of her hot flesh to the cold air. I run my finger through her wet heat, her eyes squeezing shut, she drops her head back against the brick, exhaling a long, low moan. Her silver hair sticking to the wall with the friction, she tries to grind down against my hand, forcing another evil laugh from me. I'm working her up; she's so close to getting what she wants yet so far from it. I want to take my time in watching her come undone.

"Kacey, *please*," she whines, throwing her head from side to side, needing release.

I ignore her pleas. Bending my middle finger I run my knuckle up through her slickness with a little more pressure this time, earning me a low whimper as I reach her clit. The corner of my mouth tilts up into a smile as I watch her.

"Look at me, Kyla-Rose, show me those gorgeous eyes," I demand.

Her head dropping forward, she opens her wide eyes, her gaze latching onto mine as I push a single finger into her and twist, making us both groan in appreciation.

"You're so fucking tight, Ky," I groan, the uncomfortable steel pipe in my jeans trying to burst free.

"Kacey," she cries throwing her head back as I move my finger in and out of her, the tight walls of her cunt pulsing around me, trying to suck my finger in deeper.

"Greedy," I smirk, "can you take another?" I ask hooking my finger inside her.

Her head nods in urgency, "yes! G*od,* yes! Kacey."

Slowly dragging my hooked finger out, running it over the hard nub of her clit, I add a second finger, slamming them both into her in one unrelenting thrust, grinding the heel of my hand against her aching clit, I work my fingers in and out at a punishing pace.

"*Fuck!*" she cries, her grip on my shoulders intensifying.

I work my fingers in and out harder and faster, her hot pussy clamping around my fingers, gripping me like a vice. Her nails slicing into my back, drawing blood as she rakes them up and down my exposed skin. I don't stop her, I want her to tear into me, delve inside and infect my soul with hers, our demons melding together.

"Kacey," she cries, squeezing my fingers so hard it could cut off circulation. "Fuck me." She orders on a moan her eyes flying open and locking with my own.

Sliding my fingers from inside her, I tug my jeans and boxers down so they fall just above my knees. I wrap my fist around the lace of her knickers, shredding them from her hot body with one solid tear, discarding them to the floor. I fist my aching cock, pumping it a few times, I line the tip up with her entrance.

I pause.

"FUCK!" I roar, startling her, she furrows her brow, "I haven't got a condom," I curse under my ragged breath.

"I'm clean, I'm on the pill," she pants, heaving in a breath.

"Me too, clean, I mean," I tell her, "are you sure?" I ask, my eyes darting between hers.

Please be sure.

In my twenty-eight years, I've never gone into anyone bare before and I really didn't expect to be doing it for the first time up against the side of my house, I almost laugh but now's most definitely not the time for that.

"Kacey, *please*," she begs, squirming in my arms, scraping her inked skin against the rough brick.

Flashing a feral grin I swiftly slam inside her. She cries out my name followed by a hissing string of curses, arching her back off the wall she pushes herself against me. In that one hard thrust I'm buried balls deep inside her sweet, sweet cunt.

And fuck me, I could come right now, she's so goddamn tight, I can hardly breathe let alone move.

Her pussy flutters eagerly around my hard cock, attempting to drag me deeper. I don't move for a moment, sitting fully seated inside her, I let her walls ripple around me as they try to adjust before I slowly draw out, slamming my way back in. Kyla curses out my name on a howl as I pick up speed, her tight pussy clamping down around me as I force my way in and out of her tight channel.

I slide one hand up into her hair, knotting my thick tattooed fingers through her long silver locks, I force her face down to meet mine. My lips collide with hers, teeth crashing as she breathes life into me. This kiss is like a resurrection and an exorcism all rolled into one. The push and pull, give and take, the demand, dominance and submission. Kyla-Rose's kiss rips every ounce of oxygen from my lungs and just when I think I might die, she breathes her fucking life into me until I'm full and dizzy on it.

Kyla's soul is trying to tear mine from my body and meld it with hers, intertwined in a way that will ruin me for all others. And I'm *absolutely* fucking okay with that. In fact if I never see another woman again it'll be too soon. All I need, all I *want,* is the wild girl I'm currently inside of, to want and need me in the same way because after this I'm never letting her go.

"Harder," she growls between kisses and I comply.

How could I not? She's fucking *everything*. Thrusting into her, my hips crushing our pelvic bones together so hard we could grind each other into dust. I tug her dress and bra down baring her breasts to me.

"*Fuckkk,*" I hiss biting down on my lip when I see her nipple piercings.

"More," she cries, throwing her head from side to side against the wall.

I latch my mouth onto one hard, rosy bud, tugging on the metal bar with my teeth, laving the sting with the flat of my tongue, sucking and biting on her hard nipple, her fingernails dig into my back, drawing more blood, it trickles down my spine. I take my hand from her hair, snaking it down between our sweaty bodies, I thrust into her harder and harder until my finger and thumb find her swollen clit and I pinch, *hard*.

"KACEY!" Kyla-Rose screams as she flies over the edge, her tight cunt squeezing and pulsing around me as I find my own release and come with her.

With one last thrust I let go, shooting ropes of hot cum into her, coating the entrance of her cervix, her pussy clamps down around me milking every last drop as her entire body goes lax in my arms. Her legs still wrapped around me trembling, my dick still inside her and as she wriggles against me I can already feel myself getting hard again.

Holy fuck, how's that even possible?

Neither of us moves for a beat as we pant hard trying to catch our breaths. When Kyla-Rose's legs finally relax, dropping from my waist, I slowly plant her stilettoed feet to the grass. Making sure she's steady, I tug my pants and jeans up my legs leaving the fly open, I scoop down, grab my t-shirt and drop to my knees before her. The sight of my cum dripping between her thighs has my dick immediately standing to attention.

Down, boy.

"What're you doing?" a deep crease forms between her eyebrows as she puts her bra back into place and pulls the top of her dress back up, she tries to shimmy her dress down her thighs but I stop her, pressing a hand to her knife covered thigh.

"Cleaning you up, obviously."

Gripping her wrist, I move her hand away from the hem of her dress and run my shirt between her legs cleaning up our joint mess. Wiping up as much as I can before I pull her dress back down over the curve of her arse, I cover her garter of knives, which thinking about it again just gets me hot. She bends down to collect her ruined knickers but before she can, I'm right there snatching them up and tucking them into my pocket with a wink. Her mouth hangs open a little but then she laughs. I run my hands through her hair trying to save it, I smooth it down somewhat but she grips my wrist pulling my hands away.

"It's sex hair," she shrugs her slim shoulders, "it's never going to look better than whatever it looks like now," she chuckles, lacing her dainty fingers through mine, she reaches up with her spare hand, wiping away what I can only assume is her lipstick from my face.

"I'm guessing my lipstick is non-existent now? Considering it looks like most of it is on you," she smirks and I shrug.

"Sweetheart, I like having your lipstick on me, just make sure you re-apply it when we go in," I tell her, her nose wrinkling in confusion.

"Why?"

"Because I want everyone to know that it's *your* lipstick all over me, essentially marking you and *me* off limits to every other fucker here," I shrug, my lips curling up into a sly smile.

"So, you're trying to mark your territory?" she smirks with raised eyebrows.

"No," I smile playfully making her frown in confusion, "*you're* marking *your* territory," I wink and she throws her head back with a short laugh.

"You're fucking crazy, Big Man," she smiles shaking her head, those matching dimples popping in her cheeks.

"You seem to like crazy," I state with a serious look and she smirks, her eyes dancing with mischief.

"You seem to like psycho," she tells me jerking her head in my direction and patting the knives at her thigh.

A small smile tugs at the upper corner of my mouth as I bend down to collect my screwed up ball of a shirt.

"Kyla-Rose, I already told you I like you," I laugh, "psycho is just a bonus," I beam, slinging my arm around her shoulders, turning us towards the front of the house.

"I'll re-apply my lipstick then," she confirms with a shy smile and fuck if that doesn't make my heart lurch in my chest.

She reaches her small hand up, clutching my hand hanging limply over her shoulder and linking her fingers with mine.

"Come on then," I start making our way around the side of the house towards the front door, "I need to get my girl a drink," I announce looking down at her.

She glances up at me through her lashes, her green-grey eyes watching me for any sign that I'm joking but she won't find it, I'm not joking, I just hope she gives me a shot.

CHAPTER 6

KYLA-ROSE

Okay.

I *know*.

But, just hear me out…

When I met up with Kacey earlier tonight, did I think he looked hot? Obviously, *yes*, fuck yes. He took my hand, walked me to his house and spaced out on me in the kitchen while eye-fucking me, but did I still think he was hot? *Durr*… So when he made me a drink, sat down with me *and* gave me nothing but his undivided attention, did it melt my panties a little bit? Of fucking course it did, *I'm not fucking dead*. So the fact that said knickers were -not long thereafter- torn from my very person by the above mentioned sex god?

Something like that kind of says a lot about my night so far huh?

Honestly, I don't know what it is about Kacey, but I don't feel like this was just a one night wonder, a *'one and done'* if you will. Yeah, yeah, I get that that is kind of exactly what it was, but it doesn't *feel* like that. Sure we both acted on pure lust but the demon inside me found something akin in him and latched on, that's just how it happened.

Kacey stuck up for me, he went out of his way to defend me to his friends, even though they very clearly *think* they know a lot more about me than he does, he didn't question it. He didn't ask me how I knew Gremlin -aka Tommy- and he didn't think I was a fucking loser when he brought up the whole friend thing. I couldn't exactly tell him I don't have friends because I'm a murdering, psychopathic crime lord and everyone's fucking afraid of me, could I?

I mean, I guess I could… but like, that's some seriously long conversation to be had there, I don't want to scare him off. Or not, I don't know, are these things usually simple? Are they supposed to be? Any sort of *normal* etiquette is mostly wasted on me, so I really have no clue about these things. I can't exactly look it up, get advice from the internet, I'll just type in '*how to explain to the guy you're seeing that you're a fucking criminal.'* Yeah, I'm thinking not so much.

Regardless, I like Kacey, like, genuinely *like* him –which in itself is a weird fucking feeling, I don't like *anybody*, especially not after only knowing them two days- he's a really sweet guy. He's not left my side all night, constantly making sure I'm happy and well-watered, plus, he's dead easy on the eyes so that obviously helps. And that dick, *fuck me,* that thing is a masterpiece in and of itself, especially with its little metal friend through the tip, that shit just hits different.

His tongue works magic and his cock stroked a fire inside me, that's burning so fucking brightly right now, I'm certain I must be at least fifty degrees hotter than hell –and I should know, I was fucking born of hellfire. I've never fucked anyone quite like that before and I'm not just talking about the savage act of the fucking itself, no, I mean, it was raw, dirty, hard, fucking *passionate*. It was scary how many emotions and feelings it drew out of me.

Watching Kacey across the room now, he's talking quietly with a friend, he didn't want to leave me by myself considering he couldn't convince any of his female friends to chat with me –unsurprisingly- but I forced him to go. I quite like sitting alone and just people watching.

It's clear he was always the reserved beast of a man. He keeps himself to himself, he's quiet and thoughtful, never speaking more than a few words to anyone but I don't think that's got anything to do with me being here. I think he just has his people. Like me, he has a select few that he knows he can be his complete, true self with and to everyone else there's this public version of Kacey that everybody *else* gets to see. I feel fucking privileged to see the real Kacey. He's an experience, that's for damn sure.

"How you doing, Darlin'?" a rough voice asks me, breaking me from my train of thought, I look up to find a smiling, Hux and I can't help but let my eyes dance over him.

His smooth skin has a deep caramel glow, a dark tan that's got to be tropical for sure, he's far from pasty pale like me, without all of my black ink I'm practically translucent, you may as well call me *Casper* and be done with it. His eyes are as dark as the night sky, a deep chocolate brown and dark curly hair cropped close to his scalp.

His eyebrow pierced with a silver bar, both his ears stretched the size of small pennies and one has multiple silver bars through the top of it too. Black jeans hang low on his hips and a forest green t-shirt stretches deliciously across his broad chest. I lick my lips nervously as he takes the seat on the couch beside me.

"I'm doing good," I smile politely, my heart stuttering a little in my chest as his thigh brushes up against mine.

"Good," he smiles back, his eyes taking in my face like he's refreshing himself with my features.

He drops his large arm heavily around my shoulders, his warmth almost familiar but I'm certain we've never met. Usually an action like that from a male stranger would trigger me into being stabby but I don't feel that way right now. Maybe it's all the alcohol in me making me sloppy.

"I'm Huxley, by the way," he officially introduces himself, offering me his free hand to shake.

I laugh and place my hand in his, "nice to meet you, I'm Kyla-Rose."

He smiles, all toothy and white and perfect, "nice to meet you too, Kyla-Rose," and fuck me the way he purrs my name, it drips from his tongue like honey and my tummy clenches.

Huxley's dark eyes flick between my own as he watches my face intently, I feel myself staring back as my brow creases. My brain scrambling through my memories, *why are you so familiar to me?*

"Do I know you?" I finally ask with a small shake of my head, I'm all sorts of disorientated looking at this stranger.

"*Knowing* someone is relative," he whispers, studying every inch of my face as his thumb smooths over my bare shoulder.

What the hell does that mean?

I look away quickly, taking another sip of my drink to smother my confusion and pull on my well-practised blank mask.

"Why?" he asks quietly. "Do you think you know me, Kyla-Rose?" leaning in slightly closer, the tips of his long fingers joining his thumb in grazing over my arm.

"You feel familiar," I whisper back with an unconfident shake to my voice, I look up through my lashes into his beautifully lashed onyx eyes.

My body trembling at his barely there touch, I suck in a sharp breath as his gaze locks onto mine. The way he looks at me with those ebony orbs, feels as though he's plucking all of my fractured pieces out, dragging them into the light, restructuring damaged parts of my soul and pushing them back inside. I feel vulnerable. Nervous. *Excited?* God, I'm so confused right now.

My soul screaming, *'Why do I know you?'*

"That's because we *are* familiars. Maybe we already *know* each other, perhaps in this life, perhaps in another," he shrugs as though it's the most casual statement in the world. "Perhaps it's only our bodies that are known to one another," he breathes.

His beautifully carved face barely a hair's breadth from my own, his mouth-watering scent filling my nostrils; clementine's and freshly cut grass. It reminds me of playing outside as a child at my Uncle Dee's, blissfully unaware of the world's monsters.

Huxley runs his tongue across his teeth as he unashamedly explores my face. I feel a blush start to heat my cheeks as I downcast my eyes. The way Huxley is looking at me, almost like he's assessing me, trying to figure me out, makes me feel vulnerable, like he's peeling back all my layers and examining my shadowed centre. A glint of silver catches my eye as he smiles at me, his tongue bar clinking against his teeth.

"You're his girl from the fights," Huxley bobs his head to himself with realisation.

I shrug, "uh-huh, I guess that's me," my breath catches making me stumble over my words as he distances himself from me with a smile.

My guilty eyes wander over to the kitchen searching out Kacey and I immediately find him watching me, *us*. However, despite my panicked thoughts, him seeing me with his friend in what I would describe as intimate proximity, he gives me a huge smile and mouths asking me if I'm okay to which I nod and smile back. I don't think I've ever smiled so fucking much in my life.

It's making my cheeks ache, how do people do this all the time?

"He must really like you, the miserable fucker never smiles for anyone," Huxley tells me.

"Maybe he's never had anything to really smile about before," I mumble to myself but Huxley catches my words.

Popping his knuckle under my chin he gently turns my face back to him, his ebony eyes watching my own as his gentle touch strokes alive the fire inside me.

"It's not only me who can read people well, Kyla-Rose," just the way he says my name sends another shock pulsing through me.

Huxley pushes to his feet and I instantly feel the loss of his heavy arm over my bare shoulders, a cool chill running over my warmed flesh.

Looking down at me as he stands, "go save ya boy, he's bored half to death over there," he nods, gesturing to the kitchen. "You're special, Kyla-Rose, don't let anyone tell you differently," he murmurs dropping a chaste kiss to the top of my head in a strangely affectionate way.

I watch him swagger over to a group in the corner, draping both arms around a couple of guys, making them laugh the instant he opens his mouth. I turn my attention back to my drink, knock it back and find my feet. I wander over to where Kacey leans against the kitchen counter; his large tattooed arms folded across his broad chest, his eyebrows drawn together as he focuses on whatever the guy he's talking to is saying.

Before I get the chance to enter the open-plan kitchen a tall brunette girl steps in front of me blocking my path. Her bouncy chestnut curls sit just above her shoulders, her tight blue halter-neck doing its best to contain her very large breasts. *Bloody Christ Jesus, how does she carry those bad boys around?* I wonder if she gets back ache.

"Hey!" she steps in closer, forcing me to take a small step back, she bounces on her toes excitedly, tucking a large curl behind her ear.

"Hey," I reply with uncertainty.

"Oh my god!" she squeals, "you don't know who I am! Of

course you don't! Sorry! I'm Jen!" she almost yells at me as she extends her perfectly manicured hand.

I take it lightly in my own and shake it cautiously still watching her, I recognise the name but I feel like it's more of a coincidence maybe. She's jumping around like the fucking energizer bunny, making me assume she's either high on life, or very high on a special sort of crack. I'm not sure I *ever* want to find out which. This girl is already way too much for me, I'm getting a fucking headache.

See? This is why you don't have friends.

"God, I'm such a doofus!" she squeaks loudly, *too loudly*, "as if you would know all of your empl-" a large hand clamps down over her mouth cutting off her final words as I frown.

I look to the owner of said hand finding Gremlin, he looks worried and embarrassed as fuck, either that or he thinks he's just blown it and I'm going to take him outside to put a bullet between his worried eyes.

I narrow my eyes on him, my jaw ticking as I grind my teeth together, "*discretion*," I hiss through my teeth and he quickly averts his gaze.

His eyes darting around the heavily crowded room checking for anyone who may have overheard our conversation, when he realises no one was listening his shoulders relax and he speaks into Jen's ear. It's low enough for me not to hear his words but I know it's a stern warning because her eyes grow wide and she nods her head silently.

"Sorry, boss," Gremlin hushes into my ear as he shuffles -a now very calm- Jen, out of the house.

Gremlin is head of security alongside Eli. He organises my

personal security as well as working with Eli on the security for our buildings, various family members and important members of our crew. I would rarely socialise outside of work with any of my family's employees but there are a select few we see as more a part of our extended family, luckily for him, Gremlin is one of them.

I take a deep breath in through my nose and release it slowly through my mouth just like Jacob taught me, I can't just hurt everyone who pisses me off. As I get closer, Kacey's gold eyes find mine like they called to him and he winks. When I get within a couple feet he opens up his big arms and I step into them without hesitation.

Breathing in deeply to calm my irritation, I close my eyes, leaning into him as his strong arms band around me tightly like he's holding all of my fractured pieces together. His hands slowly rub up and down my back, his chest rumbling in my ear as he speaks over my head, I'm not listening to his conversation but the vibrations from his voice roll through me soothingly.

Kacey is all man, from his muscles, to his manners all the way down to his smell, which is literally man-musk, there's not even another way I can describe the scent that is just so incredibly, Kacey, like fresh mint and damp earth, fresh and raw. Whatever the fuck it is, I'm all over it like a fucking rash.

We stand in the kitchen for god knows how long, folded into each other, I don't dare move from his embrace and his hold on me never falters even as my body relaxes so much I rely on his strength alone to keep me up.

"I don't want you to think I'm throwing you out," Kacey rumbles, "but you're literally falling asleep on your feet,

Sweetheart," he chuckles, his hot breath fanning little hairs around my face.

"You shouldn't have worn me out so early on then," I mumble back making him laugh deeply, the sound rolls through him so effortlessly, I'd love to be carefree like that.

"I seem to recall it was *I* who was doing the heavy lifting," he snorts into my hair and I pout.

"You saying I'm heavy, Big Man? Didn't think a big strong fighter like you would have had any problems," I tell him with a hard pinch to his back.

"Not at all," he chuckles, jerking forward at my pinch. "Shall I take you home? I can't drive you but we can get a cab together," he offers, "or you could stay? I promise to keep my hands to myself," he assures me and I pout harder.

"What if I don't want you to keep your hands to yourself?" I murmur, my cheek still pushed up against his chest, I smile a sleepy mischievous grin against him, forcing a thundering laugh to echo from him.

"Whatever you want, Sweetheart, so does that mean you want to stay?" he double checks and I nod my head against him.

"I need my phone."

If I don't tell Jacob that I'm not coming home tonight he'll send the fucking cavalry, he's staying with me for now until he decides where he wants to live, whether he'll want to claim a floor in the family tower or if he'll want to be separated from us, he's never really stayed in one place long enough before to have a proper home for himself.

"Where is it?"

"In my jacket," I mumble, squeezing my arms around his

waist a little tighter.

"I'll grab it if you're ready to go up now?" he speaks into my hair, pressing a kiss to the top of my head.

"Please."

Kacey uncurls my arms from around him, tucking me under his arm instead; never breaking our contact, the entire front of my body is warm and tingly where we've been pressed up against each other for so long. Kacey drapes my jacket over my shoulders, squeezing the pockets until he feels my phone.

"It's in there," he confirms with a tap to my left pocket.

"Kacey?" I mumble through my pouted lips.

"Kyla-Rose," he smiles as I look up at him with tired eyes.

"Carry me?" I frown, my lips pouting, eyes wide and pleading.

He belts out a roar of laughter, "fuck me, don't give me those eyes, they'd make me do anything for you," he promises with a chuckle, shaking his head in disbelief.

Kacey removes my jacket from my shoulders, wrapping it around my waist he effortlessly lifts me up into his arms bridal style, using the jacket to cover my naked arse –clever boy. I clasp my hands around his neck, my fingers holding my wrists; I nuzzle my face into the crook of his neck as he carries me through the –still crowded- open space of the first floor. He carries me gently up the stairs, our bodies rocking together with every step until he's fumbling around with a door handle, kicking it shut behind us as he walks in.

Kacey bends at the waist, laying me on his navy comforter. He crosses the room to his bathroom tugging the pull string, allowing light to shine in through the crack in the door. Just enough shines in for him to find me something to wear.

He drops to his knees before me, taking each of my feet into his big hands, he unbuckles my heels. Then one of his arms snakes around my waist, sitting me up and tugging my dress up and over my head, effortlessly snapping open my bra he slides it down my arms before the cool cotton of a black t-shirt is pulled over my head covering me up. I thread my arms through the sleeves before he pushes me to lie back again and slides the knife wielding garter down my leg, his fingers brushing deliciously against my inner thigh.

Kacey rummages around somewhere across the room before placing my phone into my hand, curling my fingers around the device, "is there anyone you should let know that you won't be home?" he asks me quietly and I nod my head with a groan thinking of Jacob.

"Kace?"

"Yeah?"

"Punch your address in here, will you?" I ask pushing my phone back into his hand with an open text bubble.

He takes the phone without hesitation, his fingers flying across the screen he types in his address, passing it back to me. I force myself to sit up, a delicious ache between my sore thighs radiates heat through me, sinfully reminding me of what we did together. I look down into Kacey's eyes, he's still crouched on the floor before me and as much as I know that I shouldn't this soon, all I see in him is safety.

I send the address to Frank, telling him where I am and that I'll call him in the morning when I'm ready to be picked up. Unsurprisingly, he replies almost immediately with a thumb up emoji and I chuckle –he's always looking out for me, even off-the-clock he's waited up.

I quickly check my other messages, seeing I have a missed call from Jacob only twenty minutes ago, I go with the safest option and call him back. I really don't want him tearing the city apart looking for me, that won't bode well for anyone, especially not him.

"I have to make a quick call," I sigh.

"Okay, I'll wait just outsi-"

"No, no," I startle, grabbing a fist full of his t-shirt to keep him where he is, "it'll only take a second," I smile as he relaxes back onto his haunches, it's not like I'm going to say anything to make him question me.

The call connects, Jacob answering on the first ring.

"Where the fuck are you? It's almost four-am, are you okay?" Jacob rushes out loudly.

"Okay, first of all, *ow*, that was way too loud in my ear, Jacob and second of all I'm staying out, and third of all, when am I ever not okay? This is just a courtesy call to notify my house guest of my non-return," I smile.

Kacey pinches his eyebrows together, making me run my thumb over the deep crease, trying to smooth the line away.

"You fucked him didn't you?" Jacob deadpans and I feel heat start to creep up my neck.

"Jacob-"

"Is there security where you are?" he interrupts me aggressively.

"No," I groan, "but-"

"Where are you?" Jacob demands.

"I'm fine." I say calmly, "Frank will get me first thing, I'll see you in the morning," I tell him tracing my fingers over the thick scar lining Kacey's throat, *I wonder what happened to him?*

"You're so fucking stubborn, Kyla-Rose," he snaps. "I don't give a fuck what you do but you can't sleep somewhere without security, do you even have a gun?" he sniffs, irritation clear in his voice.

"Jacob, I'm perfectly safe," I try to placate him, even though I know he's right but is it so wrong to just desperately want, *need,* one *normal* night, "I have to go, I'll talk to you in a few hours, I love you."

"Kyla-Rose, don't you dare hang up on me or I swear to g-"

I cut him off, ending the call.

"Argh," I groan, rolling my head between my shoulders to loosen the tension.

"You need me to take you home?" Kacey asks gently, from his kneeling position on the floor, his head tilting to one side assessing me, his flop of blonde hair falling over one of his gold eyes, covering the tattoo on the side of his head.

"No. I'm staying," I tell him definitively.

"Good. Now, serious question, how tired are you?" he waggles his eyebrows making me giggle, not asking me questions about my call.

"Tired… but I can last a little while longer," I shrug, "why, what did you have in mind?" I ask with a frown.

"Spread your legs for me, beautiful," he murmurs, sending a shiver up my spine, my pussy pulsing in anticipation.

His large tattooed palms slowly slide up my calves until he reaches my knees, sharply forcing them apart with nothing but hunger in his eyes. I let my legs drop open for him, giving him ample view of my bare pussy -seeing as he stole my knickers earlier and all I'm wearing now is his t-shirt- he growls, the noise thundering from his chest as he looks his fill. I should squirm under the intensity of his attention but strangely I feel no embarrassment at his assessment of my most intimate part.

His thick fingers delve into my flesh as he hooks his large hands beneath my thighs, dragging me to the edge of the bed, my t-shirt riding up with the friction, exposing more of me to him. He thrusts my knees apart as far as they'll go, the muscles screaming, he flattens them to the mattress, settling his broad shoulders between my thighs.

"Kacey," I pant, feeling breathy, my pussy already slick for him.

"*Mmm*," he moans, eyes focused on my aching core, licking his lips he murmurs, "fucking beautiful," before his gorgeous tattooed head of hair disappears between my thighs.

Kacey's tongue darts out, sliding between my already wet folds, the tip of his tongue finding my clit has me arching my back as his hot mouth closes around it and he sucks, *hard*. My fist tangles in his hair, pulling at the root I arch my back as much as I can, forcing all of my weight onto my shoulders and neck, pushing my cunt deeper into his mouth. His tongue devours my clit, darting through my folds and back up again, over and over, driving me fucking wild.

His large hand traces down the inside of my thigh, leaving a trail of goosebumps in its wake, Kacey's teeth nip at my clit, his mouth closing over it once more, sucking and licking, he drags a finger through my soaked folds before dipping it inside.

He works me in tandem, between his tongue attacking my throbbing clit and his finger twirling inside my pulsing core, I'm so overwhelmed with sensation I can hardly breathe. So when he dips that second finger inside me, I explode. Unashamedly, riding his face through my orgasm, stars erupt behind my eyelids, my thighs clamping around his head trapping him against me, my heels digging into the space between his shoulder blades as I let out a low moan.

"Kacey," I pant as he removes my trembling legs from over his solid shoulders.

"Shh, sleep," he whispers.

Pulling the comforter down, he lifts my sated body up into his strong arms, before once again placing me onto the sheet. He kicks off his shoes at the same time he pulls his t-shirt over his head, dropping it on top of his shoes. He flicks open the button of his jeans and releases the zipper, shimmying them down his legs, kicking them off to the side, leaving him in just his tented boxers.

Kacey climbs into the bed beside me, pulling the duvet up and over us. One arm sliding under my head, his other banding around my waist, dragging me into him, his hard front pressed to my back, he nuzzles his face into my hair, breathing me in deeply. I drift off easily –without sleeping pills- for the first time in a very long time, feeling warm, protected and most importantly *safe.*

CHAPTER 7

KYLA-ROSE

A trickle of sunlight peeks between the grey curtains and I groan, forcing my eyes to squeeze shut again. I stretch my arms up over my head and roll onto my back, uncurling my legs, pointing my feet, curling and uncurling my toes.

These are not my sheets.

My eyes peel open slowly as I assess my surroundings, my brow furrowing.

Where am I and what's the time?

I never sleep in after the sun's come up.

After a moment my sleep induced haze quickly clears and I remember I'm in Kacey's bedroom. Rolling onto my side, stretching my arm out into the cold space beside me, the pillow still indented from where he rested his head and his sheets engulfing me in his scent, I sigh.

Eurgh, Kacey. I bite my bottom lip, trying to smother the smile threatening to break free and that's just from *thinking* about the guy!

Sitting myself up, I crack my neck side to side, my body's aching all over but I like it. That delicious after-sex ache, muscles tense and sore, it's much nicer than the muscle ache after a heavy gym session. More fun too.

There's a neat pile of my discarded clothes on the chair in the corner and a pile of clean clothes at the bottom of the bed with a new toothbrush on top. He's so fucking cute it kills me. I smooth the sheets out, fluffing the pillows as best I can before heading into the bathroom. There's a little green sticky note on the glass door of the shower saying '**use me**'.

I snort a laugh but follow the instruction, stripping my shirt and stepping under the warm spray. I don't like hot showers, I can't stand being too hot in general, it makes me feel suffocated, just like sauna's and steam room's, I can't bear the thought of being stuffed into one of those fucking things either, quite frankly I'd rather be shoved into the boot of a car. I hiss through my teeth as the warm water hits a sore spot on my shoulder blade; I reach around to run my fingers over it but can't quite get the right angle.

I use Kacey's shampoo and body wash, thankful that he has conditioner -not many guys use conditioner, not sure why, I mean who doesn't want silky hair? When all the soap suds are washed away, I step out, wrapping myself in a large fluffy towel, I dry my body then use the towel as a turban, twisting my hair up in it so I can get dressed.

In all my naked glory I spin my back to the mirror and peek over my shoulder, sure enough down one shoulder blade peeking through my ink is a wide graze –rough sex will do that to ya- my fingers can't quite reach it but it doesn't look bad, at least it's clean now. I coat the purple toothbrush in too much toothpaste and scrub my teeth.

I pull on a pair of grey joggers which are easily four sizes too big, rolling them over at the waist I heave them up my legs, luckily for me the ankles are elasticated so that helps them stay in place. I pull on the borrowed black t-shirt and drop the towel from my head into the laundry basket sat in the corner of the room.

Grabbing my small pile of belongings I make my way downstairs, running my fingers through my wet hair as I go. The first floor of the house looks completely different today, the furniture is all back in what I assume is its rightful place, the two navy sofas are set at a ninety-degree angle in front of the large front window, angled to face the TV with a low coffee table in front of it. The dining table and chairs have been placed back on the other side of the stairs and the bar stools are back at the kitchen island.

I drop my little pile of clothes down onto the arm of the sofa and peer into the kitchen. Huxley sits on one of the stools, his bare back to me, his bare, *tattooed* back. Sweet baby Jesus, that's some impressive ink. A woman's face takes up his whole back, half skull, half flesh, with thick flowing hair, in front of a night sky, all shaded with blacks and greys. It's truly stunning.

Kacey's hulking frame is bent over, rummaging around in the bottom of the fridge, his perfect peach of an arse jutting out in the air. That boy's arse really is something to look at, I touch my own as I continue to stare at his, how is it so fucking tight?!

I suck in my bottom lip as Kacey spins around –also shirtless- using his foot he kicks the fridge door closed behind him. He cracks the top off of a sickly looking green smoothie, tipping it to his lips, his head dropping back, his eyes flick up catching a glance of me over Huxley's head. I smirk, not in the least bit upset that I've been caught staring and send him a wink, his amber-yellow eyes widening when he sees me. He inhales at the same time he tries to swallow, spluttering his drink all over his bare chest and spraying it across the counter.

"Jesus Christ, man! I don't need a fucking smoothie shower! What do you think you are a sprinkler?!" Huxley yells, jumping off of the stool to avoid being covered in the sticky green juice.

Kacey coughs; trying to breathe and cough through his choking, he plants the bottle down on the worktop and moves over to the sink still spluttering.

"Morning," I greet with a knowing smirk, catching Huxley's eye, he shakes his head.

"Honestly, dude, you gunna lose your shit every time Kyla-Rose's near? That shit's embarrassing man, get it together," he playfully teases, grabbing a paper towel, he wipes down the counter.

"Sorry, wrong hole," Kacey chokes out.

Huxley's dark eyes connect with mine across the counter and we both fly into a fit of the giggles. Kacey groans, wiping down his chin and chest, his muscles rippling under his inked skin, my head tilts to one side of its own accord and I bite my lip.

A small groan escapes me and I won't lie, I'm not embarrassed in the slightest as both men's eyes snap to mine at the same time.

"What?" I shrug, "can't I appreciate a hot body when I see one?" I ask innocently, "or *two*," I say under my breath -because let's face it, Huxley is a hot commodity too, I'd have to be blind not to notice- that final comment sends the pair of them over the edge into hysterics.

"Boys' brains are in their dicks," I mumble as I take Huxley's vacated seat at the island and spoon a large helping of his cereal into my mouth.

"I heard that you little devil!" Kacey laughs, flicking a tea towel in my direction.

He leans back onto the counter behind him facing me across the island, his huge arms fold across his chest forcing the muscles to bunch and flex.

"Yeah, well, just stating a fact, it's certainly not news to any of the superior species, you know, the women," I shrug one shoulder nonchalantly while trying to hide my mocking smile.

Both men scowl at me, I try to stifle my snickering by shovelling a second spoonful of Huxley's cereal into my mouth.

I grumble through my mouthful of soggy cardboard, "this is horrible," I complain with a grimace, "what the fuck is it?" I screw my face up in disgust as I swallow it down in a dry lump, staring down at the contents left in the bowl and flicking it around with the spoon.

Before either of them can answer, I press my toes up onto the rung of the stool and stretch my long body across the counter. Reaching for Kacey's green smoothie, I glug down a few mouthfuls to wash away the taste, wiping my lips across the back of my hand, I settle back down into the seat.

"Dude, where did you find her and how do I get one?" Huxley pants; looking between the two of us, he jokingly fans himself with his hand.

I twist my body to the side on instinct and slap him on his bare chest –which is solid as fuck by the way- "bad boy," I scold with a frown before hopping back off of the stool and skirting between the two naked torsos.

My head only comes up to the height of their chests and my god, it takes *everything* in me not to lick a nipple *or three* as I squeeze between them.

I make my way over to the fridge and pull out a vanilla yogurt; I open it and give it a sniff, scrunching my nose before tilting my head and shrugging a shoulder, deciding I'll give it a go.

"Spoon?" I say aloud to the room, both boys staring at me in shock.

"Can we *please* keep her?" Huxley whines making me snigger at the same time my stomach clenches at his use of the word *we*.

"I fucking hope so, man," Kacey's ravenous gaze slowly slides up my body with that feral hunger in his eyes, like he's mentally undressing me, devouring me and doing very, *very* naughty things to me.

"Down boy," I growl patting him on the chest like a good dog as I take Huxley's seat again.

Both men look at me like I'm some sort of alien. I raise my brows at them both; how the fuck do they expect me to eat this, with my fucking fingers?

“Sooo… spoon?”

Both of them rush to get to -what I assume is- the cutlery drawer, tussling with each other to get their hands in the drawer at the same time. Shoving each other with their elbows, each pushing the other one out of the way with their hips, they grumble at each other.

Huxley and Kacey both turn back to me at the same time. Out of breath from the struggle, they each extend their arms across the counter, holding out matching silver teaspoons. I raise an eyebrow, shaking my head as I take both spoons, doing my best to suppress my smile. Huxley and Kacey both watch me as I look between the two identical spoons. I chance a look up at them, the intensity in each of their gazes makes me shudder. I feel like by picking a spoon I’m choosing a man. *Is that what this is?* They want me to pick between them, even if it is something as simple as a teaspoon, I suddenly feel under pressure not to offend either of them.

What I have with Kacey is already this huge deal to me. I like him. He treats me like I’m this precious little gem that he wants to keep safe from the world, not to mention the sex was fucking incredible, I could totally get used to that.

Huxley and I had a rather *interesting* conversation last night which has played continuously inside my brain since, but his care-free nature is refreshing to me, everything he said to me was like he looked into my eyes and my soul was flayed by him. I felt ripped open, raw and vulnerable under his gaze but equally he whispered soothing words to it, piecing it back together, maybe a little differently, but I woke up this morning feeling *happy*.

Huxley -just as much as Kacey- is a stranger I guess, but neither of them actually *feels* like that to me. I feel like I know them both in different ways, but like I've always known them. They feel familiar and comforting to me and I can breathe easy around them both.

With one spoon in each hand, I dip both into the little yogurt pot at the same time. Lifting both to my mouth, I pop them both in, stacked one on top of the other and suck the yogurt off, looking up at the men through my lashes, both of them staring at me with heated looks.

I'm just trying to be fair…

Honestly, I'm not sure what shifted the dynamic between the three of us this morning, but the sexual tension is so thick in the room right now you could cut it with a knife, possibly the same knife that ensures I'm always bleeding, that'd be poetic as fuck wouldn't it. Thing is, it's a real possibility that my half-dead heart could start to beat itself back to life with one of the men in this room, possibly with both of them... should I just cut the bleeding bitch out right now and offer it up to them to ruin? Send the last broken pieces of me off into the ever burning blackness of damnation? Do I give this up now before it starts, before it gets *messy*?

Should have thought about that before you slid your legs open, shouldn't you Lala…

Kacey cocks his head to one side, his eyes glistening with want.

"We've never met someone like you before," Kacey's voice so low and husky it's almost a growl.

"Is that a bad thing?" I ask nervously, suddenly the pit of

my stomach feels like a brick has landed in it and that blackened organ in my chest seizes.

Long fingers tuck under my chin, tilting my gaze up to face the two men in the room.

"Darlin', it's so incredibly far from a bad thing, you have no idea just how perfect you are," Huxley tells me sincerely, his voice low and raspy, making me blush.

I can feel that damn heat crawling up my neck as I avert my gaze from Hux's dark eyes -which is a task in itself; those eyes delve into your soul if you look into them long enough- to meet Kacey's gold ones. His head still cocked to one side, he watches for my reaction, I offer him a small smile and a big sappy grin takes over his face.

"You're so fucking beautiful, Kyla-Rose, I don't know how I went my whole life not knowing you," Kacey confesses and a fragment of that ice barricade around my dying heart melts a little.

"I don't think I've ev-" the shrill ring of a cell phone cuts me off before I can say something I'd immediately wish I could take back, "oh for fuck's sake," I complain recognising the ring tone as my own.

I curse under my breath and make my way to my pile of clothes –which is really only my dress and jacket now. *I wonder where my shoes are.* I fumble through the pockets of my jacket and pull out my ringing phone. Cam's name flashes across the screen.

"Hey."

"Hey," Cam grunts.

"Oh for fuck's sake, you're not mad at me too surely?"

I release an exasperated sigh, absentmindedly twirling a wet strand of silver hair around my finger.

"Oh, no. Well, yeah, I am, I think it was reckless having a fucking *sleepover* without security but that's not why I cal- CHARLIE STOP THAT! I called beca-" a loud crash in the background cuts him off, it's so loud I can practically feel the vibrations.

"What fell?"

"Nothing, I can han- Charlie for fuck's sake put that down! DON'T TOUCH THAT!" Cam bellows.

I pull the phone away from my ear as Cam's voice hits an extreme decibel, I screw my face up at the sound.

"WILL SOMEONE PLEASE TELL ME WHAT THE FUCK IS HAPPENING?" I boom into the receiver and all goes quiet on the other end. "Well?!" I demand, my body vibrating with anger.

"When are you coming home?" Cam asks breathlessly.

I can still hear commotion in the background so I know I'm needed. I scrub a hand down my face, releasing a heavy sigh. I look over at the two guys in the kitchen who are watching me with equal parts lust, equal parts concern in their hungry eyes.

What the hell am I doing?

"I'll text Frank and I'll be right on my way, give me half an hour."

"Thanks, Ky, I am sorry to call you," Cam sighs, his expression probably similar to my own, "really."

"It's okay, I'll be as quick as I can," I tell him softly and I can imagine him nodding in that stoic way of his.

"Thank you, see you soon."

"Bye."

I move the phone from my ear, sending a text to Frank telling him to pick me up as soon as he can, he replies instantly telling me he'll arrive in three minutes. I snort a laugh, he's so fucking precise but you gotta love the guy, he's probably been sitting in the car around the corner since I sent him the address, he's reliable to a fault.

Dropping my phone back to the folded clothes, I heave a deep sigh, my shoulders tensing already, they drop with my release of breath and I pinch the bridge of my nose in frustration. Everything was perfect. I had the most incredible night with a guy who I think may actually be worth my time and my morning *was* going great, with *two* guys, until now. Comes with the territory I guess.

Large tattooed hands wrap around my waist from behind. Kacey drops a kiss to my neck, "you leaving us Sweetheart?" he murmurs, his hot minty breath fanning across my skin.

"Mmm," I close my eyes, relaxing back into his hold, laying my hands over his.

"When will I see you again?" he whispers into my hair, nuzzling his face against my cheek, marking me with his scent.

"Friday," I sigh, gently grinding my arse back against his growing erection.

"You coming to watch me fight?" he smiles against my skin, dropping another kiss to my neck, his lips lingering on my skin a little too long making me groan.

"Of course, Big Man, wouldn't miss it," I smile up at him, "I'm training there in the afternoon anyway," I shrug casually, "plus, I liked seeing you smeared with blood," I whisper.

"Oh, yeah? I'll work extra hard to make it a good fight then," he winks down at me and my tummy tightens with anticipation as he spins me in his hold. "And training for what?" he asks suspiciously.

"Nothing, just sparring."

When I got out of juvie I spent the remainder of my seventeenth year on this planet training with Cam and Fat Tony. Tony built me up and trained me hard. I had so much fucking aggression inside me I needed somewhere to channel it. Cam was practically born to be a fighter so working alongside him and Fat Tony was a fucking blessing.

Cam's trained in so many various martial arts and fighting techniques, he's always pushing himself to be more, do more, he's a slave-driver to his own body, it keeps him grounded. Just the same way the rest of us have little ticks to help keep us grounded too, mine and Charlie's just tend to be a little more *spontaneous*.

"*Fuckkkk,* Kyla! Why you gotta do shit like this to me? I'm gunna be hard all week now, thinking about you kicking someone's arse," Kacey moans, grinding his hips into mine, I slide my hands down his naked chest, biting my lip.

"You'll have to call me," I mumble, looking up into his gold eyes.

"I'm absolutely fucking calling you," he growls.

Tucking a long strand of hair behind my ear, he drops his lips to mine, devouring my mouth with his tongue. His large hands gripping my upper arms pulling me into his hard chest, I smile into our kiss and he hisses, pulling my bottom lip between his teeth, he bites down, nibbling on it before releasing it with a *pop.*

"I have to go," I tell him breathlessly, breaking our kiss.

"Give me your phone," he all but growls making me snort at his demand.

Braver men have tried to order me around, none survived very long, but like a good little soldier I hand it over before I've even thought about it.

That's new.

Kacey presses a kiss to my forehead, "I've called myself so I have your number and I've put Hux's in there too and done the same," he tells me, cupping my cheek in his big hand, wrapping me in warmth and ink, I turn my face, pressing a kiss to his palm.

"Thank you," I whisper, pressing another kiss to his bare chest, goosebumps scatter across his naked flesh, his nipples pebbling, he shivers as my hands sweep low, running my fingers teasingly along his waistband.

"Can we break this up sometime soon? Watching you two grinding all over each other is hot. I might come in my pants," Huxley whines, drawing our attention from each other back to him.

Huxley's leaning back against the counter, his hand down his joggers as he adjusts his –very large, from what I can see-cock. Laughter bubbles from my throat before I can stop it and I slap a hand over my mouth.

"See what you fucking do!" Kacey laughs, tapping the tip of my nose with his finger. "Bad girl," he whispers like the devil, nipping at my jaw, a shiver raking its way through my body.

"Sorry?" I grimace, looking to Kacey's very amused face,

before the laughter bursts free once more.

"You need to leave before we *all* start something we don't have time to finish," Kacey growls, latching his teeth onto the silken skin of my throat, not biting just holding, keeping me in place like a lion would his mate, encouraging a moan to slip from my lips in response.

"I'll call you," I promise breathlessly, breaking his hold on me and gathering my things, "but I'll definitely see you Friday."

"Your shoes," Huxley calls, walking them over to me, only he doesn't just walk, he swaggers, this cocky, self-assured, confident stride that has my eyes taking in his every subtle movement, every muscle flex, the knowing glint in his flint coloured eyes.

Oh, god, I've got it bad.

I reach out to take them, his fingers brushing mine. He drops a chaste kiss to the top of my head, breathing me in as he pulls away. I do the same to him. Freshly cut grass and sweet, sweet clementines, dizzying me with his intoxicating scent and flustering me with his contact, my brain trying desperately to get me to function.

Both men walk me to the front door, watching me trot bare-foot down the garden path lined with pretty little bluebells, the winter sun looming low in the misty, morning sky. Frank is already there, ready and waiting, holding my door open. He nods to both boys, which I'm pretty sure is a thanks and a greeting, Frank's just too goddamn nice, always acknowledging, always observing, watching, *cataloguing*.

I hop up onto the foothold of the SUV, looking over my shoulder to glance at the boys, both of them standing side by side on the doorstep, similar smiles on their faces, I throw them a little wave before dropping down into my seat.

CHAPTER 8

KYLA-ROSE

The ride home is quiet, mostly because I'm tired as shit, it's only eleven-am and although I had one of the best sleeps I've maybe *ever* had, it wasn't anywhere near long enough. Resting my forehead against the cool glass of the back window, rain aggressively pelting against it on the outside, I sigh softly, closing my eyes. Frank switched the radio on, the quiet tinkling of sound soothing me into a sleepy state, the sort of dream state where your eyes are closed but you still hear everything happening around you.

"Boss," Frank calls from the front seat, turning slightly to face me as I blink my eyes open.

"Thanks, Frank," I give him a tight smile, realising we're home and imagining what sort of fucking mess I'm about to walk into.

When Charlie gets overwhelmed it takes a lot to get him calm. I understand it because he's one of the only people who can calm me down when I hit that catatonic state too. It goes one way or the other.

Sometimes we get very calm, very quiet but agitated as fuck, murmuring and mumbling to ourselves. And other times we lose our shit completely, which involves thrashing, smashing, screaming, anything and everyone is a target, we can't differentiate between love and hate, the lines blur until they no longer exist.

Charlie and I have a uniquely special bond. We're the most similar in personality and in the way we react to things, but we're also the most damaged which is what cemented our bond even as children. He witnessed some fucked up shit as a child and so did I and then we both got fucked over as teenagers and young-adults and it all just added to our trauma. Things that we saw and endured don't only scar you physically and mentally, they damage your fucking soul.

I'm not afraid to admit that I'm not quite right in the head, there's a little black spot in there that takes over sometimes. I retreat into it on occasion too and when I go there, I'm not in control anymore. Charlie and I are a blessing and a curse for each other but we would never fit anywhere else. We need to be together. We each understand what the other one is thinking and feeling without needing any words to pass between us. Like the *Chaos Twins* we are so often referred to as, we certainly live up to our name.

Funnily enough it was actually my Uncle Dee who started using that nickname for us when we were little because everywhere we went together we raised hell and created chaos, causing him multiple headaches in the process.

Although Charlie's thirty-one -making him six years older than me- he's the youngest at heart. I've always been the baby numerically speaking but mentally out of the boys so has he.

Don't get me wrong, Charlie is one of the most intelligent people I have honestly ever met, in every aspect, he seems to syphon information without even trying. If he wasn't so volatile he could have easily run this family alone, way better than I could and if that's not what he fancied, he could have made a wicked fucking Lawyer or Judge or some shit like that. But the way Charlie is now, since the *incident*, he'd be hacking and slashing up the entire jury if shit didn't go his way. So, for Charlie, it's this family that keeps him safe and protected, always offering him a safe place to lose himself when he needs to without judgement.

I make my way to the elevator, enjoying what are probably going to be my final moments of peace for the day. The private elevator dings as it opens up into my darkened entryway.

Everything is quiet. Everything in its rightful place but something does not feel right. The air is thick, heavy, cloying, demons lurking in every corner, the devil hiding in the shadows. I slowly step out of the elevator; the hair on the back of my neck prickling to attention. I pop my pile of clothes on the round table that sits in the centre of the entryway and grab both switchblades from the garter I wore last night.

I flick open the blades and start to move on silent feet through the apartment. Working my way through each room, I clear the kitchen, formal dining room and my office before stepping back into the foyer.

A cool steel blade presses across my throat, I hold my breath, leaning back onto the heels of my feet, essentially forcing my attacker to hold my weight or push them back far enough that I gain a little wiggle room to work my way free. I flip the switchblade around in my hand, the sharp point pressing against my attacker's thigh; I don't need to look to know it's directly over his femoral artery, after all, it was this very attacker that taught me exactly how to locate it.

"What's the matter, Charlie-Boy, getting sloppy in your old age?" I tease, a sardonic smile playing on my lips.

Charlie growls low in my ear, his hot breath fanning across my face.

His demon is out to play.

But very quickly, *so is mine*.

Charlie runs his nose down my upper arm, "you smell like man," he observes with a sneer, referring to my use of Kacey's wash products and clothes. "Want to play a game, cousin?" he breathes directly into my ear, his blade digging into the delicate flesh of my throat.

"What did you have in mind, Charl?" my lips slowly curving into a feral grin at the possibilities.

"We could play hide and go stab," Charlie suggests excitedly, my eyes flash with enthusiasm.

"Ooo! *Yes!* I love that one!" I squeal with anticipation, clapping my hands together with glee, forgetting all about the knife at my throat.

"On the count of three, I'm going to release you and count to ten," Charlie sings, his rough voice like torn velvet, soft but scarred. "One," my grip tightens on my knives, "two," I suck in a deep breath, my body thrumming with adrenaline, "three!" Charlie shouts, removing his arms from where they were banded around me and I bolt, like a horse released at the races, the finish line the only thing I can see.

My bare feet slap against the wooden floor of the hallway.

"FOUR!" Charlie shouts from the foyer.

I hit the corner that leads to the guest rooms and skid around the corner, my feet trying to carry me so quickly, I move my feet without gaining any distance, running on the spot like a cartoon character. I use my hands to propel myself off of the walls as I turn the corner, I move faster as I get back on course.

"EIGHT!"

I hit the second guest room which has a large antique wardrobe inside. Slipping my open blade between my teeth, flipping the blade of my spare knife away, tucking it into my pocket, I crouch low to the floor then throw myself up as high as I can. Propelling myself from the floor, I curl my inked fingers over the top of the wardrobe, gripping the wood carvings –which is thankfully secured to the wall- and silently pull myself up.

"TEN! COMING, READY OR NOT!" Charlie roars, the delirium clear in his tone.

My adrenaline spikes as I clamber on top of the wardrobe, tucking myself as far back as I can, I close my eyes and breathe in deeply, trying to calm my breathing along with my erratic heartrate.

Like a rabbit chased by a fox, my heart beats a hundred miles a minute, threatening to exorcise itself from my heaving chest. I cover my nose and mouth with my cupped hand to hide any sounds I might be making, Charlie is nothing if not a hunter which only makes the game that much more exciting because I'll never hear him coming, I'm nowhere near as good at this game as he is and I have the scars to prove it.

The rain is still beating down heavily outside, holding the sun captive. The penthouse is already plunged in darkness but with no natural light coming in through the large windows it gives the whole place a thriller-movie vibe, ominous.

My excitement peeks as my ears prick up; I hear the door handle to the guest room I'm in twist almost silently.

"I can smell you, little Swallow, I'm hunting," Charlie whispers on a growl.

I don't move a muscle, holding my breath, silently pulling my legs up to sit beneath me. I push up into a low crouch as Charlie turns himself back to face the open doorway. I waste no time, lunging from the wardrobe, I drop down on top of him, sending him sprawling to the floor, my feet land solidly onto his back and without hesitation I plunge my blade straight into his shoulder, pinning him in place. With one splayed hand I get to my feet, spinning my spare switchblade between my fingers.

My knife still protruding from his back, I stalk around him in a circle, Charlie laughs wickedly. A maniacal chorus erupts from him into loud violent laughter as his body shakes with mirth. I smile ferociously at him, baring my teeth as I crouch down in front of him, drawing his eyes up to meet mine. I turn my head to the side so I'm face to face with him, my long silver hair curtaining around us, sheltering us from the rest of the world. I trail my spare blade down his jaw; pressing the tip of it to his bottom lip. I apply just enough pressure to pull his bottom lip away from his teeth with it.

"Want to play again?" I grin, releasing his lip so it slaps against his bottom teeth, waggling my eyebrows in question, my eyes flash with hunger.

"NO!" Jacob roars from behind us, my lips instantly pout, Charlie rolls his emerald eyes so hard he can probably see out the back of his skull.

"Party pooper," I whine.

Pressing my bare foot down in the space between Charlie's shoulder blades, I bend at the waist, getting a good grip on my knife I pluck my blade from his flushed flesh, blood seeping from the deep intrusion, I wipe my blade down his shirt before offering him my hand and help him stand.

"Next time, little Swallow, I'm going to get the jump on you," he hisses, his green eyes flaming.

"I'm counting on it, Charlie-Boy," I beam and he returns my feral grin with one of his own as I tap the flat of my blade against his solid chest.

We both turn to face Jacob at the same time, he looks *pissed.* Charlie and I both raise our eyebrows at him while we wait to hear what he has to say but instead of saying anything he grabs each of us by the wrist, dragging us along behind him like naughty children, leading us into the largest sitting room.

"SIT!" Jacob booms, making Charlie and I roll our eyes in unison.

We slump down onto the white leather, Charlie's back coating the crisp, clean furniture in hot, sticky claret. I clearly never thought this shit through when I picked my sofa, why'd I go with white, when we're both always covered in blood and entrails? I sigh dramatically, dropping my head onto his blood free shoulder.

Jacob paces back and forth; scowling over at us periodically while he traipses across the black carpet. Charlie leans back into the cushions getting comfortable, pulling me along with him, he tucks me under his arm, resting his chin on my head.

"You'd think he'd be used to us by now, honestly did he think we had personality transplants while he was in Africa or something?" Charlie whisper-snorts in his gruff voice making me chuckle.

"He's way dramatic, I didn't even stab you that bad, you'll probs only need like three or four stitches," I shrug.

"Mmm," Charlie agrees with a grunt, nodding his head, "you tired?" he asks me, all the while Jacob is still pacing across the room, making wild hand gestures to himself and rambling on at us both about how we don't have nine lives and are so irresponsible, but all I really hear is *blah, blah, blah*.

We both stopped listening to his *safety speeches* about five years ago.

"Yeah, I'm sleepy," I nod with a pout closing my achy eyelids.

I relax into Charlie's chest, banding my arms around his waist, I allow myself to be calmed by his –now- relaxed energy.

I must drift off to sleep for a while because the next sound I hear is Charlie, only he's somewhere across the room now, telling Jacob to get off of his high horse and enjoy life a little more. Then he invites him to play with us next time which earns him a scoff. I smile at that, Jacob is so serious, he would never play with us, then again, it's probably not safe for *anyone* else to play our games, we do tend to get a little carried away. I'm sure if Jacob hadn't broken up our game earlier we would have played until we were both passed out from blood loss. *A little like last time.*

"Charlie, I'm putting the final stitch in, stay still." Jacob huffs.

"Jacob, go easy on him, he had a rough morning," I smile teasingly, my eyes still closed.

"I knew you were in there, I just hadn't looked up yet when you attacked, I could *smell* you," Charlie tells me on a scoff and I snort a laugh.

"Yeah, you already told me, I smell like man," I laugh, "funniest shit I've heard in ages," I chuckle along with Charlie, earning us both a scathing look from Jacob, abruptly shutting us both up.

Jacob's large body is hunched on the little cushioned piano stool, Charlie sitting cross-legged on the floor in front of him, both with their backs to me, I watch for a few minutes while Jacob works.

"Kyla-Rose," Jacob growls suddenly.

"Yes, *Dad?*" I snicker; Charlie's shoulders shake with mirth warranting him a clip round the head from Jacob.

"Kyla-Rose, we need to have a serious conversation about last night." Jacob starts with his *superiority* tone and I deflate into the sofa cushions. "That was so fucking irresponsible, you can't do what you do and then gallivant around the city with a random man and not come home!" he chastises, "furthermore," I snort, "*furthermore*," he growls, "if you want to do all of those things I'm not going to stop you."

Here it comes –the but.

"But."

There it is.

"You must take precautions. For example," *Jesus Christ,* "when you leave the confines of this building you take a gun, no more of this fucking knife-wielding bullshit, you are not a swordsman for Christ's sake. You find yourself under attack you shoot the fucker between the eyes, no more playing games with your life. Secondly, if you go out, like you did last night," he narrows his eyes on me as he glances over his shoulder from where he's still patching up Charlie. "You take security with you, they don't have to necessarily be by your side, but they have to be there, in the shadows, waiting in the car, somewhere close by they can have eyes on you, so if shit goes south they can extract you. And lastly, no more little *slumber-parties,*" he finishes, turning back to apply a square of gauze to Charlie's shoulder.

"Okay, so here's where we're gunna have to agree to disagree," I state sitting forward. My elbows on my knees, I lean forward further, rocking on my toes, "I get all of that and I'll do it, I won't put myself in danger unnecessarily *but* and just hear me out before you go all alpha on me. *You* can't decide where I sleep, I'm twenty-five years old, I'm not stupid, I wouldn't have stayed with Kacey last night if there was even the remote possibility that I could have been exposed or in danger. I told Frank my location, he knew where I was and I trusted that if something *had* happened he would notify you, like the reliable soldier that he is, *also,* Gremlin was there for a bit, so chill the fuck out," I tell him.

"*Furthermore,*" I say sarcastically, Charlie barks a laugh and Jacob bristles. "I love you very much and I respect you and I appreciate your concern but I'm still going to live my life. I can't stay up in my tower like fucking Rapunzel, 'cause, *shit,* it would take a real fucking long time to grow my hair out." I smile over at him where he's peering at me angrily over his shoulder.

I start across the carpet, Charlie skirting around me as he goes back to his bloodied spot on the couch and I wrap my arms around Jacob's broad shoulders from behind, pressing a chaste kiss to his cheek.

"I'm sorry I worried you, thank you for giving a fuck. Oh, and I love you." I smile, hiding my face from the window reflection.

"*Argh*," he moans in defeat, rocking his head from side to side, internally warring with himself, "I love you too, I just fucking worry, it was four in the fucking morning before you even checked in and I thought something had happened to you," he confesses reluctantly, rubbing a hand down his tired face –no doubt that's also my fault.

Parting my arms from around his neck, he twists on the piano stool to face me, clasping my hands in his, his bold green eyes flick between my own.

"Does your boy know who you are?" he asks seriously and I swallow that dry lump in my throat.

"No," I whisper and Charlie's low whistle cuts through the silence.

I snap my gaze over my shoulder, glaring daggers at him and he winks, *the fucker*.

"Do you want to see him again?" Jacob asks quietly, watching my face for reaction.

I look down, pulling my foot back and forth through the thick pile, "Yeah, I think so. I don't think he's like everyone else," I mumble out, I suck at talking about personal shit.

"Then don't you think you should tell him about who you are? *Not* what you do, you don't need to put yourself in any unnecessary danger but he'll no doubt have heard about our family and don't you think it could hurt his feelings if he hears shit about you through gossip and whispers? Imagine if you started liking him and found out something that huge about him from someone else, how would that feel?" Jacob asks gently, his head tilted to one side, he gazes underneath my curtain of hair, tucking it back behind my ear and cups my jaw.

"That would really suck," I sigh.

"Call him, meet up with him," Jacob implores.

"He's fighting for Cam on Friday; I could talk to him after." I offer, hoping to put that awkward conversation off for as long as possible.

"Okay, good, we just want you to be happy, Kyla-Rose," Jacob tells me, tugging on my hands, "and *safe.*"

"What if when I tell him my last name he doesn't want me?" I bite my lip.

I'm so fucking embarrassed by this whole entire conversation right now, I can't even look Jacob in the eye but I can't seem to stop myself being vulnerable either.

"Then he's not fucking worth it," Charlie growls, making me smile.

I'm seriously the luckiest fucking person in the world,

sure I've had some really shit things happen to me but that shit doesn't *completely* control my life anymore and to have four cousins who give this much of a fuck about me makes me the luckiest woman on the planet.

"Will you," I heave a sigh trying to find my words, my mouth suddenly dry, "can you like, stay here with me for a sec while I call? If you don't, I know I'll bottle it like a fucking coward and if I don't call him to ask, I'll just never see him again," I laugh nervously, it's humourless and sounds foreign falling from my lips.

"Of course we will," Charlie walks up behind me and drops a kiss to my head as he places my phone into my palm.

"This really sucks," I cringe, "I'm literally about to puke on myself I think," Charlie snorts and Jacob rolls his forest green eyes but smiles at me all the while.

"Call him, Lala," Jacob encourages, gesturing his head to the phone in my suddenly trembling hands.

I take a deep breath and then scroll through my contacts, I hit K but Kacey's name isn't in there, "*what the fuck?*" I say under my breath, a sudden wave of unease rolls through me, he told me he put his number in my phone, he literally did it right in front of me.

"What's wrong?" Jacob asks noticing my face pale.

"I, um, I can't find his number," I say, licking my very dry lips.

I swear to god if this was all a set up and he doesn't give a fuck about me, I might die of shame. A boy fucked me over once before and I swore I'd never get close to anyone ever again, for fear of this exact same thing happening.

"Well, did you put it in yourself, maybe you misspelled his name?" Jacob tries to pacify me, his tone calming.

"No," tears sting the back of my eyes in panic but I bite down on my tongue to make pain radiate from somewhere else, anywhere else, because the pain slicing through my chest right now is unbearable.

I'm being ridiculous. Kacey is a stranger. Who cares if we fucked? Fucking means nothing. Except to me it kind of doesn't. I've only slept with three men by choice, Kacey, being one of them; it would really suck if he actually doesn't give a fuck about me. How could I have read him so wrong?

"Okay, well don't worry, maybe he just didn't hit save or something," Jacob suggests, trying to calm me.

I can't answer him for fear of a sob tearing free. I'm so fucking dumb, I thought Kacey actually liked me, he treated me like a fucking queen, why would he do all that if I was just a quick fuck? He cuddled me in his bed! Cuddled! Even now I'm trying to stick up for him and it's him who's potentially fucked *me* over.

"I'll kill him," Charlie promises and my throat closes, then I remember Huxley, Kacey said he put *both* numbers in my phone.

"Hold on," I mutter, I hastily scroll back up from K to H and exhale a shaky breath when I see Huxley's name.

Before I can change my mind, I hit dial, I place it against my ear, rolling my anxious gaze up to Jacob's.

It rings.

Once.

Twice.

The sixth ring sounds and I feel myself deflate all over again.

Kacey fucked me over, repeats itself over and over inside my head. This was all some sort of fucking game.

"Hello?" Huxley's voice hits my ear and I nearly collapse to my knees.

"Umm, hey," I say nervously.

"Darlin', why d'you sound so off, what's wrong? Are you okay? Where are you?" Huxley rushes out, clearing his throat as he speaks.

"I erm," *pull yourself together Kyla!* "I was just wondering if you were with Kacey, I need to speak to him about something and he didn't put his number in my phone like he said he did," I blurt out with false confidence, I glance my eyes back up and Jacob nods encouragingly, with a reassuring smile.

Huxley starts laughing and I furrow my brow, pain sneaks its way back into my chest and I curl my free hand into a fist, "why the fuck are you laughing at me?" I snap, instantly gaining the attention of Charlie, who almost barrels me down as he tries to grab the phone.

We tussle with it for a moment before he reluctantly gives up, throwing his arms out wide in frustration as he stalks back to the couch.

"Darlin'" he says trying to stifle his laughter, "Kacey says check under B."

"What?"

"Check under B, in your contacts,"

"Um, okay, hold on," I switch to speaker and scroll to B, sure enough there under B is a new contact.

Big Man.

I sag with relief, expelling a huge breath, Jacob gives me a wink and I smile; a real smile this time.

Kacey didn't fuck me over.

"Found it?" Kacey's deep rumble comes through the speaker.

And fuck me, if it doesn't drench my knickers.

"Yeah, I found it, Big Man," I smile, biting my lip; Jacob rolls his eyes and makes a gagging sound in his throat.

"Sooo, miss me already, cherub?" he laughs and *Jesus fuck, that sound.*

Ignoring his question –because I'm scared of my own answer- I nibble my thumb nail anxiously as I start to pace a little, "Um, can we do something Friday, after the fights? I need to talk to you about something."

"For you? I'd make myself available anywhere, any time, Sweetheart," he states so matter-of-factly, so strongly, so *honestly,* I truly believe he would too.

"Reckon, Hux, would be? It needs to be both of you," I glance back up to Jacob again for reassurance and he gives me another small nod, a tiny crease between his brows this time.

"I'd make myself free too, ya know!" Huxley shouts in the background.

"I'll take that as a yes then?" I laugh.

"That's a definitive yes," Kacey laughs.

"Cool," I chew on the inside of my cheek until it's raw.

"You're okay though, right?" Kacey checks, making me smile.

"Yeah, I'm absolutely fine, I just need to talk to you about something, but like face to face, it's nothing scary," I laugh lightly to hide my nervous tone but honestly I think I'm gunna follow through on the vomit thing.

"You don't sound fine, did I do something? This morning with both of us, did we…? I can tell something's wrong…" Kacey rushes out, blurting out all the questions that are swirling around inside his head.

"You're both great, neither of you did anything, I actually had a really nice time, so thank you, and thanks for like, taking care of me," I say shyly, I can feel that familiar heat creeping up my neck.

"As long as we didn't do anything to upset you, that's all I care about, as for taking care of you, anytime Sweetheart, any fucking time," Kacey groans and my thighs involuntarily clench together.

"Kace, I have to go, say bye to Hux for me."

"Okay, so, see you Friday then."

"You will, bye."

"Bye, Sweetheart."

I gnaw on my bottom lip trying to hide my smile but I can't help it. I'm throwing a huge part of myself out there right now, they could decide to turn and walk away and that would be it, the end, finished, kaput. I don't know how the fuck I'll feel if they don't even try for me. Should they? They don't *know* me, I don't know them, let's face it, this is an overwhelming barrage of feelings from a single nights encounter.

Isn't it?

Also, I say both of them, Huxley hasn't exactly expressed *interest* in me…has he?

How do you know?

I read an article in a magazine once that said people build a relationship slow and steady because they're happy to take their time, people that haven't lost important things or dealt with trauma in their lives don't rush, they have no need, no reason to fear for the future.

Then it said about fast-paced relationships where people have this instant connection and they throw caution to the wind, they see what they want and take it. Lay claim. Throw themselves all in with everything they have because they know what it's like to lose the thing they love the most or have some fucked up history that makes them cling to life.

Is that what I have with, Kacey? Is that something there with Huxley too? How would that work? Would I want that to work? Would they? What if they do stay? What if they're super chill about everything and then we just go back to how we were this morning?

Kacey and I.

And Huxley.

That thing inside my chest stings a little, but it's beating too, confusing emotions roll through me, do I let the tide take me? Carry me away, draw me under and drown me?

"What're you thinking?" Jacob asks, tugging me down beside him, we both squeeze on the piano stool together.

Stupid fucking piano.

"I'm nervous as shit, so I guess I'm thinking, what the fuck's wrong with me?" I snort, shaking my head.

"You know what would make you feel better?" Charlie leans forward from the couch, shirtless and still bloody. "If we play a game to relax you," he beams, his perfect white teeth flashing in the dim light of the late afternoon, his fang teeth unnaturally sharp like he files them into a point.

A fang toothed demon in the night, a devil lurking in the shadows.

"Absolutely not," Jacob booms making me jump, "Kyla-Rose needs to get changed," he tells Charlie but looks at me, his eyes roaming over my *–Kacey's-* outfit, he doesn't look impressed, that's for sure.

"Bloody hell, okay, *fashionista,*" I snort.

"Both of you do, you're both bloody, Kyla you've got a meeting and Charlie, clean that shit up," he orders, gesturing to the white leather sofa –which to be fair- looks as though someone was murdered on it, which is surprisingly something that *hasn't* happened on that couch yet.

We both huff in defeat because we know it's pointless to argue and then both of us start to move.

"I'm gunna run down to mine and change, then I'll be back, if you want me to come with?" Charlie looks at me intently for a moment.

I can see in his green eyes he doesn't fully understand the confusion of feelings in me right now because we both only really understand a few very basic emotions, we feel deep love for our family and strong hate for our enemies. Other than that we don't do feelings. They complicate even the most basic of tasks and neither of us have time for that shit.

Do we?

"Yeah come back up, I always need my partner in crime," he nods and heads to the elevator.

I run into my closet and pull out another wide leg pant suit. This time it's black so I put a red lace bodice beneath it, slipping my feet into black heels. My hair is naturally straight but since my shower at Kacey's this morning, I've fallen asleep on it in various places, so it's kinda all over the place. I comb it through removing all the knots and tangles, then run a straightener over it so it's pressed nice and straight again. I tuck it behind my ears, replacing my gold hoops from last night with simple black studs. Scooting back out of my bedroom I wander into my babies' room. Neither of them are there though.

"Brute!" I call, "Angel!"

I wander back towards the rear sitting room, finding Charlie cleaning the leather.

"That stuff stinks," I comment, wrinkling my nose.

"Tell me about it," Charlie grumbles, "but it works," he shrugs as he stands, "Brute and Angel are down in my apartment waiting for the walker."

"Oh. Thanks Charl."

Both of us tilt our heads to the right, taking a look at the sofa, I wouldn't know it was all bloody half an hour ago so I'm calling that a win.

"You two are fucking scary as shit," Eli announces.

Strolling into the room with a confident swagger, he flicks on every fucking light he can as he goes, making me hiss at him like a feral cat. There's just something about artificial light that I hate, I'm all for sitting alone in the dark, candles are okay.

"Why?" we both ask in unison, tilting our heads in the opposite direction to take him in.

Eli laughs, though it's humourless, "*that's* why," he says, pointing at us, "you look like the twins from *'The Shining'*," he snorts.

"Is that a compliment, Charl, or an insult?" Charlie narrows his eyes on Eli slightly before answering.

"I think it just confirms we're, what was it, Eli? *Fucking scary as shit.*"

Charlie and I both burst into simultaneous laughter as Eli shakes his head.

"What're we laughing at?" Cam grunts as he drops that big brutish body of his into the seat on the sofa we were just analysing, forcing even more laughter to erupt from us.

"I rest my case," Eli sighs, kicking a booted foot up against the wall, he leans against it, folding his arms over his broad chest.

The intercom bleeps.

"Yello?" Eli answers.

Franks voice responds, "I'm ready when you are, boss."

"We'll be right down, thank you, Frank," I answer before we all pile down into the car.

CHAPTER 9

KYLA-ROSE

Like any other Friday Fight Night, whether I'm a spectator or participant, I enter the warehouse through the back. This time I've got Charlie by my side and Frank bringing up the rear. Even though it's still early afternoon, fighters, trainers and staff are already arriving and setting up. I'm just here to spar with Cam, I think my fighting days are done, I drop enough bodies and spill enough blood *off* the mat, I don't think I need to up my numbers any higher.

Charlie and I walk hand in hand through the bustling maze of hallways, ignoring the busy bodies buzzing around us. We were silent on the journey here, I can't talk before I fight with Cam, he's a heavy hitter and he doesn't hold back just because it's me. I need to be inside my own headspace while I compile all of the shit that I'll need in order to really pack a punch. It hurts like fuck to drag shit up from my past but the bullshit never needs to travel from inside my head and out past my teeth, the only place that pain needs to radiate to is my knuckles.

"Cam," Charlie calls, his gruff voice scraping through the room, drawing the attention of everyone around us.

Yeah, they should be cautious around Charlie he's the most dangerous man I've ever had the pleasure of knowing. The rest of our family don't know about half the shit he gets up to, if they did I'm pretty sure Jacob would insist on having him sectioned.

Cam nods in recognition as he finishes tying back his hair.

Once Charlie's taped me up and I'm in the ring, Cam's huge body steps between the ropes. Adrenaline thrums through my veins, nervous energy bubbles up out of my throat in the form of a giggle and I hear Charlie snort behind me. He *knows* what's happening inside my body right now because it's the same thing that happens inside his. We release our monster and allow it free rein, the demonic presence that usually lies docile inside me starts to stretch and yawn, red eyes flickering alive as fire pulses through me.

"Ky, we're sparring, not fighting," Cam grumbles with a sigh as I widen my eyes and give him a full smile.

"Come at me, Cam," I chuckle darkly and he snaps his attention onto Charlie, hissing mumbled words between his teeth. "*We* don't have to fight, you could get Charlie up here instead," I suggest with pure wickedness in my tone, knowing there's no way Cam will back out, he has a monster inside him too, he just hides his better.

My six-foot-seven beast of a cousin scowls at my mocking and takes a menacing step closer as I let my crazy loose and we move together.

Just as years of sparring together have taught us, we both know each other too well. I can read him, he can read me, easily predicting each other's movements. I barely make impact with him at all and the same goes for him. Cam's fist glances off my jaw and I cackle madly as I lunge forward, throwing caution to the wind and using my smaller stature to my advantage. I fake left, then throw my body at him wrapping my arms and legs around him, pinning one of his arms into his side, I scramble up his body and noogie him with my taped fist as he tries to pry me off.

I laugh manically as he huffs a frustrated sigh, dropping his free hand to his side so he can glare at me.

"Love you," I tell him, dropping a chaste kiss to his messy head of blonde hair and ungracefully slide myself down his mountain of a body.

"Yeah, yeah, you little shit, you gave up because you're tired," he grumbles, making me laugh.

Sweat glides down my temples as I use my forearms to knock my stray hairs back.

"Whatever you say, Cam, you know I could take you," I chuckle as Frank throws me a bottle of water. "That was fun, when can we do it again?" I beam over at him and he looks to the ceiling as though asking god for strength.

Before he can answer me, a jarring girly laugh interrupts us, making my teeth grind. I'd recognise that incessant screeching anywhere.

"What the fuck is *she* doing here?" I hiss at Charlie who smirks back at me, lounging casually against one of the steel beams holding the warehouse together.

"I dunno, ask boss man, Cam," he chuckles darkly as I glare across at Cam with a raised eyebrow.

"Don't look at me like that," he complains, his voice low as he stalks toward me. "She wanted a fight but I couldn't get anyone to go up against her, you know what she's like, she just hangs around," Cam sighs and I fight the intense urge to pull Franks gun free and put a bullet between her beady fucking eyes.

"No one would go up against her?" I murmur, more to myself than Cam, as I tap my taped knuckles against my lips.

"Kyla-Rose Swallow," the screechy voice continues, making my eyes roll.

I plaster a fake grin on my face before turning to eye the irritating bitch.

"Michaela Kensington, what a *pleasure*," I lie, sarcasm dripping like venom from every word I spit in her direction.

"Thought you'd retired, *baby Swallow*," a red eyebrow drawing high on her head as she smirks at me, "I heard you took too many knocks to your head, had you sent off to the loony-bin," she winks with an insinuating tap to her temple.

Charlie growls from his position in the shadows, making her stiffen slightly and glance over her shoulder at him. He straightens his posture and looks to me, I give him a firm shake of my head. We don't need to be killing anyone here, well, not *today* anyway and not with this many witnesses. I slowly turn my attention back to the ballsy red head and raise an eyebrow at her tangerine-tanned skin and shitty attitude.

"Well, you *heard* wrong, *Micky*," I smirk, using the

nickname I know she hates; she bravely shoots me a scowl, turning my smirk turn into a full mocking grin.

"Oh, yeah? When you fighting next then?" she asks cockily, planting her hand on her cocked hip, her pale blue eyes raking up and down my sweaty form, a sneer on her curled upper lip.

I cock my head to one side as I survey her. Her tight body dressed in a sports bra and matching shorts, defined abs and overly pushed up tits. *Where does she even find a sports bra that can do that?* I scoff at her and turn away, essentially dismissing her, ending the pointless conversation.

"Just leave it, Ky, ignore her," Cam murmurs to me as I step over to him to remove my tape.

"Yeah, *baby Swallow*, just *leave* it," Michaela taunts, my eyes narrowing as I glance up at Cam.

Cam firmly shakes his head at me and continues to hiss at me to ignore her, even as she continues to call me out. I stop focusing on Cam's words, flippantly turning back to the gobby bitch.

"Tonight, *Swallow,* you and me, come out of your *non-existent* retirement," she laughs, I sniff at her words.

"That's not how my fights work," Cam bellows from behind me, asserting his authority, making her flinch.

The usually silent Swallow brother can really belt out his words when he wants to. Michaela's eyes widen with *fear?* Or is that panic? *Ooo*, she wants to get in Cam's pants! Hah! Classic! She sneers, fires insults at the Swallow family name but still wants to fuck one of us! Fucking hilarious, I feel a grin split my face as my insides heat.

"'Kay."

"'Kay?" She repeats as a question, her voice a little flustered.

"Yeah, I said okay, I'll fight you," I mock as I slip my way between the ropes, dropping to the ground beside her.

"Tonight?" Her small blue eyes peer up at me, her five-ten height not quite matching my six, but she does a good job with her scowl, even I'm impressed.

"No, now, ten minutes, I don't need to fight you in front of an audience to make a point. Gear up," I finger wave over my shoulder chuckling as I hit the door for the locker room.

So much for a closed fight...

Apparently, after I disappeared into the locker room to wipe myself down and ready myself for my fight with Michaela, she bitched and whined and made a huge fuss about money from the bets and how she needs our fight to be on the card, blah, blah, *blah*. Although, her incessant whining eventually worked, Cam took pity on her and agreed to put us on tonight. Not exactly what *I* wanted but I'm no coward, I won't back down, so if she needs an audience to perform for, so be it.

I'm not cocky enough to say I'll win because to be honest I think our skillsets are pretty evenly matched as long as I keep a straight head. I just need to keep in the *here and now* and make sure I don't accidently kill her. That's why I don't fight anymore. I get too lost inside my own head and shit gets confusing.

Sitting in the backseat of the SUV, I rest my forehead against the cool glass of the window. Rain hammers down against the glass, the sound filling the car as Frank, Charlie and I travel in comfortable silence. I can't chit-chat before a fight, I can't really do much of anything, I just want to get it over and done with, I hate waiting around. I don't thrive off this shit anymore, beating on someone for no reason, honestly brings me no joy.

Don't get me wrong, I fucking *love* watching. The grunts, the blood, the sweat, everything about being a spectator thrills me, I just don't have the same desire to actually fight anymore. So this is all about Michaela, which I'm sure she's ecstatic over, always one craving the spotlight. There's nothing particularly wrong with her, she's just an arsehole and her whinging drives me insane, that shrill tone to her voice just grates on me and every time I hear it I want to slap my hands over my ears and cringe.

My door opens and Charlie takes my hand as I hop down onto the puddled gravel. Cars are parked haphazardly, people hanging around outside smoking but I pay them no mind. I just want to get in and get ready.

Clutching Charlie's hand, he leads me through the back door. The stifling heat hits me, the roar of the crowd penetrating my already buzzing ears as we near the main room. Kacey's fight is up a fair few before mine and I made a promise to watch him and I intend to follow that through. I don't usually watch any before my own because I don't need the distraction but I'd more or less do anything to get one of those golden eyed, soppy grins slapped on Kacey's face.

I haven't seen Kacey since Sunday when I left his after the party, but we've spoken on the phone every night since. We each talk about our day, or rather, we talk about *his* day and I tell him I've been completing boring spreadsheets and paperwork shit for the family business, he hasn't asked me what it is yet though, so for that I'm at least grateful.

Turns out, when Kacey isn't bare knuckle fighting in an illegal underground circuit, he's a mechanic that dabbles in the occasional private security job. He tried to tell me it wasn't interesting and I wouldn't want to know about it –which he'd be right about when it came to boring security shit- but I squealed about the mechanic part and started telling him about the custom cars my Uncle Dee, used to own. He laughed and told me that he knew he liked me for a reason.

He told me about a custom build he's working on and I groaned at the details for which he chastised me for because apparently the noises I make, make his dick hard. I cackled in response, then continued to antagonise the beast. Turns out I can get him hard as a rock using a whole array of sounds, even the one where I got my hair tangled around my earring and I huffed in irritation, *yeah*, he got a hard on at that too… said it reminded him of a noise I might make if I was sexually frustrated. I mean, whatever floats your boat I guess.

Equally, I've been texting with Huxley all week too. He sends me the most random shit throughout the day, some of it funny, some of it downright weird and some of it entirely fucking questionable, but he never fails to put a smile on my face.

We've been playing a made up game of *emoji chat* too. We build sentences using emoji's and the other person has three guesses to work out what the other's trying to say. It's fucking hilarious.

I've been getting to know them both. We've even got our own group chat which Kacey appropriately named '*three-way'*. We've been playing games of twenty-questions to get to know each other better but each time we attempt it we never seem to make it past question five before the questions take a dramatic turn down '*Dirty Avenue'* and once we head in that direction, everything ends up in the gutter and it's game over. I mean there's only so many times Huxley can ask me what colour knickers I'm wearing before ten in the morning and still maintain that it's *'part of the game'*.

Charlie pulls me through the staff door out into the main room, leading me through the shadows along the back wall until we hit the locker rooms. Frank takes up position outside the door as Charlie tugs me inside, dropping my bag to the bench in the centre of the room.

"Cam said you're on last," Charlie informs me, shucking his leather jacket off and hanging it on the coat hooks, leaving him bare chested once again.

He leans against the wall on the inside of the door, kicking his booted foot up against it, he folds his large arms across his chest. Charlie's tattoos are almost identical to mine but slightly more twisted. We both have swallows, roses and thorns and the ink covers his upper body the same way mine does. His back, chest, abs and both arms are dripping in black ink, where my swallow birds are alive and in flight, Charlie's are half skeletons, somewhat decayed, blood drips from them and the roses down his forearms are dying and wilted with eyeballs in the centre of them, giving all of his tattoos a much darker vibe than mine.

They're fucking beautiful all the same.

That was something we bonded over a lot when I got out of juvie. Tattoos. Charlie already had a few large pieces but nothing like the ink he's sporting now. When I decided I wanted this huge piece that more or less covers my entire upper body, Charlie found the perfect guy to do it and then we both decided we wanted more or less the same.

We sat together for those long arse sessions, Morrie –our artist- always works with blaring headphones shoved in his ears and he always cleared the shop out when it was our appointments so we could talk freely without being overheard. Charlie just sat and listened to everything I had to say without judgement on the premise that, what we spoke about went no further.

Morrie was working in a seedy little back alley shop that the average Joe wouldn't dare step foot in for fear of tetanus or some shit but we strolled right up in there and got the best ink I've ever imagined. He heard our vision and literally brought it to life. We regularly visit him even now for ink although we're both rapidly running out of space.

I draw my hair up into a high ponytail and secure it with a few elastics then I twist my rope of hair up, wrapping it around the ties in a tight bun, securing it with a black silk scrunchie so it stays nice and secure and can't be used against me. Women love the hair pulling, even in bare knuckle fighting, it's such a fucking bitch move and if you've got as much hair on your head as I have, you need to make sure that shit stays tucked up right out of the fucking way. I didn't spend the last six fucking years growing it to this length just to have tufts of it yanked out of my scalp, I'd cut a bitch for less.

I wriggle into a tight as fuck sports bra over my already taped nipples –I really don't want my piercings being ripped out- and then put on another over the top, gotta keep the twins happy. They're not exactly *huge,* but they're bigger than the average handful and on my slim frame, well let's put it this way; have you ever tried to run up the stairs without a bra on and gotten black eyes in the process? Yeah, exactly, I rest my case. So double up on the sports bra it is, plus it's not a fucking strip-tease, I don't want these babies randomly popping out to say hello. Lastly, I pull on my high-waisted leggings and trainers.

I'm dressed head to toe in white which makes my already pale complexion look even more shocking. My black ink stands out against the stark white and a small smile creeps over my lips. *Dramatic.* I always wear a white outfit when I fight, that way when I come out of the ring covered in my opponent's blood; it's a harsh reminder not to fuck with me. Sick I know, but it comes with the territory. If I don't instil fear in every fucker around me, some fuckwit will try to take me out and we can't have that now, can we?

A knock on the door draws my attention but I don't move my gaze from the girl staring back at me in the mirror. Charlie cracks the door, nodding over his shoulder before it closes again. He raises an eyebrow at me.

"You ready to watch your boy? Frank says he's on next."

"Who's he fighting?" I ask, my tummy immediately doing summersaults.

"Butcher," he shrugs.

Kacey will destroy him, I have no doubts about that.

Butcher's a good fighter, don't get me wrong he's one

of the best, he's huge but he's slow. If Kacey's last fight was anything to go by, he's huge *and* fast. He's gunna make his way to the top of the card so easily over the next few weeks if he keeps fighting for Cam. Thinking about it, I still haven't asked Cam where he found Kacey.

I shrug and turn to face, Charl. A slow, wicked grin starts to bloom on his lips as he eyes my outfit. He raises an eyebrow at me before releasing a rumbling laugh.

"Come on, killa, let's get out there and wish your boy luck yeah?"

Charlie walks out, still shirtless and I follow closely behind still gripping his hand, the crowd automatically parts for him, *us.* With Frank bringing up the rear, Gremlin silently moves in to flank me on the left with Rubble –Gremlin's second- bringing up the right, we move in practiced formation through the sweaty bodies until we reach the ring. Charlie tugs me forward as Gremlin, Rubble and Frank crowd in at my back, their eyes darting all around, checking and surveying for any threats.

When we get to the ropes, my eyes dance around as I peer over Charlies shoulder until I spot Cam. He gives me a nod from where he stands on the opposite side of the ring, which I'm sure is paired with some sort of grunt –not that I could hear it over the noise of the crowd, but it seems fitting for Cam. It's packed in here tonight, even more so than normal, people are squashed together like tinned sardines but no one seems to mind, they all came here for the same thing, after all.

To see blood.

We're a violent species, humans. Blood, violence, fighting. All of those things society frowns at and discourages but we need it. Whether it's a fist fight down a back alley, an MMA organised event or underground bare-knuckle fighting, we need it. Even those who actively fight against it, thrive on it in the shadows, secretly enjoying the chaos.

Charlie's crushing grip on my knuckles tugs me forward until he plants his big hands on my shoulders, moving me to stand in front of him. When I glance up, my eyes connect with a pair of pretty gold ones, my heart skips a beat in my chest, my breath hitching at the mere sight of him.

Kacey leans his weight forward on the thick ropes so his face is level with mine. His scent engulfs me, my head swims, tummy flutters, my thighs clench and my tongue darts out to wet my suddenly dry lips.

"Can I get a good luck kiss?" he smirks with a cocky lift of a blonde eyebrow.

"These lips aren't a good luck charm, Big Man," I snort, as desperate as I am to kiss him, I'm not making it that easy.

"No?" he teases, his mouth mere inches from mine, his hot breath fanning over my face, his eyes flicking between my own.

I hike my chin in defiance.

"Not a chance in hell. All I bring is destruction. These lips are like poison, they don't bring luck, they bring suffering and death."

"So, kiss me, *Angel of Death*," he winks unfazed, dipping his face down to meet my own, he presses his soft lips against mine. I rise up on my tip-toes deepening the kiss, my fingers gripping the back of his neck before he breaks the kiss leaving me wanting and breathless, "*God*, you're fucking beautiful, Kyla-Rose," he smiles, pushing off of the ropes and taking his corner.

I quickly feel another pair of eyes on me, heating my skin, the hair on the back of my neck prickling with awareness. I look across the ring and there, to the left, is Huxley. He sends me a devilish wink and I feel my cheeks heat which must be obvious because he shakes his head before throwing it back with laughter. Charlie's low whistle behind me gets my attention, I peer at him over my shoulder, spotting Gremlin, Rubble and Frank all trying hard to avert their gazes.

"What?" I scowl, prodding my finger into Charlie's naked chest.

"Nothing," Charlie answers coolly with a smirk, I narrow my eyes on him but he just gives me a wink and looks over the top of my head to watch the fight.

Cam calls the start. The two fighters circle each other, both trying to get a feel for their opponent. Butcher has fought here for years, his dark hair shorn close to his scalp, his bright blue eyes almost haunting in the dark, his huge fists like sledge hammers and his attitude is that of a cocky motherfucker. Nonetheless, he's a good fighter but I'm still convinced my boy's gunna win.

Kacey grins wide. Moving in from the side he throws out a few teasing body shots, getting a feel for Butcher's reach – he's got long fucking arms. Butcher, swings out mercilessly, barrelling a fist toward Kacey's ribs. Kacey dances on light feet out of the way and as Butcher's only guarding himself with one arm, Kacey lands a punishing blow to the side of his face, his head whips round as blood and spittle flies from his open mouth.

Butcher has his hands back up in an instant; working his jaw a few times, telling me what I already know -that hurt like a bitch- then all bets are off. They both get good shots on each other. Butcher catches Kacey on the brow splitting it open, he blinks the blood from his eye trying to clear it. Through the river of blood, now flowing down his beautiful face, a grin takes over, a maniacal one at that, crimson covering his teeth.

And that's when I see his demon again, it calls out to my own, my heart pounding so hard in my chest it could shatter my ribs. Big Man glances over at me, winking his bloodied eye, setting my soul on fire, my blood screams through my veins and all other sounds are blocked out until all I can hear is the thud of my own erratic heart pounding in my ears.

With a roar Kacey dives at Butcher, he pummels into Butcher's ribs before landing a solid kick to the back of his calf, the slap of his foot against flesh is deafening. The crowd roars, drinks fly from cup, bottles soaring up into the air all around us, bodies bustle as they surge forward trying to get a better look.

Butcher's knee buckles but he manages to stay upright, he latches hold of Kacey as he tries to pin Kacey's arms between them, essentially stopping Kacey from getting any more shots off. But Butcher's breathing hard, his large size weighing him down and making him slow. He's trying to give himself a break but Big Man's having none of it.

Kacey lands blows to Butcher's ribs while still trapped to him, forcing the movement to create some wiggle room. Big Man rears back and finishes him with a roundhouse kick to the temple, Butcher drops like a sack of shit, out for the fucking count.

Cam's guys step in, dragging Butchers unconscious body from the ring as Cam steps up, he grips Kacey's wrist thrusting his hand into the air in victory. As my hearing slowly returns, the noise is tumultuous, people are screaming Kacey's name and I stare at him in awe.

He's mine.

Cam releases him allowing Kacey to cross the ring in three long strides, people are screaming to get his attention but he only has eyes for me. Leaning down over the ropes, his large tattooed hands grip my waist, effortlessly heaving me up into the air, the thick ropes crushed between our hot bodies, his lips crash into mine with possessive need. A low growl rumbles from his chest as my mouth opens for him greedily, the tang of salt and copper sweeps in with the movement of his tongue, only making me hotter for him. My fingers snake their way up into his mess of blonde hair as I cling onto him like he's my lifeline.

Then I realise that this is it.

In this very moment he's claiming me as his prize. Publicly announcing, without words, that I am his. I should be rearing back, breaking the kiss and stopping this, I should have stopped it before it even started but I find myself so completely consumed by everything that is Kacey, that it only drives my wanton desires deeper, hooking into my flesh and sucking me under.

Then all too soon it's over. He removes his warm lips from mine, gently lowering me back to the floor, never taking his eyes from my own he smiles, not his usual big soppy grin, no, this smile tells me things I'm too afraid to even speak aloud.

CHAPTER 10

KACEY

I look down from the ring into a pair of glistening emerald eyes, the usual grey storm clouds banished from her perfect orbs. My rich blood stains her pretty face, the thick crimson smeared across her lips and over her pale jaw and I'm certain I've never seen anything more beautiful in my life. I want to take her right here, throw her down onto all fours, strip those white leggings over her peach of an arse and ram my raging hot cock into that tight little cunt, like a fucking rabid animal, I'm salivating. Everyone else be damned because I'm never giving Kyla-Rose up, I'm addicted to her like a drug of the highest quality.

Her big green eyes stare up into mine, she doesn't try to clean my mark from her face, though I'm sure she can feel it sticky and drying on her ivory skin. Yet she wears it like war paint, like a warrior heading into battle, she stands tall and confident as she looks up at me, something inside me demands I get my hands back on her as quickly as is humanly possible but I can't right now, she's got a fight too.

She turns away from the ring, a tall muscular guy with similar features to hers, eyes me warily before turning and following behind her, the crowd parts like the sea, allowing them to pass. People here must already know her, I guess she must have been fighting here for a while before she stopped. I move to the back of the ring and step under the ropes.

"Good fight, Kacey," Cam slaps me on the shoulder, passing me a bulging envelope with the other. "Think about coming back next week, you did good," he tells me with a grunt.

I'm not sure the guy's capable of many words, so I figure that's a compliment in itself. I make my way through the crowd, people slap me on the back, grip my hand and congratulate me. Blood still streams down my face but I ignore it, I can't even feel it if I'm honest, I'm running on the high of my win right now.

"Kace!" Huxley calls from up ahead, I make my way over to him as we both move into the locker room, "let's get you cleaned up man, you don't wanna miss, Kyla-Rose."

"When's she on?"

"Last," he states with a smirk, a cocky lift to one of his dark eyebrows.

"Last?"

"Yeah man, the crowd's fucking buzzing, apparently she doesn't fight often but when she does, it's a bloodbath."

I can see that. My wild girl definitely has a savage streak in her and I'd bet my life on the fact that she doesn't go down easy.

Huxley pushes me to sit on the wooden bench in the centre of the white locker room while he tips a bottle of water over my split eyebrow, he flushes it out, instructing me to get in the shower. I wash myself, quickly shampooing my hair before drying off.

After Huxley applies glue to my eyebrow, I hike black joggers up my legs and thread my arms through a clean white t-shirt. I feather my fingers through my mess of wet blonde hair and kick on black trainers. We step out into the main room, two guys are fighting it out in the ring and there seems to be even more people crowding the space than there was before.

The whole warehouse is buzzing, people push and shove each other, trying to get enough elbow room to tip their beers back, girls are dressed up to the nines, men discussing and placing bets on who they think will make them the most money.

"Oi, you! Fighter boy!" a man's voice calls. I turn my head in the direction it came from, my eyes landing on a short bald headed man with stark blue eyes, standing behind a bar top table taking bets. "Wanna put some money on your girl?" he smirks. When I don't immediately answer, he eyeballs me a moment, "unless you wanna bet against her?" a cruel smile curves his thin lips and a growl rips free from my throat.

I stomp over, shoving a roll of hundreds into his meaty palm and watch as his hollow eyes gleam, he counts it out quickly before passing me a slip of paper, without looking at it I shove it deep in my pocket and turn away.

"I wanna get as close as possible, Kace," Huxley beams, pushing on my shoulder as we weave through the crowd.

"You never get this fucking excited when I fight," I laugh.

He scoffs, "you don't have tits or a pussy, what's there to be excited about?"

I roll my head back, barking a laugh, "honestly Hux, you're never gunna build a relationship with her if the only thing you ever think or talk about is her cunt," I deadpan.

He spins on his heel so fast, I don't see it coming when he punches me square in the chest. I move my hand up to rub the now sore spot with a frown.

"I do not only think about her cunt, you fucking arsehole, I actually fucking like her, the same as you do, so don't be a fucking dick about it," he growls at me, all traces of humour abandoning him as a snarl falls from his lips.

"She might not fucking like you anyway, you dick," I mumble under my breath, already knowing that's not the case.

The conversations the three of us have shared this week gave me a good idea on how Kyla-Rose feels about the both of us and I'm almost certain there's more than friendship there with her and Huxley.

He shrugs as though he hasn't a care in the world, "If not then that's fine and I'll be happy with whatever makes her happy," he says confidently like it wouldn't affect him if she wasn't into him.

I know that's fucking bullshit.

I saw him and Kyla-Rose talking at our party, he had her undivided attention as soon as she clapped eyes on him and she looked comfortable enough around him. I wonder if maybe she'd met him first I wouldn't even be in the running at a chance with her.

"Yeah, well, just keep walking dipshit," I mumble pushing him in the chest to turn him around, he doesn't stumble like I intend and he barks a laugh, shaking his head as he turns and continues shoving his way forward.

I would never willingly share my girl with anyone, but Huxley's…*different*. He's my best friend, my brother. We've saved each other's lives countless times when we were deployed. When you're forged in fire, nothing could ruin that friendship. That's why him, Nox and I are so inseparable, when you've been out in the desert with nothing but each other and your hopes and prayers, you build something no one else could ever comprehend.

As strange as it is, the thought of him also being interested in Kyla-Rose doesn't make me rage with jealousy like I guess it should, it actually makes me sort of happy I 'spose, knowing that my best friend could be as happy as I feel right now. I don't feel weird about it at all and if that says something about me then fuck it, I don't give a damn what anyone thinks.

We've shared women before, don't get me wrong, we're both always up for a good time but we haven't had an actual *relationship* with the same woman, sex is sex, relationships take work and it would take a special woman to even consider dating the both of us, if that's even a thing, if that's even what they want? It's not like Hux and I have discussed anything, not *too* seriously anyway but I know he has feelings for her, even if he's not sure what those feelings are, I think I know him better than he knows himself sometimes.

The fight before Kyla's wraps up as we approach the ring; both guys look bloody and tired as they're half-carried away.

Someone gets up onto the mat, mopping the blood away before drying it and clearing the space.

A busty red head steps up into the ring wearing a matching purple shorts set, her toned stomach and legs on full display and her breasts hitched up so high they look like they might burst out at any second. She must think this is a fashion show because she's literally wearing a full face of makeup and I'm no expert, but I'm sure fake tan runs when mixed with sweat?

When Cam waves her over, she practically hangs off of him like a desperate leech. As he speaks into her ear, he uncurls her fingers from his bicep making me snort, he's clearly not much of a fan either. Honestly, I hope I'm wrong and this is a good fight but this girl looks like she's trying to win a beauty contest not a fucking fist fight.

The crowd around the outskirts of the warehouse suddenly start to silence, noise slowly diminishing in waves like the calm before a storm, until all that can be heard inside the warehouse is the rain battering against the tin roof and the collective breathing of the crowd.

In the dark –because the only lights not focused on the ring itself are on the bars and dotted around, so just enough light stops you falling over your own feet- it's an eerie feeling. Being surrounded by so many bodies all waiting with baited breath for what's to come next. In all my years of fighting I can honestly say I have never witnessed a competitor walk out to pure silence. It's so quiet around the room that you could hear a pin drop.

A door opens at the back somewhere to my right and the hordes begin to part, the echo of feet shuffling against concrete fills the silence as people move out of the way. The tall, shirtless guy -who was with Kyla-Rose earlier- walks through first, closely followed by my girl.

Taking real notice of her appearance now and not viewing her through a haze of adrenaline, her thick rope of silver hair is wrapped up tightly on top of her head. All loose hairs combed back from her heart shaped face making her usual green-grey eyes stand out like deep emeralds in the low light. She's wearing high-waisted white leggings and a matching sports bra, it's so basic but it's shocking against her pale skin and the harsh black ink adorning the rest of her.

Kyla-Rose doesn't look at those around her and nobody tries to touch her as she passes, not like they usually would with their favourite fighter. As far as I can tell her pretty eyes don't blink the entire way across the floor, her focus straight ahead. Much like everyone else's in the room, my eyes are glued to her lean ink covered body as she heads to the ring, a lioness prowling toward a gazelle.

The guy in front of her parts the ropes allowing her to gracefully slip between them, bouncing on her feet lightly as she enters, her eyes glued to Cam, he gives her a nod which is more recognition than he usually gives any of his other fighters. Kyla-Rose limbers slightly, still bouncing softly on her toes, her hips swaying with the motion, her arse practically begging me to sink my teeth into it.

Later.

The warehouse still engulfed in silence, the red head steps forward a little, her stance strong and overly cocky, she runs her eyes up the length of Kyla's tall frame, sneering when her eyes fall on Kyla's face. Kyla-Rose slowly tilts her head to one side, assessing her opponent, her whole body freezes, her muscles locking tight for a moment before she releases a long deep breath, easing the tension in her shoulders.

That's the moment everything changes.

Murmurs begin to drift through the sea of people as the two women stand off against each other. Cam calls the start of the fight and the crowd erupts as though they've just been given permission to speak again. Kyla-Rose's opponent moves, but Kyla doesn't, I'm not sure by looking at her that she's even breathing.

The red head launches forward on the attack, landing a decent punch to the side of Kyla's face, her head whipping to one side at the impact but she makes no attempt to move, her feet firmly planted to the floor. Red hammers jabs to Kyla-Rose's sides, landing a particularly nasty kidney shot but still, Kyla-Rose doesn't move a muscle, she doesn't flinch or even rock on her feet with the impact, taking hit after hit without reaction.

"What the fuck is she doing, Kace? She's not even moving!" Huxley shouts in my ear, panic evident in his voice as he shouts her name.

I don't answer him though. I can't. I'm still trying to work it all out for myself.

Red backs off, a little out of breath where she's put so much energy into her shots and looks to Cam standing off at the side, her face appears just as confused as I feel. Appearing unfazed, Cam simply nods for her to carry on. The crowd starts to amp up their volume, the shouts and cheers deafening.

The red head –leaving herself completely unguarded- saunters across the ring towards Kyla-Rose, -who still hasn't moved a muscle since the fight started- like an apex predator, Red gets right in Kyla's face, I see her mouth moving as she says something into Kyla's ear. Without a moment's hesitation, at whatever shit Red's spewed in her ear, Kyla-Rose rears her head back, smashing it forward into the red head's face.

The crowd thunders with roars as blood pours in rivulets from Red's nose. Kyla-Rose pulls her arm back, throwing her elbow into the red head's face, pounding into her, over and over, never letting up. As she pulls back her right fist, her left hits its target, never giving Red a chance to defend herself, let alone fight back.

Eventually, the red head manages to throw her arms up in an attempt to block the barbaric assault but Kyla-Rose just continues on in her savagery, Red takes so many hits it's impossible to even tell which hits are the ones that start to finish her. All she can do is try to cover her face and pray it's over quickly.

Kyla-Rose takes a step back, blood soaking her white clothes, her chest heaving rapidly, she backs off, but that doesn't mean it's over. The red head shouts something at Cam, who just shrugs at her words, the fight's aren't declared over until someone's out cold or taps out and as much of a beating as this girl's taken, I can already see the determination in her. This girl will never tap out.

The red head wipes her sweaty forearm across her bloodied face, gingerly moving forward again, spouting her mouth off as she goes, this girl might be able to win verbal wars but she's certainly not about to win any fist fights –not today anyway.

Kyla-Rose waits patiently, biding her time, letting the red head's words soak in until she gets within grappling distance. Throwing an arm around her chest, Kyla spins so that she's standing behind her and swiftly flips her to the ground onto her back. She wastes no time pouncing on top of her writhing form, her knee pressed firmly on the inside of Red's thigh while she presses her foot into the inside of the other.

Kyla-Rose pins the struggling red head's arms above her head with one hand before head butting the woman in the face again, this time her opponents' nose cracks. Her nose broken, twisted on her already bloody, swollen face, crimson flows down her. The woman screams in agony as Kyla uses her one free hand to land punch after punishing punch to her face. The red head's body now lifeless beneath her, knocked out cold but Kyla doesn't stop she continues to batter her knocked-out opponent. The crowd roars even louder, demanding more blood.

None of Cam's team steps in to stop her savage attack, Cam aggressively shouting off to one side at the bare chested guy from before. He casually hops up into the ring, effortlessly hauling Kyla-Rose away, her entire outfit now stained with red, she kicks and punches as she goes. As soon as she's clear of the ring, Cam's team jump in and attend to the bloodied mess of a woman left behind.

No one bats an eyelid at the bloody scene before them, all cheering and chanting as Kyla-Rose gets dragged away, still fighting to break free from the tattooed arms restraining her.

My mouth slightly agape at what I've just witnessed, I honestly don't know what to think. I'm both enthralled *and* turned on at the prospect of that dangerous woman. The way she moved through that fight was like she released the darkest part of herself, the part akin to mine, the part that's always there beneath the relatively calm exterior but is constantly screaming to be let out. A demonic presence begging to escape, scratching and clawing beneath the surface until it's freed, just waiting to take control.

My Wild Girl.

Huxley's voice bulldozes through my train of thought.

"I think I'm in love."

Just five short words.

Five, seemingly innocent words but one of which packs a punch.

Is that what this is, is it too early to tell? This can't just be lust, I've felt lust before, it's hot and fleeting, over before it's started, it's breakable and easily shatters under pressure. I don't think that's what this is.

But, love…

HUXLEY

Kacey and I grab a beer while we wait for Kyla-Rose. Now the fights are over for the night, a few people have cleared out while the rest stay on to party. The drinks flowing, the music pounding but I can hardly hear it over the residual ringing in my ears from watching Kyla-Rose's fight.

Honestly, I'm in awe. Everything about that girl captivates

my attention like no one ever has before her. She's sexy and smart, confident and funny, she says how she feels and has a wicked sense of humour. I *know* there's so much about her that we *don't* know but that's okay, there's a fair few things she doesn't know about us either. But we'll get there, hopefully tonight's chat will maybe help clear up a few things, Kacey and I have shit we want to discuss with her too.

I'm desperate to see Kyla-Rose, those big grey-green eyes filled with shadows, the way her long hair falls around her soft, heart shaped face when she laughs. And that laugh, *god,* it sends every last drop of blood in my veins surging straight to my dick when she makes that giggling sound.

Kyla-Rose's fight ended about half an hour ago. We talked on the phone this morning, it's honestly the only thing that got me out of bed, she asked us to hang around and said she'd find us, so that's what we'll do, honestly I'd wait here all night if it ended with me clapping eyes on her.

From my observations tonight, I'd say she's kind of a big deal… the crowd went wild for her. I've never seen an audience so in tune with one of its fighter's. Kyla-Rose let that red haired woman pummel her for at least a full minute without reacting. That's a really long fucking time to be beaten on without reaction. I honestly think I held my breath the entire time.

To see that man jump in and drag her away afterwards, the way everyone around the ring steered clear of them as he carried her off, no one else intervened, it was unusual, teams usually dive straight in at knockout but that's not what happened tonight. I'm beginning to realise there's a lot more to all of this than we can even begin to imagine.

Kacey thumps me in the side with his beer free fist, essentially drawing me back into the room. He nods gesturing for me to look up at something in front of us. My eyes snap up and I watch as a tall, suited, dark haired man approaches. The closer he gets the easier it is to see him in the dim light, I'm pretty sure this is the guy who picked Kyla-Rose up from our house.

"Boys," he greets with a firm nod, "Kyla-Rose is ready for you now. Follow me."

Trailing along behind *Lurch,* we silently follow as instructed. Not something either of us would usually do without question, considering our line of work but it seems we'll already do just about anything for this girl. He takes us through a door marked *staff only*, then through a maze of hallways, each piled high with crates of liquor and empty glass bottles until he stops in front of a large blue door and raps his knuckles against it. Without waiting for a response from the inside he clicks it open, pushing it wide.

There, sitting on top of the desk is Kyla-Rose.

"Hello, boys," she grins with a wiggle of her perfectly sculpted brows, "thank you, Frank," she says, dismissing the big guy, she locks eyes with him as she speaks and all I see there is respect, he exits, clicking the door closed behind him.

I doubt he's gone far, though.

Kyla's wearing a long sleeve white dress shirt, buttoned all the way up to the hollow at the base of her throat, a sleeveless black sweatshirt dress pulled over the top, the little white collar of her shirt poking out. Her long tattooed legs swinging back and forth over the edge of the mahogany desk, her feet in cherry red biker boots.

Her long silver hair hangs perfectly straight with a central part, tucked neatly away behind her ears which hold large black skull earrings studded through the lobes; they're large and just brush along her jawline. They're totally ridiculous and over the top but they suit her, I don't think anyone else could pull them off the way she does. Her eyes rimmed with black kohl and her perfect cupid's bow lips painted a deep cherry red that matches her boots. She looks fucking spectacular even with the small crescent shape bruise blossoming on the apple of her cheekbone and the two inked hands with split knuckles. She's still so fucking beautiful.

Kacey gravitates towards her, his feet moving him unconsciously, like she tugged on an invisible string. Her legs part automatically as he buries his hips between them, hitching her dress up slightly at the motion, forcing her to show even more of those long lean legs. He crowds her in, palms lying flat either side of her thighs, his head dips, his lips meeting hers in a hard dominating kiss, her head drops back as he brings a large hand up, gripping her jaw tightly in thick tattooed fingers.

He guides her where he wants her, devouring her mouth with his, a small whimper escaping her lips as he pushes himself back from the desk, a shit-eating grin upon his smug face, looking exactly like the cat that got the cream. Her thighs snap shut, her legs crossing at the ankles as she continues swinging her booted feet.

When Kyla-Rose gets her breathing under control, she slowly peels her gaze from Kacey's –who looks equally as tortured as her at having to stop at only a kiss. Her grey-green eyes connect with mine like a magnet snapping them into place and she smiles shyly.

"Hello, Huxley," she purrs, reaching out a hand for me.

I glance at Kacey from the corner of my eye but the big lummox just stands there staring at Kyla-Rose with that soppy as fuck grin slapped across his face. Kyla-Rose tilts her head slightly as I slowly stalk towards her, her eyes dragging up the length of my body as she takes in her fill. A single eyebrow raised, her plump, cherry red lips tilt up at the corners as I lace my fingers through hers.

"Hey," I whisper, suddenly finding it hard to find my voice, when I'm in Kyla's presence I turn back into that teenage boy who fancied his young, hot high school teacher.

She tugs me closer, my insides turning to liquid at her flush skin on my own. Turning her face away from me, she taps her cheek with a long, painted black fingernail, gesturing for me to plant my lips there. I lean into her, my already hardening crotch brushing against the outside of her thigh, the rough denim scratching over her supple skin. Such pale, delicate silk covering her body, I can't wait to see how prettily she bruises. I pucker my lips, pressing a feather light kiss to her bruised cheek, my lips lingering against her coconut scented skin just a little longer than necessary as I breathe her in.

Unlacing our entwined fingers I move back to where I was standing beside Kacey.

Kyla-Rose's eyes flick between the pair of us, "have a seat boys," she instructs waving her bloodied hand in the direction of the two large armchairs sitting opposite her.

That goddamn desk, all I can think about is throwing

her down on that fucking thing, stripping her bare and tongue fucking her sweet little cunt until she comes all over my tongue. I shake my head, running a hand through my hair, I've really got to stop thinking about her like that.

She eyes us both as we settle into our seats before she crosses her long legs, one knee over the other. Clasping her hands atop her knee she looks at us both with an intensity so strong it's hard not to squirm under her unyielding gaze.

"So, I need to talk to you both about something," she starts, swallowing hard she looks between the pair of us, "it might change how you look at me and how you feel about me and that's okay!" she quickly reassures, "but what I have to say needs to be said before we take this… *thing* any further."

We both frown at her, "nothing you tell us will make us feel differently about you," I growl, earning me a sympathetic smile, her twin dimples carving deeply into her cheeks.

"Well, let's not start making promises we can't keep, okay, Hux?" she laughs lightly but there's no humour to it, it's a nervous laugh, one that says her heart's contorted with the words she has to say.

She twists her fingers together in her lap, a nervous gesture, her eyes creasing as she looks down at them, thinking through what it is she wants to say. I want to go to her and give her comfort in whatever way I can, just hold her and protect her from the world, which is silly really because this woman is clearly not weak. Not in any sense of the word.

"My last name is Swallow," she announces boldly, "and so that makes me part of the Swallow family crime syndicate."

Her big grey-green eyes peer up at us from beneath her

black lashes, her gaze flicking between the two of us awaiting our recognition. We both know the name, we're not stupid, we've danced with this devil before, our best friend Nox has had some dealings with Elliot Swallow in the past. I didn't think *that* was what she was going to say though… I'm kinda intrigued.

"Okay," Kacey says, drawing the word out a little with a raised brow, "and…?"

"*And?*" she splutters, big doe eyes widening even more as she looks right at him, "that's all you have to say? You don't have questions?" her gaze darts between us, her perfect cupids-bow lips parting on a breath.

"Um, yeah? What did you want us to do? Scream? Flee and run, cower? We couldn't give a fuck what family you belong to, criminal, aristocratic or otherwise, Darlin'. We just want *you*, shit like that ain't gunna scare us off. And of course we'll have questions but none of them are really important right now," I shrug my shoulder casually as Kacey nods his agreement.

"Also, kinda makes the shit we need to say easier too," Kacey laughs casually.

"Why? What do you need to tell me?" she asks nervously, like anything we could tell her could top that.

I look to Kacey as he looks at me, both shrugging in unison. This is definitely not a difficult thing to explain now.

"I'm not just a mechanic, Sweetheart, and Huxley's not just '*working with computers*'," he does little quotations with his fingers when he says that last part which makes me snort. "You remember how I said we sometimes take on security work?"

"Yeah, you're like bouncers and stuff, right?" she frowns slightly.

"Yeah," he smiles at her, "but we *actually* run a private security firm and I guess you could say we *find* people," he cringes but gives her the information confidently.

"Sooo… you're like bounty hunters on the side too?" Kyla asks blankly and I curl my lips in between my teeth to stop my laugh as Kacey nods.

The bluntness of her question and lack of reaction or even expression has me wanting to burst out laughing. She's so unfazed by it all, it should probably scare me but it doesn't, if anything it makes me want to get inside of her head even more.

"So, you're not like scared off or whatever? I'm worried once you see the real me you'll be frightened off," she finishes quietly, sucking in a deep shuddery breath, her eyes once again dropping to her lap.

Showing us her insecurity is kind of a big thing. There's a trust there and I'm not about to fuck it up.

"So," I start, "I can't stand here and promise you that shit you may do, won't intimidate me or shock me sometimes. Just in the same way that I can't promise you that stuff that we do," I gesture with my hand between Kacey and I, "won't intimidate or shock *you* sometimes. This is new. All of *this,*" I gesture between the three of us, "is new. We'll get on each other's nerves sometimes, we'll upset each other, hell, we'll most likely piss each other off all the damn time, but don't think for one second that anything you do or say will ever scare the likes of us off," I smile honestly, meaning every single word.

"I know this is all kind of happening fast but I think it's more than obvious that I like you. Kacey is like a big puppy when it comes to you and I mean I'd like this thing to at least have a chance, regardless of our careers. Think you're willing to give this dynamic a go? I mean, sure it's unconventional but like, I'm game if you guys are?" I say the last part as a question as I look between the two of them.

This is the make or break moment now. I had to throw it out there, I'm already serious and I'm at an age where I just need to be honest about what I want. Are we all on the same page inside our heads? I think I already feel some connection and I don't want to ruin it all because I'm not honest straight off the bat.

"I think what Hux is trying to say is, we're not going anywhere unless you tell us otherwise and we'd both like to see where our relationship with you could go. What d'you think, Sweetheart, wanna give this thing a chance?"

We both glance at each other nervously while Kyla-Rose kicks her legs back and forth over the desk in thought. We've been open and honest by laying it all out there and although we hadn't discussed this in detail, we both know each other so well we can speak for one another easily. We've both been fucking around with relationships for so long, why -when we find someone we're both genuinely interested in- not at least see if we could give it a go? I don't want to fall out with my best friend over us both liking the same woman when we could just *share* the right woman instead. I want Kacey to be happy just as much as I want myself to be, so what have we got to lose other than this spitfire of a woman before us.

"Huh, soo… have I got like two boyfriends now or…?" she suddenly asks.

That sinfully seductive smile of hers back on her tempting

lips. That smile, *fuck,* it could literally kill a man where he stood.

I look to Kacey with raised brows and he beams back at me.

"If that's what you want, then most fucking definitely," Kacey growls making her giggle the lightest, most carefree, if not slightly unhinged sound, I've possibly ever heard.

It's fucking *beautiful.*

"And the thing with security, bounty hunting, all that stuff," she flaps a hand in the air like it means nothing, "that shit's all fine in my world, there shouldn't be any issues in that respect. I mean unless some idiot puts a bounty on me or my family's heads, that could definitely be a conflict of interest," she laughs. "It kind of makes sense now," she smiles at Kacey, "I guess that's why Big Man got all turned on by the possibility of having his brains blown out when we first met. All that adrenaline and excitement, huh?" she grins wide, shrugging a shoulder before looking to me. "Any other secrets boys or are we done here?" she asks casually, so casually I almost laugh.

"No, think that's it," Kacey says as she jumps off the desk to her booted feet.

"Want to think over what I've said?"

"Nope," we both reply in unison.

"Do you?" I ask her and she smiles, the corners of her lips prick up with amusement, the green in her eyes glittering to life eradicating the stormy grey.

"I think I'm the bigger baddie out of the three of us, so I'm confidently going with no, if you don't need to consider what I've told you then I'm good too." She shrugs again as she saunters towards us. "But just know, I'm fucking loopy, so I hope you're prepared for a wild fucking ride," she says, slipping between the two of us, her long tattooed fingers curling around the door handle. "Want to party with me boys or are you just gunna sit up here all night?" she tosses over her shoulder, skipping merrily out into the corridor, humming a cheery tune as she goes.

CHAPTER 11

KYLA-ROSE

I feel surprisingly light after getting that all off my chest. I feel like I can really move forward with Kacey now. I see something in him or rather *feel* something in him, which is also in me, I feel as though my monster and his are one and the same. Kacey carries this like, alpha-male, cocksure, big dick energy around with him but shutters it with his silence. Being around his friends he's the quiet type, he doesn't seem to show much in way of emotions, he's stoic, expressionless, almost looks disinterested but he's not that way with me, it's in the eyes. Those liquid gold eyes make my heart flutter and my toes curl and my demon claws at my chest to spring free, she can feel Kacey's monster and she wants it.

As weird as it might sound, besides our crazy seemingly on par, he makes me feel comfortable. I'd even go as far as to say he makes me feel *safe*. When he puts those giant Orangutan length arms around me, I feel like nothing in the world could ever hurt me.

I haven't wanted to date since I got out of juvie after everything that happened and I definitely haven't wanted to pursue a *relationship* -I shudder at the mere thought- but then I met Kacey and in a whirlwind of a week I have feelings for him that are definitely supposed to develop over a much longer time period than that, but somehow I think he feels just as strongly about me. Maybe if you just know you know? Don't ask me, I'm definitely no expert.

And then there's Huxley. Kacey's best friend, house mate, brother and now my what?

Second Boyfriend.

That's a damn weird thought in itself. When I casually threw out the boyfriend question I was joking, *well*, half-joking anyway but the way they both just sort of nodded in agreement like it was the most normal thing in the world to suddenly have a boyfriend after knowing them a week but not only that also getting a second one on top of the first is definitely not the most *normal* way to do things. *Unconventional.* I'm sure Charlie will find this whole thing hilarious. I mean, my family and I are certainly not normal or in the least bit conventional but still, two boyfriends *is* a little weird.

I won't even try and lie here because let's be honest, Huxley is fucking gorgeous, anyone can see that with those deep brown eyes that are as black as the nights sky. His short brown curls that I'm just dying to run my fingers through, his eyebrow piercing and cocksure smile. And *fuck me,* that body, he's got this ripped, athletic, swimmers body, he's tall and lean, not built like a brick shithouse like Kacey, but he's got broad shoulders, ripped arms, shredded abs and strong thighs. All of that caramel coloured skin wrapped around those flexing muscles quite literally makes my greedy mouth water, I'm just aching to run my tongue over his inked eight-pack. Not that I only like him for his looks. I've been speaking to him all goddamn week and he constantly has me crying tears of laughter. He's funny and kind and really fucking perceptive too.

So that's the crux of it, isn't it? That I spend nine fucking years not in a relationship, not dating and not being the least bit interested in anyone. Only to have two seemingly perfect guys, turn up all at once. And worse than that, they turn up together, complete and utter opposites of one another and my greedy cunt can't even begin to get a grip on herself. Imagine me in a relationship?

How in the fuck am I gunna make this shit work?

Kacey's standing at one of the bars deep in conversation with Eli, I only know that because Elijah has this cute little crease that forms between his blonde eyebrows and one always twitches when he's trying hard to focus on something, just like he's doing now. Kacey just nods along at whatever he's saying but they're both relaxed and drinking beer quite comfortably together so that makes me feel a bit better.

You see, I come from a family of *all* men and well, they're really rather *protective* of me, even though I'm more than capable of looking after myself, but god knows they won't be told. There's my dad, Uncle Dee and my four cousins, Jacob, Charlie, Cam and Eli and then there's me, just little old me who is treated like their fragile treasure, the only girl in the entire family. The boys used to absolutely terrorise any male I was even friends with at school, so forget about dating. Not that I was ever interested in anyone except *him* anyway, but that's a shit storm to dissect another day.

Charlie made himself scarce as soon as I brought my boys out, *see*, I'm doing it already*, my* boys, boys, *plural*, I scoff at myself and roll my eyes, *greedy bitch.* Charlie's not too good around strangers, I don't doubt he's got eyes on me though, I can practically feel them burning into me, he'll be stalking in the shadows close by I'm sure of it.

Cam's in his office with Uncle Dee. I was summoned earlier but I think Dee's overly concerned about me, sure, I got that weird fucking note and I won't lie, it did unsettle me a little but as far as I'm aware all's been quiet on that front since, so maybe it was just some kind of weird joke. Only time will tell.

"Dance with me," Huxley's voice whispers in my ear, his hot breath fanning my hair across my face.

A shiver works its way up my spine at the closeness of him, he's not physically touching me anywhere but I can *feel* him *everywhere.* My soul reacts to him like we're familiars, my body heats, my skin tingles as my chest fills with warmth. Like we're already known to one another, but I don't know how that can be when I've never met him before last weekend.

I look over to Kacey who instantly locks those pretty gold eyes with me, a small smile curves his lips as he gives a single nod of his head, as if he already knows exactly what I'm asking, *is this okay?*

"He's okay with this, if you are," my breathing hitches,

my heartrate erratic, I swear it's beating faster than that of a hummingbird, shortening my life with every thump it makes. "You're *ours,*" he breathes into my ear, my whole body trembling with awareness.

Placing one large hand on my hip, the heat from his long fingers sets my entire body aflame like he's thrown a match and I'm the accelerant. My mouth suddenly dry, I lick my red painted lips to try and regain some moisture.

Huxley's turns me in the direction of the mass of writhing bodies, the bass music heavy and slightly tinny from the old speakers, he weaves me through the crowd, guiding me from behind, his hands on my hips, moving us until we hit the centre of the floor.

By this point in the night no one takes any notice of me now, all too far gone with the weed they've smoked and the booze they've drunk, only paying attention to the people they're dancing with or grinding on, ensuring they don't leave here alone tonight.

Huxley starts to move with the beat, it's not really dance music, it's more like the symphony to a pre-fuck ritual, heavy, grinding and relentless. Nevertheless, Huxley moves me with him, his long fingers firmly curled around my hips, guiding my body to flow with his. Arching back into him, my arse pressed firmly against his growing erection that neither of us comments on, we just let the music flow through us like the waves of the ocean.

My head lolls back onto his hard shoulder, my eyes slipping closed, his hands never straying from my hips. His fingertips dig deeper into my flesh with a delicious sort of pinch. *I want more.*

I bring my arm up, wrapping my fingers around the back of his neck, my black fingernails catching on the piercing there. I move with him, applying light pressure to his neck, bringing his head down towards me until his lips just brush the side of my throat.

I've only ever danced like this with one other guy before. The hooded man from *The Pit.* Recognition suddenly hits me, my body stiffens, my eyes popping open as I look up at his handsome face.

"This isn't the first time we've danced together," I whisper, my voice breathy and wanton, giving away just exactly how turned on I am.

"You remember," he smiles down at me, his hand sliding around me, drawing me back into him, his long fingers splaying over my lower belly.

"You knew all this time?" I question gently.

"No," he chuckles, "but I had a suspicion. When you were at my house, you seemed too familiar and I couldn't work out how I might know you, then it clicked. But I didn't say anything, what would I say? Nothing happened between us, it's irrelevant," he shrugs one shoulder with that same reassuring smile.

This smile says I'm safe in his arms, this smile tells me he wanted me to figure it out on my own. That two years ago he was the man in a dank underground rave that I almost willingly gave myself to, for the first time in my adult life, a man I chose to have sex with and Charlie interrupted me with a goddamn SOS torture text message. Oh, how life seems to be coming full circle.

"I want you," Huxley admits in a breathy moan, like he didn't want to make that honest admission but just couldn't stop the words slipping free.

But I can't form my own. At this point it's information overload and all I can do is groan as he grinds his hard length into the bottom of my spine. I thrust myself back into him, arching my back and pressing my shoulder blades into his solid chest. My nails digging into the soft skin of his neck as I flick the cool metal bar there, his soft lips feather over the soft skin of my throat before fully connecting with the point between my neck and shoulder. It's only contact over my clothes but I feel it penetrate my skin like a bullet, I breathe out a slow heavy sigh, silently begging for more.

One of his hands snakes up my side, fingertips running over my ribs. His thick arm bands around my waist, dragging me back into him and gripping me tightly against his rock hard body. His lips glide over my throat, kissing and sucking as he works me over with his hot mouth, making my eyes shamelessly slip closed once again. Sweeping my hair over my shoulder he sucks on that sweet spot behind my ear and I melt, like ice cream on sun-kissed concrete in the heat of a summer's day.

With my eyes still closed, I don't see anyone approach us until I feel another pair of large hands run over my already trembling body, it's hot as hell in this warehouse and I'm in long fucking sleeves but a cold shiver rattles through me, goosebumps sprouting all over my skin.

I draw my eyes open to slits as a familiar hulking body presses me in from the front. Familiar eyes stare back at me with fire in them, lustful flames flickering to life in his gold irises. I'm deliciously crushed between two perfect specimens, two hard bodies grinding up against me, Kacey's thick thigh slips between my own, the heat of my core rubbing against the soft fabric of his sweatpants.

Kacey pulls me towards him and I gasp as he flips me around like a rag doll, his chest plastered to my back, my breasts brushing against Huxley's chest. Kacey dips his head down, pressing his lips against the shell of my ear as my eyes lock with the coal coloured ones before me.

"Does he get you hot, wild girl?" Kacey asks me, his new nickname for me sending liquid heat straight to my already flooded core.

I nod my head silently, never taking my eyes from Huxley's, my chest heaving with rapid breaths. Kacey nips at my earlobe, roughly pulling it between his teeth.

"Do you want him to touch you?" Big Man's husky voice penetrates through my skull, his naughty words flooding my insides, I can't help the groan that slips past my lips.

Kacey's big hand massages my breast over my clothes, his thumb focusing on my sensitive nipple, moving it in slow circles until it's so hard it's almost painful. His thick fingers massage me, the black lace of my bra rough against my sensitive skin.

Huxley's hands start to roam over me at the same time, his palms running down my arms, he takes my wrists, lifting my hands to lie flat against his chest. Leaning in he presses his heavenly lips to mine, electricity pulses through me as his pierced tongue flicks over the seam of my lips making them part for him on a groan. My fists clenching at the fabric of his t-shirt, holding him to me like my life depends on it. Time stops, the room falling away, the crowd evaporates as Huxley kisses me, his kiss sucking the life from me and replacing it with his own essence, all I want, all I feel is him.

"I need more," I choke out breathlessly between kisses.

Kacey steps away from my back, leaving a cold space where his big body was, my head snaps in his direction at the loss of contact. I look over my shoulder as he winks with a smirk, backing away from us, disappearing into the crowd.

Before I can even think about it, Huxley's attention is back on me. His lips crush mine, our tongues dancing and teeth clashing, the cool metal of his piercing sliding against my tongue, only making me kiss him harder. I'm digging my nails into his shoulders so hard it's like I'm subconsciously trying to claw my way beneath his smooth, dark skin. I gasp into his mouth as his teeth nip my bottom lip, his fingers tangling in my hair whilst the other gropes my backside, his large hands tucking me firmly into his body.

Huxley softens the kiss, his hands less demanding as he gently pulls back, resting his forehead against my own, our breaths mingling, both of our chests heaving.

"Hux?" I whisper, as I try desperately to get a grip on reality.

"Mmm?"

"What're we doing?" I ask, my stomach suddenly drops with thoughts of upsetting Kacey, *but* he was here, he encouraged it, so it's gotta be fine, right?

We're together, they're with me, *both* of them, *this* is the new normal. I think.

My heart twists painfully inside my chest, phantom hands

wrapping around the fragile organ and squeezing the life from it. Nothing's been discussed, we've not talked about how this is going to work, does it warrant a discussion, is it just anything goes? Now my heart's pounding for a completely different reason. Pure panic.

"You're thinking about it too much, this is fine, you already mean everything to Kacey and I'm starting to think you could mean the same for me," he whispers.

As though reading my mind, Huxley cups my face, his forehead still resting against my own, his ink coloured eyes bore into me, his unyielding raven gaze stripping me bare, until he's speaking directly to my raw, bloodied soul.

"If you don't want this, if it's moving too fast, we can stop, just say the word, Darlin', you're in control," Huxley tells me so sincerely all air escapes my lungs, leaving them shrivelled like overripe grapes left unpicked on the vine, wilting in the hot sun.

"I like you," I tell him, a small smile perking up the corners of his mouth, "both of you," I breathe, closing my eyes.

"Look at me," Huxley demands, my eyes slowly peeling open as he traces the line of my jaw with his nose, breathing me in and marking me with his short stubble as his cheek rubs against my own. "You're so fucking beautiful, Kyla-Rose," he breathes, my insides take flight until I'm weightless, floating on a cloud, drifting off into eternal bliss, "you deserve two men who will worship you like the goddess you are."

And that's when I die. His words completely shatter my soul, forcing the tiny pieces to float off into the skies, leaving my boneless body behind. Well, not *literally*, but that's what it feels like.

"You don't have to declare feelings because you feel like you should, Darlin'. This is all new and everyone feels things at a different rate. There's no pressure on you to say or do things as quickly as us," Huxley offers, but I don't need time to decide, my heart, *the little traitor*, speaks the words for me.

"I don't need to think about it, I already know I want you both, to try. To see where things go," I breathe anxiously.

My eyes flicking between his coal coloured ones, as deep and dark as thunder clouds. He presses the lightest of kisses against my lips, pulling back with a smile.

"You honestly have no fucking idea how perfect you are, do you," he murmurs more to himself than to me but his words make my breath catch all the same.

Huxley takes a step back, separating our body's and laces his fingers through mine, leading us back through the crowd, back to where Kacey, Eli and now, Cam, are all standing.

"Well, that was quite the show," Eli mumbles in my ear and I swat at his chest.

"Fuck off, *Elijah*," I hiss making his chest rumble with laughter.

"So, there's two now?" Cam asks, which is more words than he usually utters in the presence of company.

So I guess something I've done has finally shocked him enough to speak, although, of all the things I've done, I think having two boyfriends is possibly the most tame.

I look to Kacey, who has that soppy grin I love so much plastered on his handsome face, he beams at me and Huxley.

"Yeah, she has the two of us," Kacey answers for me and I swear I've never seen anyone look happier.

I can feel my cheeks heat but I suppress myself into business mode, just so I don't have to listen to Eli tease me about it for the next fifty fucking years.

A short while later, we're all perched on some low scaffolding used for the stands, I'm perched between Eli and Huxley, the latter of which has his hand high on my thigh, his fingers massaging little circles on the inside of it. Kacey and Cam –after Cam filled himself with a shit-ton of cheap beer- are laughing and joking together like they're long lost brothers. It does funny things to my heart if I'm honest, Cam never really takes to anyone but maybe he too see's something in Kacey that makes him feel like he isn't really a stranger.

Eli and Huxley are easily bantering back and forth about American ice-hockey teams while I sit comfortably and watch the still partying hordes. This is my favourite part of the night, when it's started to die down a little, just enough that you can breathe a little easier and don't have to scour the room for a sliver of space.

I look over into the shadows, I sent Frank home a little while ago so he's not here now but I spot a few members of Gremlin's team, they won't leave until I'm home safely. My eyes still scanning the shadows for Charlie, they instead land on a pair of bright blue ones on the opposite side of the room, staring straight back at me. My stomach drops, my blood running cold. I feel every muscle in my body tense up as a single bead of sweat races down my spine, my bones locking into place.

This cannot be happening.

This isn't *happening.*

Close your eyes Lala, it's in your head.

I squeeze my eyes shut tight, my hands trembling as I drag in a painful breath.

Those blue eyes stared into yours while he held you down and let those men do those heinous things to you. You screamed at him to help you and he did nothing but force his hand over your mouth. He might not have touched you like they did but he didn't help you either, did he?

My ears buzz as I force myself to stumble up to my unsteady feet, I'm somewhat conscious that someone tries to speak to me, Huxley's hand slips from my trembling thigh but I can't focus on that right now. In fact, I can't seem to focus on anything right now but the single pair of piercing blue eyes still locked on me from across the room.

And then in the blink of an eye, my fear is replaced with rage. Pure, raw, unfiltered fury floods through my veins, sending my heart rattling around inside my quaking chest, like a rocket ship preparing for take-off, my whole body vibrates. My fists curl and uncurl as I dig my nails so deep into my palms that little beads of blood swell to the surface. Rubble abruptly steps up in front of me, blocking my view of the room with his large body.

His lips move as he speaks to me, a deep set scowl marring his young face but I can't hear his words. In one swift movement, my fingers wrap around the grip of the revolver in his underarm holster, I thrust it free and move, gliding as fluidly as a ballerina, I drift across the crowded room.

Unconsciously shoving my way between the grinding

bodies, using my elbows like oars of a rowing boat, I force myself through the sea of sweaty dancers as I seek out my target. I'm vaguely aware of screams in the background as people start to move out of my way, scattering like scavenging rats disturbed in a seedy alleyway. As I reach the middle of the crowd, the people left dancing are still oblivious that anything's happening around them. I still. Closing my eyes I take a long deep breath. Sound starts to filter back into me and then my eyes snap open.

My head whips round, taking in all of the terrified faces surrounding me, I watch my security team pushing people away from me as I spin around and around on the spot, searching. He has to have gone outside.

Find him!

I sprint, full pelt, running as fast as my legs will carry me towards the one and only entry and exit door. I push the two heavyweight security guys out of my way, bursting free into the cold night air. The wind attacks my hot skin, feeling like a thousand tiny paper cuts, cutting me so sharply that I sting all over. Like a starving wolf following a scent, I rush forward, people scattering out of my way as I fly through them, my head snapping erratically in every direction as I try to relocate my prey.

He has no shame. He came here knowing who you are and that you would be here, he didn't hide, he was bold, he isn't *afraid of you.*

I start to see his slimy face form on every person around me.

Everyone looks the fucking same!

I spin around and around trying to find my target.

He was here! He was fucking here!

He can't have gotten far, he must still be here somewhere, there's no fucking way he could've gotten away from me that quickly.

I shove my way through the haphazardly parked cars, slamming peoples open doors shut as I rush past. Running straight for the burnt down warehouse, the one that's beyond repair, the one that *I* destroyed, it would make the most sense, to hide in there. It's dark and out of the way.

No one will hear his screams if you find him in there.

My psyche whispers rotten things, the torturous revenge ideas rush through me, burning my brain and pushing me to move faster.

My heavy boots pounding against the wet concrete, the rain has stopped now but I can sense another storm brewing, *unless that storm's in me?* I silently slip inside the abandoned warehouse, skirting the edge of the building, keeping to the shadows as I hunt. I try to slow my breathing until I'm sure I'm silent enough to move out into the open space but I can't, there's too much adrenaline coursing through my panicked veins. In my hysteria to get to my target I've completely abandoned all of my meticulous hours of training, to help me deal with a situation exactly like this. Instead I'm fumbling around in the dark on unsteady feet like a complete amateur.

Stupid, stupid, Lala!

I stumble into the wide open space, engulfed in pitch dark, my eyes still not adjusting to the complete absence of light, not even the moon is lighting my path tonight, smothered by thick rain clouds, it appears even that has given up on me.

I trip over the cracked concrete, coming down hard onto my bare knees, I pick myself back up before falling again and again. I hit the ground so hard this time, my knees screaming in agony, I can't get back up, I can't see, all I can hear is the fuzzy thudding of my own heartbeat roaring inside my ears. I press my forehead against the cold concrete to try and catch my breath.

He held you down while you screamed. He watched while they attacked you. He let them hurt you for their own pleasure. He watched you cry. You were helpless, *less than helpless. You were nothing. They made you* nothing. *Vengeance, Kyla-Rose. You must seek revenge.*

But you can't, can you? You're too weak, look at you, crawling around in the filth.

"No, no, no," I tremble, slamming my forehead into the concrete, "leave me alone," I whisper into the dark but the voices don't stop coming.

Damaged.

Used.

Pathetic.

Dirty.

"NO!" I scream as I bash my head into the floor again, I see stars for a moment but it's still not enough.

Broken.

Trash.

Worthless.

The voices hiss into my ears as hot blood pools beneath my face.

I release the gun, throwing it away from me, placing both palms flat against the concrete, the skin of my knees grazing as

I rock myself on the rough concrete.

"No, no, no, no, no," for every no, I slam my head into the concrete, harder and harder just trying to feel or to not feel, I don't even know anymore.

But I can't feel anything. I'm weak. Numb. Broken. Sad. *Dirty.*

A large hand wraps around my face, cupping my bleeding forehead, the pressure making me scream, strong arms band my hands behind the small of my back, pulling me into them, my arse hitting thick thighs as someone pulls me into their lap, their other hand still putting pressure on my wet forehead.

I can't see in the dark and I scream again.

I scream and fight until I can't breathe anymore, thrashing my body in every direction as my head pounds and my face pulses, until the entire world just falls away. Soft voices whisper in my ears but I'm too far gone to hear their words, a sob rips free from my throat, clawing it raw as I tremble violently, from the cold, blood loss, shock, *fear.*

"Take a deep breath," I hear someone say, their words echoing around inside my mangled brain but I can't, I'm shaking too hard for my lungs to work.

Just as I feel I'm about to pass out, a familiar scent fills my nostrils.

"CHARLIE!" I scream as loud as I can.

I don't know how loud I am or if I'm even screaming at all because I can't hear anything properly. My head aching, my pulse thumping in the wound on my forehead, blood gushing violently down my face, my thoughts fuzzy and dark. Charlie's rough hands wrap around my cheeks and he speaks to me so softly, it's like his soul is speaking directly to mine.

"Open your eyes, Lala. Look at me, Rose," he tells me and I do.

I strain my heavy eyelids open through the pain, until all I can see are his emerald orbs glowing under torchlight.

"They're coming for me, Charl, don't let them touch me again," I sob my plea, my words sounding shattered and disjointed.

"No one's coming for you," Charlie murmurs, his gruff rumble echoing around my brain.

I'm still sitting, cradled in someone's lap but It's like I'm not really here, I'm not really anywhere at all.

"They are, Charl, I saw him, you have to get him, Charlie, *please*," I beg.

"She's most definitely going to have a concussion, she could have internal damage, there could be bleeding on the brain, swelling, anything," I hear someone say, their words broken and far away as my eye lids start to droop.

God, I'm tired.

"He was here, Charlie, please, don't let them touch me," I attempt to say but my tongue feels heavy in my mouth, my eyes falling shut, the world drifting away from me.

The last thing I feel before I submit to the darkness is a pair of strong hands banded around my broken body, like they're trying to hold me together. But the thing is, you can't fix what's already broken.

And I, I'm already broken beyond repair.

CHAPTER 12

KYLA-ROSE

TWO WEEKS LATER

"I am fucking fine! Stop fussing," I snap, "stop prodding me. I swear to god, so help me, I will skin you alive. I. Am. *Fine*!" I growl impatiently. "Just get these fucking stitches out of my goddamn skull before I get irritated," I snarl and Jacob scowls.

"You are not fucking fine, bossy boots, you have a head injury, dipshit, so stop being so fucking aggressive. I'm trying to fucking help you," Jacob snaps back, his anger palpable but his practised Doctor hands perfectly steady as he carefully snips and pulls the dark stiches free from my forehead.

"I *had* a head injury," I shrug, "concussion is so lame, it's literally nothing and I am not bossy, you're just an arse," I huff, breathing through my nose like a raging bull, seems appropriate really, all I tend to see is red lately.

Jacob pulls back from me, his green eyes staring me down from beneath his thick eyelashes.

"Concussion *is* serious, especially when you had a case as severe as yours, now, just shut the fuck up and let me get on with it. The quicker you sit still the quicker I can release you back into the wild, okay you little beast?"

I try hard to hide my smirk but it's near impossible as a bubble of laughter escapes my throat, I wipe the tears from under my eyes with my index fingers.

G*od, I need a manicure.*

"Little beast?" I laugh, never has an insult felt so perfect before.

Jacob slaps his frustrated hands against his thighs, dropping his head back with a groan.

"You *would* take that as a compliment wouldn't you, you're a pain in my arse you heathen," Jacob growls, "please can we just get on with this? I've only got a few more to go," he whinges, which really only makes me laugh harder.

I'm sitting up in bed, Brute and Angel beside me, their huge bodies lying the length of it and hogging all of the blankets. Jacob's perched himself on my other side while he tries to remove my stitches, *tries* being the operative word. I fucked my head up pretty bad and I'm gunna have some whack scar like that boy wizard with a lightning bolt on his forehead, but shit happens, scars aren't that much of a big deal, I mean I have enough of them already, what's one more?

"Okay, *okay*," I stifle my giggles and close my eyes.

Tilting my head in the direction Jacob moves it. The little tweezers and silver scissors cold against my flush skin as he works, my nails digging into my thighs, it doesn't *hurt*, it just stings a bit and tugs, it feels fucking weird. I hate it.

"How's our patient today?" Huxley sings, waltzing into the room like he owns the place, which to be honest is sorta nice.

He and Kacey haven't slept in their own house even *once* since I had my little *episode* -as Jacob keeps referring to it- I internally roll my eyes at that.

Huxley, Kacey and I have been camped out in the penthouse for the last two weeks and for a new relationship it should probably have been a bit *weird*? Intense? I don't know how these things are supposed to be, anyway, it was anything but, you would have thought the two of them had lived here forever. Plus, being sandwiched between the two of them every night has done wonders for my usually terrifying sleep patterns, I mean, I've actually slept, *without* sleeping pills. I'm still not sleeping for long, but it's much better.

Having their warmth pressed up against my back and curled into my front is like being cocooned in the sexiest motherfucking chrysalis there ever was. *Unfortunately,* I did not emerge from it this morning like a beautiful butterfly, rather, I woke up like a pissed off, angry squirrel who's missing tufts of fur and just found out his nut stash has been discovered by another irritable rodent-type creature. Oh and is also in desperate fucking need of a trip to the salon.

Angel growls lowly as Jacob continues to fiddle with my head and I place my hand gently on top of her to settle her down. I run what's left of my nails up and down her smooth snout, she's getting used to the two boys coming and going now, they're not her favourite pair but she's not actively trying to eat them anymore, so I call that a win. She's just sensitive and doesn't particularly *like* change.

"I am not a fucking patient!" I snap aggressively.

Can you tell I'm fed up of being stuck in the house?

"Oh, Darlin', you so are, just enjoy it while it lasts," he laughs, placing a vase of sunflowers on my bedside table, adding to the already ridiculous collection.

Huxley's bought me a vase full of flowers every single day since I lost my shit and thought it a good idea to crack my own skull open, I'm seriously lucky I didn't do any proper damage.

"You are on a ban," I hiss through my teeth as Jacob pulls at a stitch particularly hard.

I open my eyes to glare at him but he ignores me, I see the slight tilt to his lips though, he's fucking enjoying this.

I flick my gaze over to the cocky delinquent and narrow my eyes on him leaning against the dresser, his smooth caramel skin, rippling over the muscles in his forearms as he crosses them over his deliciously broad chest.

Yum.

"A *ban*?" Huxley echoes with an amused smirk, like that's not the most annoying but sexiest thing in the world, "and what, *pray tell,* sort of ban would that be exactly?" he teases, his pierced eyebrow arched and a shit-eating grin slapped on his smug face.

I can't order a sex ban because there would have had to have been sex previously and unfortunately for me, there hasn't.

Yet.

"An everything ban," I snap back, "no communicating with me at all for the rest of the fucking year, you're all irritating me to fuck," I frown, causing the skin on my face to pull, "ow!" I yell in Jacob's face and he smirks.

Told you he was enjoying this.

"Stop moving, brat," he tuts with that evil gleam in his eye.

I scowl even harder at him, glaring into those emeralds like I could make his head explode, splattering brain matter over the walls, using nothing but my thoughts.

"I can live with that, I mean, it's already December there's not much of the year left to be fair," Huxley shrugs, his smirk getting impossibly wider.

I narrow my eyes on him until they're nothing more than slits, using my finger to slowly slide it across my throat, indicating exactly what I'll do to him if he isn't careful. Huxley's head rolls back with a bark of laughter.

Honestly, boys.

Kacey's hulking frame appears, leaning in the doorjamb, his posture mimicking that of his friend's, one corner of his mouth kicks up when he sees the murderous look on my face.

"What did you do to upset her now?" Kacey asks with a small smile, directing his line of sight over to his best friend.

"Me? Nothing," Huxley slaps a splayed palm over his heart, as if he's personally offended at such a wild accusation, like he wouldn't ever dream of doing such a thing.

I scoff with a heavy roll of my eyes before deciding to change tactics.

"They're being mean to me," I pout heavily at Kacey, jutting my bottom lip out dramatically and he smiles.

That fucking smile, man, it gets me every goddamn time. My knickers are fucking drenched in zero-point-two seconds, which feels particularly uncomfortable, what with my cousin currently plucking shit out of my face and all.

“Oh, Sweetheart,” Kacey pouts back before throwing a wild wink in my direction, forcing a saucy smile to my face.

“Done,” Jacob declares aggressively, standing from the bed, he takes the little silver kidney dish with my bloody stiches in it away as he stands.

I shove the covers aside, jumping to my feet, stretching my arms high above my head before I start crossing the room towards my bathroom.

“Err, what d’you think you’re doing?” he frowns, blocking my path and towering over me.

“Err,” I mimic, making him frown harder, “taking a shower, now that I’m allowed to get my face wet, I really need to wash my hair,” dry shampoo is a god send but it gets all itchy after a couple of days, there’s nothing like a good hair wash to make you feel better.

“Okay, shower, but then straight back into bed, you’re not going anywhere,” he instructs as I step around him.

I ignore his words because I am so totally getting the fuck out of here.

“Everyone knows not to take direct orders from you for another two weeks so don’t even think about fucking trying anything, Kyla-Rose.”

I almost growl but force myself to keep walking into the en-suite, if I react, he’ll know I’m gunna try to escape and I don’t wanna give the game away this early on.

I step into the warm water, letting the gentle rainfall wash over my slightly aching face, using a pair of exfoliating gloves,

I lather up my body with coconut soap and start the meticulous task of shampooing and conditioning my hair until my naturally white blonde strands are clean and shiny, just begging to be re-toned back to that shimmery grey-silver I like so much. Luckily the salon I frequent always makes an appointment available for me whenever I call.

As I step out of the little steam produced by the warm water, Kacey's there waiting with a big fluffy towel. I step into it, letting him wrap me up as he presses a gentle kiss to my new scar and smiles down at me.

"What are your plans today, you little escape artist?" he murmurs and I pull away from him, trying to hide my frown.

I bet Jacob's told them not to let me out of their sight and that's fine but I swear to god, I will scale this motherfucking building to get out of here today if I have to, I'm not fucking around. I need to breathe.

I move over to the twin sinks and pick up my green toothbrush, scrubbing my teeth as Kacey's heavy gaze bores into me. I try not to look because there is something I most certainly am *not* good at and that's lying. If I meet his eyes he'll know what I'm planning instantly and then I'll be really fucked.

"I can see your devious mind working away beneath those pretty eyes," he all but purrs at me.

I feel my irritation spike.

I spit and wash my face, dabbing my chin dry on a hand towel as my eyes meet Kacey's gold ones in the mirror.

"I want to get my nails and hair done and I want a wax and I want an espresso, in a coffee shop, in a proper glass, in a public place, where other strangers are happily milling about. I'm not going to go back to work," *today* anyway. "I'm not asking you, I'm telling you. That's my plan, I will call Frank, he can take me to my appointments which I have *already* made, he can wait for me outside and then and *only* then will I be coming home," I fold my arms across my towel covered chest and raise a brow.

Kacey narrows his eyes on me before a barrel of laughter spills out of him, curling in on himself he clutches his ribs with laughter, his entire body shaking with mirth.

Fucker.

"You are so demanding," he carries on laughing and I can feel my trigger fingers flexing, "good luck getting to any of those appointments, you're on a total fucking lockdown, you won't even get down the hall. Cam's watching your entryway like a hellhound."

I huff and wrinkle my nose, the new skin on my head tightening. That's going to be a little bitch to fully heal, I can already tell.

I push past him back into my bedroom. Huxley lying where I was a short while ago, he's got both dogs lying across him as he strokes their smooth fur.

"*Traitors,*" I spit in their direction but only Angel reacts, peeling her eyes open to glare at me before yawning heavily and closing her eyes again.

Brute on the other hand, the big lummox is lying on his back in submission while Huxley rubs his big pink belly.

"Kyla-Rose thinks she's going to the salon," Kacey tells Huxley, talking about me like I'm not even here, which just adds further to my annoyance.

"I am."

I step into my walk-in, grabbing some black, ripped skinny jeans and an off the shoulder black sweatshirt. I throw my wet hair up into a messy pile on top of my head using a red silk scrunchie and pull heeled boots with little silver studs, onto my socked feet. I walk out into the bedroom, opening the top drawer to my dresser where Kacey is now leaning himself; I thoroughly ignore him. Pulling out my leather underarm holster I slip my arms through it, filling both sides of it with loaded revolvers, neither of my boys even bat an eyelid.

I stride through the open door, neither one of them tries to stop me as I march my way out into the entrance hall.

"No." Cam's deep voice rumbles, eyeing my weaponry from his position against the wall.

"Move," I say firmly as I slip my arms through the sleeves of my leather jacket, I'm getting out of here even if I have to fucking shoot him to do so.

"Kyla-Rose," Cam growls but I ignore him and press the button for my private elevator.

The doors open and I step inside, no one even tries to stop me. *Smart move on their part,* I'm feeling rather *twitchy* today, in case you hadn't noticed.

The elevator doors slide open as I step out into the underground parking lot, where I'm instantly met with what can only be described as an entire fucking army.

Charlie is standing front and centre, his arms folded across his bare chest -it's the middle of fucking winter and the boy still doesn't know how to find a shirt- Gremlin and Rubble stand either side of him, flanking his position and a dozen other guys on our security team are fanned out behind them in a sort of arrowhead formation. I roll my eyes heavily and move towards the cars.

"Where the fuck do you think you're going?" Eli asks me casually, he's leaning his tall body against the rear passenger side of Franks SUV with a shit-eating smirk on his face.

"If you must know, cousin dearest," I bat my lashes at him with a saccharine smile. "I want to get my cunt waxed," I deadpan with a cock of my head and a raised brow, the fake smile nowhere to be found as I fold my arms across my chest and cross my feet at the ankles.

"Tough shit. You're not going anywhere," he says calmly, making me want to throat punch him, I glare at him as I stalk over and poke him with a finger to the chest.

"Get out of my fucking way, I have shit to fucking do today," I snarl getting in his face, I know they're trying to look out for me but this is ridiculous.

"No. You've got a head injury, you need to take it easy, you haven't been cleared by the Doc."

I snort a laugh, *the Doc*, in question, is fucking Jacob, he wouldn't clear me as fit for purpose for an entire fucking year if he thought he could get away with it.

"I'm going to get my claws redone. I'm not going into battle, get out of my fucking way Elijah or I swear to god I will drop you where you stand."

What can I say? I'm feeling extra stabby today.

We have an intense stand-off for a moment where we both glare at each other and try not to blink, I almost want to laugh at the ridiculousness of it but I don't, you know, in case I accidently blink first or something, 'cause that would really suck.

"Fucking fine!" Eli shouts exasperatedly, throwing his hands up into the air, "fine! You do whatever the fuck you want, like fucking always! Don't mind the people who actually give a shit about you!"

"This is a little dramatic for only wanting to go to a salon isn't it?" I ask with a yawn.

It's a fake yawn but he doesn't need to know that.

"You're being a brat."

"Elijah, get out of the way," I shove Eli to the side with my shoulder and pause with my hand on the door handle, glancing back over my shoulder. "Boys, it's been real, let's all do this again real soon," I toss over my shoulder with a smirk before thrusting the door open.

"Hello, Kyla-Rose," My Uncle Dee's voice filters through to me from the other side of the back seat.

"Oh, for fuck's sake," I groan, hearing Charlie chuckle behind me, just he wait until I get my hands around his fat neck later, I'm going to murder him.

"Hello, Uncle," I return with a sickly sweet fake smile.

"Get in the car, Kyla-Rose," he instructs with a sigh and my shoulders slump as I begrudgingly get in the backseat beside him.

"Boss," Frank greets me from the driver's seat and I frown.

"Are you taking me to my appointments?" I ask with -what I'm well aware is- a childish attitude.

"As soon as Mr Swallow has said what he needs to say, I'm authorised to do just that."

The way he says authorised, like *I'm* not his boss, really grates me. I hold my tongue as I grit my teeth, taking calming breaths in through my nose. Frank starts to pull away and I buckle my seatbelt, Uncle Dee turns to face me with a deep frown on his slightly wrinkled face, he looks great for a man in his late fifties, the definition of a silver fox if I ever saw one.

"Kyla-Rose, I'm not trying to patronise you but you had an episode and hurt yourself not more than a fortnight ago and less than twenty-five minutes after having your stiches removed you're attempting to go gallivanting off around the city. The boys are worried about you, your security team is worried about you," I narrow my eyes on the back of Franks head, likely he can feel my gaze on him but he doesn't look at me in the rear-view mirror, probably knowing I'm plotting a hundred and one ways to kill him. "*I'm* worried about you," Uncle Dee finishes and I roll my eyes over to him.

It pisses me off knowing that my mental health has been discussed with my fucking employees, like, do I actually need to be viewed as weak right now? When someone is sending me threatening notes and abusers from my past are rearing their ugly mugs?

"I'm *fine*, I just had a bad night, I let my *crazy* take over, it won't happen again. You can trust me to run my shit, Dee, I swear it, I'm still up to the job."

"I'm not saying you're not," he says simply, his swift sweep of greying hair is pushed back and over to one side, his navy pin-stripe suit pressed to perfection, his shoes freshly polished, he's the definition of put together. I used to be like that.

Once.

"You are more than up for the job, but I would like you to take the next two weeks off to rest. I've got cover for you while you take some time out, you need it," he tells me but I don't mistake this for advice, this is a direct order, I release a heavy sigh.

"But I really am okay, I *swear*, I'll take the rest of the weekend off and get back to work Monday, I've got shit to do and there's a shipment tha-"

"No." he cuts me off midsentence with a hand in the air. "I've got everything handled, the boys have been given their instructions this morning and the decisions have been taken out of your control for the next *fourteen days*. During that time you will *not* involve yourself in any activities, jobs or tasks, if you do I will know. Everyone has been told to divert everything through Eli and Charlie and they will come to me with anything else. You *are* going to do as I say, so kick your feet up, rest and recuperate. Your boyfriends have even offered to help in making sure you do as you're told. They actually have a very impressive security firm, have you looked at their business plans?"

What in the hell?

That's just my Uncle in a nutshell.

Business, business, business.

Well, that's all fucking great isn't it? Everyone's been fucking planning, plotting and talking about me behind my back.

"Is this a punishment?" I ask, "because it sure as shit feels like it," he just took away the last thing keeping me *somewhat* sane.

"No, it's a vacation," Uncle Dee tells me authoritatively.

"I don't need a vacation, I need to get back to fucking work," I slam my fist into the door panel, silently screaming, *because fuck me that hurt.* Then I narrow my eyes on him, "if you want to retake full control just fucking tell me I'm doing a shit job," I bite, "the jobs fucking yours if you want it all back."

"Kyla-Rose," his dangerously low voice warns, "don't be ridiculous, we're just looking after you, the decisions have been made. You need a rest, you *will* take a rest and then everything will go back to our usual, routine scheduled programming," he tells me calmly, just as Frank pulls up alongside another blacked out SUV, identical to this one.

Frank steps out opening the door for Dee.

"Be good," Uncle Dee demands, with a softness in his eyes he places a kiss on the top of my head, "you're a good girl, Lala," he tells me as he steps out of the car, stepping straight into another.

"Where to, boss?" Frank calls over his shoulder as he retakes his seat and I bristle.

"Call me, *Kyla*, I'm not your boss the next fourteen days, didn't you hear?" I say sarcastically –well aware I'm being a brat- making Frank sigh.

"Look, bo-" I snap my gaze to the front, meeting his blue eyes in the rear-view mirror, he sighs again. "Look, *Kyla*, I'm on your side and I mean this with the upmost respect so I hope I'm not crossing a line here," he swallows. "I care about you and I can see they're just trying to look after you because they care for you, but you're still my boss and I will still keep you safe and follow your instructions, however at the same time my hands may be a little tied in some aspects, so we'll have to just try and make it through these next two weeks however we can, until everything returns to normal."

I pinch the bridge of my nose, resting my head against the window, “can we go to my appointments now please?” I request quietly.

Frank nods, offering me a warm smile as we begin moving down the street.

CHAPTER 13

KYLA-ROSE

Okay, I have to admit, I *do* feel better. Not because I've been forced into taking a vacation that I don't want to take, *obviously,* but because I'm once again hairless all over –bar my eyebrows and head- my body's like a slippery sea lion that's been tossed around in baby oil, *mmm,* those visuals, am I right? My nails are fresh and just this side of disturbing with long pointed tips, painted in gloss black, the underside of them a nasty shade of blood red. And my naturally white blonde hair is toned into majestic, shimmery silver and I finally feel like myself again.

I got Frank to take me shopping after all of my appointments, which I never normally have time to do because, well, I'm normally working. So the car is filled to the brim with shit I liked and probably don't really need, but like who makes the rules on how many leather jackets are *too* many leather jackets, am I right? Plus, Christmas is coming up in a couple of weeks, so I got a lot of my holiday shopping out of the way too.

Sitting up front on the way home, we divert to a coffee shop where we decide on take-out rather than sitting in because it's getting a little late and as much as I hate to admit it, I'm starting to miss my boys. Yeah, I know, gross, but having spent the last two weeks with either one or both of them attached at the hip, I feel the way I would if I were missing my favourite knife. You know the saying 'a workman's tool is an extension of his arm', *or something*. Well, that's how I feel without my favourite knife and I guess now without my favourite boys… It's probably how Charlie feels without Dillon.

Dillon is Charlie's pet duck, well, not pet, Dillon is, *was*, his companion. Dillon died a really fucking long time ago but the thing about Charlie is that he can't let anything go. Once he has something that is his, it's not going anywhere, even in death. So, Eli had Dillon taxidermied, taxidermed? Is that a word? Oh, fuck, I don't know! But he had him stuffed and shit so he was preserved and then Eli made wooden training wheels for him, sort of like a little cart, so Charl can drag him around his torture dungeon without having to touch his pretty white feathers with bloodied hands.

And that's how I feel about my boys. I feel the same way about them as Charlie feels about Dillon.

I'm never letting them go. Even if I have to kill them and stuff them and drag their lifeless, *beautiful* corpses around on wooden wheels for the rest of my life then I will.

Deciding on grabbing coffee's for everyone on shift at

home, Frank climbs out with me and we hustle into the shop where I pick out a whole array of sweet treats too because like Uncle Dee said *I am on vacation,* and people on vacation eat sweets. *I think*. I've never actually had a vacation before but I guess there's always a first time for everything.

Three boxes of treats and sixteen cups of coffee later, we're finally loading everything into the car. Frank and I have had a good laugh together today, I mean the man's a real trooper. He sat in the nail bar with me, cracking jokes and telling me stories about when he was younger, all the while his eyes scanned all entries and exits and he observed everyone around us. He really is such a great guy, well, I mean I already knew that but it was just nice to relax and hang out.

"I'll call ahead and let the team know we're gunna need help with all this *stuff*," Frank gestures wildly to the packed vehicle and chuckles as he moves around to the driver's side of the car.

I wrench my door open, stepping up onto the little foot ledge to peer up at him over the roof, folding my arms over the cool metal I rest my chin on my forearms, "yeah, that, and tell them how nice we are, getting them all co-"

I blink.

Once.

Twice.

Three times, before my hearing comes back and the static leaves my ears.

"Boss?" Frank stares back at me, his face tight with concern.

"Frank," I swallow; my mouth and throat as dry as the

Sahara, despite the extra-large ice water I just downed while we waited for our order. My tongue feeling three times too big for my mouth, "do you see that man?" I whisper, hating that my voice cracks and gesture with my chin as cautiously as possible to a tall guy standing behind him, on the opposite side of the car park.

Since it's early winter it gets dark out by four, but I can still very clearly see the disturbingly familiar figure under the glow of the orange streetlamp.

My entire body trembles uncontrollably as I try to not freak the fuck out. Frank strategically drops his keys to the floor in a bid to stand and look behind him. As he straightens up and looks over the top of the other parked cars, the guy's gone. I watch Frank searching for a face, a figure, a shadow, *anything*, but I can already tell from the drop in his shoulders that he doesn't see anything, he doesn't *believe* me.

Frank turns back to me with a sad smile. It's one of those smiles that says, *damn girl, you're really losing it*, but it's also a smile that says he cares about me which is why he's worried and he wishes he could see what I see. I swallow the bile climbing up the back of my throat and squeeze my eyes shut.

No.

"I don't see anyone, boss, I'm sorry," he says clearing his throat and my heart lurches in my chest, "let's get home, yeah?" he says softly and I instantly know he thinks I'm imagining it, like they all thought about the guy I saw at the warehouse.

'Emotional trauma manifests itself from irrational fear, that's what this is, Kyla-Rose, PTSD. It's not real.'

That's what Jacob said, they all think that guy at the

warehouse was a figment of my imagination.

It wasn't.

He wasn't.

I was just too slow to catch up to him. He's lucky I didn't because I would have killed the fucker in the worst way imaginable.

I sit myself down in the front seat, defeated, and buckle up as I cradle the tower of hot coffees. The heat should probably be scolding my legs by the time we're fifteen minutes into our drive home, even through the thick denim of my jeans, but I can't really feel anything.

In fact, I feel completely fucking numb, numb like I've been sitting outside, naked, in the middle of winter up to my knees in snow, so much so that I can't hear a single word that Frank says when he calls the boys. I strain my ears so hard trying to pay attention but I can't make any of it out. Frank keeps glancing over at me, I don't see him but I can feel his eyes studying me, watching the crazy girl who's seeing imaginary monsters in the shadows.

He thinks you're losing it, Kyla-Rose.

It's weird isn't it? That voice inside your head that's actually just you but that feels like someone else? Like there isn't *actually* a person sitting up there prattling out shit to me, it's just me, my subconscious spewing shit that doesn't make it from my brain to my tongue, shit that's better left unsaid or words that aren't socially acceptable. Things that Charlie and I say and do together that the *normal* people would deem unacceptable, like drinking martini's with paedophile's eyeballs in, playing hide and go stab, throwing knives at each other with our eyes closed, pin the python on the paedo, that kind of fun shit we do when we hang out together.

I have a demon inside of me. But is it just an extension of myself or something else entirely? Is the demon really just my tarnished, shadowed soul? Will I ever really know? Half the time my demon is my shield, my weapon, my guardian angel. And other times, it has me flinging myself recklessly into the fire, consuming me in its glorious flames and scorching me to the bone. It's either calming and soothing or panicking and terrorising me. And it's really just *me*. Self-torture I guess.

It's completely normal behaviour to me, in this life –ruling the underworld and all of its devil worshippers- it's not even something one would bat an eyelid at, but in *real life,* normal society, I'd be declared unsafe, unfit for purpose. Be forced to swallow pills to control my immoral inhibitions, pills that make me drowsy and unable to function without help and a padded cell.

That's my worst nightmare. A padded cell in a mental facility haunts my dreams constantly. Just because I'm not like everybody else doesn't mean I should be deemed crazy and be locked up. I'm doing the world a service even if my methods are *unusual*.

I protect little boys and girls; I obliterate their tormentors and the predators that stalk them in the dark. I do unspeakable things to them because they fucking deserve to feel even an ounce of pain that they so ruthlessly inflict, my inner demon needs an outlet and by unleashing it on abusing scum, I'm essentially using my darkness for something good. Why is that so wrong? I'm not hurting the innocent, far fucking from it.

So to have my family –of all people- not believe in me when I tell them I see someone or something, it cuts me to the bone, straight to my motherfucking core and it *hurts*. I'm bleeding from a wound that can't be treated, a wound that maybe will never stop bleeding.

Because that's what I am, even on my good days; bleeding.

Always fucking bleeding.

I don't even realise we're home until Frank is pulling my door open in the underground garage and taking the mountain of coffee's from my quaking hands, he gives me one of those sad smiles again and it pangs my heart. My subconscious crafting and adding yet another block of ice to the foundations of the wall erected around it. I did see that monster; he was there, one of my tormentors, abusers. A piece of my heart cracks inside my chest leaving me gasping for air, I can hardly draw in breath yet I'm breathing perfectly normally. Inside I want to scream but on the outside my body is my biggest enemy, it's almost given up the fight.

Weak.

No one is going to believe you.

"Hi, Sweetheart," I roll my head at the sound to see Kacey, standing in my open doorway.

I'm still buckled into my seat as I slowly look up; it takes every ounce of strength in me to move my head to look at him. My energy severely lacking, draining out through the gaping wound in my chest, he gives me a beaming smile like the one he always reserves just for me, but this one? This one's tainted with sadness. He reaches across me, unbuckling my seatbelt he offers me his hand but I just stare at his open palm, willing my arm to move but it doesn't. I just blink.

I know I need to get the fuck up, hold my head high and march into my building, then I can fall apart without the eyes of my employees on me, watching, judging or worst of all feeling *sorry* for me. I'm the fucking boss, I'm a ruthless leader, I'm respected for my decisions even when they're really fucking hard to make, they trust me to lead them. I need to show everyone that I'm fucking strong and shit like this doesn't affect me. But then, here we are; my legs numb and my body shaking so violently that my teeth are crashing together in an unshakable chatter. *I'm so fucking cold.*

"I can't walk," I choke out the whisper, only just loud enough for my safety net to hear me, my mouth so dry, the weak words taste like ash on my tongue and the brick in my stomach is joined by two more.

Without saying a word Kacey places one arm under my knees, the other sliding behind my back, lifting me with ease he cradles me to his chest, I let my eyes slip shut as I try to block out the world around me. Kacey's huge body drawing me into him, crushing me to his chest, shielding me from my monsters, melding our bodies together, I hang limply in his strong arms. My fingers aching to cling to him but they can't, my energy depleted, defeated.

I'm not crazy.

I chant it over and over in my head until my brain hurts and my heart aches harder. That familiar smell of my house hits me, orange blossom and lime scented air fresheners are all over my apartment, I find the tangy scent calming and refreshing. It also hides the copper scent of blood that I so often trail through the halls.

I take in long steady breaths as Kacey moves us through the house, I let the smell of him wrap me up, mint and earth, it's the scent of my protector, raw and harsh and perfect and I let that keep me grounded to him because the only thing tethering me to this plane right now is him, Kacey. Gripping me tightly with his huge, tattooed arms, holding all of my broken pieces together, I wonder if there's a glue strong enough to put me back together after this.

When he sits on the white leather couch with me in his lap someone drops a blanket over me and gives my knee a gentle squeeze, it's a gesture that's meant to be comforting, letting me know that someone's there for me but it doesn't feel that way, it feels far too much like sympathy and I hate it. I don't need or want it, I'm not broken. *Am I?*

"We brought coffee," I whisper to Kacey through clattering teeth, his large hand coming up to cup my face, his thumb stroking over the apple of my bruised cheekbone.

My bruising is just a mottled amber-yellow now and easy to cover up but it's still a little tender.

"I saw, how d'you remember fourteen guys' coffee orders?" he chuckles, the sound soothing me.

"I know everything about my employees," I breathe and he laughs again.

I try to learn as much as possible about every single person that works for me. I want to know every single thing, right down to their cousins twice removed and what their dream job was as a child. If you always know every detail of the people you surround yourself with, it makes it very difficult for them to ever get one over on you.

That's why I keep all my secrets to myself. No one can fuck me over if they have nothing to use against me.

That's one of the reasons I'll never bear a child, no one should be forcibly dragged into this hell dimension I rule, I'd never force anything so dark on an innocent. I always dreamed of being a mum one day, I wanted to be a better mother than what I had growing up, I wanted to give someone the world and show them true kindness and love. But circumstances change and mine did dramatically.

My mother never did that for me, love me, I mean. It wasn't her fault, she had a sickness, then used illegal drugs as a coping mechanism. She never loved me but I still loved her. That's fucked up isn't it? Unrequited love, be it in the form of a parent, sibling or lover. Nothing is more gut-wrenching than that of a broken heart. Trust me. I know. I've had mine broken over and over.

Uncle Dee never let me go without though, he gave me this life and I'll never resent him for that.

"That's 'cause you're good at your fucking job," he rumbles, "only the best employers take time to learn that much about their employees," Kacey praises as I steal all the warmth from his chest.

He's like a big grizzly bear –minus the fur- his huge body keeping me safe and clutched to his firm chest whilst simultaneously scaring everyone else away.

"It's only so I know what colour poison I can use in their coffee, should the need ever arise," I rasp.

Kacey's large body rocks with mirth beneath mine but he

knows as well as I do that I'm serious.

"How's our girl, still cracking jokes, huh?" Huxley says calmly with a light laugh, his normal tone comforting.

And I'm so exhausted I can't even really appreciate the way he so naturally says '*our girl.*'

I feel him move into the space beside Kacey and he runs his fingers through my hair. His hot fingertips trailing over my scalp, my skin prickling with want, I nuzzle against his palm as he drags it to my jaw, cupping my other cheek, my face held safely between my two saviours. Because that's what they are, they just don't know it yet, and neither do I, not really. I don't realise in this very moment just how much they'll save me, over and over again, *from myself.*

"Your hair looks good, Darlin', I missed the silver," Huxley tells me in an appreciative purr.

His voice sends shivers racking through my already trembling body but it's a good shiver, I always get this feeling around Hux, he's a smooth fucking talker and definitely a ladies man. He commands the room with his mere presence, he's a confident speaker, fucking cock-sure of himself without a doubt but I think that's what I love about him. He makes me feel safe with his confidence; he's never frightened or nervous of anything. He reassures me like no one else ever could. He's invincible. Danger doesn't scare him, neither does death.

Spending the last two weeks with him just solidified the fact that I need him, I need someone to bring light and laughter into my life, someone who doesn't take life so seriously all the time and is genuinely unafraid of what's to come. That's Huxley in a nut-shell.

He's everything I wish I were.

Brave, strong, unafraid.

I peel my heavy eyes open to look at him and all I find in my line of vision is the two men who have bitten off way more than they can chew, this is certainly not what they signed up for, some crazy, haunted nut-job.

"There she is," Huxley beams, his smile bright like a childhood summer's dream, smiles and laughter and sunshine, he runs his thumb over my bottom lip, "fucking beautiful," he whispers with a wink and I feel myself smile, it's small but it's real.

"Kyla-Rose," Jacob's deep voice rattles me and I jump at the sound of it.

Jacob is strong, loud, large and in charge. His very essence permeates the room as he enters, making all those around him cower and bow down. Submit.

I let my head lull gently to the left, resting my cheek against Kacey's ripped forearm, to see him perched against the gloss black grand piano. It's the biggest waste of money I ever spent. The only reason I got it is because I'm seriously fucked in the head and enjoy torturing myself with memories of the past.

When I was a little girl the boy who lived a few houses down, -who I had a supreme love-hate relationship with until I was sixteen- had an old piano in his Grandma's living room, his Grandma had got it from a church charity sale and taught him to play. When I would go over, he would always sit me next to him on the little worn bench seat and play for me, then he'd lay his hands atop mine and try to teach me the tune.

I'm very clearly emotionally damaged by the whole history

of that little boy. The little boy I loved more than the world until I just couldn't anymore. When I went to juvie I had to push all thoughts of him from my mind, I replaced the space that held my love for him, with a small, empty black crevice, the place I would crawl to when I needed to disconnect my brain from the things happening to my body, things I couldn't stop.

Then I moved into this apartment and there it was, the emotions resurfacing, forcing themselves to burn through me like the string to a stick of dynamite, I just had to have a fucking piano. I still sit at it sometimes, just to lay my fingers against the smooth keys, even when the only song I still remember how to play is '*twinkle, twinkle, little star*'.

Kacey and Huxley have helped mend that little piece in me that was shattered by my first love, they're healing me without even realising it and that scares me more than anything, because if they fix something inside me and then decide to toss me away, will there be anything left of me when they're gone?

"I hate that piano," I rasp, my voice cracking and dry, wobbling as I bite back my tears. "I fucking, *fucking* hate it," I whisper.

"Are you listening to me?" Jacob snarls irritably, I tear my eyes from the piano to look at him.

He's passing his big hand through his short blonde hair, his brow creased, lips pinched and turned down. His nose wrinkles in distaste, he looks like an irritable little bunny rabbit that has a carrot dangling just out of its reach and instead of lunging for the carrot, he's thinking about lunging for the person dangling it and tearing their fucking fingers off.

"No." I snap at Jacob, "no, I am not fucking listening to

you and your bullshit analysis of me and my, what was it you called it? *My fragile mind?*" I spit, wrestling free of Kacey's ridiculously sized arms. "In-fucking-fact, I am *sick* of your psychoanalysis crap, I know what I fucking saw and nothing you or anyone else says will change my fucking *fragile* mind. I lost my shit. I fucking know that. I know what I did, I fucking *know*. But I also fucking know *who* I fucking saw!" I scream, my hands balling into fists, my new pointed fingernails digging into my palms angrily, biting at the pale skin.

Charlie followed by Cam and Eli, step through the archway from the hallway, all of them wearing various looks of concern on their faces. Whether those looks are for me or the situation, I'm not quite sure.

"Do you know what, you don't believe me, that's all fucking fine, I don't need you to, I have my own resources, I'll hunt the cunts down myself, they think popping up and making me think I'm losing my mind is going to work, it's fucking not, I fucking dare you to try and stop me," I seethe.

I'm panting and pacing like a caged tiger, practically pulling my hair out but I'm fed up now, I'm not that weak, vulnerable, easy target that I was in juvie, no I'm the biggest bad there ever was this side of fucking Southbrook, if not further than that and I'm not taking this lying down.

"Kyla-Rose," Charlie growls softly, not a growl because he's aggressive, no, that's just how his voice is, a deep, low, gravelly growl, menacing and unsettling to everyone who doesn't know him, but to me it's like the growl coming from a kitty cat, cute but with sharp teeth and claws.

I snap my attention to him as he crosses the room, curling

his tatted fingers around my upper arms, his emeralds bore into mine, flicking between the two, he licks his lips and then turns around, tucking me behind him protectively. Putting himself in the line of fire, just like he has since I was seventeen years old.

When I came home and didn't know who I was anymore, he's the only one who knows, the only one who will ever know the full story of what happened to me over those two years. Because Charlie? He's the other half to my deranged, fractured soul. We are the same, him and I. We are one. We kill for each other and would die for each other, no questions asked. I would go to hell for him and drag him with me if he asked. We could rule it together.

"I believe her," Charlie rumbles at the same time Eli punches the wall, his knuckles piercing the drywall, Cam sighs and Jacob clenches his teeth so hard I swear I hear a tooth crack.

"What?" Jacob spits through gritted teeth, his carefully constructed, put-together persona tearing at the very seams, the real man finally rearing his head.

He tries so hard to hide his monster. But deep down, beneath those iron bars he uses to keep himself in check, he's just like us. A true Swallow through and through. Because Jacob? His demon might be the worst one of us all.

"You 'eard, I said I believe her," Charlie replies calmly, gruffly, evenly.

Even as his muscles tighten in his shoulders -the fact that he never wears a shirt helps with that visual- his strong arms still binding me to him, hands clasped together behind my back, protecting me, drawing me into his back, shielding me from the room, just as he always has.

"You are not helping her by buying into her delusions," Jacob scoffs.

Charlie and I both stiffen but Jacob doesn't seem to notice, that, or he doesn't care.

"You're only going to make her psychosis worse! Can't you fucking see that! I know you always just *have* to take her side, but this is ridiculous! She's sick, Charlie! Fucking sick! Just like her *mother* and look how that ended! She needs professional help!" Jacob snarls, Charlie's grip on me tightens to the point it's crushing and borderline painful, but I don't react, he's the only thing keeping me on my feet right now.

My mother.

I can hardly believe he would compare me to her.

I've never tried so hard not to cry in my entire life.

And all of that coming from Jacob, the one who's supposed to protect me, his brothers, his family.

The room erupts into heated discussion, Cam grunts, Eli paces, Huxley sounds pissed, Kacey is clenching and unclenching his fists trying to keep his shit together, all while Jacob throws his *professional opinion* in everyone's faces.

Honestly, not everyone is on my side right now and I truly get it, I am a little *unhinged* I can see why me *seeing* things is a reasonable explanation, but I don't think anyone in this room wants to hear me called crazy, delusional, *sick*. I am most definitely sick, but not in the way Jacob means.

After a few minutes of heated discussion, "I'm not staying here," I whisper and the room falls silent.

Charlie turns me in his arms to look at me, he watches me for a moment, silent communication passing between the two of us and then he nods, turning back to face the room. He understands me maybe more than anyone else I've ever known and yes I do realise just how goddamn fucking lucky I am, truly, I know.

Charlie is my entire life. He means everything to me. *Everything.*

Huxley and Kacey stand in front of the couch, side by side, just how I imagine them doing on a job, backs slightly turned toward one another, analysing the room and its occupants, never having their backs to the exit, eyes roving everywhere. I'd love to know how it works; their security team, like how do they get jobs? Do they take every one of them or do they decline some? What standard of rules and morals do they follow? Do they have any at all?

Charlie sees it too, "I'll take the dogs," he announces and I breathe a sigh of relief, my babies do not like change.

"Whoa, whoa, no, where the fuck will you go? You can't be serious right now. Kyla-Rose, stop being stupid," Jacob scolds, yet again, like I'm a child needing parental permission, not an independent twenty-five year old woman with more kills under her belt than the fucking government.

Finding my strength I steel my spine and step out from behind Charlie. Looking between everyone in the room, Cam's large ink-free hands are tucked deep into his jean pockets. His face stern and masked, but I can read him, he's worried about me and although he's a fighter, he hates confrontation, especially with his family. This whole thing is making him uncomfortable; he'll probably hit the gym after this and work out his stress for a few hours.

Eli is the easiest to read, he's the most emotional, open with his feelings, he wears his heart on his sleeve and is the one out of all of us who takes the least amount of risks. He's safety tied up in a neat little silk bow, that's why he's so perfect to run security. He thinks of everything and right now I'm a flight risk, one he wants to eliminate and smother with twenty armed guards.

Then there's Jacob, he thinks of himself as a parent to us because he's got his PhD and Doctor's name tag. He just looks angry and pissed off and stressed. Jacob's only problem is that pesky conscience of a do-gooder, he see's everything as very black and white, he's so far removed from this life that he just doesn't know how to deal with anything that can't be given a clinical diagnosis. But I love him for it, we all do, he's the only good left in any of us.

I walk towards him, stopping a foot before him. I look up into those harsh green eyes and reach out to cup his face.

"I love you, Jacob," I tell him seriously, his jaw clenches beneath my palm, "but you cannot control me, I know you're trying to look out for me, I know that, but you can't stop me doing this. I'm off work for two weeks, I'm supposed to be taking a vacation, so that's what I'll do, I'll come home on Christmas Day and we can re-evaluate my role," I tell him softly. "Uncle Dee's right, I need a break, I'm over worked and I'm stressed, you boys have this shit handled right?" I ask the room, trying to stop the arguing, Cam nods, Eli sighs with a mumbled yes and Charlie, gives me a very, *very* scary wink before I look back to Jacob.

He sighs heavily, exhaling through his nose sharply; he

pinches his eyes closed and cracks his neck from side to side.

"Fine, but you better be at home Christmas morning or I'll hunt you the fuck down," he mumbles on a growl.

"You got it," I smile, dropping my hand from his stubbly face.

I reach up on tip-toes, dropping a kiss to his cheek before stepping back, instantly finding myself wrapped up in four thick arms.

"You can stay with us," Hux smiles, as I crane my neck back to look up at him, resting my head against his chest.

Kacey squeezes my arm, kissing the top of my head, enveloping me in his masculine scent. Everything about these two men makes it easier to breathe, even if it's just a little, it helps.

CHAPTER 14

KYLA-ROSE

Once I'd packed a bag with essentials and said goodbye to my fur babies –who will love staying with their Uncle Charlie, because he feeds those dogs peanut butter like it's going out of fashion. Frank followed Huxley's car over to their house and helped unload all of the shopping we did earlier, I mean, I *need* it here because most of it's Christmas presents and I'm not going home before then.

Eli's got ten men watching the perimeter on rotation. I won't see them and they won't bother me but they'll be watching the house from the shadows to make sure I'm safe, all of it was agreed *without* my input, but I let it go, I know I can protect myself regardless.

I'm standing in the middle of the open plan living room feeling awkward as fuck. I shove my hands into my back pockets, not really knowing what to do with myself. I feel like I've forced myself on their space and they've taken me in by default because let's face it, where else would I have gone? A hotel?

"Darlin', why are you standing there like that?" Huxley asks me with a tilt to his head, a lazy smirk on his full lips. Standing behind the kitchen island, his hands splayed on the worktop, he leans forward, "you look like a little lost lamb, all vulnerable and unsure of herself," he chuckles with a wink.

"I feel like I'm imposing," I say honestly, ignoring his vulnerable comment that makes my chest ache, shifting my weight from one foot to the other, I offer him a one shouldered shrug.

Thing is, I feel like I've been imposing on my own fucking family the last couple of weeks, so where do I even go from here? It's been a long time since I felt like I don't belong, it's a feeling you never really want to have, let alone go back to, I guess I've learnt to hide my awkwardness but obviously not well enough, not lately anyway.

Huxley's brow creases deeply, releasing a heavy sigh.

"We want you here, you're not imposing, not at all," he tuts, running a hand over his face, "we wouldn't have offered to have you stay here if we didn't want you, when are you gunna realise we want to be around you *all* the time? If living with you the last two weeks hasn't already told you that then we're not doing a very good job. I guess I'll have to get extra creative with showing you just how much I want you around," he smirks.

Heat climbs up my chest, the pink blush spreading to my heated cheeks. I avert my gaze, my eyes dropping to the floor.

I haven't ever had anyone that's not family want me around before, people usually keep their distance and want to avoid being near me at all costs.

"This is not exactly what you signed up for," I mumble, running my tattooed fingers through my hair, the ends feel nice and silky now that I've had it cut, they're not rough like scraggly little rat tails anymore.

"Babe, we signed up for it all, we just want to be with you, come rain or shine, we'll take it all if it means we get to be with you. I wish you could see what we see."

Huxley moves around the island, stopping before me, his big arms wrap around me allowing me to lay my cheek against his firm chest. I let the sound of his steady heartbeat calm me as he nuzzles his face into my curtain of silver hair.

"I'm scared," I whisper with a shudder, my arms wrapping themselves around his waist, he takes a deep breath and releases it slowly until I find myself matching my breaths to his.

"Tell me what you're scared of, Darlin'," Huxley murmurs into my hair, his fingers rubbing circles into my back as I let my eyes close.

"Everything," I heave, releasing my confession on a deep sigh.

I feel like I can be the most vulnerable version of myself around Huxley, he's not afraid of *anything* and if I'm honest I've been afraid of *everything* for a really long time. I just pretend to be brave; really I'm still that frightened teenage girl getting her arse hauled off to juvie.

"I'm not imagining this, Huxley. I know it's hard to believe given my track record. I'm well aware I'm not functioning quite right or firing on all cylinders but I swear it, I did see those men." My whole body trembles like an earthquake's struck, the floor feels unsteady beneath my feet and I bite into my lip to stop my teeth from chattering.

"Okay, here's what we're gunna do," Huxley grips my upper arms and leans back from me to look at my face, I tilt my head back, looking up at him, needing his reassurance. "We're gunna spend the next two weeks making sure that you have fun. We're gunna go for dinner, to the movies, bowling, *shit*, I don't know, whatever the fuck you wanna do we're gunna do it. We're gunna make the most of your once in a lifetime vacation and relax and then re-evaluate it all after you've had a break. I'm not saying I don't believe you, nobody is saying that-"

"Except Jacob," I interrupt, I feel like he's just itching to dope me up and lock me away in that fucking tower we call home.

"Okay… don't worry about that right now, but I believe you. If you say you saw those men, then you saw them, how can I argue with that? I didn't see them, so I can't say they were there, but I also can't say they weren't just because I didn't see them, you know what I'm saying?" his big brown eyes lock onto mine, a hint of gold I've not noticed before shining through the darkness, his eyes are normally so dark they look black but not tonight. A small smile tugs at his lips, "plus, I'm really happy you're here for super selfish reasons," he smirks and I roll my eyes.

"And those would be?" I carry out the last word and raise an eyebrow.

Huxley bursts into laughter before bringing his face down

to rest against mine, brushing his sharp jaw along my own, marking me with his scent, laying claim to his mate. It's such a dominant move and I fucking love it.

"We don't have a bed big enough for the three of us in this house, means I'll get to have you all to myself," he whispers and I swear to god my knickers are instantly drenched as he lets go of me and takes a step back.

My spine tingles and my knees almost buckle as he releases me, I just want to be enveloped by everything that is Huxley.

"Pizza?" Kacey calls out as he thumps down the stairs in nothing but a pair of jeans and boots, seeing him shirtless quite literally makes my mouth water, *am I dribbling?* I reach a finger up to swipe at the corner of my mouth, *I can't help it okay?!* "All of your stuff is, well, kind of everywhere, but it's upstairs anyway," Kacey laughs, "we have a chest of drawers at the end of the hall that was more or less empty, so I've emptied out the crap that was in it and put your clothes away in there, some shits hung up between our wardrobes though, but you can move whatever you want," he informs me, dropping an obnoxiously large arm over my shoulders, forcing me onto the navy couch with him.

Kicking his booted feet up onto the low coffee table, he switches on the TV. I peer past him to Huxley back in the kitchen who throws me a suggestive wink before burying his head inside the fridge. My cheeks heat and I'm sure I must be the colour of a cherry. Why do these boys make me blush so fucking much?

Kacey's large hand cups the side of my face, turning me to face him, he drops his lips to mine in a feather-light kiss and I immediately melt into him, this is what we've been doing the last two weeks.

Kissing.

Just fucking kissing.

God, I'm a thirsty fucking bitch.

Both boys are so fucking intoxicating, I completely lose my head every time one of them so much as breathes near me.

Kacey's thumb digs into my chin, my hand running up over his exposed abs, the tight muscles rippling and flexing beneath his tattooed skin, my hand rests on his bare chest feeling his heart thrash wildly beneath my palm.

I do that to him.

Make his heart thump like a race horse.

Me.

My tongue demands entry, licking over the seam of his mouth, he opens for me and I delve in, feasting on his very essence. Kacey kisses me with such passion that I can hardly catch my breath. Kissing Kacey is like dropping to the bottom of the pool, expelling all the air in my lungs and then just sitting there, waiting until my body forces its way to the surface for air. I hold out as long as possible and then just as I think I'm about to pass out, Kacey's right there breathing the life back into me, forcing that oxygen back into my burning lungs. He kisses me until I'm dizzy and panting and in need of *so* much more.

"You're so delicious, I could dine on you for the rest of my life and never get bored of the taste," Kacey breathes, a shiver rakes its way dangerously up my spine and I shudder.

Kacey laughs loudly at my body's reaction to his, his tongue darting out to lick over my top lip before he pulls away, laying his head back against the sofa, his gold eyes lazily rolling to look at me, "what pizza d'you want, Sweetheart?"

He winks one of those glorious gold eyes at me, burying the orb beneath a fan of thick black lashes, they're far too long those lashes, too dark and thick to have been created for such a beast of a man, such a feminine feature on a hard face with a vicious cut jawline.

I shove my hand into his solid chest, that familiar zap of electricity passing between us at the touch as I shuffle away. Kacey's laugh reverberates around the room, his body shaking with mirth as Huxley drops into the newly created space between us.

"Hey!" Kacey yells, protesting at the separation.

I snuggle myself into Huxley's side, his big arm effortlessly wrapping around me. I tuck my feet up onto the couch beneath me, laying my head against his chest, my ear resting over his heart.

"What's up, Big Man?" I ask innocently, batting my eyelashes at him.

Holding Kacey's gaze I run my hand dangerously low along Huxley's hips, his stomach muscles contracting beneath my gentle touch. I latch my hand around his hip, nuzzling my face into his homely scent. Huxley always smells like the outdoors, like a mixture of freshly cut grass, oranges and a fresh outdoorsy, woodsy scent that I love.

Huxley laughs, tilting my jaw up, breaking my eye contact with his brother as his lips press against mine, I open for him on a groan. His long fingers comb through my hair, latching on at the ends, tugging my head further back, his tongue piercing cool against my hot, swollen lips as he licks over them, teasing and tasting me, tasting Kacey on me, exploring my body with his other hand as it runs down my spine.

His long fingers quickly find the hem of my shirt and he effortlessly glides beneath the tight fabric, his warm palm running flat across my ribs until he's cupping the heavy weight of my breast through my flimsy lace bra. The pad of his thumb drags over the sensitive skin of my nipple, flicking at my piercing until it's worked into a hard point, he continues teasing it, running his thumb over and over in small tantalising circles to the point I feel like I'm about to explode.

Never breaking our kiss, my leg swings over his thighs as I move to straddle him, he deepens the kiss as I grind myself down over his hardening length. Huxley's hard body beneath mine lights a fire inside me, stroking the ember in the pit of my belly to life.

I tug at Hux's shirt and he allows me to tear it over his head, I drop it to the floor, arching my back, pressing myself further into him, groaning when my oversensitive nipples brush against his hard chest. His big hands run down my back from shoulders to hips until his fingers are biting at the skin of my hip bones in a punishing hold, sure to leave bruises. That thought alone makes me groan, seeing his mark on me makes something primal inside of me roar to life.

One of Huxley's hands snakes between our melded bodies, flicking open the button on my jeans, slowly dragging the zipper down, his fingers delve beneath the lace of my knickers, finding the evidence of what he does to me.

I groan into our kiss with a rough nip to his bottom lip, his fingers sliding through my slick folds, teasing me, gliding up and down, circling around my clit. He never once touches it, not once, the ultimate tease, my body's on fucking fire and I let out a frustrated growl making him chuckle darkly.

"God, you're so fucking wet for me, Darlin'," Huxley breathes into me, tearing his lips from mine, resting our foreheads together as his fingers continue to explore.

I rock myself against his hand, his black eyes flick up to meet mine and I swear to god it almost pushes me over the edge, he's barely touching me at all but just one look from him sends my brain into overload, my stomach muscles clench, a cold sweat breaking out all over my flushed skin.

"Huxley, please," I plead on a whimper, my hands gripping the short curls at the base of his pierced nape, tugging him back to look up at me above him.

His long fingers continue their slow, lazy pace against my greedy core before dipping a single finger into me making me gasp.

"Fuck, you're so tight," his voice strained, Huxley's other hand grips my hip so tightly it feels like the bone is protruding through the skin at the pressure.

He uses his grip on me to move me with his other hand, grinding me against him as his finger curls inside me, bumping against that sweet spot before adding a second.

I bite down on my lip so hard the skin tears filling my mouth with the tangy copper of blood, I suck it down, our foreheads still pressed together as we share the small amount of air between us. For every breath he exhales, I draw it in, sharing a single life force, one can't exist without the other.

And that's how I feel in this moment, as I grind myself down against the heel of his hand on the navy velvet sofa in the middle of his living room. I can't ever imagine us being separated. In fact I don't think I'd survive it, we've only known each other a short time and although we've spent so much time together the last couple of weeks I surely shouldn't feel this strongly about him. Should I?

Who sets the rules on relationships anyway? Can't I just feel whatever I feel?

In one lightning fast move Huxley shifts our position so I'm flat on my back and he's hovering above me, resting between my thighs, his lips taste me all over. He kisses me on the mouth, working his way along my jaw and down my neck, all the while his hands are exploring me, touching me all over, searing my skin as his long fingers dance up the insides of my thighs, white hot flames licking at my insides as he expertly covers my body with his own.

Huxley sits up on his haunches, his long fingers curling beneath the waistband of my skinny jeans, he shimmies them over my arse and down my thighs, edging himself off of the sofa, ripping my boots, jeans and knickers off in one single tug like he's done this a million times before. But I shove that thought to the back of my mind; I *really* don't want to think about him with anyone else.

Then in a desperate fervour that can only be described as verging on idolatry, his fingers curl around the inside of my knees, tearing them apart, his face instantly dropping between my parted thighs.

His sinful lips suck their way along my wet folds, his

pierced tongue slipping between them before he's lapping at me, my back arching away from the soft velvet of the sofa, my fingers digging into the armrest behind my head. Huxley works my clit like he's on a mission, feasting on me like he'll never get enough, my hips buck into him, one hand sliding into the short dark curls on his head, holding onto them like I'm drowning and he's my life preserver.

"You're so fucking delicious, I could eat you all day and night and never come up for anything else," he says against my pulsing core.

His naughty words muffled against my heated skin, I can *feel* how wet I am, I could come from his dirty, whispered words alone. Huxley works me with his devil tongue, worshipping me like I'm a dark goddess until I'm shivering and shaking beneath him, unable to catch my breath, every time that cool metal piercing of his bumps against my clit I almost die.

I'm just about to throw myself willingly over the cliff's edge when he abruptly pulls back. My fingers fumble together with his as we unbutton his jeans, our minds both in sync with one another. Once his zipper is all the way down, I lick my hand, the flat of my tongue slathering my palm before I force my fingers inside my mouth, letting Huxley's eyes watch as I slowly wet them, lazily rolling my tongue over each one, before pulling them out with a pop.

Huxley's eyes follow my movement with hunger and carnal excitement as I guide my wet palm beneath his tented black boxers, gripping his thick, pulsing cock. My fingers wrap around his silky skin, I can't quite join them together with my thumb around him, Huxley is *big*, like, *I'm kind of a little scared, is this thing actually going to fit inside of me?* Big.

I pump him slowly in my hand a few times, getting the true feel of him, he's long and thick and hard as steel, satin covering a steel pipe. Unsurprisingly, a cold bar of metal is also pierced through the tip, Hux, has a lot of piercings and I'm sure I'll discover more over time.

His dark brown eyes focus on mine as I touch him, his eyes never leaving me as I give him a gentle squeeze, but when I draw my hand up and swipe my thumb over his tip, slowly dragging the glistening pre-cum down his heavy shaft. My fingernails grazing over his balls, his eyes change dramatically turning a deep coal black, like the animal he's been trying so hard to contain has just been released.

Oops?

Huxley grips my wrist, forcibly removing my touch from his body, he shoves his jeans and boxers down over his hips in one swift motion. Pinning my hands above my head with one of his, pressing them into the cushions as he slides his beautiful thick cock inside me, thrusting into me all the way to the hilt, his pierced tip hitting the entrance to my cervix.

I cry out, my eyes squeezing closed, back arching into him, plastering my front to his, our pelvic bones slamming into each other. He settles inside me, allowing my body to conform to his, stretching my walls with the most delicious bite of pain.

"*Fuuuuckkkk*," Huxley hisses through his teeth, his head dropping back, his other hand still gripping my hip, his long fingers digging into my soft flesh.

Our breathing wild and erratic, Huxley starts to move, his long, thick cock, sliding into me over and over. Heat surges through me like an unstoppable force, goosebumps break out over my skin with a cold sweat, my nails clawing into the back of his hand holding mine captive above my head as he thrusts deeper and deeper, stroking deliciously inside me until white dots speckle the edges of my vision.

Our groans create a sexual symphony, bouncing the sound around the room like a fucking string quartet. Huxley releases my hands, turning my face to the side, exposing my neck, giving ample room for his tongue as it glides up the side of my throat, his teeth latching onto my earlobe as he bites and sucks it into his mouth, his finger and thumb pinching my chin as he controls my movements.

"You're so goddamn beautiful," he whispers into my ear sending yet another shiver up my spine, my whole body quivers beneath him, "just like this, spread out beneath me, hair laid out around your head like a silver halo," he murmurs.

Pushing my t-shirt until it's bunched up exposing my breasts, the black lace of my bra barely containing the heavy flesh, he dips his face down, his teeth latching onto one of my piercings.

I cry out at the sting, the pain rippling through me, my nails clawing at his bare back.

"These tits," he says, "pierced," he groans, biting his lip while moving his hot, wet mouth from one to the other, "are fucking incredible," he breathes, sucking the supple flesh into his mouth, still pumping into me, his other hand kneading my other breast, sharing his attention equally, he goes back and forth between the two. "God, I could fuck you like this forever," he tells me, dropping his lips to mine, his thrusts deeper, sharper, faster until we're both trembling.

Our breaths mingling and skin slapping skin, I roll my hips up to meet his punishing thrusts until we're both crying out as we reach a combined climax, Huxley shoots ropes of hot cum into me, stars bloom behind my eyelids, splattering my vision with black orbs.

Still seated inside me, Hux collapses down on top of me, breathing hard but still holding up his own weight on his forearms, like he's trying not to crush me beneath that rock solid body of his, is it weird I kind of want him too? Crush me beneath him, meld us together, so I can syphon his strength. I couldn't think of a safer place to be.

My shaking legs wrap around his waist, crossed feet digging into his spine, drawing his firm body into mine, bringing him as close as two people can possibly be. I run my fingers lazily over his scalp, gently clawing my way through his dark curls, he rests his head against my chest as we both start to come down from our high.

After we both settle somewhat, the only sound in the room our combined breathing, Huxley kisses my chest, sliding out of me and sitting up. I'm still lying spread eagle on the couch, trying to get myself together but I can't lie, I have been well and truly fucked. I don't even think my legs work anymore. I'm not sure they ever will again.

Huxley looks me over as I drop an arm above my head, not bothering to cover up, what's the point? He's had his face in my most intimate places, what's left for him to see? He shoots me a wicked smirk like he knows exactly what he's just done to me. I can't even gather enough energy to shoot him a sarcastic comment about his serious case of smugness. I mean after fucking me like that? He *should* be fucking smug, it was incredible.

"What?" I eventually manage to spit out, my chest still rising and falling dramatically, my breasts heaving.

"Nothing," he smirks with a twitch to his dark eyebrow, the silver ring pierced through it glinting in the low light from the lamp in the corner. "Just looking at you like this is getting me hard all over again," he admits, adjusting himself in his open jeans as I gape at him.

"You cannot be serious right now!" I squeal tucking my knees together in an attempt to tell that twitchy dick of his that I'm closed for business.

"Darlin', you should see you right now, you're the most beautiful, freshly fucked woman I've ever laid eyes on, I can't help getting hard again," he laughs, that deep, over-confident laugh where he throws his head back and his shoulders shake with mirth.

I frown at him, kicking my foot out, he catches it easily just before it makes impact with his chest and laughs even harder. I wrestle my boobs back into the flimsy lace bra and tug my t-shirt back down. Huxley tucks his already hardening cock away *–thank god-* as I scramble around the floor to find my jeans.

"Urgh," I moan, looking down at my bare thighs as his cum drips down them. "I need to shower," I laugh, but when I look back up at Huxley, all I see is hunger in his eyes, raw, primal need washes over his face, his black eyes stark against his smooth caramel skin as they hone in on the space between my slick thighs.

I snap my fingers to get his attention, slowly, *ever so slowly,* he drags his eyes up to meet mine, a lazy smirk covers his pink lips.

"Eyes up here, pervert," I scold and in typical Huxley fashion he just laughs at me, shaking his head.

I tug my ruined knickers and jeans back up my shaking legs before throwing myself back on the couch beside him, his hand latches onto my thigh instantly like he can't stand to be so close and *not* touch me. It's a weird feeling to *want* to be touched like this and actually enjoy it.

"Umm, where'd Kacey go?" I ask whipping my head around the room, suddenly realising he was right next to us before this whole thing started.

Huxley laughs, "don't sound so worried, Darlin', we both need to spend time with you alone as well as together, we share a lot better than you'd think, he's okay, don't worry." Huxley tells me, tipping my chin up so he can press a soft kiss to my swollen lips. "Just let us worry about the dynamics okay? We don't want you worrying about stuff like that, this will work, as long as you don't stress about it, just do what feels right to you and let us worry about the other stuff." Huxley smiles, reassuring me and I do feel better knowing these men are sensible, this can all work out if I learn to relax into it.

But then the fuck-head ruins the entire moment with a dirty wink that has me flying up from the sofa and pounding up the stairs towards the door that I know leads to Kacey's room.

I rap my knuckles gently against the wood, it's open ajar but I don't want to just barge in.

"Yeah?" Kacey's deep rumble calls out.

I push my way in, only opening the door halfway, sticking my head around the door to look at him.

He's laid out on top of his bed, feet crossed at the ankles, huge arms folded beneath his head, muscles flexed and delicious. His face lights up when he sees me and he turns to face me, dropping his legs over the side of the bed, resting his elbows on his knees.

"Hey, beautiful girl," he smiles as I step fully into the room.

The way Kacey always looks at me makes me feel like the only person in his world, as though he doesn't look at anyone else on the planet quite like this; the whole thing is reserved just for me. That beaming soppy grin and the naughty glint in his gold eyes, I hope he always looks at me like this. Just in case, I commit a mental image of this moment to memory.

"Hey, Big Man," I reply with a smile, "I feel like I need to say something but I don't know what," I laugh nervously, knotting my fingers together, I've never been so unsure of myself.

Kacey narrows his eyes at me slightly before getting up and stalking across the carpet with intent.

"No," Kacey says as he wraps me up in his masculine scent, overwhelming my senses and filling my nostrils with it. "You don't need to say anything, there's nothing to say, we both need alone time with you as well as together, you and Hux, you needed that," he tells me just as relaxed as Huxley was about the whole thing, I'm already breathing easier. "I won't lie though, listening to you, I was jealous as fuck. I just needed to see your face, you have the most delectable expression when you come," he winks and my face heats to at least fifty degrees hotter than hell.

I groan, burying my face in my hands as he chuckles deeply, the sound vibrating through his chest.

"Trust me, you'd get a boner too if you saw what we see when we look at you," he laughs, drawing me in closer to his chest.

"I need to shower," I grumble against his solid form and although my words are muffled he seems to understand and releases me before walking into his bathroom. I hear the spray of the shower, cupboard doors opening and closing before joining me back in his bedroom. "All your girly shit's in there," Kacey says rolling his eyes, "honestly, I don't understand how you need that many products, my little sister has an obsession with beauty products that I don't understand too, I thought it was just her but apparently not," he shakes his head, gesturing to the bathroom with a wave of his hand.

That blonde flop of hair dropping into his eyes as he pushes his huge hand through it, brushing it off of his face and smoothing his hand over the tattoo on the side of his skull.

"How old is she?" I ask, tilting my head to one side, his eyes light up so she must mean a lot to him.

I always wanted a sister, I was really jealous of the girl who lived next door to me when I was little, one day her parents came home with a baby in a car seat and since the minute that baby could toddle the two girls were inseparable, I'd love to have had a sister bond like that.

"Lila's seven," Kacey shrugs, but a smile tilts up the corner of his lips, his eyes faraway as he thinks of her.

"What's she like?" I ask dropping my arse to the end of his bed.

"She's a special kid, shy, quiet, reserved, too fucking smart for her own good too. My mum remarried ten years ago, my dad wasn't a nice guy and he just fucked off one day when I was little so it was always just me and her until she met Nick," Kacey toes the carpet dropping his gaze to the floor, his jaw clenching tight.

"You don't like him?"

Kacey's gold eyes meet mine with a short nod of his head; that flop of blonde hair dropping over one eye again, hiding it from view. He looks, sad?

"She seems happy anyway, my mum, so who am I to judge?" he shrugs, pushing his hair back from his face again. "What about you? Your mum and dad?" he asks changing the subject onto me, he does so, so causally like this is just a normal question asked and answered between normal people.

It is usually isn't it? Asking about your lovers parents, just through interest, trying to find out where the person you care about came from, or rather who they came from, like parentage actually contributes to defining a person. I hope it doesn't.

"My, urr," I lick my lips and swallow, my mouth suddenly dry, "my dad's in prison, got sent down for a triple homicide when I was just a baby," I shrug like it's no big deal, cause it kind of isn't. I've killed more men than that in a weekend sometimes. "He's a good man," I frown, why the fuck am I defending him like Kacey's one to judge? Kacey would never judge me, that's one of the things I like about him actually.

Kacey never judges a book by its cover, he lets the soul of

a person speak to him before he makes judgement, he seems to always try to hunt out the sliver of good in a person before he chooses to write them off.

"He's a good man," I repeat, gnawing on my bottom lip, I really should visit him soon.

It's a weird thing isn't it, having a parent in prison? My daddy raised me from behind bars. I would visit him with my Uncle Dee every Saturday morning. They would talk business and I'd take my daddy paintings I'd made for him and show him my cuts and bruises from my adventures with the boys throughout the week, he'd always sit me on his lap and run his calloused hands over my white blonde hair, cup my face and kiss me on the top of the head while he listened intently to all my stories.

Kacey disappears into the steamy bathroom, switching off the shower, emerging to come and sit beside me, his large tattooed hand dropping to my thigh, his thick fingers giving it a comforting squeeze.

"What's he like?" Kacey asks, tucking my silver curtain of hair behind my ear.

A laugh escapes me, how could I even describe that brute of a man?

"He, well, he's hard as nails, I think he rules that fucking prison," I laugh but it's a nervous laugh, I worry about him behind bars, it's already been twenty-four years. "He's strong and huge, kind of like you I guess if we're talking weight class," Kacey chuckles as I prod his solid abs with my finger. "I think he loves me more than anyone has ever loved another person," I say honestly, so honestly that I even shock myself.

Wow.

That was a raw confession, *where the fuck did that come from?*

Kacey grips my chin, forcing my face up to meet his, he drops a kiss to my lips that still taste like Huxley, but Kacey doesn't seem to care, neither of them do to be honest, they're not shy around each other.

"My mum's dead," I whisper against his lips when Kacey breaks our kiss, still, he doesn't say anything, he's good like that, patient. "She overdosed when I was sixteen," I swallow the lump of sawdust on my tongue before continuing. "I tried to look after her as best I could, she was a junkie, ya know," I shrug looking up into those beautiful golden eyes that look like spun gold and sunshine. "She had bad depression, like real bad, she was sad a lot, always so fucking sad," I whisper just as Huxley makes his way into the room.

"Why you crying, Mummy?" I ask as she rests her forehead against the steering wheel of our car, her skinny body wracked with sobs. "Did I make you sad?" I ask innocently, my bottom lip already trembling with the very thought of upsetting the woman I love the most in the world.

She has long gold hair, not like mine and Daddy's, ours is like snow, Mummy's is too yellow, it's a little curly too and she always keeps it tucked behind her ears. Her eyes are pale blue, so pale they're almost grey, like sad little rainclouds.

She just picked me up from my friend's Grandma's house, Maxi's been teaching me to play twinkle, twinkle little star on the piano, I'm no good at it but he tells me I am, he always says I'm good at something even when I'm not. I didn't get my clothes dirty because we didn't play outside so Mummy can't be upset with me about that, she always gets upset when I get muddy.

"Mummy's just sad today," she tells me quietly, coldly, detached.

Snuffling as she sits upright before starting the car. I feel the engine sputter to life, a horrible smell filling the car making me wrinkle my nose, Uncle Dee's car never smells funny.

"I need you to be quiet tonight, Mummy has a headache," she tells me firmly and I nod.

I always have to be quiet when we're at home, Mummy doesn't like noise, especially from me. I think sometimes she would like it better if I weren't there at all.

The drive home is short and when we pull onto the crumbling concrete driveway there's a man I don't recognise leaning up against the side of the house.

"Stay in the car," Mummy snaps and I know not to answer or I'll make her mad.

I sit quietly in my car seat, watching the man follow her inside our house.

It gets darker the longer I wait for her and cold, really cold. I wrap my arms around myself, rubbing my arms with my little hands to try and get warmer. I don't really like the dark and it's getting really dark now, my tummy's rumbly and my teeth are chattering.

I unbuckle my seat clips, dropping my feet to the floor, I try the door handle but I can't get out. She will come back for me soon, *I tell myself and then I climb back up onto the back seat. I really need to use the bathroom, I drank lots of apple juice at Maxi's Grandma's house, she made us cookies with the little rainbow coloured chocolates in them; they turned Maxi's tongue blue! Maxi's Grandma, is so nice, she's got really warm hands and a kind smile and she always smells like cookies, I wish she were my Grandma.*

"She left me in the car that night, I wet myself twice, crying until morning, she only found me in the car then because she was looking for something that had fallen out of her bag the day before, she didn't even remember she'd left me in there," I scoff with a shake of my head. "Then she dragged me inside, her nails bit into my cold skin, little crescents of blood pooled on the surface. I remember counting them later on that day when she screamed at me, told me off for wetting myself, told me I was a dirty girl and she should send me off to live with someone else, how she wished she could swap me for a good little girl who did as she was told."

"It's sick isn't it? How much I loved her and how much she hated me. And yet I still clung to the hope that maybe she did love me, maybe I was just a bad girl and it was my fault she was always so sad. I took care of her my whole life," I sigh, thick wet tears slide down my face but neither of my men say a word, just listening, waiting, patiently letting me tell them my story.

"I would bathe her after she got so fucking high she'd throw up all over herself, I'd clean the house after she trashed it in a rage, I'd wash and cook and clean. I'd put her to bed and all the while she would shout and hit and spit venom at me, told me how I was worthless and how I ruined her life, she was thirty-one when she died, fucking thirty-one," I scoff, swiping at my wet face.

"I came home from school and found her OD'd on heroin, the needle still sticking out of her throat, eyes cold and dead staring up at the ceiling, I just stared at her like that until it got dark. I didn't even move over to her, I couldn't tear my gaze from her dead grey eyes, they fucking haunt me those eyes, even now I sometimes see them in the dark," I swallow. "Sometimes in the mirror," I choke a disbelieving laugh.

Looking up to see Huxley opposite me, his foot kicked up against the wall, his thick arms folded across his bare chest, he's sad for me, his dark eyes don't look black anymore they're just that beautiful chocolate brown with little honey flecks, all of his bullshit and humour firmly put away, *for me*.

Kacey's large hands cup my hot face, his thumbs wiping away wet tears, he gives me a small smile, "I feel like there's more to this story," he murmurs with a tilt to his head, his flop of blonde hair dropping back over one eye, I reach up and push it back, my fingers tracing over his sharp jaw.

"Mmm," I agree, my mind still far away. "May as well get it over with right?" I laugh caustically. "I fucked up my whole life that night, that's where the old Kyla-Rose died, right there with her mother, the woman she loved the most in the world, the woman's daughter she wished she'd never had, they both died together in that house and I was born. A monster."

"What d'you mean, Darlin'?" Huxley asks moving toward me, dropping to his knees on the worn carpet at my feet, his hands resting comfortingly atop my knees.

Kacey wraps an arm around my lower back, resting his

thick fingers on my hip.

"I loved a boy once, when I was really young." I almost whisper, not really sure that's the bit I should start with but hey, here we are. "I found my mum and then stood there staring at her for hours," I repeat, like my brain can't compute the next part of my downfall. "I didn't even call my Uncle, I just left the house and walked, for ages, in the dark, stole a car and drove it around aimlessly until I stopped in the warehouse district."

"The one we fight in?" Kacey asks and I nod.

My eyes meeting his, those beautiful gold irises shining back at me, *so fucking beautiful.* I reach up running my thumb across Kacey's cheekbone. I can't seem to help myself around these boys. I've gone from touching no one to constantly having to touch these two huge men.

"We used to party in them, abandoned, empty, away from any houses, they were shit heaps but you know, we were kids, we didn't care. Anyway I went inside one and then after a while that boy, well man, he was a man at this stage of the story, he took my virginity right there, fucked me, said he had to do something and would come straight back, to wait there for him. I waited. Hours. Until daybreak and he didn't come back for me," I release a sharp laugh. "I know right, what a fucking idiot I was," I shake my head but neither of my men look at me like they think that, they don't think that, *at fucking all.*

"Anyway, I started a fire, I set the car I *borrowed* on fire, crashed it into the warehouse and burnt that shit to the fucking ground, I laughed as I watched it burn. I thought I was cleansing my soul, setting my rage free, releasing it into the ether, purging myself of it all but I think all I really did was unleash the beast."

"So, I got arrested, theft, arson, property damage, they found a joint on me too, so they added drug possession to my list of criminal activities and then threw the book at me because of my last name, like father like daughter. I went to juvie for eighteen months and lived through hell." I shiver at the thought, but I won't bring that up. Especially not now, maybe never, who knows? "How I survived that place I'll never know and now I'm here." I shrug and pull my fingers through my fresh silver strands.

"I've never told anyone except Charlie that shit before, sorry if that's just solidified the fact I'm a damaged psychopath, but here we sit," I laugh but it's humourless, if I don't laugh I might cry and I've done enough of that today.

Kacey kisses my temple as Huxley leans forward on his knees, kissing my lips, both of them worshipping me even though I've told them some of my fucked up, sordid history.

The boys don't leave my side the rest of the night, they shower with me, both of them and pretend they don't see me cry. We eat pizza *with* pineapple, and watch stand-up comedy until we all fall asleep together in Kacey's bed, me sandwiched in the middle of the two men who I think I might need more than I ever realised was possible.

CHAPTER 15

KYLA-ROSE

Just leave Kyla-Rose, don't look at her anymore, this isn't your fault, you were at school, you couldn't have stopped this from happening. I tell myself over and over as I walk, my black combat boots stomping through the muddy puddles along the uneven path, splashing filth up my bare legs. The only light from the flickering orange street lamps -the ones that still work that is- everything in this shitty city is plunged into darkness even in the middle of the day, everything and everyone that live here are like rot, a fungus, stealing the goodness and light from everything.

After walking for too long, I take a little joy-ride in an unlocked car, hot-wired of course, I learnt that little skill from my older cousin Charlie; he's a genius he is, a motherfucking genius, he's going to fucking MIT next year, all the way over in

America.

I park up when I find myself in the warehouse district.

It's completely abandoned, empty for years. This is where the dodgy fuckers come to make their drug deals, deliver goods and make illegal trades. We also come here to party sometimes, we're sixteen what else are we gunna do in the poorest part of this scummy city?

Venturing inside one of the buildings, I clamber my way up a large pile of rubble -broken concrete slabs, trash, even a shopping trolley is dumped in amongst this shit heap- once I get to the top I stretch up, wrapping my fingers around the support beam, swinging myself up to perch on the heavy red steel, one of the one's that's still holding this particular shit heap together. There's a large piece of flooring behind me, what I assume is left of the second floor that would have been here at some point, it's just a large ledge now really, held up by the steel beams like the one I'm sitting on.

I sit on the beam, the cold metal biting at my bare thighs and swing my legs below me as I pull a cigarette from the packet stuffed in the pocket of my scuffed leather jacket. I bring it to my lips with shaky hands, slipping the lighter from the other pocket, I spark up until the end is red and crackling -the only light inside this shadowed tin house. I inhale deeply, letting my eyes drop closed, holding the smoke in my lungs until they're screaming at me to release the toxins. I exhale the plume of thick white smoke and take in a deep steadying breath of the icy night air.

It's November, a cold one at that, and here I am in the middle of the fucking night, in a dark, abandoned warehouse in a mini-dress, boots and a leather jacket -that's so old it keeps the cold in rather than out. I scoff at myself before taking another drag on my cigarette. I chain smoke through my jitters, on my fourth cigarette I hear something below me.

My mind must have been a million miles away because I know *I would have heard someone approaching long before they ever got this close. When you're a young female and live in a shithole of a city like I do, you grow up fast, knowing what to listen out for and how to not leave yourself vulnerable. Guess I forgot even the basic rules tonight. I'll let myself off though I think; I mean I just found my mum dead.*

My mum's dead.

The head of a familiar boy continues to muddle his way up the heap of rubble before he heaves himself up easily to sit beside me.

Maddox Sharpe.

I say boy, but he's a man now, eighteen and all *man. He hasn't got that familiar body of the little boy I grew up with anymore. His tall, gangly frame has been replaced with a hard, unforgiving build of broad shoulders and tight muscles all wrapped up in pale inked skin, how does someone so young even make time to cram in so many sittings? I mean I have a couple of tattoos –illegally done of course since I'm underage- but like, the array of ink on Max's body is absolutely insane.*

"What ya doin' up here, Rosie?" he asks me.

His deep voice smooth as silk, that's how he speaks, Max, like he owns the damn world, he probably could one day, all he'd have to do is reach out and take it and it'd be his. When he speaks, he speaks to grab and hold your attention until his words suffocate you with their horror stories and fill you with pretty lies.

"Smoking," I say on an exhale without looking at him.

"Yeah, I can see that," he scoffs.

He's irritated with me a lot lately, everything I do or say seems to be wrong, I don't know why he hates me so much now, we used to be inseparable and then one day, he just cut me out.

"What the fuck do you want?" I snap at him, still keeping my line of sight straight ahead into the darkness, I know if I look at him I'll break down and I can't let him see me vulnerable, not anymore.

My mum's dead.

"You shouldn't be out here this late by yourself, you know that," he growls back and my hackles rise as I bristle.

Without looking, I flick the end of my cigarette at him. Out the corner of my eye I see him quickly brush it off his denim covered crotch as I light up another, my hands still trembling, I try to hide it, but Max? He sees everything; he's like the fucking all-seeing eye that kid.

"What's happened, Lala?" he asks me, his tone of voice rapidly changing, this time he's soft, well, as soft as someone with a soul as dark as Maddox Sharpe's can be.

"Why d'you give a fuck? Don't you have better shit to be doing than sitting here with me *of all people?" I spit, the venom on my demonic forked-tongue flaying him alive.*

If only.

"No actually, I don't," he snatches the freshly lit cigarette from between my red painted lips, tucking it between his own, they're pink and plump his lips, slightly bigger on the bottom than the top, perfect for someone with a jaw as square and

defined as his, "and in answer to your first question, I don't *give a fuck."*

I scoff so hard I have to wrap my fingers around the steel beam beneath me just to stop myself from toppling over the edge, "of course you don't, but then, you never fucking did," I spit, more in irritation at myself than at him.

I'm the fool that thought our friendship was real. I thought we had something real. Fuck. I thought he loved me. But that's just it isn't it? He's a man now and I'm some silly little girl that he left behind in his righteous journey to manhood.

"Don't talk about shit you don't understand," he spits back and I swear I could throat punch him off this fucking beam and cackle like a witch while I watch him fall.

"Then explain it, arsehole!" I scream back, my relative calm snapped and non-existent, my screech bouncing around the empty warehouse.

I finally look at him as he reaches up, running his tattooed hands through his thick black hair; it's longer than it was the last time I saw him, too short to tuck behind his ears but long enough to tangle my fingers in.

Jesus Christ.

The cigarette still hanging from his bottom lip, his bright blue eyes cut to mine and I suck in a sharp breath. Those eyes are the colour of the deepest ocean on a bright summers day, a deep, dark turquoise that makes his pale skin even whiter and his black hair even darker, eyes that blue and hair as black as the nights sky, that combination should be fucking illegal.

Max, watches me for a minute in the dark, his blue orbs studying every inch of my face like he hasn't looked at me properly in years and he's committing my shadowed face to memory. His gaze so intense I can't even breathe, I'm not sure I've even blinked, I'm not sure I'd even know how *to if I could. This is the man who was always going to be there for me, look after me,* love *me. He told me as much at his Grandma's funeral.*

'We're endgame, Lala, you and me. Soulmates of the darkest kind, you'll always be mine.'

That's what he told me.

More bullshit.

Maddox leans into me, I don't dare move, or breathe or, fuck, even think. His scent instantly overwhelms me, tobacco and something familiarly sweet like icing sugar. Maddox is the definition of man, there's probably a picture of him in the dictionary next to the damn word, everything about him screams, 'I am male, hear me roar'.

He's an apex predator, everything about him is designed to draw you in, his scent, his voice, his perfect fucking face, every fucking thing about him makes him irresistible and once you fall he strikes like a viper, going in for the kill. He's violent and sadistic and so fucking right for me, I hate him.

But I hate myself more.

I hate that I love him.

With trembling fingers I reach up taking the dangling cigarette from his lips and he lets me, I drop it to the heap of rubble beneath us before twisting myself to face him. Max reaches up slowly, tucking a strand of white blonde hair behind my ear, his warm knuckles grazing against my cold cheek sending a shockwave straight to my core.

I close my eyes taking in a deep, steadying breath through my nose. All of this is too much, it's too overwhelming, he's *too overwhelming, he hates me now, whatever I think I see in him right now is not really there. It's all in my head.*

"Look at me, Lala," Max whispers, a single knuckle lifts my chin as I flutter my lashes open and look up at him, blinking back unshed tears. "Fuck, don't look at me like that, I can't stand it," he grits out, turning away from me, sucking his bottom lip into his mouth, he runs his free hand back through his thick hair.

"Like what?" my voice quiet and breathy, I can't seem to get my words out any louder than that.

"Like you love me," his entire body shivers as he whispers the words to me.

My black painted fingernails dig into the red steel as I clench my hands into fists.

How fucking dare he make me say this.

"But I do," I exhale sharply, my gaze still studying my bare knees, "and no matter what I do I can't stop, I don't think I'd stop even if I were dead, Maxi."

I daren't look at him right now, I can already feel him tensing up, he's going to crush me for good this time, I can feel it, mind, body and shadowed soul. But that's okay because if someone is going to do it who better than, Maddox fucking Sharpe? The boy I've loved all my life. Maybe this will help me get over him. If he destroys me like I know he can maybe it'll be for the best. Maybe I won't have to worry about falling from this beam, maybe I'll just fling myself from it instead.

Even though that little boy is gone now there's a little piece of him buried somewhere inside this man, beneath this hardened exterior my childhood best friend Maxi still lives, fighting to see another day. It's probably a silly pipe-dream but I latch onto the idea because if I'm right then my Max is still here, his body just looks different is all, but souls never look different to each other; they still see each other for who they really are. No matter how twisted and tortured and fucked up, they still love each other. Don't they?

"You shouldn't, Kyla," he growls and that hurts, calling me my name like that.

Max never calls me Kyla. It's always been Lala, Rose or Rosie, fuck, even my full name, it wouldn't hurt so much to just be called Kyla-Rose but Kyla is harsh coming from Max.

"Fuck you!" I snap. "What are you even doing here? Just fuck off and leave me alone," I snarl, turning myself away from him, I swear being in such close proximity to him is slowly killing me.

"Don't do that, don't push me away," he pleads, but his voice is still cold as ice, my top lip curls up over my teeth.

*I scoff, "you have got to be fucking kidding me right now?" I almost scream, "*me *pushing* you *away?! What the actual fuck is wrong with you?" I twist myself back to look at him, I move so fast I almost throw myself off this fucking beam but I manage to keep myself up. "You've got some fucking nerve, you attach yourself to me for thirteen fucking years and then just fuck off and cut me out for two? Now you're sitting here telling* ME *not to push you away?! God, you're a fucking arsehole."*

I twist my hands around so I can turn my body and drop back down onto the pile of shit beneath our feet. As I go to slip my arse off the cold metal, Max's huge hands grip my waist, hauling me back up and onto his lap, my thighs either side of his, my breath catches in my throat as my breasts brush against his chest.

"I was trying to protect you, Lala," Max breathes into me, his forehead resting against my own, his turquoise pools boring into my grey-green ones.

Max's large hands grip my hips in a punishing hold, the rough denim of his jeans scratching against the soft, untouched skin of my inner thighs; he adjusts me against him until his lips graze against mine as he speaks.

"Everything I've ever done has been for you, Lala. I've just joined the army, I'm gunna make something of myself, for us, I want to give you the world, it's just, I've just got myself involved in something and it's not safe for you to be around me right now. That's why I've been pushing you away, I'm sorry, Rosie, I'm so fucking sorry," his huge hands squeeze my hips so tight I'm sure he's leaving bruises but I daren't move, I can't, I don't know what to make of his words.

"Are these just more of your pretty lies?" I whisper against his perfect pink lips, my hands smoothing their way up his leather encased arms.

He shivers under my touch as I drag my fingers down, resting my hands flat against his hard chest, I can feel his heart hammering against my cold palms, he's so warm even through his t-shirt I can feel his heat. It's something I loved when we were little and would play outside, whenever it got cold, Max would wrap me up against him and loan me his warmth.

"I swear to you, I just need time to make it work, Lala," he swallows as I watch his Adam's apple bob in the pale column of his throat.

His hands move up until they sit on my waist beneath my jacket, a shiver rips through me as his fingers gently caress me through the thin fabric of my black mini-dress.

"I've loved you since I was five years old, Kyla-Rose," he tells me softly and even if these are all lies, they're pretty ones, beautiful ones and I intend on cherishing them for the rest of my days.

"I've loved you longer than I can even remember, there is nothing *before you," I choke out almost silently.*

A single hot tear rolls down my cheek and although it's pitch dark in here, Max sees it, the rough pad of his thumb catching it, his eyes never leave mine as he sucks his thumb into his mouth, swallowing my tear, the tear for him, for me, for us, my mum.

My Mum's dead. *I think again, why can't I just say the words?*

Max's lips collide with mine in a hot, desperate kiss, one he's been waiting for, one I've been longing for, he kisses me with every childhood memory and lonely separated day.

He tastes like dark corners in haunted houses and nightmares, ice cream on a hot summers day and love, so much fucking love that it physically hurts. This kiss is ripping me open and I'm bleeding out. For everything we should have had, everything we could have, there's so much blood, covering everything in deep, dark crimson. Everything in this kiss is a deep, desperate love. It's in this moment that I realise just how hard I've fallen for Maddox Sharpe. I would give this world just to be pulled into his.

My lips part for him and he wastes no time as his hot

tongue delves in deep, his hand cradling the back of my head, pulling me closer and closer until we're sharing breath, there's no room between us for air, only each other. My fingers curl over his broad shoulders, my black painted nails digging in as my hips grind down against him. His hand tightens on my waist as he pulls back.

"We're not doing that, Lala," he breathes into me and I flush, of course we're not*, stupid, stupid, stupid. "You're barely legal, I don't want your mum finding out and calling me in on rape charges, I'm in enough shit as it is, you understand that, don't you?" he pleads and the thing is I do.*

I do understand, but I still can't help feeling his rejection. Although I'm sixteen, which is the legal age of consent in England, that's what my mum's like, or was *like, she hates Max.*

"Don't you want me?" I breathe, our lips still brushing against one another with our words.

"Of course I fucking do, but not like this," he shakes his head, his thick black hair dropping into his eyes, I reach out, brushing it back from his beautiful face.

He really is striking to look at even in little light, now that my eyes have fully adjusted to the dark, the moonlight reflects off of his pale skin, his hair as black as night against the electric turquoise of his big eyes, hidden beneath thick eyelashes and perfectly arched brows.

"I want you, just for tonight, if you're going away with the army I'll be here all by myself, can't we just forget about everything else? Just let us have this moment, the world owes us this much." I look into those eyes, those endless pools of blue. "I want you to be my first," I breathe against him and he lets

out a low groan.

"Fucking hell, Lala, you have no idea what you're doing to me right now, I'm trying to be a good man," his fingers flex on my waist as we teeter on the metal beam, but neither of us seems concerned with being suspended twenty feet in the air.

"I don't want a good man, I just want you," I whisper, my words laced with wanton desire, my heart rate kicks up, the damaged organ galloping in my chest.

"Kyla-Rose," he warns with a low growl making me shiver with the use of my full name.

I adjust myself in his lap, shamelessly grinding down over his lap as I shift my weight around. I know he wants this too, I can feel how hard he is beneath me. I lean in pressing my lips to his, he kisses me back, slowly, testing, unsure. I slide my hands beneath his jacket, pushing it free from his shoulders, he allows me to slide it down his arms, letting it fall over his hands, dropping to the dusty floor beneath us; hitting the ground with a gentle thud.

I run my greedy hands down his cotton covered chest, clawing gently over his abs. I trace my fingers beneath the hem of his shirt, running my hands up and over his tight muscles, I let them rest against his chest, skin to skin, his nipples turn into fine points beneath my freezing hands and he shivers.

I smile against his mouth as he bites into my bottom lip, nipping at it before sucking it into his hot mouth, releasing it with a loud pop, a low groan rumbles free from his chest. My breathing is so ragged and uncontrolled, I lift my hips up, grinding them back down against his hard length, his punishing grip on me tightens almost to the point of unbearable but I need it, the pain.

I revel in it, it's where we live, me and Max, in the shadows, the darkness in the thick filth of the underground, we thrive in the gutters we were slung into and we're rising up. We will rise up, together.

Max and I.

Even if it's all just an illusion for tonight, I'll take it anyway. The dream, the memory, I'll take this selfishly because deep down I know this is our beginning and our end. He feels it too. It's in every breath he takes. This is the start of our downfall.

Max grips my hips, motioning for me to stand above him, balancing either side of his thighs I slowly rise to my feet. He looks up at me, eyes full of unspoken promises.

"Jump over to that platform," he instructs me, his voice low, one of his huge hands runs up my calf, gripping the back of my thigh, keeping me balanced.

I launch myself across the small gap landing in a crouch, what's left of this second story thankfully feels solid beneath my feet.

Max follows behind me and then his solid body slams into mine, knocking the wind straight from my lungs. His arms wrap around me, one pulling my hip toward him, our pelvis's grinding into one another as his other hand cups the back of my head, he deepens our kiss, his lips and mine were made to fit together, they dance together effortlessly, like a well-rehearsed performance.

Max's hands move suddenly, stripping me free of my jacket, it hits the floor hard and then he's ripping his t-shirt up and over his head with one hand, the other still crushing my hip. My hands desperate to run over his hot flesh reach out, roaming his heated skin, tracing the unfamiliar body of an all too familiar soul.

Max drops a chaste kiss to my bare collarbone before running his tongue down my throat and along to my shoulder, kissing, nipping and sucking his way there. My head drops back in ecstasy as he pillages my mouth once again, stealing my breath and assaulting my tongue.

His big hands glide down my back, over the soft curve of my arse, his fingers tracing the bare skin at the crease between bum and thigh, before he's pushing my dress up and over that hump, the cold air hits my skin feeling like a thousand splinters, goosebumps breaking out all over my skin as I shiver beneath his touch.

Max walks me backwards until my back slams into the metal wall, I gasp as my bare arse slaps against it.

"You're sure about this?" Max asks me gruffly, drawing back an inch; just enough to get a good look at my face.

"Don't stop," I demand, fisting a handful of dark hair and forcing his lips back to mine.

His forearms slide to the back of my thighs and then he's holding my weight up for me against the tin wall, my legs automatically wrapping around his waist.

Max kisses me all over, along my jaw, down my throat, across my collarbone until he reaches my heaving chest, leaving a scorching trail in his wake. One hand holding me up he uses the other to drag my dress down, baring my lace covered breasts to him. He sucks one of my hardened nipples through the flimsy material into his hot mouth and I arch into him, a whimper escaping my lips as I drop my head back, crashing into the cold metal.

His free hand runs up my inner thigh, teasing the sensitive skin before he reaches my molten core. His fingers run over the lace of my drenched knickers, teasing, barely grazing me with his touch. I wriggle in his arms and he releases my nipple with a low chuckle.

"Patience," he growls into the crook of my neck and then I'm crying out as he sinks his teeth into me, drawing blood and letting it trail down my arm.

Marking me, claiming me, making me bleed for him, for us, I hope it scars. I want his teeth permanently imprinted in my skin. So he'll always know and I'll always know that I belong to him. Maddox Sharpe. That I bled for him, bleed *for him.*

The experts say there's only three types of bleeding, capillary, arterial and venous.

But there's a fourth

Emotionally.

And I'm always fucking bleeding.

Lapping the trickle of blood away, sucking on my throat, he tears my knickers to one side, running a single digit through my slick folds.

"Fuck, you're so wet," he hisses, suddenly dropping my unsteady feet back to the floor, "I need to taste you," he growls falling to his knees before me.

His fingers shred through the scrap of black lace -RIP to what used to be my favourite knickers- then his hot mouth is on me, we groan in unison as soon as his lips hit my core, the vibrations from him making my knees wobble. Max splays a hand against my lower belly, pinning me to the wall, holding my jelly like legs up. Pretty sure if he didn't have hold of me right now I'd be sliding to the floor.

Max feasts on me, his hot tongue violently lashing my clit, rolling back down to dive deep, he fucks me with his mouth unceremoniously, it's loud and sloppy and so fucking good.

I cry out when one of his heavy inked fingers pushes into me, not too far, only to the second knuckle but fuck, the wave that crashes over me, has me trembling and shaking and crying out Max's name over and over, singing my devil's name like a prayer.

Before I can even blink, his lips are back on mine, tasting myself on him only makes me crave him more. My fingers tremble as I struggle with his zipper but he's right there with me as he frees himself. My cold fingers curling around his hot, thick shaft. I stroke him in my hand lazily, dropping his face forward, his forehead resting in the crook of my neck.

I've never touched a man before and I literally have no idea what I'm doing but whatever I'm doing, Max seems to like because the noises falling from his throat can only be that of pleasure.

Max's warm hand slides to the back of my thigh, lifting my leg so it's bent at the knee and resting in the crook of his elbow. He replaces my hand on his hard cock with his own, lining himself up with my entrance.

Max looks deep into my eyes and for a second I just stop breathing. I could almost swear that he's telling the truth, that in this moment he loves me, I'm his reason for breathing, like the planets orbit the sun and I'm his sun.

His long shaft pushes into me slowly at first, Max grits his teeth as he melds his body with mine, once the tip's in he slows his movements, his eyes flicking between my own seeking silent permission or to witness my hesitation, he wants me to be sure.

"Do it," I whisper, the fire in my belly burning white hot.

Max braces a hand against the wall beside my head, his other still clutching my thigh, he presses his lips to mine in a searing hot kiss, pushing the rest of his way inside. He continues kissing me, swallowing all of my moans, gulping them down as if they were his own.

I guess they kind of are his, in a way, every noise I make belongs to him, is for him, I am more his than I am my own. Maddox Sharpe owns me, so completely, body, mind and soul. His to kiss, his to touch, his to love, his to destroy, I'm so completely ruined by everything that is him, in all the good ways and the bad.

Max glides himself in and out of me, thrusting slow and steady, his entire body tense, every muscle taut, I know he's holding back, trying not to hurt me, but I need this, I need him. I need it to hurt because it's what we do together, we hurt.

"Max," I breathe, breaking our lips apart, "don't hold back," I run my hand along his jaw, cupping his cheek in my hand, "fuck me like you never will again," I whisper, because deep down I know this is it, this is our beginning and our end, oh, how I wish I were wrong, but I just know.

This is his goodbye.

Max draws his face back from me, his turquoise eyes flicking between my own before he thrusts into me in one hard punishing move, bottoming out, his hips slamming into mine as he works me over. My hands gripping onto him as I try to hold myself up, Max fucks me into the metal wall, the cold of it biting at my exposed skin.

Then he's lifting up my other leg, wrapping both around his waist, massaging my arse cheeks with rough hands as he slams into me over and over, hitting the end of me with every savage thrust he makes. His lips suck and bite a vicious trail down my neck, leaving his mark for the world and everyone in it to see. I drop my head back against the cold metal as he forces pleasure through me in thick waves.

Our whole lives have been leading up to this very moment; everything we've ever said and done has bought us both to this. Everything from here on out is going to change. I just wish it were for the better.

Holding me up with one hand, Max slides his hand between our sweat covered bodies, "come for me, Lala," he demands between breathy moans.

He rubs my clit in harsh circles with his thumb and I immediately cry out, my head thrashing from side to side as he continues to fuck me into oblivion and then he's right there with me, he thrusts into me one last time so hard I see stars, filling me with his hot cum, dropping his head to my shoulder.

Neither of us moves as we try to get our breath back, me still pinned to the wall with his large hands, his entire body slumped against my own, every muscle aching and tingly and so fucking alive.

"I have to go, Lala," Max mumbles against my neck between kisses, "I have to do something," he sighs. "I'll come back, I won't be long, just... just stay here and wait for me 'kay?"

"Okay," I whisper obediently with a nod, he slowly lowers my feet to the floor, holding me up, waiting until I'm steady.

He tugs my dress back into place before throwing his t-shirt back on and brushing it down with his hands to remove the thick layer of dust.

"I love you, you know that, don't you, princess?" he asks me, using the endearment from our childhood, when I was locked in the castle and he was my knight that tore the city apart and slayed the dragon to get to his princess.

He cups my face in his large hands, the skin rough against my flushed cheeks.

"I do," I tell him, my eyes opening and connecting with his, he presses soft kisses against my lips, pecking at me over and over until I giggle, smiling up at him.

He draws back still cupping my face and gives me one back, Max never smiles, he has a hard face, it's intimidating and harsh and I can see how people are easily frightened of him. But when he smiles, angels sing and birds fly and the sun beams just that little bit brighter.

"I'll be back," he promises, "as soon as I can, just wait for me here, I won't be long."

I nod and with one last kiss to my lips he jumps the small gap from the platform to the beam and shimmies himself down, dropping back to the big pile of rubble. I watch him as he scoops down to grab his jacket and my eyes follow him until he's swallowed by shadows.

Then I sit and wait.

I wait and I wait and I wait.

Did he lie to me?

Is everything he said untrue?

What could be so important that he just had to leave me right after that?

He's not coming back.

He never was.

Stupid. Stupid. Stupid.

I wait until the sun starts revealing herself and it's apparent to me then, he's not coming back for me.

My heart quite literally shatters inside my chest, splintering into sharp jagged pieces, piercing me from the inside out, my lungs scream at me as I sob. I heave trying to force some of the icy air into my lungs. Dropping to my hands and knees I rock myself.

Breathe.

Just take a breath and everything will feel better.

Breathe.

I repeat the mantra over and over until on a gasp I finally manage to pull in some much needed oxygen. I fall back on my haunches and cry. When I finally run out of tears I dry my cheeks with the backs of my hands, dusting myself off. Pushing to my feet I make the small hop back across to the red beam, lowering myself to the pile of rubble beneath.

I wander back to the car I borrowed, I always intended on taking it back, I made sure I knew where I pinched it from but plans change and it can all happen in the blink of an eye. One singular moment can redefine everything. I climb behind the wheel and start the engine, buckling my seatbelt because I'm not completely reckless and then I back the car up as far as I can.

With one last steadying breath I slam my foot down onto the clutch, hammering my way through all five gear changes and then thrust my foot flat to the floor. I ram the car into that shit heap in the middle of the warehouse, this car is such an old piece of shit it doesn't even have air bags, my head slams into the steering wheel on impact. I sit for a minute to get my bearings, blinking my way through the haze, I manage to unclip my seatbelt but the door's jammed.

I turn in the seat, lie on my back and draw my legs into my chest, I boot the door as hard as I can, kicking at it until it finally creaks open in protest. I drag myself from the mangled vehicle and sit a few feet away from the smoking mess. In shaking hands I tuck a cigarette between my lips and light it up, ruining that car didn't make me feel any better, in fact all I've done is twist my rage into something even darker, more deadly.

He left me.

He's not coming back.

I stumble to my feet, my fingers finding the hot stream of blood trickling down the side of my face, I feel through the hot liquid and touch a gash on my forehead, I poke my fingers into it, forcing the torn flesh apart and feel nothing.

I feel absolutely fucking nothing.

In a moment of weakness, I hear my cousin Charlie's voice inside my head, 'burn it to the ground, burn it all, burn the world, show them you won't take their shit lying down, burn it all down.'

So I do.

I tear the bottom off of my dress, pop open the petrol cap and tuck the fabric inside before lighting the end with my lighter,

I watch as the flame quickly climbs the length of the fabric and then I turn, slowly walking away from everything that happened in this god-forsaken place. When I'm about twenty feet away the car explodes. The impact throwing me forwards, heat licks over my back as the whole thing starts to burn. I turn myself over on the gravel and watch as the flames engulf the building. Red and orange flames flicker, lighting up the pink early morning sky.

I hear the sirens as they approach, but I don't move, I don't have anything left to move for. I know I should be getting the fuck out of here, no one would ever know this was me, there's no evidence here, no cameras we're deep in the underground dwellings of the city here, no one would ask questions, this is just the same old shit that happens all the time.

But I don't move, in fact I lie back onto my elbows, kick my feet over one another and laugh. I laugh until I cry and even then I don't stop laughing.

Not when I get dragged up from the floor, not when I get handcuffed and thrown into the back of a pig's car, not even when they take my fingerprints at the station and throw me into a cell. No, I laugh until I'm standing up in court and get told I'm going to prison.

I'll never forget that first night in juvie.

That was the beginning of the end for me.

Fresh meat.

CHAPTER 16

KYLA-ROSE

I shoot bolt upright in bed, a sharp gasp escaping me, my skin beaded with sweat, tendrils of long silver hair plastered to my sweaty face and my palms so slick I could squeeze the sweat from them into a glass. I scrub my wet hands down my face, smoothing my hair back, the sheets all twisted beneath me, my ankles knotted up in my pushed down pyjama pants.

What the fuck?

"Morning, Darlin'," I jump at Huxley's cheery voice and hiss a string of curses as my heart gallops in my chest, I flip onto my other side to face him.

"Jesus Christ, Hux, you scared the shit out of me," I say, slapping a hand over my thundering heart to the feel of it beating three-times its usual speed.

Huxley chuckles at me, clutching my wrist and dragging it

away from my chest. He tugs me down so I'm lying face to face with him in the pillows, Hux's hands in a prayer position tucked beneath the side of his face, I mimic his position as I get comfy and stare back at him.

"Huxley…" I drawl with a smirk and a raised eyebrow, he stays silent, smirking right back, "why are my pyjama bottoms around my ankles?" I ask as suspiciously as I can while trying hard not to laugh.

We've been playing these games you see, on the nights I've been sleeping in bed with Huxley this past week, he and I seem to naturally gravitate towards each other in our sleep, meaning I usually wake up with his dick in me, *somewhere…* we seem to subconsciously take it in turns with the initiation side of things.

Jesus, I'm a thirsty bitch.

"Well," he starts with a grin that's just far too smug for first thing in the morning, "you tossed and turned all night, so obviously that kept me awake."

"Mm-hmm…" I hum with two raised brows, tucking my lips between my teeth to hide my smile.

"So, being the gentleman that I am, I pinned you to the mattress with my arms and legs to try and keep you still so I could at least *try* and get some shut eye, I mean look at me! I know I'm super good looking and all but I still need my beauty sleep, goddamn it!" he cries in outrage and I snort.

"Get to the point, Huxley Harrington-Griffin," I growl and he laughs a deep chuckle.

I love using his full name, the way it always makes his eyes narrow.

Huxley's mum is like some super fancy politician, he

comes from wealth, a lot of it by the sounds of it, his family even have gold mines. No, I'm not kidding, literally they own some, more than a few by the sounds of it too, pretty crazy shit if you ask me.

Huxley's mum is half African; she came to England when *her* mum –Hux's grandmother- moved here. She met her would-be husband in her home town, he was filming a documentary about wildlife. They fell madly in love and married, she moved back here with him and the rest is history, hence the source of Huxley's beautiful caramel skin and pretty curls, he's a whole quarter African, he's been there a bunch of times too and he's been telling me all about it. I'd love to travel with him one day.

"Well you must have gotten hot being entrapped by my wrestlers hold on you and you started shoving your clothes off, I got an elbow to the ear and everything. Honestly, you usually sleep like the dead, I sometimes prod you in the night just to see if you're still breathing but last night was like a motherfucking mattress rave, some unspoken dance competition, just you against the bed," he tsks with a shake of his head. "I have to wonder though, were you dreaming about the first time we met," he smirks, waggling his eyebrows at me and I can't help but laugh. "Your arse wriggled against me so violently, you were like a giant caterpillar trying to shimmy out of its shell! I feel violated by the whole thing if we're being totally honest," he cries in mock outrage.

"You mean cocoon," I correct on a giggle and he narrows those deep brown eyes on me.

"You think you're so clever don't you little Pilly?"

"Pilly?" I question, sitting up with a cocked brow, the

sheets pooling around my waist.

"Caterpillar, durrrr," Huxley rolls his eyes dramatically then sits up, "sheesh, I thought you were *clever*!" he snorts, darting from the bed just as I go to grab him.

"I will get you," I promise, "when you least expect it!" I call after him as he escapes into the bathroom, he doesn't lock the door though, neither of them ever do.

I lie on my back still wrapped up in everything that is Huxley, his humour refreshing and light. He makes every day I wake up next to him feel like a blessing and I never leave the bed without a smile on my lips.

Thinking over my nightmare -or rather memory- from last night I cringe at myself. I haven't dreamt about that night or Maddox fucking Sharpe for weeks. Meeting Kacey and Huxley seemed to distract me from his memory so much that I started to rest easier at night.

One less thing haunting me in the dark or so I thought.

I think talking about my mum the first night I was here last week triggered me a little. A lot happened that night. I wonder sometimes about Max. I wonder where he went when he left me that night, I wonder if he got in an accident and he really did mean to come back for me but then I remember I was just a gullible, naïve, stupidly in love teenager who had just found her mum's dead body on the floor of her living room.

That's called trauma. My nightmares are due to PTSD apparently, but all that really means is I have triggers I may or may not be aware of and when those little switches get flipped, how I react or behave in certain situations is entirely dependent on my *fragile* mind. Three guesses who spewed all that doctory shit…

The brain is a funny thing, it can do so many clever things but it can also act as a cage, a darkened prison of your own making, a place filled with rot and decay.

I read somewhere that people who have survived sexual abuse often create a little safe place inside their head, like a happy little room filled with all their favourite things and the people they love. Good and happy memories to remove themselves from a situation that they physically have no control over, a warm, safe place to escape to during stressful situations.

I didn't create a space like that when I was raped in juvie. I carved out a pitch dark hole, just big enough for me to crawl inside, empty and barren and cold. The light in my grey-green gaze would fade and I'd often come to with a harsh slap to my face, it's no fun you see. Raping someone who plays dead, that doesn't excite these perverts, paedophiles and rapists.

They want you to scream, struggle and react, to fight. They want everything from you and more, it's not enough that they're already stealing your dignity, no, they want it all. Take, take, take. And that's why eventually I stopped doing those things, I quickly learnt that no matter how loudly I screamed, how hard I fought back and how much I struggled. They ultimately always won.

No one was coming to save me, even the men who held me down while the ring-leaders tore my body apart and violated me in ways you wouldn't want to imagine, they may not have performed the act but they had a part in it. They all did. There was not a single staff member in that facility that didn't know what was happening and not one fucking person did a thing to stop it.

"Are you joining me in this shower or not, *Pilly*?" Huxley chuckles, the sound dragging me from my poisoned thoughts.

A soft smile marks my lips, kicking my pyjama bottoms all the way off, I roll myself out of bed, scuffing my feet along the thread-bare carpet. I push open the door into his en-suite, steam billowing out around me and I fan a hand across my screwed up face.

"I'm not getting in that, the steam will suffocate me!" I protest, my hands on my hips as I hover in the doorframe, I seriously hate hot water.

Huxley points a finger at me, gesturing to me with his chin that I should follow his eye line's direction of travel, I watch as he spins the temperature dial down from nine to four and then raises both eyebrows at me in silent challenge. As if to say, *'hah! Now what you gunna do about it?'*

Decision made, I drop my knickers to the floor, kicking them aside to join the pile of Huxley's clothes by the sink, gripping the hem of my oversized t-shirt I slowly drag it up and over my head, I reach my arm out still clutching the fabric and dramatically drop it to the heap on the floor giving him a show.

Huxley wolf-whistles at me, his coal black eyes raking up my naked body in appreciation.

"Get the fuck in here," he orders with a smirk.

I sashay my way over to him, making sure to emphasise the wiggle in my hips, sliding open the shower door I attempt to step in but before I can even place my other foot inside, Huxley's dragging me against his strong body.

Kissing me hard, he gropes my breasts with long practised

fingers, teasing my peaked nipples, the rainfall of water pounding against the back of his head as he protects my face from the harsh spray. His hands dance across my wet skin, touching and teasing me in all the right spots. Who knew the inside of the elbow or the back of the knee were such erotic spots of pleasure? I for sure fucking didn't, I'm certainly not complaining though.

Then he's spinning me around, placing my hands on the tiles and holding them there as he drags my hips back to meet his, his hard cock brushing against my already soaked core and no, it's not wet from the shower, everything about Huxley turns me on, I'm wet between the thighs at the mere thought of him.

Huxley uses his knee, tapping my thighs apart, spreading me wide for him.

"Don't move your hands," he growls in my ear before nipping at my lobe, goosebumps racing across my slippery skin.

Keeping my palms flat against the white tiles, Huxley's hands fall away from me, I whimper at the loss of contact, all I can feel is the harsh pounding of water against my flesh.

Huxley takes my hip in a punishing hold at the same time his other hand knots through my silver hair, pulling my head backward at a sharp angle, my neck curved and back arched. The bite of pain sending a shiver up my spine, I am *dripping* wet for him, I swear to god if he doesn't fuck me soon I may actually die.

I don't have to wait long before Huxley's beautifully thick cock is slamming into me; a guttural moan escapes his throat as he wrenches my head back even harder. Then he fucks me, pounding into me relentlessly, the piercing through his tip hammering into my cervix as he curves my spine back so far I'm afraid it might snap, he hits a new spot inside me and a low groan spills from my throat.

"Come for me, Darlin'," he orders through gritted teeth, his unrelenting thrusts deep and hard and reckless, there's no method to his madness he's just going at it hard and fast and I am *here* for it.

It's dizzying and enthralling and crazy stimulating all at the same time, when he releases his fistful of my hair and reaches around to pinch my clit I come so hard I see stars. Huxley finishes a few hard thrusts later with a roar so deafening as he fills me with his cum, I'm a million percent certain the neighbours three streets away heard him.

His wet body collapses over me as he kisses my bare shoulders, trailing his lips down my spine.

"Hmm, you seem to be all dirty again, Miss Swallow, may I be of some assistance?"

He squeezes my arse cheeks before slapping them both, one after the other, the sound loud and dramatic against my wet skin.

I spin around, my back against the wall as I try to catch my breath, the water hitting Huxley, gently dusting me with the warm spray. Huxley drops his lips to mine in a kiss filled with passion and raw hunger; I think we could fuck like this all day every day for the next fifty years and never get enough of each other.

"You appear to be correct, Mr Harrington-Griffin, I would very much appreciate your assistance," I say in a fake posh accent, I mean, I'm common as fuck and proud, I don't wanna pretend I'm from fucking Kensington or some shit.

We all have money and we could buy pretty much whatever we wanted but me and my family, just like my two men, we're more than the money that lines our pockets, we all came from nothing –bar, Hux- so I guess that's why it hasn't changed us. We don't care if we're rich or poor, we all just want the same things, to be safe, happy, loved.

Huxley snorts, lathering up a loofah with coconut scented soap. It's one of those fancy imported, organic ones with actual pieces of coconut inside, weird as fuck if you ask me, but Huxley likes it so whatever. He dragged me around the department store the other day when we did some Christmas shopping, he only took us to the fanciest places but it was fun strolling around the place acting like we belonged there, buying all our gifts and laughing raucously while travelling on the escalators.

Kacey and I started going up and Huxley started going down, when he realised he was going in the complete opposite direction he turned and started running back up as the thing filled with people continued taking him down. I laughed so hard I nearly tumbled over the edge when I looked down at him, the only thing that saved me was Kacey's iron-clad grip on my arm.

Gotta give it to him though, the boy made it all the way back up before he made his way to us and he only knocked into one lady on his mission in getting back to us. I'm honestly impressed with his stamina, when he sets his mind to something he follows through, *every single time*. Both boys have been taking me all over the place the last week, we've spent every evening together, even the days Kacey had to work at the garage.

After another round of shower sex, Huxley leaves me to

actually wash. When I emerge I tug on a black sports bra and a pair of acid-wash grey joggers. I dry my hair, shade in my eyebrows and lacquer on some mascara before I bounce my way down the stairs. When I reach the bottom, Kacey's hanging multi-coloured Christmas lights around the ceiling.

"Cute," I smile.

Slipping between Kacey's bare chest and the wall, I reach up onto tippy toes and pucker my lips for a kiss. Kacey's thick fingers immediately wrap around my throat as he presses me into the wall, one arm still above his head holding up the little coloured lights, he kisses me so hard and demanding that I melt into a hot little puddle right at his feet. When he finally breaks our kiss he smiles down at me, that big soppy grin that I love so much and drops another quick kiss to the tip of my nose.

"Hey, Big Man," I smile as he releases my throat and I almost slide down the wall.

"Mornin', Sweetheart, how's my wild girl this morning?" he asks, reaching back up to continue tacking the coloured lights up.

"Happy," I shrug, skirting back around him I park my arse on one of the navy couches so I can shamelessly watch my man work.

His bulging muscles ripple as he moves, the defined muscles in his back flexing beneath the confines of tight inked skin. And when he stretches both arms up above his head I can't help but tilt my head and bite my bottom lip with a groan. Kacey whips around to face me but I don't remove my gaze from him, instead I circle a single finger in the air.

"Turn around and get back to work, Big Man, you're

ruining the show," I frown dramatically and he chuckles, his whole body shaking with the motion but he does as he's told and turns back to the task at hand.

"Where's Hux?" I ask after a beat, I've gotta stop looking or I'm gunna make him take me right here.

"Getting the tree, we thought you might wanna decorate it with us," Kacey looks over his shoulder at me and I tip my head so hard to the right to stare at all of that manly goodness that I almost topple off the couch.

"Kyla-Rose," he growls in warning and I straighten my gaze to focus on those golden-amber orbs in his beautiful face.

"Yeah?" I smile and bat my eyelashes at him innocently; he shakes his head, turning back to his lights.

"I said, d'you wanna decorate the tree with us?" he repeats like I didn't actually hear him, I did *hear* him, I just wasn't *listening*, two very different things right there.

"Have you already got decorations to go on it?" I mumble absently, my mind still ninety-percent focused on his delectable body.

I lick my lips and smack them together loudly re-drawing his attention to me.

I stand up, confidently strolling over to my golden eyed beast, my skin prickling at his closeness. I run my cool hands up his back before roughly scraping my nails down his skin, a shiver runs through his huge body but with his arms still up above his head with the last of the lights I loop my arms around his waist and snuggle into him from behind, pressing the side of my face against the solid planes of his back. His warm skin heating my own as I nuzzle against him, squeezing him just a tiny bit tighter, my hands linked across his abs.

"You okay, Sweetheart?" Kacey's deep voice rumbles, the sound vibrates through me all the way down to my toes.

"Mm-hmm, I just missed you," I tell him honestly, he worked all day yesterday at the garage and I slept in bed with Huxley last night.

I hate having to switch between the two rooms. I want to be with both of them all the time. As much as I like our individual alone time, I would much rather be in a permanent Hux and Kacey sandwich.

Yum.

Just the thought of the two of them together, four wandering hands, two hard cocks and two desperately hot mouths, it's enough to push a girl over the edge. Know what I mean?

Christ almighty, I need to get a grip.

"I missed you too," he says, finally dropping the remaining end of lights and covering my hands with his own, "and yeah, we have stuff to decorate it with, Huxley's mum gets all these ridiculous decorator people in over the Christmas period, their mansion is lit up so bright you can see it from space," he laughs and I chuckle with him. "Anyway, she always ends up with way too many decorations, so she sends a box over for us to pick through."

"I see, so really, you don't decorate, Huxley's mum does and you just hang shit she gives you on a tree?" I sass, teasing in my tone as I nibble my bottom lip to keep from smiling.

"You see right through me, huh?" he chuckles removing my arms from around his waist.

I frown at him but his grin only gets wider.

"You know," he drawls, turning away from me again and bending to grab the loose end of the string lights. "We could play a little before Huxley gets back," his eyebrows lift in question as he turns back to face me.

"What kind of game?" I ask cautiously.

Cocking my head to one side, I eye him warily, earning me a wild chuckle. The sound makes me pause and raise both my eyebrows in surprise. That laugh sounded just a little bit psycho…

"Do you trust me, Sweetheart?" Kacey asks, mirroring my head tilt as he swings the string of lights around.

I take a step back. He follows my movements, taking a step closer for every single one I take until my calves hit the soft velvet of the couch and I drop to my bum with an *oof*. Kacey leans into me, his large hands resting on either side of my thighs. I crane my neck back to look at him, his amber eyes flash with excitement, my pussy clenching in anticipation.

I will never stop wanting Kacey.

He drops his lips to my ear; his words whispered almost silently.

"How d'you feel about being tied up, baby girl?"

Involuntarily I suck in a sharp breath, a small gasp leaving me almost instantly as his thick fingers wrap around my throat, restricting my air flow just the smallest amount. He tugs me up from my sitting position, my body trembling with need.

"I'm so fucking hard for you, Kyla-Rose. Are you going to be a good girl for me and take my cock?" he growls.

Leaving me in just my underwear, he strips me free of my clothes moving us back over to the wall, slamming me chest first into it, he presses himself against my back.

Every single plane of muscle digs into my bare, soft flesh as he holds me against the wall with his weight. His grip still tight around my throat, his fingers flexing against my pulse point, I groan, pushing my arse back into him, shamelessly grinding against his erection.

"You're so fucking beautiful. Every time you bite into your lip when you look at me you make me so fucking insane with need that I almost come in my boxers. Do you like teasing me? Getting me worked up and desperate to slide into your slick cunt? How wet are you, Sweetheart?" Kacey's voice grows huskier, his low tone animalistic, wild, getting me hot and wet in all the right places. "WELL?!" he bellows demanding an answer, his body sending waves of vibration through me.

I flinch but not in fear, with desire. Kacey taking charge isn't new, but like this? This, *this* is definitely new. And I have a feeling this is only the beginning, he's been taking it easy on me the last couple of weeks but now that my heads healed and I'm feeling better in myself, it seems all bets are finally off.

"Yes!" I squeal in response, my voice tight, earning me a harsh slap to my arse.

"Good girl," he rumbles against my ear. "Now, place your palms flat against the wall and slide them up above you head," he orders in a growl, stepping just slightly back from me, still keeping a firm grip on my throat.

As instructed, I very slowly slide my hands up the wall, Kacey's breathing becoming harsher as he watches my tantalisingly slow movements.

When my hands meet each other above my head, "spread

your legs," he barks, so I do.

I widen my stance, spreading my feet wide apart, bending slightly to separate them further, sticking my arse out a little just as a harsh slap lands against my cool skin, making me yelp before Kacey quickly massages the sting away.

I'm panting now and it's got nothing to do with Kacey restricting my breathing. My legs feel like jelly, shaking as they try to keep my needy body upright. My pussy clenches as he runs his thick fingers down my spine before spanking my arse again and nipping my neck harshly with his teeth.

"I'm going to make you come now, Sweetheart," Kacey breathes into me, a tremor instantly working its way through my trembling body before he releases me from his hold.

Cool air hits my back as Kacey's hot body moves away from me. I involuntarily slump against the wall, my cheek resting against it as my eyes slip closed, my chest rising and falling rapidly with uneven breaths. My eyes snap open as Kacey grabs my wrists. Holding them tightly in one of his large hands still above my head, he flips me to face him, my back now plastered against the wall.

Kacey wrenches my arms up as high as my tip-toes will take me, pinning me against the wall with his huge body, my shoulders pinching as they're stretched to their limit. His other hand comes up, twisting the loose end of Christmas lights around my wrists, binding them together. He tugs them sharply, the plastic cord pinching my delicate skin.

Kacey releases my hands, taking a large step back, leaving the thick cord of coloured lights to bind me to the ceiling. My legs spread wide and pale skin flushed, heat working its way up from my chest, clawing its way up my neck and settling in my heated cheeks. He cocks his head, a smirk slowly making its way to his lips, his dimples creating perfect little crescents in his cheeks as he rakes his eyes up my exposed body.

I've never allowed myself to be this vulnerable for *anyone* before but I already know I'd do anything with Kacey, I think deep down my soul knows I can trust him. No matter what the situation. His demon is akin to mine in that way.

I shift on my toes as much as is possible, trying to balance my weight evenly as the arches of my feet scream in protest; I'm definitely not ballerina material, that's for fucking sure. I hold my breath as Kacey stalks closer. His huge body, broad and intimidating, glides towards me like he's the lion and I'm the injured gazelle. The muscles in his forearms bunch and ripple beneath his inked skin as he shoves his joggers down, kicking them away, his thick cock springing free and standing to attention, the silver glint of his piercing catching my eye.

I drop my gaze, taking my time to appreciate the glorious sight that is his rock hard body. His calves and thighs thick and wide, tattoos starting at his toes, his sculpted hips, that delicious pelvic V leading to a thick, long cock, glistening with pre-cum and pierced at the tip, tattoos curling around the base. Ripped abs, solid pecs, broad shoulders, thick biceps and corded forearms, every visible inch of skin wrapped in ink. Inked vines and ivy climbing up the shaved side of his head, blonde hair hanging over one of his gold eyes the other, I lick my lips, sucking my bottom lip into my mouth as my eyes finally lock onto his.

I exhale a sharp breath as his eyebrows twitch at me, his smirk morphing into a sick, satisfied grin. My stomach clenches, my knees wobbling as a grin splits his face, a wild, manic glint burning behind his gold eyes.

And then he's there, towering over me, his hands relaxed at his sides as he drops his face into my mess of silver hair. Breathing me in deeply, he runs his nose down my neck and along my shoulder, inhaling my scent before rolling his eyes into the back of his head with a groan. My breath catches, his gaze snapping up to meet mine, a low rumble echoing through his clenched teeth.

"Tell me you're mine," he demands roughly before sinking his teeth into the exposed skin of my neck.

I tug at my binds, whimpering as the cord snags my skin. I arch off of the wall trying to get closer to Kacey, make him touch me, *something.* My pussy dripping down my thighs, clenching at nothing as Kacey pulls back and laps up the trickle of blood from his teeth.

His large tattooed hand runs up my other arm, grazing his knuckles across my jaw, cupping my flushed face. His golden eyes, the colour of the sun, flick between my grey-green gaze as he thumbs my bottom lip.

"I'm yours," I manage to admit in a breathy whisper, meaning the words with every fibre of my being.

Something snaps inside Kacey at my confession, I see the change in his eyes, the feral, demonic part of him fully surfacing and he's suddenly on me like a man possessed.

My bra and knickers are torn from my body, the flimsy silk shredding in his big hands as he tosses the useless fabric aside. He runs his hands up my flat belly, his rough palms kneading the heavy flesh of my breasts. His thumbs torturing the piercings in my nipples as he flicks them over and over. His thigh pressing between my own, just out of reach for me to be able to get some relief, I exhale my irritation as Kacey chuckles darkly in my ear before biting into my neck again. I cry out, bouncing on my toes as my cunt gushes juices down my thighs at the pain.

"Fuck me!" I snap in frustration through gritted teeth.

He crashes a hand against the wall, smacking his palm against the spot next to my face, his dark chuckle vibrating through his chest, filling us both up with the demonic sound. He leans back from me, his eyes boring into my own. Taking me by surprise his other hand snaps up gripping my throat, my breathing cut off completely as he squeezes. My windpipe closed off and burning, he slams his cock into me with a tortured grunt, his fingers flex on my throat allowing me to suck in a sliver of air as he starts to fuck me, pulling out of me almost entirely before ramming his thick length back in.

My mind goes completely blank.

Thinking and feeling nothing but Kacey and his control over me. That's what I've given him, complete control over my mind, body and soul. Allowing him to control me and fuck me so violently that he purges us both of our demons. Everything about Kacey is intoxicating, infecting me like a fast acting poison. Dragging me in, like the sand with the tide, he pulls me in and takes me under.

Black spots creep into my vision as he continues to hammer into me, my body slick with sweat, knees trembling. Just as I think I'm about to slip into the darkness, Kacey releases his hold on my throat. My head falling forward as I heave in breaths, my lungs screaming and chest heaving, I suck in a lungful of air just in time for Kacey's lips to slam down on mine.

He kisses me hard, sucking the breath right out of me before sinking his teeth into my bottom lip. I kiss him back just as ferociously, our blood mixing on our tongues. Praying I had the use of my hands so I could tear my nails down his back. Kacey suddenly lifts me, dragging me over to the dining room, tearing the lights from the ceiling in the process as my wrists remain bound, the little tacks firing around the room like missiles.

Kacey drops my arse onto the dining table, the cool wood making me jolt as it meets my hot skin. He wraps the torn down string of lights around my torso, all the way down, avoiding my legs, linking them around my ankles. Forcing my knees open with his large hands he drags me to the edge of the wood, roughly shoving my body down onto the table he slams back inside of me.

I cry out at the intrusion, the tip of his dick hits my cervix battering my insides as he pounds into me. The dining table screeching in protest as it scrapes across the floor, jumping in time with his punishing thrusts. I squirm in my bindings, my arms bound above my head, the string of lit lights wrapped down and around my upper body, Kacey growls, attacking my clit with his thumb.

"Come. Right fucking now, come for me, Kyla-Rose!" he roars as he twists the bundle of nerves between his thumb and finger.

I scream out my release, my head rocking side to side as Kacey finishes with a grunt, coating my insides with his cum. His huge body drops onto mine, his fingers absently reaching up to release my hands before he cradles himself to me. My fingers run through his hair, my nails gently clawing over his scalp as I clutch his head to me, his cheek pressed tightly against my heaving chest. Without pulling himself free, he shifts slightly, his chin resting against my sternum so he can look at me.

"Are you happy here?" he asks me and I smile at him softly.

"How could I not be? I feel like the luckiest woman alive right now," I chuckle lightly.

"I want you to always be this happy, with us," he murmurs, pulling me up with him, his thick fingers winding themselves into my hair, he tugs gently on the ends, unwinding the lights from my body and tilting my head back. "I think I'm falling in love with you," Kacey whispers and I freeze, I don't fucking mean to but I fucking freeze and he feels it too, I know he does, there's no way he couldn't, not with his dick still inside me.

His gold eyes flick between mine, my heart stutters to a stop inside my chest as my breath catches and my spine stiffens.

Fuck.

Fuck.

Fuck.

Loves me? I never expected a man to say those three – seemingly innocent- words to me. Let alone actually mean them. And I can see it in his eyes, he does, he means those words more than he's ever meant anything before. Do I even know how to love? Do I have the capacity? There's a difference between loving my family and *this.* This? What is this? Okay, boyfriend, *boyfriends*, like, relationships are messy at the best of times but love?

Love hurts. Love cuts and breaks and torments. Love shatters even the most solid of people. I've done love before.

Only once, but I've done it. And it destroyed me, but this is *Kacey*, could Kacey ever hurt me like that? *Would he?*

Before I get a chance to speak and fuck everything up, he presses his lips to mine silencing me with a searing hot kiss. One that tells me he's serious, one that tells me he can wait, one that tells me he doesn't need me to say it back right now, a kiss that wreaks havoc on my soul and tortures the half-dead organ in my chest. I think it's this kiss that makes me realise that even if I'm not ready to say those words, I'm already there anyway, because I know in this very moment that I could never get Kacey Baker out of my head or my heart for as long as I live, be that a day, a week, a year or a hundred. Kacey Baker has well and truly imprinted himself on my bloodied soul and carved his name into my damaged heart.

Huxley brings the most perfect little tree back just as Kacey finishes putting up the lights, *again*. It sits in the corner of the room beside the front window, a real pine, about five feet high and chunky, it's a dumpy little thing and as soon as Hux dragged it across the floor and freed it from its net I loved it. I can't have real trees in my penthouse because Brute likes to chew them. The first Christmas I had him he demolished the entire tree and half of its decorations in seven seconds flat. It took me and Charlie nearly all night to get him to release the tree trunk, well, what was left of it.

Anyway, this tree is perfect. It's not like the obnoxious one we always have at Uncle Dee's house. The one's we have at home –well my old home which is still Uncle Dee's current house- are always ostentatious, fifteen feet tall, decorated by professionals and lit up like the empire state building and they're always shiny and perfect and it's great because it suits him, he loves Christmas so to be able to have a tree like that is his dream come true.

Looking at the short, stubby tree with its uneven branches and slight tilt has me coming over all emotional. These men, they're sharing their Christmas with me. My favourite time of the year and one of the most special, it's about family and love and that's what I think I may have found here, in this house with two beautifully heroic boys, one of which only a short while ago half declared his love for me. I mean fucking hell, what the fuck did I do to deserve this?

Me and Huxley wrestle with the lights for the tree, hanging glass baubles on the spindly branches, topping it off with a gold star. I take a step back to look at our very first Christmas tree together.

Engulfed by the scent of pine and mint as I suck on the end of a candy cane, Kacey's big body drapes over mine; his thick arms band around my waist from behind, his chin resting on my shoulder. Huxley reaches into another paper bag, pulling out a few small boxes.

"We've got some extra ones," Hux tells me, gesturing to the little red boxes in his hands. "For our first Christmas with you," he winks, jerking his chin, gesturing for me to move toward him.

I lay my head back against the hard planes of Kacey's chest, looking up into his unusual amber-yellow eyes, he gives me a smile and a wink -much like Huxley's- and releases me. I eye the small packages carefully, raising my gaze to Huxley's. He gives me one of his infamous cocky smirks, tugging the half eaten candy cane from between my lips, I release it with a pop. He sticks it between his teeth, snapping off the end and crunching on it raucously.

"You're an animal," I growl, swatting his chest, making him laugh.

"You know it," he winks, "open this one first," he instructs, offering me up a little red gift box.

I lift the lid, unfolding the dark green tissue paper, revealing a small, gold caterpillar made of fine glass on a thick red ribbon. I burst into laughter, laughing so hard, literal tears pour from my eyes as I swipe at them with the backs of my hands.

"When the fuck did you get this? You only called me that for the first time this morning!" I laugh again shaking my head in disbelief.

Huxley seriously does everything he puts his mind to, this boy is definitely determined, that's for sure.

"Mum's decorating team," he shrugs, "they can get fucking anything, do you like it?" he asks almost nervously.

I place the little box down onto the coffee table, turn and wrap my arms around his neck, leaning up onto my tippy-toes, I press a kiss to his lips.

"I love it," I whisper against his mouth.

I kiss him again and then drop back down onto flat feet. Crossing over to the tree, I hang the little glass caterpillar on a sturdy branch near the top, front and centre for all to see.

"This one's for you, Kace," Huxley says, passing over

another small red box.

Kacey opens it up and pulls out another glass ornament, only this time it's a little pair of red boxing gloves on a glittery gold ribbon loop.

"Thanks man," Kacey says, looking up and over at Hux. "I love it," he beams as he passes it to me to hang opposite the little caterpillar. "Err, we also got you one when we were out the other day, it was too *you* for us to not get it," Kacey tells me, eyeing Huxley over the top of my head.

Kacey moves to stand beside his brother as Huxley passes me another box. It's similar to the last two but slightly sturdier with a thick gold ribbon tied on the top; it's weightier than the last two too.

I untie the silk ribbon, lifting the top off, my eyes popping wide as my breath catches. I flick my gaze up to meet the eyes of the two men who continuously surprise me over and over. Their beautiful eyes a stark contrast from one another, one as bright as the sun, the other as black as night.

My heart pounds extra hard in my chest and I bite my bottom lip to fight off the threatening tears. With a shaky hand I reach into the box, pinching the thin black silk loop, using delicate fingers I lift the crystal ornament out of its box and hold it up to the light from the window, watching the black crystal reflect a rainbow of colours across the ceiling as I rock it back and forth over the palm of my hand.

A small, black crystal swallow bird, its wings spread wide in flight, forked tail and short beak, it's the most beautiful thing I've ever seen. It sits in the palm of my hand, no bigger than a compact mirror and it's absolutely fucking perfect. And for the first time in my life I genuinely don't know what to say. I just blink back my tears a few times, swallowing the thick lump of emotion in my throat.

"Thank you, it's beautiful," I manage to choke out and when I finally look back at them both, they're looking at me with expressions that scare the hell out of me.

Expressions that say they would burn the world and everyone in it for me.

"Hang it on the tree then," Huxley laughs encouragingly, already knowing how to break the tension when I'm overwhelmed.

He already knows me so well, I wonder how it's only been a few weeks that we've known each other, it feels like forever and that thought alone scares me half to death. I give him a grateful smile crossing back to our perfect little tree, hanging the shadowed swallow beneath the gold star on the top. I take a few steps back until I'm wrapped up in four big arms, enveloped in their combined scent of mint, earth and clementine's.

We stand there for a moment, just the three of us tangled up in each other's arms and I wonder what it is that I'm so afraid of. Why am I so frightened of letting these men in, when it's obvious to anyone looking that they truly care for me.

Kacey told me just this morning that he thinks he's falling in love with me and I didn't say anything back. Yet I feel so comfortable with Kacey, so secure and safe. He's always holding my hand and making sure that I'm not on the road side when we walk down the street. Stepping in front of me and shielding me from possible danger when there are lots of people around and he can't survey our surroundings in the way that he'd most like.

And when he cuddles me, wrapping me up in his long, thick arms and murmuring comforting words in my ear. Even leaving me out his thick, thermal socks on the end of the bed because he knows after I shower I like to keep my toes toasty. So many little things that he does without hesitation just because he wants me to be happy. Because he *loves* me.

And it's obvious; the way Huxley feels about me, just by looking at all the caring little things that he does for me on a daily basis. He makes sure to have the fridge stocked with those little yogurts I like because he knows I can't stomach too much first thing in the morning. He wears a scrunchie around his wrist whenever we go out because he knows the likelihood of me wanting to shove my hair up when we eat is high. He watches me when he thinks I don't notice, scoping out the room to make sure I'm safe. And he's always, *always* making sure, whatever we're doing or wherever we are, that I'm smiling, which is an easy one because no matter how I'm feeling as long as I'm with Huxley, I smile. And I smile because I *love* him.

I love them both.

CHAPTER 17

KYLA-ROSE

"Ready to party?" Kacey asks me, stepping through his bedroom door.

It's the last Saturday before Christmas, so of course, the boys are throwing one of their parties. I swear, I don't know how they party every week, I'd be dead, but I won't lie, I am kind of excited. I'm really in the Christmas spirit this year, even more so than normal and this time I'll have my two men at my side.

I feel comfortable in the space that I've been living in for the last week and a half, the boys are very in tune with my emotions and my reactions to things now too, so they can sense if I'm getting overwhelmed or I need a cigarette break or five minutes away for some fresh air. They're both completely in sync with each other from years of friendship which makes reading me a slightly easier task, between the two of them they always seem to work out what I need before even I do.

I've tried really hard to let my guard down around them. I know I'm safe with them and I've allowed myself to be vulnerable with them both, together and separately and in lots of ways. I told them about my family, my job, the fire and the virginity disaster. I bristle at the mere thought of that royal fuck up but I'm also kind of thankful it happened because at least I didn't lose my virginity by rape to a correctional facility officer, so I guess that part was kind of a blessing in disguise, in a *really* fucked up way.

Anyway, onto better and brighter things, I'm not going to think about Max tonight, or that place or anything in the past. I'm going to have fun and relax and then try to convince both of my men to share the bed with me again. I know they will if I pout enough but it really is a tight squeeze with the two of them because they're both such big guys.

Kacey is an immovable hulk of a man -I honestly wonder how he fits through regular width doors- and Huxley is stacked just in a different way, so although he's not as wide as Kacey, he's still one hell of a big guy. So it's more like sleeping between two super-hot marble pillars than men, they're just solid. And the bed did protest in very unnerving ways the last time we shared. I was scared to breathe as I wondered if at some point in the night the bed would cave in and I'd wake up in a pile of wooden splinters and knotted sheets.

"Yeah, I'm ready," I smile at Kacey's reflection in the mirror, smacking my red painted lips together.

"You are so fucking hot," Kacey groans, "maybe we should

just stay up here and have a private party instead," he murmurs, biting his bottom lip as his amber-yellow eyes rake over my body appreciatively.

I turn to face him, twisting and re-capping my lipstick; this one is waterproof and supposedly kiss proof, *maybe I should try it out?* I sway my hips a little extra as I walk bare foot across the worn carpet, stepping into Kacey's embrace. His arms are so long and so thick that when he holds me close, I feel like I'm in the safest place in the world. Nothing can touch me when he's got me like this; I'm totally shielded from the darkness by being engulfed in his light.

"Maybe you should get some shoes on and I'll go wait downstairs for you, where I can keep my hands to myself. You know, so we actually *do* make it down there at some point tonight," he laughs but I can feel the tightness of his shoulders.

"Okay, go!" I chuckle, swatting his arse. "I'm coming," I say, releasing his waist and turning away from him to find myself some shoes.

"Eurgh, please don't say *coming* like that," he groans readjusting himself in his tight black jeans.

I spin around, lobbing a rogue shoe at him, which of course he catches effortlessly before it can hit its target.

"I did not say it in any *way!*" I protest with a cluck of my tongue.

Parking myself on the edge of the bed I slip my feet into some blood red stilettoes with a pointed toe and a heel so high that I may very well break my neck in them if I lean a little too far to one side, but I also know how Huxley feels about these shoes. In fact it was only two nights ago that he bent me over the sofa and fucked me in them and by *in them* I mean, in *only* them. I wonder if he's up for a repeat of that…

Tonight I've got on the highest heels and the tightest dress known to man, the boys picked it out when we were shopping last week. It's a spaghetti strap, blood red mini dress with a nineteen-twenty's inspired fringe, so when I move the little tassels dance in the opposite direction. My hair's straight -as usual- hanging past my waist and I've paired it all with gold jewellery, far too many rings on every finger, a thin gold chain sits at the hollow of my throat and thick gold hoops. *What?* I fucking love a hoop, okay? Quit judging me.

People have already arrived, the music has been pounding out of the speakers for the last two hours. Huxley really is a party animal, he's a social butterfly, the mere mention of a party and he's there, that boy can fucking dance too. I remember all too well the night he danced with me at The Pit –when I didn't know who he was- and then at fight night at the warehouse. It was like sex without taking our clothes off; the boy knows how to work his body that's for fucking sure.

One last spritz of perfume and a quick puckering of my lips to check my lipstick and I'm good to go. I close Kacey's door behind me and take a deep breath. I just need to get myself ready for a house full of people that I don't know again. After last time at least Kacey gets now, why some of his friends kept their distance, they obviously recognised me and were wary. I get it, stories about me are bad enough let alone the gossip attached to them, we all know the re-telling of stories are often exaggerated.

I just want to have a nice fun evening with my two boys.

But should it go south at some point, I've hidden a bunch of weapons around the house –it's a comfort thing, okay?- so should the need arise I'm very well prepared. I'm praying that I won't have to stab a bitch though; I mean I'll try very hard to behave myself, but I won't make any promises that I *know* I can't keep.

I take the stairs down finding the first floor crammed full of people already. The first one of my guys I spot is Huxley. His head thrown back, arms out wide as he tells his story, laughing at himself as everyone else joins in, it's hard not to, his laugh really is infectious. As though he can sense my presence, his eyes divert to my direction and without a word he immediately abandons his guests to meet me at the bottom of the stairs.

"You are fucking stunning," he whistles lowly, taking my hand in his.

I finish walking down the last two steps and as I reach the bottom he spins me to get a good look at me before devouring my mouth with his. His kiss leaves me panting and breathless and aching in all the right places. Knowing exactly what he's done to me, he smirks, dropping his arm around my shoulders he leads me across the room to Kacey.

"Yo! Kace!" he shouts over the crowd dancing in the living room. The boys moved the furniture out of the way again so the open-plan floor space is free of any obstacles. "Get our girl a drink," he yells, Kacey giving him a two finger salute in acknowledgment, his golden eyed gaze sweeping over me with desire before disappearing behind the open fridge door.

"Are your friends gunna think this is weird?" I question, looking up at Hux he drops his chin and frowns.

"I couldn't give a fuck what they think," he growls, "you're fucking ours, they can fuck off if they don't like it, you're my number one priority, fuck everyone else," he scoffs confidently.

Huxley grips my chin between his thumb and forefinger kissing me hard on the mouth, giving, giving, giving, but never taking. When he finally draws back I quickly inspect his lips. *Huh,* guess this shit really is kiss proof. Still not sure if it's worth the thirty-six quid I paid for it though. But oh well, you win some you lose some.

The front door opens, a dark haired guy with a keg shouts Huxley's name, drawing both of our attention.

"Go," I tell him as his head whips round, "I've got Kacey," I smile up at him and he looks torn.

Not because he's giving me over to Kacey, but more like because he doesn't wanna stop touching me. It makes me feel all warm and weird and so not like myself that I blush.

"I'm fine," I reassure him with a gentle nudge to the side of his chest as I try to free myself from his embrace.

Reluctantly he drops his arm from my shoulders, taps me on the arse and turns back towards the front door.

"Your Majesty," Kacey bows as I enter the kitchen space, holding my drink out in his big palm of one hand, the other he dramatically waves in the air in little circles, presenting me with my drink, like he's presenting the goddamn crown jewels.

"Stand up you big idiot," I chuckle; shaking my head I take the drink from his hand and swat him on the shoulder with a giggle. "Why are you calling me *'your majesty'* you weirdo?"

"Because you're my queen and I'm gunna make sure to treat you like it," he shrugs casually and I gape at him.

"I don't know how I'm going to survive you two," I laugh taking a sip of my drink, "you're too much," I murmur with a shy shake of my head as my cheeks start to heat.

Kacey leans across the island, his forearms resting on the countertop. He really is beautiful, with his broad shoulders and inked skin, glittering gold eyes, swirls of ink down one side of his skull and thick flop of blonde hair. I tilt my head to study him as I think about last night.

Last night Kacey pulled me out into the back garden. He sat cross legged on the wet grass in nothing more than a pair of joggers and trainers, it was freezing cold but he didn't care, he didn't want to miss having a clear sky.

He pulled me down into his lap, so I didn't get wet, wrapping his arms tightly around me, telling me to look up. There were a million stars in the sky and it's the first night in ages there've been no rain clouds blocking the view.

He pointed out a bunch of constellations, although he definitely made some up, I'm a hundred percent certain that there's not a 'big dick' or a 'pasta twist' constellation. Then he made my tummy flip. He told me that no matter where we are, whether together or apart, if we both look up at the stars when we miss one another, wherever the other one of us is, we can rest easy knowing that we're both looking up at the same sky. Kacey told me he takes comfort in that because he looks for the light in all the dark places. I think, until then, I'd forgotten how to do that, well, I'm not sure if I ever knew *how* to before if I'm honest, but it made me want to start trying.

Both Kacey and Huxley have been teaching me a lot of things about myself and the way I look at things, even when they stayed with me at my house they taught me things and told me things that made me look at shit differently. I think this overwhelming feeling I keep getting in my chest is actually happiness. They make me smile and laugh every day, making me feel warm and safe and *happy*.

"Get over here," Kacey growls and I raise my eyebrows at him, trying to hide my smile.

"Is that anyway to speak to one's queen?" I deadpan with an exaggerated blink making Kacey drops his head back with a raspy laugh.

"My queen, if you would please draggeth thy sexy arse in this direction; thou shalt be greatly rewarded," he winks and I can't hide my smile any longer, I snort a laugh and skirt around the island.

Kacey grabs the back of my head in one hand, wrapping an arm around my waist, he dips me backwards making me grip his forearm with a squeal and kisses me. He takes his time exploring me, tasting me, our tongues dance together until he straightens us up, breaking our kiss with an expression that promises *later*. I tap his chest with a smile and break free from his hold. When I turn back to grab my drink a familiar brunette is standing on the other side of the counter with a meek expression on her face.

"Hi," I smile at her and she smiles back shyly, as soon as she smiles I realise who she is, "you're Jen," I say, remembering her as Gremlin's girl, or rather the energizer bunny who was way too much for me to handle last time we met.

"Yeah, I am. Hey," she smiles more confidently and it suits her face much better than the mild expression she walked over here with.

Her honey brown curls bounce just above her shoulders and her pretty blue eyes are lined lightly with brown liner, her cheekbones dusted rosy pink, a matching shade on her lips. She's wearing a cream, A-line mini-dress with bright blue heels.

"Boss," Gremlin nods coming up behind his girlfriend. "Kace," he greets, reaching out his fist to tap Kacey's.

Kacey moves to grab them both drinks and I sit at the island to chat with Jen. She's actually a pretty cool girl, she's a personal shopper for some fancy department store and says she loves her job because she gets all the celebrity gossip before anyone else, which makes me laugh, I've never really cared for anyone else's drama. We sit together for a couple of hours; the boys coming by every now and again refilling our drinks and checking on me, which involves more groping and kissing than actual words, not that I'm complaining. The music is so fucking loud we have to shout at each other to hear but neither one of us seems to mind.

I've never had a girlfriend before, it's kinda, *nice?* It's weird but I think I like it, it might be nice to have a female friend. I even start to let my guard down a little, feeling comfortable… until I don't.

I'm leaning into Jen to hear her better when someone whacks into my stool sending the fresh drink in my hand sloshing over my wrist and fingers. Jen grabs a napkin and leans over me, patting it against my skin to soak up the red liquid. I look up to see what happened finding the sneering face of a woman who I vaguely recognise but like a blast from the fucking past kind of recognition, I can't quite place her.

The woman is tall, not quite as tall as me, maybe five-ten

but with her heels she's taller, her bottle tanned skin making her look like she's just returned from a six-week vacation in Barbados. Her nails manicured perfectly and her bouncy gold curls hang over one shoulder, wearing a strapless pink top and tight black skirt.

"Once a slut always a slut, huh, Kyla-Rose?" she sneers at me with a curled lip.

"Err, excuse me?" I bristle, clenching my free hand into a fist in my lap, the other having a death grip on my crystal tumbler.

"You heard me," she pops a hip and scowls, looking me up and down, like she's less than impressed by what she sees.

"What the fuck?" I frown in confusion.

She throws her head back, laughing loudly, crossing her arms over her chest, pushing her already bulging tits up even higher in her tiny top.

"Of course, *Princess Kyla,* doesn't remember me, why would you? You never gave anyone attention unless they had a dick you wanted to sit on," she almost shouts at me and I blanch at that, I don't think I have *ever* chased after a guy or vied for male attention, it's just not something I do.

The noise in the room seems to quiet some, like those standing and dancing nearest are trying to listen in on the unfolding drama.

I recognise her irritating voice more than her face but then she's got so much botox shoved into her that she probably finds it hard to even recognise herself. Not that I have any issue with plastic surgery, If you want it and can afford to have it done then you go girl, but this definitely screams botched job or perhaps it's just the ugliness of her personality –or lack thereof- shining through the expensive procedures.

I push my anger down, twisting in my seat so I'm facing her head on. Tilting my head to one side, I drag my eyes slowly up her body until they rest on her face and *click.*

"Chelsea Harris," I smirk with recollection, folding my arms across my chest, I feel much more comfortable now I know the bitch I'm dealing with.

This particular mean girl was always jealous of my relationship with Max. When we were younger Chelsea was in Max's year at school and she pined after him, always following him around like a little puppy dog. It doesn't matter that he gave her absolutely zero attention because he just wasn't interested, no; obviously it was all my fault that he didn't want her.

That's the thing with girls, they can never just accept that the guy they want might not want them back and rather than be like, okay whatever, they have to blame it on a fellow female. Pathetic if you ask me but girls like Chelsea will never change.

"You never were good at hiding your jealousy were you? Which one is it you're after that doesn't want you, Kacey or Huxley?" I taunt, "I'm sure that'll be my fault as well, will it?" I ask sarcastically, running my tongue across my teeth, I cluck my tongue as I look at her, equally as unimpressed by her as she is me.

"Shall I get one of the boys?" Jen whispers into my hair and I give her a firm shake of my head but I immediately feel cool air at my back so I know she's scurried off to do exactly that anyway.

"You little bitch!" she snaps, "you walk around this house

like you fucking own it. Kacey and Huxley, I *know* them, they don't give a fuck about you! You're just a warm cunt they can slip their dicks into. You're still some trashy little slut, always have been trash though, haven't you? Poor little Kyla-Rose, Daddy banged up, dead Mummy," she mocks sticking her bottom lip out, "now you're what? Fucking two best friends to ruin their relationship too? You're a waste of breath, Kyla-Rose Swallow, you're not worth the dirt beneath my shoe," she spits, turning to help herself to another drink from the fridge.

I let her, sitting silently, silently seething but silent all the same, trying really fucking hard to keep my shit together. I suck in a calming breath but I don't know how long I'm going to be able to keep my cool. I can feel my demon clawing at my insides, snarling and chomping at the bit to be set free.

All I can think about is ramming my head into her overpriced face and watching her bleed for me. There's something so satisfying about head butting a bitch in the face, the beautiful crunching of bone and cartilage is one of my favourite sounds, music to my ears if you will and totally worth the headache every fucking time.

"He never wanted you, ya know," she starts as soon as she closes the fridge door, turning back to face me, resting her back against it.

She opens one of those sickly sweet cans of pre-mixed cocktail and takes a sip, her eyes snapping back to mine as she presses her body forward across the counter, casually rocking back and forth on her heels as she leans in.

"He just felt sorry for you, you always followed him around like a little lost puppy dog, but no matter how many times he kicked you, you always came back for more. He chose me in the end," she smirks viciously, that statement whether true or false making my chest ache. "It was *always* going to be me because let's face it you are *nothing* but a desperate little whore," she tuts. "It's sad really, isn't it, that he never wanted you and you still pined after him like a little bitch in heat," she smirks nastily and it's possibly the ugliest expression I've ever seen on a person's face.

And then everything happens really fast.

My demon explodes from my chest as I see fucking red, I didn't need any reminder tonight of Maddox fucking Sharpe, but she just had to go there.

I press up on my toes, resting my heeled feet against the rung of the stool and stretch across the counter. Backhanding the can of drink from her perfectly manicured fingers I send it flying to the floor, the liquid splashes down her leg as it falls and hits the tile. She turns her head to look at it, giving me the perfect opportunity to grab a fistful of her hair, tangling my fingers into its length I slam her face forward into the countertop as hard as I can. Blood spurts across the counter as her perfect nose explodes, hot crimson pours down her face, dripping from her chin and splashing onto the counter as she screeches at the pain. Chelsea wails, reaching up with a shaking hand to touch her very, *very* shattered nose, but I'm too quick for her and I'm not done yet, nowhere near done.

I pounce from my stool slamming her back into the fridge door, my forearm pressing against her chest, her head ricochets off of the door as she hits it and she screams. *Fucking idiot.* She raises a hand to me, to do what I'm not quite sure, slap me maybe? But she doesn't get the chance, I'm a professional killer after all and violence, it's in my blood.

I grab her wrist, immediately snapping her middle finger back with one forceful twist of my hand making her howl in pain, I feel the feral grin split my face in two as I give my demon free rein. There's no coming back from this now. Grabbing another handful of hair I kick her legs out from beneath her, knocking her to her knees.

I can't hear or see anyone or anything around me. I'm so far gone now, nothing is gunna bring me back from this. My breathing even and calm, the adrenaline flowing but it's relatively under control and all the shaking from it is nicely hidden from the outside world. Inside I'm a jittery mess but I've been trained well. You don't show your emotional responses or reactions on the outside, you must be an emotionless leader, instilling fear and demanding respect.

With a fistful of gold hair I spin on my too-high heels and start to drag her, she flails behind me, trying to hold her damaged face and claw at my hand with the other but I'm far too in control of the situation to care, she doesn't stand a chance.

The crowd parts for me like the red sea, all of them trying to get as far out of my way as possible. I drag her bleeding, howling mess of a body across the carpet, thrusting open the front door. Releasing my grip on her hair I prod her with the toe of my foot. Chelsea tumbles down the two steps, hitting the concrete path in a ball, she's still screaming at me but I can't hear a fucking word of it, I'm too angry, all I can hear is the buzzing static inside my ears, it's all white noise.

"Get the fuck up you snivelling bitch," I demand lazily

with a hand on my hip.

My face tells the world this is boring as fuck to have had to do but the demon inside me is screaming for more violence.

Always screaming for more blood.

"You fucking cunt!" she screams, teeter-tottering unsteadily to her feet, wobbling in her heels, "you can't throw me out of here, you don't fucking live here!" she screams, but the gurgling sound in the back of her throat is too distracting for her pathetic words to have any real impact.

I cock my head to look at her. All I see is a nasty, broken girl. I probably didn't need to bash her face in like that, I'm sure I could have shut her up with words but nearly four weeks without any violence and I'm slowly losing control.

"And please, for the love of god, don't step on Huxley's flowers or I'll have to break the rest of your fucking fingers," I warn her as she stumbles to keep her feet under her. "Oh, and I'll be sure to send you the cleaning bill for the carpet," I call out to her, folding my arms and resting my shoulder in the door jamb.

As she wobbles down the path I catch sight of Kacey perched on the garden wall, a couple of other guys with him as he stares back at me, his mouth open a little, his eyes darting between me and Chelsea. I just raise my hand, wiggling my fingers at him in a little wave with a coy smile, not really sure what he's gunna make of all this.

He looks to Chelsea then back to me, clearly having missed the whole encounter, he looks up at me and beams. That big soppy grin he saves just for me, so even though he can see it was most certainly me that inflicted the damage and then threw her out, he's still looking at me the same way.

Chelsea gets to the end of the path turning to face Kacey, they exchange words that my adrenaline flooded body doesn't allow me to hear. He shakes his head at whatever she says before returning his attention back to his friends. She stamps her foot in temper before storming off down the road.

I step back into the house, slamming the door closed behind me as I clap my hands together. Huxley and Jen are stopped on the stairs before me, clearly having only just caught the last part of my little drama. I swipe my bloody knuckles down the front of my dress.

"I can't leave you alone for five minutes can I, Darlin'?" Huxley asks me as he re-settles me at the kitchen counter, mixing me a fresh drink.

"No, probably not a good idea," I agree. "I'm not going to say it wasn't my fault, but I'm also not going to apologise," I tell him with a quirked brow.

Huxley runs a wedge of lime around the rim of my glass before dropping it in and sliding it over to me, just the way I like it.

"Not going to ask you to, this house is as much yours as it is ours," he shrugs, like *that* isn't a really big fucking deal. "Plus, I fucking *hate* Chelsea Harris with a passion so it was nice to see her finally put in her place," he scrubs a hand down his face, fiddling with his eyebrow piercing before looking up at me. "What did she say to you?" he releases a sharp breath, waiting while I think about what I want to say.

Huxley knows about my history with Max, I've told both of the boys a very clean cut, shortened version of the whole thing, I don't ever wanna go into full detail about it all but they know enough for now.

"She was just being Chelsea," I shrug, taking a large swig of my drink and letting the tartness of the lime sour my next words. "She was dragging up shit about the past," I say with a furrowed brow, dropping my glass down on the counter, heaving in a deep breath.

"You know her?" Huxley asks innocently, trying to understand without pressing for details I don't want to give.

"Yeah," I sigh squeezing my eyes shut, "she err, well," I take a deep breath, my eyes connecting with his dark mahogany ones. "You remember my story about that boy?" I ask nibbling on my bottom lip, my leg jumping beneath the counter at the mere mention of *him*.

"Yeah, I remember," he says with a grimace, a small flash of anger in his eyes.

"Well, Chelsea was always after him, always picking on me because she was jealous, she was just saying shit about that. It's no big deal, I just don't want to think about that shit anymore, it sends me to a dark place, Hux," he nods more to himself than me.

Twisting away from me he snatches two shot glasses from the cupboard, filling them with smooth honey-brown liquid and slides one across to me.

"Fuck 'em," he says, raising his glass to me with a smirk and I swallow my shot at the same time he does, our eyes never leaving each other's.

A large, hot body closes in on the space behind me, glancing over my shoulder to see Kacey, just as his big hand slides around my waist.

"Upstairs, now," is all he says before he's releasing me and turning away, heading for the stairs.

I look back to Huxley with a puzzled look but he's moving too, he's next to me in less than a second, his hand sliding into mine as he helps me from the stool. He leads me through the crowd and up the stairs until we're stood in front of his bedroom door. He looks back at me over his shoulder, his eyes almost black before twisting the handle and swinging the door open.

The ceiling is strung up with little Christmas lights just like the ones Kacey hung downstairs, except these ones are a warm white instead of coloured. They're the only light in the room but it's lit up enough for me to see Kacey lounging back on Huxley's bed. Huxley kicks the door shut behind him, twisting the lock into place, the only sound the click of the lock sliding into place and my quickening breaths with the faintest trickle of bass from the music still pounding downstairs.

"What are you doing?" I almost whisper but it doesn't sound like me, it's raspy and breathy and it's a stupid fucking question because all three of us know exactly what's about to happen in this room. Even if my brain hasn't quite caught up yet, my body is already there.

"We want to love on you, Sweetheart," Kacey tells me casually, "*together*," his mouth playfully lifts up at one corner as he tags that on the end. From his relaxed position on the bed, his feet crossed at the ankles, one bulging bicep tucked behind his head propping him up, "will you let us?"

Huxley's fingers still grip mine and I feel myself squeeze his hand for reassurance as I look up at him. He's looking down at me with a soft smile and dark eyes that want to devour me. I look back to Kacey, who's shifted his position now, sitting on the edge of the bed, his knees spread wide, forearms atop his thighs, he looks at me through his flop of blonde hair and smiles. I'm not worried, I know these two boys, *men,* will look after me, even when I don't want them to they will, because that's how much I mean to them.

Huxley gives me one of his classic cheeky winks as he unlaces his fingers from mine, nudging me toward Kacey.

"Come here, Sweetheart," Kacey instructs.

I wipe my sweaty palms down the fringe of my dress as I walk across the worn carpet, stepping between his spread thighs and into his open arms.

Kacey's thick fingers dig into my ribcage as he grips my waist, flexing his fingers against my body, he looks up at me, his eyes flicking between my own as he takes my chin between his thumb and finger of the other hand.

"So fucking beautiful," he murmurs to me before bringing my face down to meet his.

His lips scorch mine as he kisses me, my hand sliding up into his thick hair, the other gripping his shoulder as he delves his tongue between my lips, spearing my mouth with it, our tongues sliding against one another as he crushes me in his hold.

Huxley presses up against my back, the heat from his firm body sparking me to life, his long fingers massage my shoulders before he slides them down my arms, leaving a trail of goosebumps in his wake. Huxley's lips drop to my bare shoulder, attacking my exposed skin with his teeth and lips, his tongue darting out to soothe the sting of his bites. He brings his hands back up, slipping them beneath the thin straps of my dress, sliding them down my arms.

Kacey continues destroying my soul with his kiss, removing my hands from him and forcing them to remain at my sides as Huxley lets my dress drop into a pool of heavy red fabric at my ankles, leaving me in nothing but a scrap of lace. I forwent a bra because this dress was cut too low in the back to accommodate the strap.

"Fuck, Kyla-Rose," Huxley growls appreciatively into my ear, nipping at the lobe.

Curling his arms around me he cups the heavy weight of my breasts, massaging them in warm hands, tweaking the piercings through my pebbled nipples.

Kacey breaks our kiss. Huxley removes one hand from my breast, Kacey's hot, greedy mouth immediately replacing it. He sucks on my flesh, his teeth grazing over the hardened point as Huxley turns my head and devours my mouth with his tongue.

I gasp as they both play my body, their hands, teeth and tongues worshipping every desperate inch of me.

One of my hands tangles in Kacey's hair forcing him to take more of me into his hot mouth. My other hand reaching up and wrapping around the back of Huxley's neck as he kisses me, I groan into his mouth as my legs start to shake.

"You're both wearing too many clothes," I say breathlessly between kisses.

"D'you hear that, Kace? Apparently we're wearing too many clothes," Huxley teases with a laugh and I feel the vibration of Kacey's laugh rumble through my chest where his mouth is still feasting on my puckered nipple, his tongue lashing around my piercing and his teeth grazing the soft flesh.

Synchronised as though it's been planned like a well-rehearsed dance, the two men detach themselves from my body, leaving me gasping and wobbly on my heels, my knees threatening to buckle at the mere thought of their impending onslaught.

They simultaneously strip their shirts, slinging them onto the chair in the corner of the room then perfectly in sync with one another they pop the buttons and release the zippers on their jeans, hauling them down their legs and sending them flying in the same direction as their shirts.

Both men stand before me, their eyes such a stark contrast from one another but their gaze's the same, hunger, desire, the need to devour, conquer, *claim.* And I'm their target, their prey, their willing victim, *sacrifice.*

They stride towards me in step with each other like the militant men they are and then their hands are back on my naked flesh. Huxley drops to his knees before me as Kacey claims my mouth like I'm a prize to be won, like he has to give this his all or die trying, he kisses me like his life depends on it.

Huxley's long fingers slide into the waistband of my lace knickers dragging them painfully slowly down my legs, his fingers burning a trail in their wake as he glides them down my thighs, past my knees and to my ankles. Carefully he lifts one of my heeled feet from the floor, slipping the lace over my foot, doing the same with the other, discarding the scrap of fabric, throwing it into the growing pile of clothing in the chair.

Kacey's large hands roam over my torso, pinching at my nipples and massaging the heavy flesh, he forces his knee between mine, tapping them apart, widening my stance for Huxley. Huxley's hot breath fans across the sensitive flesh of my inner thigh as his long fingers trace a pattern up my calves, stopping at the back of my thighs; his fingers dig deep into my supple flesh forcing a moan to escape my throat as his hot mouth finally closes over my aching core.

Huxley's tongue dives deep between my folds, spearing my entrance, he fucks me relentlessly with his mouth while I grip Kacey's shoulders to keep me on my feet. Kacey bites and sucks across my jaw, down the column of my throat and over my collarbone as Huxley's teeth graze my clit. My legs shake uncontrollably at the onslaught, his tongue ravages my cunt, sliding two fingers inside me without warning and I cry out as he sucks my clit with abandon.

My head drops back, Kacey's arm banding around my waist, holding up my weight like it's no effort at all. My orgasm hits me suddenly, hard and fast, I see stars and I can do nothing but ride it out. Huxley's tongue laps up the evidence of my release like he'll never get enough. Kacey's mouth still sucking across my flushed chest, leaving a trail of red and purple bite marks before sweeping me up into his strong arms and placing me down in the centre of the bed.

My chest rising and falling rapidly, I crack my eyes open as both men loom over me, both now freed of their boxers and as bared to me as I am to them. Huxley flashes me a wicked smirk, a brow cocked in challenge, while Kacey looks at me like he wants to consume me and I have no doubt he will. I want him to, I want them both to take everything from me, everything I have left to give is for them after all. All of my cracked and severed pieces belong to them, however they want to take them, are theirs.

Kacey crawls onto the bed until he's behind me, his back against the headboard; he hauls me up so I'm laid between his spread thighs, my back to his front, his very real, very hard erection digging into the base of my spine. He hooks my feet over his calves and then slowly, torturously slowly, he drags his legs apart taking mine with him. My breath hitches and the words I want to choke out die on my tongue as Huxley stalks forward, eyes on me as his best friend opens me up to him.

"Such a pretty pussy," Huxley praises as he gets his knees on the bed, "you taste like peaches, you know that, Darlin'," he tells me, I shake my head at him but I don't take my eyes away from the predator in front of me, those black eyes focused on mine, tearing into my soul.

Kacey wraps his arms under mine, pulling them away from me, trapping me, leaving me open and vulnerable and helpless. Being in a position like this should trigger me, being restrained, but instead it makes me feel empowered. The way Huxley's looking at me like I'm his most favourite thing in the world and he lives purely to please me, makes me feel confident and safe. These two men would never hurt me, that much I'm now certain.

I let my head fall back against Kacey's powerful chest, my heavy-lidded eyes still locked on Huxley as I watch the muscles in his shoulders bunch and flex as he crawls towards me. His head drops between my open thighs, his hot pierced tongue teasing my wet folds, sucking on my juices as he looks up into my eyes.

"Fucking delicious," he smiles, his hot breath fanning against my wet flesh and I feel all my muscles tense as a whimper escapes my lips.

"I'm going to fuck you now, Darlin', I want you to come for me, for *us*," Huxley tells me and my god the way he says *us* makes me almost combust from his words alone, I'm already so close to another orgasm, it really wouldn't take much.

Kacey kisses and sucks on the side of my throat as my eyes stay firmly fixed on the caramel skinned god before me. Without breaking eye contact he drives into me in one hard thrust, hitting the end of me with his pierced tip, making both of us groan, slamming my body back into Kacey, his painfully hard cock digging into my spine. Fully seated inside me, Huxley stills, allowing my walls time to adjust to the intrusion. Huxley is very, *very*, well endowed, like really, he's *big*. It takes me a second and a bite of pain before he starts to move and then the waves of pleasure overtake everything else, like the ocean crashing into the cliffs, inevitable and oh, so powerful.

My hands wrap around Kacey's forearms, my wrists curling, my nails biting his flesh, I crane my head back capturing his lips. Kacey kisses me slow, steady, unhurried, as his brother destroys me with his swollen cock. Our tongues dance and teeth graze, as the motion of Huxley pounding into me thrusts us closer together.

"So beautiful," he tells me as he sucks my bottom lip into his mouth, "such a good girl, taking Huxley's cock," he murmurs against my lips, the praise making my pussy clench.

Huxley's movements intensify as his long, thick shaft continues to penetrate my molten core. Kacey releases one of my arms, letting it drop to the mattress. Kacey snakes his big hand down my body, gliding his rough palm across the silken skin of my tummy, his fingers teasing my clit. Using his middle finger he rubs the hardened nub in rough circles while Huxley pounds into me over and over. When Kacey pinches my clit it's all over. I explode, crying out both men's names followed by a string of mumbled curses.

Before I get a chance to recover, my exhausted body's being dragged forwards. Huxley drops onto his back, hauling me on top of him, spearing me once again on his thick cock, I groan as the sensations of my orgasm continue to wash over me. Kacey moves up behind me on his knees and I hear the distinctive click of a plastic lid. My eyes snap open at the sound and instantly connect with Huxley's.

"Think you can take both of us at the same time, baby girl?" he asks me and I tremble.

I know I can say no if I wanted to but I don't, I want them both, always, together, in any way I can have them.

"Yes," I say quietly as Kacey's fingers run up my spine, unsure of myself but not unsure of my men.

"Good girl," Huxley smiles, his thumb tracing over my bottom lip, his praise making butterflies flutter inside my tummy.

"Have you done this before?" Kacey asks me and I shiver as his voice washes over my flushed skin.

I want to say something sarcastic like, *'what? Have two boyfriends at the same time? Or did you just mean anal?'* but I don't, instead I just shake my head, Huxley's eyes lighting up at the admission. I glance over my shoulder to look back at Kacey, his eyes telling me everything I need to know. I take in a deep, steadying breath and close my eyes.

"We'll go slow, just let us take care of you," Kacey promises, dropping a punishing kiss to my lips that has my pussy clenching around Huxley's shaft which has him moaning and squirming beneath me.

Kacey's large hand rests between my shoulder blades as he applies pressure, encouraging me to lie forward until I'm chest to chest with Huxley. Huxley kisses me like his life depends on it, his breath filling me up as though I might drown without it. Thick cold liquid runs between my cheeks and I tense on instinct, Huxley breaks our kiss as his hands gently run up and down my spine, soothing and reassuring me.

"Just kiss me and try to relax, I promise it'll feel good," Huxley tells me, his eyes watching my own, making sure that I really am okay.

I nod dropping my lips back to his, his hands still roving over my clammy skin. Kacey carefully pushes a finger inside my pussy alongside Huxley's cock, pumping it a few times before he runs it up to my puckered hole, using my own juices mixed with the lube to make sure I'm nice and wet. Huxley kisses me deep, his tongue putting on a display of dominance as he devours my mouth with his, desperate and wanting as he waits patiently for his own release.

Kacey pushes a finger inside of me as Huxley starts to move again instantly making me forget about the unfamiliar intrusion. The zinging sensation pulsing through me is indescribable as Kacey starts to slowly fuck me with his finger. Huxley's hands tease my pebbled nipples, flicking the metal bars with his thumbs. Kacey slowly adds another finger, scissoring them inside me, his other hand still holding me forward; he leans over me, his hot breath fanning over my skin as he whispers in my ear.

"That's it, Sweetheart, let Huxley look after you, you're such a good girl, good girls get rewards, Kyla-Rose," Kacey murmurs behind me, his breath blowing tendrils of my hair across Huxley's face.

Hearing him encourage me to fuck his best friend does something to me that I'm not entirely sure how to put into words. The way he speaks is so full of love and affection, as much for Huxley as it is for me. These two men love each other like brothers, they've saved each other's lives on more than one occasion and now they're sharing me with each other. That's how much they care about each other. That's how much they care about *me*.

Kacey removes his fingers and I feel the hot head of his cock replace them, the cool metal of his piercing pressing against me. His large hands splayed on my cheeks he pulls the flesh apart, nudging at my opening. I kiss Huxley, distracting myself and focus on my breathing, Huxley stops moving inside me as he lets his brother take his time. Kacey pushes the tip in and I still, both boys stop moving, giving me a second to relax again and when I do, Kacey starts to push further in, once he's about half way I tear my lips from Huxley's.

"I don't know if I can," I say on a frantic breath, panic setting in as I lose control of my breathing.

Huxley runs his hands up and down my arms soothingly, his thumbs rubbing small circles into my skin.

"You're doing so good, Sweetheart, you've nearly done it.

You look so fucking beautiful with my cock in your arse, such a good girl, taking us together," Kacey praises, continuing to push into me.

His voice pinched and strained as he does, it's taking a lot for him too, he's not exactly small in the cock department either, both of my boys are seriously packing.

"I'm okay," I finally nod, taking another steadying breath which is unsurprisingly difficult considering how full I am.

Huxley works my mouth with his, his hands caressing my breasts until Kacey is finally fully seated. Everything inside me feels like it's being rearranged, trying to accommodate and make space but fuck me am I full.

"Fucking hell, you're so tight," Kacey chokes out, "I can feel you dude," he whispers to Huxley and I smile.

Having both my men like this, together at the same time is simply the greatest feeling, they're both such different lovers but work together perfectly.

The three of us together are perfect.

Kacey drops his lips to my shoulder at the same time Huxley recaptures my lips and then they both start to move. As Huxley slides in, Kacey glides out and then they both move in sync, sliding in together at the same time and then pulling out. I feel so fucking empty before they slam back in and fill me up, it's almost hard to breathe.

It's like being inflated and deflated before being blown back up again and it feels fucking amazing. Kacey grips my hips in his tattooed hands, his thick fingers digging into my supple flesh as Huxley kneads my breasts, leaning up and sucking each nipple into his mouth while flicking the piercing in the other with his thumb.

We collectively groan a chorus of sexual desire, every intake of breath, every thrust of hips and every bolt of electricity that floods through me, flows through the three of us simultaneously, all connected, intertwined with each other, I move, they move, I bleed, they bleed.

Huxley's hand glides down my flat tummy, the heel of his hand resting on my mound as his fingers find my overly sensitive clit. Kacey picks up his pace and Huxley quickly falls into step with him as he massages my clit with rough fingers. They suddenly both move so hard and fast that all I can do is hold on as they fuck me into oblivion and then I'm coming.

"Fuck, fuck, fuck, *fuck*," I say on a breathy moan, my nails biting into Huxley's shoulders as Kacey's cock pulses inside of me, my body squeezing around both of theirs.

Huxley shudders as he lifts his hips, hitting me at a different angle, he comes hard, still rubbing my clit with frenzied fingers as I cry out, screaming both their names, over and over, Kacey grunts behind me. Pumping into me one final time, he comes with a roar before his head drops to my shoulder, our combined weight lying heavily on Huxley.

"Fuck," I breathe making both boys laugh, the sound vibrating through me.

Essentially crushed between them, our combined breathing ragged and heavy in the otherwise quiet space, the music from downstairs softly filters up through the floor as we regain our breath. Kacey drops a kiss to my shoulder as he rolls over taking me with him and dropping me between the two of them on the bed. My back plastered to his sweat soaked chest and my front facing Hux as he lies on his back, his face turned to me but dark eyes closed.

"Well," I say when I finally get my breathing more or less under control, "that was," I pause as Huxley looks at me, wondering what I'm going to say. "When can we do that again?" I question breathlessly with a raised brow causing both men to burst into laughter.

"You were fucking made for us, holy fuck," Kacey laughs, turning my face back so he can kiss me, his kiss tasting like the future and all the pretty promises he made me starting to come true.

Huxley snatches my face from Kacey's grip kissing me just as hard, putting a piece of his soul into the kiss silently promising me the world. I lie on my back with my men either side and close my eyes with a smile on my face.

These two men, so different yet so similar in so many ways, they make me feel safe, fuck I don't *feel* safe, I *am* safe. And I don't just mean physical safety, I mean mentally too, the mind is fragile, as fragile as my heart and those are two things I know I never have to worry about in the presence of these two.

Kacey, a giant, scary looking teddy bear who only smiles for me and Huxley, a cock-sure, smooth talking, social butterfly who cuts out all the bullshit for me. They breathe for me, live for me, everything we've done over the last five weeks feels like a lifetimes worth of relationship building, neither one of them feels unfamiliar to me. In some strange sort of way, my soul knows them, whether from another life or not, I don't know. But when their souls meld with mine they're like the kindling to my flame, they spark something inside me that no one else could ever replace and continuously build me up.

"Boys," I say, drawing the attention of the two dangerous men either side of me.

"Yeah?" they both ask in unison, always so very in tune with one another.

I feel their gazes turn on me, my skin burning everywhere their eyes rove and I don't even need to open my own to know they're both staring at me.

"I love you," I whisper, "both of you."

And then my stomach bottoms out and my breath catches and I daren't open my eyes in case they're both staring at me and I don't like what I see. Why did I say that?

Stupid.

Stupid.

Stupid.

Fuck.

They've been quiet for too long and if I don't start breathing soon I might actually die from lack of oxygen.

"Sweetheart, open your eyes," Kacey says softly and I already know this was the worst thing to say ever; maybe he's changed his mind!

Fuck my stupid sex clouded brain! Why, why, why?!

"Darlin', look at us, please," Huxley whispers and my heart clenches in my chest, it's battering my ribcage like a sledgehammer trying to crack through.

Reluctantly, I slowly peel my eyes open and stare at the ceiling, my body refusing to let me look at either one of the boys that I'm so desperate to be loved by. Both men sit up on an elbow and lean over my face making me wince as their intense gazes lock on mine.

"Sorry, I didn't mean," I breathe out and bite down on my tongue so hard I taste copper, "I shouldn't have said anything, please just," I swallow, "forget I said anything, it was stupid, you shouldn't fuck me like that and not gag me, honestly, seriously, next time, if there ever is a next time I mean, gagging is the way forward or maybe I should just cut out my tongue now, someone please, for the love of all that is holy, stop me," I cringe, babbling, inhaling sharply as both boys burst into laughter.

"Darlin', I'm all for the gagging you but not because I don't wanna hear that beautiful voice of yours, especially after sex, you're all husky and sexy an-"

"And we're getting off topic," Kacey interrupts shooting a stern look at his brother.

Something silent passes between the two of them as my heart tries to rocket out of my chest and then they both look down at me again and I reflectively cover my face with my hands as I let out an embarrassed groan.

"We love you too," they say in unison and then they're each pulling a hand away from my face.

"Please don't just say that because I said it," I whisper, the raw vulnerability I feel in my chest bleeding into every word.

And there it is again, that open wound, always fucking bleeding.

"I've loved you from the minute you held a gun to my head and told me you were going to shoot me," Kacey beams, his crazed, soppy grin splitting his face in two.

"You're a crazy bastard," I giggle, reaching out and cupping his dimpled cheek in my hand.

"I love you," Kacey tells me and my body tingles all over as he presses a gentle kiss to my lips.

I turn my head to find Huxley waiting patiently for me, he's so beautiful, his short brown curls soft as silk, his mixed skin tone a beautiful dark caramel, those high cheekbones and deep coal coloured eyes. I catch myself smiling every time I look at him.

"I love you, Darlin'. I'm not worthy, honestly, I don't know who sent you to me, but if there is a god out there I'm undeniably indebted for eternity. I fell for you the moment I saw that soppy bastard grin like a fucking sap," he laughs as I cup his face with my other hand; he presses a kiss to my palm then bites the pad of my thumb.

"Okay! I need to shower this sticky, well, everything, and no you can't join me, I want to get back downstairs. I was actually enjoying myself before I was so rudely dragged away," I mock scold and both men make a face.

"You beat a girl up, honestly, what are you missing out on?" Huxley jokes and I scowl.

"I did not *beat a girl up*," I growl, "I smacked a woman in the face and broke her finger, that is not a *beating*," I protest, sitting up and sliding off the bed.

"And you rolled her out the door, it was hot," Kacey grins.

I spin to face them, both lying naked on the crumpled sheets, ignoring Kacey's comment, "and I was having fun *before* that, so, hurry, get washed, get dressed, we have guests!" I order as I dive into the shower before the men can get in first.

Twenty minutes later, we're all washed and re-dressed in

our same outfits including my shoes -when they came off, I'm not sure- my makeup touched up, bar my lipstick, that shit is totally worth the extortionate amount of money I paid for it, I take back everything bad I said about it. It's not just kiss proof, it's fuck proof, threesome proof, now *that* is something they should advertise it with.

Huxley taps me on the arse as he passes by the mirror I'm standing in front of and Kacey drops a kiss to the top of my head, lacing his fingers through mine.

"Ready?" Hux turns back from the door and I give him a nod, "come on then gang, up and at 'em, let's go, move, move, move soldiers!" he orders, circling his hand in the air above his head as he ushers us from the room.

Kacey releases my hand as we pass his room, grabbing a spritz of aftershave as I bounce off ahead, the two boys bantering behind me. I hop down the first couple of steps and turn my head back to check my boys are following; they are they're just taking their sweet time.

I'm so fucking happy, I don't think even the apocalypse could ruin my good mood right now, I've got two men who *love* me, *two*. I mean, I didn't think I'd ever find anyone again after Max, I thought that boy was my entire life, my past, present, future, but it just wasn't meant to be. And then everything that happened after that I didn't think shit like this was even a possibility for me but here I am, sickly sweet, picture perfect happy.

Well, I don't know anyone else that has two boyfriends but I'm totally recommending it when I meet literally anyone. Four hot hands, two mouths means two tongues and two men equal's two thick, hard cocks and they're *always* ready and waiting. I bite my lip and close my eyes pausing at the top of the stairs, *fuck,* I'm one lucky bitch.

I take in a deep breath and allow the smile desperately trying to break free appear on my lips. I'm so happy, giddy even, I couldn't care less about schooling my features right now, let the world see, I don't care. I'm on fucking vacation after all.

I hop down the stairs, my hand sliding along the polished white wood of the bannister stopping dead in my tracks as I hit the third from bottom step. My stomach drops, my head spinning as all the air escapes my lungs. There, standing in the open front doorway is a ghost; a tall, dark, menacing ghost with turquoise eyes and raven black hair.

"Max?"

AFTERWORD

So, I'm sitting here -not so silently- praying that you, yes, you, the reader, have made it this far! And if you have… are hopefully not hating on me too much for that little, teeny, tiny cliffhanger? Either way, hate or no hate, I really hope you enjoyed the start of this story and its characters so far.

This is my debut novel and these characters demanded -more loudly than the rest- that they be written and published first. So here we are! I'm hoping you won't have to wait too long for book two of this trilogy, as of right now it's more than half way done, so fingers crossed all goes well and it's out sooner rather than later because I honestly cannot wait for you to meet Maddox *fucking* Sharpe!

I won't ramble on any more than I already have but I will say just once more, thank you, thank you, thank you! Okay, that was three times but who's counting?! But seriously, thank you, you have no idea how much it means to me that you've chosen to pick up my book and make it this far. Whether you loved it or hated it or just thought it was okay, I appreciate you giving it (and me) a chance. And if this one wasn't for you, perhaps my next series will be.

It would mean the world to me if you could leave me an honest review on Amazon and/or Goodreads. Any and all feedback is welcomed and appreciated! Even little one line reviews can go a long way in helping indie authors get their next book out, so I'd appreciate anything you have to say.

Thank you from the bottom of my heart and hopefully see you in book 2!

ACKNOWLEDGMENTS

Firstly, to my other half, my soulmate, thank you for believing in me and pushing me to put myself out there, without you I would have done none of those things and I'd still have all my stories just saved on a memory stick! Without you I don't know where I'd be. I love you so much.

To my mum and dad. Mummy, Pops, thank you for everything you do for me, thank you for not pressuring me into a hobby or sport I had no interest in as a child, you helped me find what I enjoyed by letting me work it out for myself. You will never know how much I love and appreciate you.

To my baby sister, you honestly inspire me every day, you work so hard, you put your absolute all into everything you do and you always look amazing doing it! You drive me to want to do better, push harder, get myself out there and do the scary things I'm afraid of. Thank you for being my cheerleader. For always rooting for me and believing in me and praising even my smallest achievements. And for having my back –like *you* were the big sister- for my entire life, I love you more than you will ever know.

And my bestie, Daisy, without whom this story would never have been written let alone published. Thank you for always talking me through my ideas and ironing them out, for always pushing me and saying yes to my slightly crazed ideas and never judging me for it! I love you so much.

A huge thank you to my Beta readers! You guys took a

chance on me and for that I'll forever be thankful! Unfortunately, for you, you are now stuck with me… So I wish you luck with that!

Kiyahnah, you are so lovely! You're such a kind soul, your edits are beautiful and you are so conscientious in everything you do. You always make me feel so comfortable and I'm so grateful for our chats!

Laura, you are devious! You're my evil twin, devilish partner in crime and you always manage to convince me into doing all the naughty things! I will never be able to write a Charlie chapter again without thinking of you encouraging the worst! Not that I'll complain because it just gives me someone else to blame! *shines halo* Soul Sistaaa, love you, girl!

Cat at TRC cover designs, you have been so helpful and so lovely! I would still have no idea what to do without all of your help, thank you so much, I can't wait to work with you again soon!

And finally, to you, the reader, who I couldn't do this without, I'm eternally grateful.

ALSO BY K.L. TAYLOR-LANE

SWALLOWS AND PSYCHOS
A DARK REVERSE HAREM ROMANCE

BOOK 1 – PURGATORY
BOOK 2 – UNTITLED (coming early 2022)
BOOK 3 – UNTITLED (coming mid 2022)

CHARLIE (TBC)
A DARK ROMANCE

FIND K.L. ON

Amazon – K. L. Taylor-Lane
Goodreads – K. L. Taylor-Lane
Instagram – kltaylorlane_author
Facebook – KL Taylor-Lane
Facebook Reader Group – KL's Southbrook Psychos

Printed in Great Britain
by Amazon

87380596R00231